To Paul

# THE SPACE NEEDLER'S INTERGALACTIC BAR GUIDE

## by Scott Fulks and Will Viharo

Cheers,
Will V.

Cover art by Michael Fleming: http://www.tweedlebop.com

ISBN-13: 978-1-5121-3127-7

*THE SPACE NEEDLER'S INTERGALACTIC BAR GUIDE* is a fictional satire, with no malicious intent. The authors have invented all names and situations in this book, except in cases when public figures or places are being satirized. Any use of real names is either accidental and coincidental, or used as a fictional depiction or personality parody. References to, and short excerpts from books, songs, movies, and TV shows are handled according to the doctrine of transformative fair use. Please support the legitimate distribution of classic print, music, film, and televised content.

This book contains fantasy depictions of unsafe sexual practices and irresponsible substance abuse. DO NOT TRY THIS AT HOME.

The science and math content in this book is intended to stimulate critical thinking around certain elements of current "Standard Model" physics. The theories advanced are the intellectual property of Scott Fulks, and *THE SPACE NEEDLER'S INTERGALACTIC BAR GUIDE* is the first publishing of this academic work. This content has not been peer-reviewed prior to publishing. Academically-inclined readers are encouraged to extend these theories in their own published work. If footnote references are used, an appropriate format is "*THE SPACE NEEDLER'S INTERGALACTIC BAR GUIDE* © 2015 by Scott Fulks and Will Viharo."

Scott contributed the high-minded science, Will provided the lowbrow pulp, and Becca provided cocktails and inspiration. Enjoy at your own risk.

Special thanks to Michael Thanos, proprietor of Forbidden Island Tiki Lounge in Alameda, CA. Please visit when on "the island": http://www.forbiddenislandalameda.com

*In Memory of Leonard Nimoy:*
*Live Long and Prosper*

*He made science look cool.*

# "THE SPACE NEEDLER"

*1 oz lemon juice*
*1 oz Tang syrup (1:1 Tang powder with water)*
*1 oz cinnamon/vanilla flavored simple syrup*
*½ oz Cherry Heering*
*2 oz pineapple juice*
*1 oz Angostura 5 Year rum*
*1 oz Rhum Clement Premiere Canne*
*2 oz soda water*

*Moisten the rim of a 16 oz glass and dip in Tang powder. Shake everything but the soda with ice and pour into tall glass, top with soda. Garnish with a tall straw topped horizontally with the top dome slice of a lemon, like the saucer on the Space Needle.*

Cocktail created by Becca Morris, Forbidden Island Tiki Lounge.

Featured at Tiki Oasis 2015 "Yesterday's Future, Today": http://www.tikioasis.com

Thanks to the House of Angostura for their continued support of the art of the craft cocktail: http://www.angostura.com

## Caution!

The custom drink recipes heading each chapter of The Space Needler's Intergalactic Bar Guide are *strong* (mostly hard alcohol) and feature exotic flavor combinations and intoxicating qualities not generally found on Earth. What can we say, the universe is just full of heavy drinkers! Brand-name ingredients have been used where they provide a unique flavor component; otherwise we have kept things as generic as possible. Those who are new to cocktails should start with the classics at the end of each chapter, and move up from there. For convenience, in the table of contents the custom cocktails are listed in quotes, while the classics are not.

# "RESERVATIONS"

*1½ oz rye whiskey*
*½ oz Gran Classico Bitter*
*½ oz simple syrup*

*Pour ingredients neat into a 6-oz Old Fashioned glass, stir until clear.*

*Seattle, 1982*
Hilburne Chase was lost in space.

A car honking behind him interrupted his mental orbit, bringing him immediately back down to Earth, and he continued driving through a strangely quiet and seemingly abandoned downtown Seattle toward his destination. It was a cool, crisp, beautiful spring day, with cherry and apple blossoms blooming everywhere and Puget Sound shimmering in the soft rays of sunlight penetrating the fleecy cumulous clouds, so the almost complete absence of foot and street traffic was bizarre, to say the least. And the faces of the few folks he did see walking and driving around appeared either preoccupied or stoned. Even odder, no birds were flying or chirping. Hilburne thought of that old billboard that popped up near Sea-Tac airport a decade earlier, back in 1971, in response to the recession infamously known as the Boeing Bust: "*Will the Last Person Leaving Seattle Turn Out the Lights.*" Hilburne never imagined that might be *him.*

But he had no time to stop and soak in the supernaturally serene scenery. It was almost noon and he didn't want to be late for lunch, especially since he was an honored guest. Plus his morning coffee had worn off and he really, *really* needed a cocktail.

The forever-futuristic sight of the Space Needle loomed before him as he cruised up through the Queen Anne District in his vintage, powder blue, 1957 Thunderbird. The car was in pristine condition, with lower mileage than its original owner, Hilburne himself.

The song on the radio, "Rock Lobster," by a band called the B-52s, had brought back some disturbing memories for him, even though it was only three years old and he had never heard it before. Images of creepy, crawly, crustacean creatures had been occupying his nightmares for years. However, he also cherished a twinge of warm nostalgia, since the tune's twangy guitar hook reminded him of the instrumentals that were popular when the Space Needle was first revealed at the 1962 World's Fair, twenty years earlier.

But he had seen it long before that.

Another recent song called "Atomic" by the band Blondie, featuring a similarly retro reverb, was playing as Hilburne pulled up in front of the Space Needle. This song likewise conjured disturbing memories of mushroom clouds and mutated monsters, and yet he couldn't bring himself to turn off the radio, mesmerized by the mental imagery. Once the song had ended he switched off the dial, killed the engine, and climbed out. He took a ticket in exchange for the keys and a ten spot, which was a generous tip, though the valet barely nodded in response. He was the only one on duty, too, which was unusual.

When Hilburne walked into the lobby he was greeted with another sonic blast from the past: "Telstar" by The Tornados was playing as he went up the elevator to the revolving restaurant, which was called Eye of the Needle. Besides the oddly apathetic attitude of the lone valet, Hilburne was struck by the fact that no one else was around—no clerks, no elevator attendant, no tourists, even though it was midday and the place was obviously open for business. In fact, a strange stillness permeated the place. Hilburne was dressed in an immaculately pressed, shiny, dark green suit with an impeccable white shirt and skinny black tie, which was conveniently back in style now even though he had never succumbed to '70s fashion trends. Additionally he wore Ray-Ban sunglasses—originals, a gift from his friend, the late John F. Kennedy—which he kept on as the rare rays of Seattle sunshine shot through the glass. In his younger days, Hilburne—now in his mid-50s, with graying temples but otherwise a full head of slickly combed hair—had often been described as "the real" James Bond, but that was back when Sean Connery owned the role of 007. Now, with Roger Moore packing the Walter PPK on big screens worldwide, Hilburne wouldn't take that as a compliment anymore. Pretty Boy Moore was better suited to play The Saint, anyway, at least according to Hilly.

Only his friends called him Hilly, ever since his days at Harvard, where he was a brilliant student with a triple major:

History, Science, Art, plus an unofficial, unaccredited minor in which he still excelled: Sex Education. He was also a popular TA for that latter course. As it were.

When the elevator door opened and suave, erudite Hilburne stepped out from his solitary ride, there was one of his old friends to greet him: Hank "The Tank" Mahoney, a former gridiron star and ex-Marine from Houston, whom Hilly hadn't seen in over a decade.

"*Hank*!" Hilburne said with genuine surprise, extending his hand for a shake.

"*Hilly*!" Hank said with a smile before punching Hilburne right in the face, almost breaking his shades and possibly his nose, which immediately began to swell. When the pain shot through his face, Hilburne instinctively dropped his hand towards his right hip, fingers grasping for his sidearm in a practiced motion. But his pants only packed one weapon at the time, and it was useless in the current conflict.

As Hilburne fell, a stunningly beautiful, shapely, middle-aged blonde woman dressed in a tight, silk purple dress and high-heeled pumps raced to his side to help him up. As soon as Hilburne was on his feet, the woman slapped him sharply across the face. Luckily, she hit his jaw rather than further abusing his swollen nose.

"*Mara*!" Hilburne moaned with a wan smile as he massaged his aching jaw, recognizing his ex-wife, former B movie screen queen/pinup model Mara Vickers, originally from San Francisco, who obviously recognized him too. She was older now, but hadn't lost her taut, voluptuous figure. She also spent a lot of time working out, as evidenced by the power of her punch.

Hilburne's dumbstruck daze was broken by another familiar, but friendlier, voice. "Hey, is that any way to greet an old friend?"

"*Tony!*" Hilburne said as Tony Landon, a boyishly handsome, middle-aged yet youthful-looking man from Philadelphia with a thick, black pompadour, pushed his way past Hank and Mara to hug his former mentor. Hilburne joked, "Hey, is that a bear rug or what?"

"No way, man," Tony said, sifting through his thick locks. "Not dyed either," he added proudly. "Just keep it nice 'n' greased, like always."

"Hey, I still got my original carpeting too!" Hilburne laughed.

"Remember me too, Hilly?" interrupted another deep,

resonant voice. Hilburne let go of Tony to embrace a tall, muscular, middle-aged, African American ex-New Orleans cop named John Shift. His painfully sexy wife Patricia—Patti—Grier-Shift, formerly Miss Black Chicago, was standing by his side, radiating sensuality in her tiger-striped patterned halter top and tight, black slacks.

"What the hell are all of *you* doing here?" Hilburne asked, looking around the assemblage of acquaintances from his past, obviously bringing along old baggage for the trip. "I thought we were never supposed to meet again. *Ever*."

"That's a good question," said Jimmy Honda, an athletic, slickly groomed Japanese-American native Seattleite of the same general age group, working his way through the crowd. He politely shook Hilburne's hand, both eschewing their customary masculine embrace for this more traditional but impersonal salutation. There was some tension evident there too, but at least no immediate physical abuse. In fact, Jimmy would have preferred a more intimately affectionate expression, but decided against it, given present company and circumstances.

"Jimmy!" Hilburne said while shaking his hand. "So... what's the answer? I don't even know who invited me!"

"Neither do we," Tony Landon said. "Come, we have a table by the window. Join us, and we'll figure this out."

"It seems the food and drinks are on the house, too," John Shift added. "Which is okay by me, whatever we're doin' here. Just as long as this thing doesn't take off while we're *in* it."

"Glad you tested the drinks first for poison," Hank said only half-jokingly as he followed them back to their window-side seats, two tables pushed together to accommodate the large group. The restaurant was slowly spinning as the single waiter brought two more complementary martinis to the table, both for Hilburne. His reputation obviously preceded him. The sound system was playing the usual mix of Frank Sinatra, Dean Martin, Sammy Davis Jr., Ella Fitzgerald, Julie London, June Christy, Bobby Darin, Nat King Cole, and other crooners popular during the Space Age, in keeping with the theme. The vibe was vintage supper club with a healthy dose of retro-futurism. It was like a rotating museum with a full bar menu. Hilburne felt right at home. He hadn't been to this restaurant—either the Eye of the Needle or its companion, the Emerald Suite—in at least a decade, even though he lived over in a posh Ballard neighborhood called Olympic Manor, an enclave of midcentury modernism which Hilburne likened to "Palm Springs with water." Looking around, he noticed nothing had changed much inside, much less outside the Space Needle, except for one alarming detail:

Besides the sole waiter, who resembled and behaved like an androgynous mannequin, and the aforementioned guests, all dressed like to the nines for the mystery occasion, no one else was there, just like the eerily empty lobby. *No one.*

"Where the hell is everyone else?" Hilburne asked rather rhetorically. "Is this a private party? In the middle of the day?"

"We have the joint to ourselves!" Tony said, slapping Hilburne on the back with cheerful confirmation. "Who cares why? I say we deserve it, for all the sacrifices we made that *no one* will ever hear about it. Not here on Earth, anyway."

"Hey, wait for me!" said a swarthy, suave but subtly menacing dark-haired man emerging from the men's room, pulling up his zipper.

Hilburne got up to hug him. Jimmy Honda noticed.

"Jake!" Hilburne said. "The gang's all here now! Well, *almost.*"

Jake Luna—a Cuban-American born Joaquin Romero Luna in Miami, Florida, the same month Hilburne was born up in Manhattan—pulled away gently from the man-hug and sat next to Hank, who had his arm around Mara, now smoking her sixth cigarette of the day as she downed her second martini since breakfast, which had consisted of two Bloody Marys and four cigarettes.

Hilburne noticed how cozy Hank and Mara were behaving but made no comment, especially since he didn't want to invite any more physical abuse. They were obviously an item, which was news to him, but news that no longer concerned him.

"It *is* very odd that no one else is here," Jimmy Honda observed uneasily. "I mean, it's unsettling enough we're finally allowed to congregate like this in a public place. Only this feels more *private,* doesn't it?"

"Maybe the lunch crowd hasn't arrived yet," Hilburne said, looking at his watch. "And my invitation said I should be here at noon sharp, yet you all beat me here, and except for Jimmy, whom I haven't seen in ages, I'm the only local here now."

"Most of us were coming from out of town," Jake Luna said. "Flew in last night and wanted to get here early, out of curiosity, to find out what this is all about. None of us knew it was a secretly organized rendezvous until we all showed up at once, from all parts of the country and different phases of our lives. Me, I just flew in from Miami. I've got my old life back, for what it's worth, teaching Spanish at the University. Boring, but stable."

"I should've never quit football for *any* of this crap," Hank chimed in. "Then I would've never met any of you to begin with. I had to fly all the way from Texas just to see you clowns! I didn't even know you'd be here, otherwise I wouldn't have made it! Me, I was doing fine with drudging up the past." Mara continued to silently sulk by Hank's side.

"C'mon, Hank, don't be that way," Jake said, patting Hank on the shoulder with condescending consolation. "We can all get along, now that it's all behind us, and maybe even share some stories. We're bonded by our common experiences."

"Speak for *yourselves*," Mara mumbled into her glass.

"So we're all together again, for the first time since it began," Hilburne said.

"All except the one who never made it back," Jake said. "She's either still MIA, or wasn't invited to this party, for some reason."

"Or just couldn't make it," Tony said.

"I'm afraid she's lost *forever*," Hilburne said grimly. "Hopefully she's someplace *safe,* at least."

"I still have nightmares," Jimmy said softly, but audibly. "Just being inside this place creeps me out. Brings it all back."

"The interior is a lot different," John Shift said, looking around the fancy restaurant. "But then this one wasn't designed to travel through space, was it?"

"Ours were equipped with better bars, too," Hilburne said. "But then *our* booze was, shall we say, 'imported,' right? Hey, I wonder if our old friend put this together?"

"You mean that mad scientist who sucked us into this whole mess?" Tony said with a wan grin.

"That *bastard*," Patti said, hugging John's round, hard arm. "I almost lost you because of him. No man had any business out there. *Or* woman."

"I wouldn't trade those experiences, even the disturbing and dangerous ones, for anything in the world," Hilburne said. "Well, not in *this* world, anyway."

"You're a cad," Mara hissed.

Hilburne frowned, and moved on. "I think all of us owe a debt to that so-called mad scientist, and his whole clandestine program. I mean, what else would we have done in our lives that would've even come close to these accomplishments?"

"But if we can't brag about 'em to anybody but each other, what the hell good are they?" Hank growled.

"Just memories," Jimmy said, as if in a trance. "Memories, and nightmares. I can't even tell the difference anymore."

"Hey, there was an unlimited supply of booze and broads in space!" Hilburne said enthusiastically. "No complaints here!"

Mara threw what was left of her martini across the table, right in Hilburne's face. He simply smiled wiped it away with a napkin. Everyone at the table laughed with discomfort, except Hank, who reveled in the display of disgust. Mara scowled and signaled the waiter, patiently waiting by, for a fresh replacement.

Licking his lips, Hilburne said, "I'm tasting… Hangar One Vodka, from a distillery called St. George's Spirits that just opened down in Alameda, California. Talk about a cutting edge menu—that was fast! Can't believe they stocked it already! Compliments to the bar manager, or whoever organized this little powwow. Good stuff, by Earth's standards. But nothing here compares to the liquor out there. You have to admit I'm right about that. *Right*?" He raised his own barely touched martini for a toast.

No one joined him.

"Cheers anyway!" he said, sipping the drink judiciously. "Vodka Martini. Three olives. Very dry. Shaken not stirred. Perfect, at least by local standards. Just how Bond would like it."

"That's only in the movies—the *real* Bond cocktail is the Vesper, at least in the books," Tony said, sipping his drink, then belatedly clinking glasses with Hilburne's. "Here's to 007. I'll drink to *that.*"

"We should all switch to Vespers! *Waiter!*"

"Those Vespers will knock you on your ass," John said. "I had a few of those back in Nawlins once, while on a stakeout, yet. Stopped at a bar in the Quarter just to kill time. I got totally blitzed and blew the bust."

"So they promoted you to an astronaut?" Hank asked sarcastically.

John ignored the hostility from his flank, and addressed the group. "*Any*way, it's one part gin, two parts vodka, no wait, the other way around, then a dash of, what's it called…"

"Lillet Blanc," Patti said. "I know. I was there, remember? That's how we met. At that same bar."

"Yea," John grinned. "You were dancin' on stage!"

"You mean *stripping*," Mara said.

"Hey, who invited you here anyway, bitch?" Patti shot back.

"Who invited *you*, jigaboo?" Hank spat.

John reflexively turned and rammed his elbow harshly into Hank's jaw, knocking him backward, as Mara and Patti lunged at one another, pulling each other's hair, clawing at each other's clothes, their large, pointy breasts jiggling loose from their dresses. The waiter just stood by passively with Mara's fresh martini on a tray, waiting for the ruckus to die down so he could serve it properly.

The combined forces of Hilburne, Tony, Jake and Jimmy finally managed to separate John from Hank and Patti from Mara, but not before the nearby tables and chairs were knocked over.

Disheveled but subdued, wiping blood from their noses and lips, adjusting ties and covering overly exposed cleavage, the battling quartet finally sat back down, but further apart than before.

"Sorry I let him get to me," John said to the group.

"Yea, I guess I was out of line," Hank added rather insincerely, massaging his sore jaw, the true source of his regret. "Sorry."

Patti and Mara just glowered at each other for a moment, then did their best to avoid any eye contact.

"I'd really like to know who thought that bringing us all back together after all this time was a good idea," Jimmy said.

"I'm telling you, it's the mad scientist," Tony said. "I just *know* it."

"How could he even still be alive?" Jake said. "He looked old thirty years ago!"

"Last I heard he was back in Boston," Hilburne said. "But that was ages ago, right after we got back."

"A lot has changed since then," Jake said.

"Not enough," said Jimmy. "The world has changed, as was predicted, but we haven't, apparently."

"We *all* changed forever the moment we signed those papers," John said. "That's all the change we needed. *More* than we needed. Or wanted. None of us counted on any of this wild shit."

Hilburne waved him off. "I must be in the minority—sorry, John, so to speak—but I still look back on everything like a pleasant dream, even if much of it gave us nightmares. It was all quite traumatic in many ways, true. But no one else in history, at least no human being, can claim these experiences. And since the program was cancelled, probably never will."

"Yes, but it was cancelled because of what happened to *us*," Jimmy pointed out. "Because of what we found out there."

"Way more than I bargained for, that's for sure," Hank said. "Things down here just went all the hell while we were away, and just got worse when we got back."

"You saying it's all *our* fault?" Jake asked Hank.

Hank just shrugged. "Who knows. I still believe I brought back a virus that infected the population. Now it's too late anyway, so what difference does it make?"

"Imagine our planet if we had have been able to share what we discovered," Hilburne said. "Being sworn to secrecy may prevent widespread panic, but it also deprives our world of many precious secrets. Imagine a Mai Tai that can cure cancer! *Man*, I wish I still had that recipe!"

"You have a point there," Jimmy conceded thoughtfully. "Gene Roddenberry had no idea how close he was to the truth."

"Or George Lucas, for that matter," Jake added.

"Or Steven Spielberg," John said.

"Hell, even Rod Serling," Tony chimed in. "That guy was so on the money it's scary."

"'The Outer Limits,' 'Lost in Space'... *all* those shows were basically documentaries sold as mass entertainment," Hilburne said, nodding his head in agreement. "But I believe they had consultants from our program working with them, guiding the productions, shaping and informing the scripts, so not *too* much was given away, even subliminally. The producers and writers all knew the same people we did."

"No, I think the consultants were working in a strictly creative capacity, without divulging any actual facts," Tony said.

"Yea, you may be right about that," Hilburne said. "Good point. They probably had no idea that what they were selling was the results of scientific research. Our scientific research."

Everyone nodded in reluctant agreement.

"I actually wrote my own treatment proposing a new

television series, but got shot down by the powers that be," Tony said.

"What was it called?" asked Hilburne.

"'The X Files.'"

"Nicely non-descriptive and vague. I like it."

"I bet they'll pitch it to a producer themselves and totally rip me off," Tony said with bitter resignation. "That's Hollywood. Right, Mara?"

The former actress just rolled her eyes and said, "Don't get me started, kid."

"Mankind owes a great debt to us," Hilburne said, quickly interrupting her. "And to the man who started it all, with one impossible dream—the exploration and colonization of outer space...."

## VESPER

*3 oz gin*
*1 oz vodka*
*½ oz Lillet Blanc (or blonde Lillet)*

*Stir with cracked ice, strain then serve with lemon peel garnish.*

* * *

*Riddles of the Unmind I*

The Great Unmind pondered the riddles of the universe. "What is it, that is everywhere the same, and everywhere different?"

As in all ponderings of the Unmind, it answered itself. It was in communication with no other. "The speed of light."

The Unmind was a riddle in its own right, being what appeared to be a single immense intellect, yet comprised solely of the unmindful biological processes of an uncountable number of fungal cells. All over the Earth, vast colonies of yeasts, molds, and mushrooms contributed their biological activity to the Unmind, bound together by subtle chemical signals. Each cell was an automaton, merely eating, reproducing, and dying in response to its local environment, but the sum total of all of that cellular activity resulted in the organized entity that was the Great Unmind. It did not think, so much as recognize and react to the forces of the natural world, but that instinctive reaction to nature imbued the Unmind with a strange internal mirror of reality. All things that were experienced by its myriad cells resulted in a pattern of information, which was able to alter its internal state by self-reflection. In turn, that self-reflection subtly guided the actions of the cells that made up its form. Considering that about a quarter of the biomass of living things on Earth is fungi, the number of cells making up the Unmind was vastly larger than those of any other intellect on the planet. Abstract scientific thought was therefore a rather trivial exercise for the Unmind.

"In what way is the speed of light everywhere the same?"

"In its measurement at the smallest of scales. Everywhere that the measurement is taken, in that specific locale the numeric value of the speed is always the same."

"In what way is the speed of light everywhere different?"

"It is different when measured from one locale to another."

"So cell A can measure the speed of light at A, and cell B can measure the speed of light at B, and their measurements will be the same, but if cell A measures the speed of light at B, it will be different?"

"Yes, and if cell B measures the speed of light at A it will also differ, though it will be the inverse of the measurement from A to B. For example, assume cell A measures the speed of light as one light-second per second at A, but measures the speed as one-half light-second per second at B. Then, cell B will measure the speed of light as one light-second per second at B, but two light-seconds per second at A." The Unmind did not use the time unit of "seconds" or distance units of "light-seconds", as those are arbitrary human constructs, but the terms have been substituted for ease of understanding, in this translation.

"What is the purpose of measurement, if it differs so?"

"The measurement of the speed of light is most useful as a relative measure. If one measures the speed of light in a variety of locales, one can then choose to move in the path where the speed of light is the greatest, which will provide a faster mode of travel." This sort of practicality was typical of the Unmind, as it always was seeking ways to optimize the actions of its component fungi. Though fungal colonies are not generally motile, they do rely on various external transport methods for distributing their spores.

"The riddle is not fully answered. These relative measurements seem arbitrary and unexplained. What is the mechanism for the differences?"

"The speed of light is a ratio like any speed, of some distance traveled in an amount of time. However, the speed of light is also a fundamental aspect of the universe, which determines how matter and energy behave. As the speed of light changes between locales, other fundamental properties of matter will change along with it."

"What properties are those?"

"In the current discussion, it is distance which is the most profound change. Any physical object composed of atoms is held together by electromagnetic forces which propagate at the speed of light. Increasing or decreasing the speed of light will alter those forces, and cause objects to get bigger or smaller. So, any physical measurement device which is calibrated for distance will grow in size where the speed of light is larger, and shrink in size where the speed of light is less. If cell A measures the speed of light as half speed at B, it is because A's measurement device is twice the size of B's measurement device."

"How can cells A and B ever agree on the sizes of their measuring devices?"

"Assume cell A and cell B start at the same time in the same locale A, with two identical measuring devices. Cell B then takes one measuring device and moves to region B, which we have defined as having half the speed of light than at A. To A's eye both cell B and B's measuring device would shrink to be half the length that they originally were. Cell B would, on the other hand, see cell A, and A's measuring device, grow to twice their original size."

"Very well. I see now how the speed of light can be everywhere the same, and yet everywhere different." The Unmind was satisfied with this riddle. Lacking true consciousness, it didn't realize that its choice of this specific riddle was a direct result of the odd congregation of humans in a Seattle restaurant. That was just one input in a sea of diverse experiences being aggregated into the Unmind by all of its daughter cells around the Earth. The Unmind did not assign significance to such events. It permitted Nature to assess the impact, in the ebb and flow of natural selection. The Unmind merely pondered, and directed its component cells accordingly.

# "IMPOSSIBLE"

*2 oz bourbon*
*2 tablespoons powdered sweetened lemon iced tea mix*
*2 oz unsweetened cranberry juice*
*2 oz root beer*

*Shake everything but the root beer thoroughly with plenty of ice, pour into 12 oz glass. Top with root beer, stir.*

*Washington, D.C., 1961*
Professor Wilhelm Falkenstein was walking though the Rose Garden at the White House with the newly elected President of the United States, John Fitzgerald Kennedy. They were discussing the secret launch of the Space Needle Program, based in the *other* Washington, clear across the country.

It was early February, shortly after the inauguration, and JFK was still basking in his narrow victory after a very close election against his Republican challenger Richard M. Nixon.

"It pays to know people, I guess," Professor Falkenstein—a tall, bald, foreboding man in his 60s with large, penetrating, ice blue eyes—said to the president.

"You mean my asshole father?" Kennedy said. "I owe him nothing."

"I was thinking more of Frank Sinatra," Falkenstein said with a grin.

"Oh. Well, I *do* owe Frank a small debt of gratitude for his support."

"Frank and his friends."

"Dean and Sammy. Of course."

"And?"

"Okay, Joey and Peter, too."

"You're conveniently leaving out the crucial members of the extended Rat Pack, Mister President. And I don't mean Bogart, Tony, Janet, or Shirley."

"Again, I don't know what you mean, sir."

The professor shrugged. "Doesn't matter now. The best man won. Or at least the right man at the right time. Your opponent would not have been an adequate ally in this particularly crucial venture. For one thing, he would have balked at the necessary further funding to complete the project. He's much more conservative than your predecessor. And therefore more resistant to change."

Kennedy nodded. "Yes. Ike almost gave it all away with that parting remark about the Military Industrial Complex, though."

"I trust your lips won't be as loose."

"You can trust me, sir. I'm very good at keeping secrets."

Just then, JFK looked up and saw his wife Jackie standing in the window of the Oval Office, waving, and the president and professor waved back politely.

"She keeps a very close eye on you, I see," Falkenstein observed.

"But not even she knows the truth about where I spend many of my evenings."

"On official business."

"Exactly."

"Like your cabinet meetings with Marilyn Monroe in cabin number three at Sinatra's Cal-Neva Resort in North Lake Tahoe?"

Kennedy stopped and looked at Falkenstein with a rigid expression. "How did you know that?"

"Just letting you know that we have my own friends in high places, even higher than yours, Mister President. And they precede your successful promotion by many, many years."

"I must make sure not to piss them off," Kennedy said with a nervous chuckle.

"That would be wise. Especially since they know a lot of the same people you know, but have greater influence over them. There are elements within our organization that disagree on tactics, and whose motives are grounded more in fear than in hope, but I am confident calmer heads and more peaceful minds will eventually prevail, and uniformly dictate the direction both of our agenda and the future of mankind, especially since shaping mankind's future *is* our agenda. After all, we learned many hard lessons from the insane, futile megalomania of Adolph Hitler. At least I'd like to think so. One day, if all goes according to plan, we will all co-exist in perfect harmony, not just on our world, but within our universe. But meantime, just watch what you say, and whom you say it to."

"Professor, you're a mysterious man and frankly, you're wigging me out a little bit."

"No need to worry, Mister President. We consider you a personal friend, as well as a colleague."

"'We?' You keep saying that."

Falkenstein found Kennedy's paranoia bemusing, but withheld his mirth so as not to appear patronizing. "NASA, of course."

"That's Ike's baby, though."

"But you've adopted it. Nominally, of course. As long as you let us run it as we see fit, there won't be any, shall we say, conflict of interests."

"This office really is only a figurehead, isn't it? Ike was right. The president is merely a pawn."

"You were briefed on that before you even launched your campaign. So no complaints now. Look at it this way. If you can't be the actual owner, better to be tapped as coach of the team than merely stand by helplessly watching the game unfold, just another faceless voice in the stands, with no power over any of the plays on the field."

"Yes. Hopefully I can at least advance some of my pet causes, like Civil Rights."

"Bigotry is bad for business. And besides, it's merely cynically exploited ignorance, just another corporate driven device to control the masses by dividing them into tribalistic factions. Divide and conquer, the oldest trick in the proverbial book. This fostering of the mob mentality is finally backfiring, as evidenced by the growing unrest among the oppressed. Your impassioned support for equality is another reason we chose you over your opponent."

"*Chose* me?"

"Would you rather give credit to Sinatra's Chicago friends? Although they are our friends too, when needed. We have lots of friends for lots of different reasons. Your brother Robert's investigations into the Mafia will be permitted as long as they bear no actual fruit or cause any structural harm to this carefully calculated paradigm. We need to maintain a certain balance to achieve our ends, at least for now."

"'We' meaning NASA."

"That's one branch of our organization, yes."

"Of the Military Industrial Complex?"

"That's one name for it. Not ours. But we're not nationalists. We're humanists. At least most of us. The ones that truly matter. So it doesn't matter what we're called. Not to me, anyway." Falkenstein pointed to one of the roses and said, "As the Bard wrote, 'by any other name'…"

Kennedy nodded and sighed. "Like 'Apollo.' It's all becoming very clear to me, I'm afraid."

From behind the rosebushes, with a shy giggle, erupted the President's three-year old daughter Caroline. She ran to her father, who stooped down to hug her tenderly. She smiled broadly, but kept politely quiet, as if recognizing the solemnity of the adult discussion she had interrupted, even at her young age.

JFK broke that silence by lifting her up in his arms, then suddenly whirling around in a circle, faster and faster, holding out his daughter at arms length. He and the girl laughed wildly. "Faster, Daddy, faster!" squealed Caroline, "Faster than light!"

After a few rapid turns, Kennedy slowed and set Caroline back down on the grass, where she quickly ran off behind the bushes. The President suppressed his grin as he caught his breath. He put his hand on a fencepost, a little unsteady from dizziness. "Pardon me, that was a bit fast. My head is still spinning."

"It is a pleasure seeing you with your delightful family. The entire country looks to you as a model of the American Dream. Such a smart girl too, how old?"

"Three last November."

"And yet she already knows the term 'faster than light'. Impressive. She'll be a force to be reckoned with one day."

"Yes, though I think she was a bit generous with her assessment of my speed of rotation. I'm a bit slower than light." The president grinned at the thought.

Falkenstein considered a moment. "On the contrary, she was right on the money. You were indeed spinning faster than light, at least in relation to most of the universe."

Kennedy retorted, "That's absurd. Einstein proved nothing can go faster than light."

"A common misconception. As you spun with your daughter in your arms, relative to you, the Sun itself was going much faster than light. Let me explain. The Sun is about 8.3 light-minutes from the Earth. That means light takes over eight minutes to get from the surface of the sun to the surface of the Earth. When you spun around, the Sun was whirling around you in a circular arc, with a radius of 8.3 light-minutes."

The President looked puzzled. "I don't see how...."

Falkenstein continued, "All motion is relative. You can say that you were spinning and the Sun was stationary, or that you were stationary and the Sun was spinning around you. The concepts are mathematically equivalent, in the absence of any 'preferred' frame of reference. But if the Sun spins around a radius of 8.3 light-minutes in a couple of seconds, it must traverse the circumference of 2 times 8.3 times pi, or about 50 light-minutes, in 2 seconds. That's hundreds of times the speed of light, which is only one light-second per second. If you think of the stars and galaxies similarly spinning at their longer distances, they must have been traveling millions of times the speed of light relative to you and your daughter."

Kennedy looked dubious. "Why haven't I ever heard of this? I thought light was the limit?"

"Einstein's relativity theory was incomplete. It only worked well when there was no rotation or gravity involved. Add those in and the theory starts to break down, yielding inconsistent results. Scientists discount such objections with mumbo-jumbo about 'non-inertial reference frames' and 'motion relative to the fixed stars', but the fact is, there's no rigorous mathematical explanation on the quantum physics level, of how you can spin your daughter that fast in relation to the rest of the universe. Yet, it is an everyday occurrence."

The President considered the ramifications of this. "Wait, if Einstein's theories aren't fully proven, then aren't we taking a big gamble with these new NASA programs? Shouldn't we prove the science first?"

"We don't have the time, if we're to beat the Russians. They excel at putting abstract ideas into practice, as they showed with Sputnik. Whatever their ideology, they are a robust people who have conquered much adversity through perseverance. Their rockets are crude but rock-solid; I don't doubt they'll be launching the same rocket systems they are building today for 100 years to come, when Apollo is nothing but a distant memory. We, as the envoys of freedom, must forge ahead. You have, however, just realized the reason why our space program must be a two-pronged approach. Conventional science leads to the Apollo moon landing. Unconventional science drives the Space Needle Program. We suspect things we have yet to prove, but the Space Needles will give us certainty."

"I don't see how the American people will consent to funding two space programs."

Professor Falkenstein just smiled and patted Kennedy reassuringly on the shoulder. "We're all in this together, Mister President. The many real and immediate threats that face our nation pale in comparison to the possible threats posed by unknown entities in our vast galaxy. Our common enemies may finally unify our species. Or we will be chastened by the revelation of our common friends in the universe, both humbled and emboldened by the knowledge we are not alone. Our future depends on which they happen to be, even if it's a challenging combination of both. In any case, there's only one way to find out."

"The Space Needle Program."

"Exactly. It was only the Space Needle Project when we first started developing it after the war. But now that we've entered the final phase, it's officially a program that will permanently and positively change the course of human history like nothing else before it. It is being kept under wraps, sharing the same funding as the Apollo program, to avoid awkward questions. As the public face of the project, once it's revealed to the public (if it's ever made public), you will get much of the credit."

"Or the blame, depending on how it works out."

"Precisely."

"And the prototype being unveiled next year at the Seattle World's Fair, concurrent with the launch of this secret program, is designed to divert the public's attention and negate any brewing theories about its true purpose."

"Bingo," the professor said.

Kennedy nodded and sighed again. This was way more than he bargained for. But it was too late to back out now. He was trapped, with only two possible exit strategies. He preferred the first one, meaning serving two terms before comfortable retirement, basking in a legacy that would glorify his family name forever. That was the plan, anyway.

"So despite the charade of a democratic election, I was basically selected by secret committee due to my willful if uninformed compliance to this program?"

"And your damn fine head of hair. I admit, I'm jealous!"

Kennedy just gave Falkenstein a blank stare. Then the professor slapped him on the shoulder and laughed, and Kennedy reluctantly joined in the joke at his own expense. The professor reminded Kennedy of a villain bent on world domination from one of those Ian Fleming spy thrillers he loved so much. Basically, the president couldn't figure out whether Falkenstein was sinisterly subversive or artfully ambiguous. Either way, the president was anxious to end this meeting.

"We should go back inside soon," Kennedy said. "Jackie is waiting. And she's been drinking. Alone."

"She must never, ever know about this," the professor said solemnly. "At least, not before the rest of humanity. If it ever even comes to that."

"I understand. No pillow talk from me about sensitive matters. I have a lot of practice with that, too. And not just with my wife, as you apparently know."

"None of your trusted confidantes, in or out of bed, must prematurely discover anything about this program, or frankly, it will put you *all* in serious jeopardy."

"Is that a threat, professor?"

"More like a promise. And not one I'll be in charge of enforcing, either. I'm only a scientist. And I abhor violence, even as a means to an end. But others with more authority in our organization are being quite strictly vigilant, and they are not to be contradicted or betrayed. Keep in mind this is all being done for the sake of the greater good, even if in the short time, there will be some unfortunate but necessary casualties."

Kennedy shook his head and said, "It's amazing, and frightening, how little power any of us actually have over anyone's fate, including our own."

"We're trying to change that, Mister President, by initiating first contact and then making any diplomatic or, only if necessary, I'm assured, militaristic maneuvers the situation may call for. All of our mutual interests are intertwined, Mister President. It all comes down to National Security. From civil liberties to the exploration of outer space. Peaceful engagement will be the preferred protocol. After all, if we don't encounter the aliens on their own turf first, much less colonize uninhabited or at least friendly worlds before we destroy our own, the Russians will. We have intelligence that claims they are planning a similar program, but reportedly without the benefit of our accidentally acquired, extra-terrestrial knowledge. Sputnik was merely a taunt, a devious ruse. They are as ambitious as we are, if not more so. Their goal is conquest, not exploration. We're just lucky their research isn't as advanced, restricted to earthbound science. But, being communists and despots, if they happen to beat us to the punch, as it were, their intentions and interactions will not be as benign as ours. Look how the Reds completely ruined the beautiful island of Cuba, effectively cutting it off from the rest of civilization. Think of what they'd do to a celestial paradise! We need to pre-emptively introduce and spread democracy across the galaxy, even I we have to do it by force. That, as you know, is the American way. It's a race against time, Mister President."

"Yes. I often feel my own clock ticking. It scares me, frankly. My hourglass feels less than half full, despite my much touted, relatively youthful age, at least for *this* office. Can't shake this feeling of… mortality. I am consumed with a sense of urgency."

"Then we have no time to waste, do we?"

"No. Keep me posted on any changes to the launch schedule."

"Oh, believe me, Mister President, we will. You are our handsome, charming, eloquent ambassador to the entire world. It will be up to you to either reveal the happy truth, heralding a new era in interstellar relations, with all the scientific and practical benefits that implies, or prevent a widespread panic and total breakdown of the system if we encounter hostile races and forces. At every step of the process, you will be kept abreast. In more ways than one, I take it."

Kennedy smiled wanly. He was weary of the professor's innuendos, despite or rather because of their veracity. But the professor was not all he seemed to be, in anyone's presence, and for very specific reasons.

Though semi-retired from the halls of higher education, Professor Falkenstein retained a position of academic authority at MIT, and still maintained a residence in his long time hometown of Boston, though he had been born and raised in Berlin. Fleeing Germany shortly after the Nazi occupation as a "conscientious objector" to the racial genocide, he had always been a firm believer in the ultimate integration of all human cultures. The refugee was granted asylum via his contacts in the US science community, and after a thorough vetting he was swiftly recruited by the Pentagon for the fledgling Space Needle Project, since the military was already looking beyond the Axis into outer space for its next challenge. This was concurrent with Falkenstein's authoritatively arranged induction as an instructor of the advanced PhD program in Advanced Rocket Science at MIT, to help him assimilate into American society. Fluent in several languages, Falkenstein quickly mastered an American accent and, to avoid any suspicious controversy or patriotic bigotry, claimed he had been raised in a Swedish boarding school, hence his penchant for Scandinavian architecture, which influenced the modernist "futurism" movement already sweeping the culture. In fact, the Space Needle rocket ships were all designed in this modernist mode, though the genesis for the concept was alien technology culled from a crashed "flying saucer," recovered by the U.S. military after several eyewitness accounts of a UFO in the skies over the New Mexico desert, shortly after the end of the war.

The top-secret Space Needle project, first conceived by Falkenstein and a small group of like-minded scientists in an underground research facility located deep beneath Roswell, constructed almost immediately following the discovery and study of the UFO and its two deceased passengers, was very much a matter of carefully protected national security. Though Falkenstein was an integral part of the project's development, he was not the ultimate authority, and in fact took his orders through a clandestine chain of command. Not even he knew who, or what, was ultimately calling the shots.

For the past decade, to continue the pattern of strategic deception, Falkenstein had been an honorary member of the University of Washington faculty, primarily as a researcher, even though this was not a matter of public knowledge. His capacity at UDub was often explained as "guest lecturer," and indeed, he often held forth publicly on matters of physics and astronomy, his professional fields of study and expertise. But that was not his true purpose for being there, or anywhere.

John F. Kennedy was learning that this program was likewise his true purpose for being president, or rather the titular head of an allegedly altruistic puppet regime, to help usher in the manifest destiny of humanity at a rapidly accelerated pace.

As the president and the professor walked into the Oval Office, the First Lady was already on her second cocktail, a French 75. She was standing next to the president's desk on which an ornate, expensive silver tray with a pitcher and two more glasses, ready to serve.

"Have you tried these?" she asked Falkenstein, handing him a champagne glass filled to the bubbly brim with the requisite fluids, which he immediately sipped. "It's called a French 75. Jack and I were introduced to them on a trip to France a few years ago. I did my research and discovered it was created at the New York Bar in Paris in 1915. It's such a lovely drink, don't you think?"

Falkenstein nodded in agreement. "Oh yes, I am quite familiar with this little concoction. Smooth and potent, but not too strong for a, shall we say, midday matinee. Excellent choice, Mrs. Kennedy."

"Please, call me Jackie. Cheers!" They clinked glasses.

The president took a glass off the tray and drank as well, belatedly joining the impromptu toast, though with a look of quiet consternation. "Okay, but no more after that one, all right, dear?"

She ignored her husband, a habit she had honed over the years strictly as a defense mechanism, and asked the professor, "So what were you and Jack talking about out there?"

"Politics, what else?" Falkenstein answered quickly, pre-empting the president's awkward attempt at admittedly skilled subterfuge.

The president nodded and continued sipping his drink.

After taking his final sip, Falkenstein said, "Now, I must leave you two beautiful people. I have to make a lot of telephone calls today. I'm rounding up…a team. For our next assignment."

"Which is?"

"Let's just call it… an experiment in cultural diversity."

"That's wonderful!" Jackie said. "But too bad you have to leave so soon. We barely had a chance to talk!"

"Well, these calls are very private, and they can't wait any longer."

The First Lady was suddenly flustered. "If only someone would invent a portable pocket phone you could carry around with you, like a camera! Maybe it would even *have* a camera! And you could do other things on it as well, like look up directions or research the origins of a cocktail!"

"I'm working on it," Falkenstein said. "But first things first…."

## FRENCH 75

*2 oz champagne*
*1 oz gin*
*½ oz lemon juice*
*2 dashes simple syrup*

*Mix gin, syrup, and lemon juice in cocktail shaker with ice, then strain into glass and top with champagne.*

* * *

*Riddles of the Unmind II*

The fungal Unmind pondered riddles. "I am a series of boxes, each larger than the last. All contain nothing, save one that contains everything. I can perform only one action, which is to dump the contents of the box of everything into the next larger box, leaving nothing behind. When I do this, the contents of the box are slightly re-arranged; otherwise they remain motionless. What am I?"

The Unmind answered itself from another portion of its being, "You are all of space and time, containing the universe."

"What does each box in the riddle symbolize?"

"The three dimensions of space."

:What does the sequence of different boxes symbolize?"

"The dimension of time."

"Why does the size of the boxes increase in the sequence?"

"The universe expands in spatial extent over time."

"How is it that space and time are both dimensions of the universe, but have distinctly different qualities? Why are space and time not in all ways equivalent?"

"In space we have freedom of movement, but in time we are always constrained to move ever forward at the same rate," the Unmind answered.

"What constrains our movement in time?"

"It is the Law of Conservation of Energy which constrains our movement through time."

"What is this law?"

"It states that the energy of things in the universe is always the same. If energy changes in one locality, then that energy must simply have moved to an adjacent locale, or altered its nature, as from mass energy to light energy. The total amount of energy at any time in the universe cannot change."

"This is comprehensible, but how does this constrain us in time?"

"To better understand time and space, using an analogy to our perceptions of three spatial dimensions, let us reduce space to two dimensions, like a photograph, and let time be the third dimension." The Unmind actually had no concept of a photograph as humans know it; it used instead a representation of the projection of shadows of objects from a distant light source upon a surface. To avoid confusion, that concept is translated here as a 'photograph'.

The Unmind continued its pondering. "I believe I comprehend the analogy. Time-space is like a stack of such photographs, each indicating a moment in time where the two dimensions of space are captured."

"Yes, the photographs of the past start with the Big Bang, and progress forward to the photograph of present time. The photographs of the future are unexposed, blank canvases, yet to be written."

"If we have this big stack of photographs representing the whole history of the universe, what keeps us from moving around as we wish? Why can't we visit the past and future as easily as east and west?" Again, the terminology of "east" and "west" is a substitution for the Unmind's true designations for the directions of sunrise and sunset.

"That is the difference between space and time. In space we can go anywhere, east, west, north, south, up, down; but in time we march in lockstep with everyone else. In time, we have no choice."

"But can't we travel in time at different rates, some slower and some faster?"

"No, that is an illusion. In space we have such options, to travel faster or slower, backwards or forwards. Time is rigid. As an example, assume two cells A and B are in the same locale, and both decide to leave. A chooses to move at a fast pace, while B progresses more slowly. Soon A will outdistance B. When A gets to her destination, B will be nowhere to be found."

"That seems in accordance with experience."

"Now imagine the same movement in time. If cell A could move faster than cell B in time, A would progress to the next photograph of the universe before B could get there. To A's view, B wouldn't be in that universe at all. Cell A could make any changes A wanted without B's intervention, and then move on to the next photograph in line. As for cell B, she would arrive late into a photograph already taken, where A's actions had been recorded before B ever got there. Cell B could have no effect on that universe that was B's 'now'."

"That does seem at odds with experience."

"Not just 'at odds', impossible, due to the Law of Conservation of Energy. At any moment the energy of cell B could be transformed to another form, for example by a disintegrator ray, but the energy at least must remain constant. Energy cannot be created or destroyed, only transformed. If B had fallen behind A's timeline and disappeared to A's worldview, no trace of cell B or her intrinsic energy would remain. The Law of Conservation of Energy would be violated. Cell B must always exist in cell A's 'now'; A can never move faster than B through time."

"Cannot cell A and cell B have differing perceptions of the passage of time?"

"Whatever the *perception* of the rate of time may be, cells A and B must always exist in the same 'now', able to make changes to the future universe together, though B may make changes at a slower pace than A. Even if their perceptions of time vary, when one advances to the next photograph of the universe, the other must always be there, and able to act at its own rate of change. Every cell's passage through time is immutable and fixed."

"So every being in the universe must advance at the same rate through time, to arrive at the next photograph in concert with all other beings in the universe, so that all may make their personal stamp on the 'now'?"

"Exactly. No one may move faster in time than another. No one has a 'now' that is not shared by everyone. They may choose to be far in *distance* from others, by moving through space at a faster rate, but no one may escape the rigid march of time."

"I begin to see. Is travel backwards through time similarly precluded?"

"By the same Law of Conservation of Energy, an entity traveling backwards in time would appear on a photograph already taken with her forward-traveling self, doubling her energy in that snapshot of time. Conservation of energy would be violated."

"How is it that this effect of the immutability of time is not immediately perceived by all organisms, if it is an inviolate rule of the universe?"

"The observational signatures of time and space are easily confused, so it is comparatively easy for an unsophisticated being to decide that the distortions they see in quantum phenomena are from the dilation of time as well as space, instead of the purely spatial distortions that are the true case."

"Explain how such a misinterpretation could be made."

"If the local invariance of the speed of light is misinterpreted as an absolute measure of that speed, it may be perceived that it is distance and time that must change between localities, instead of distance and the speed of light. Two of the three factors (time, distance, and speed) must change for the mathematics to balance correctly. The correct interpretation is that time is fixed, and the spatial dimensions and the speed of light are variable. To a lesser mind, it may appear more likely that the speed of light is fixed, and so time *and* space must be variable."

"It would appear that such a misinterpretation would have negative effects on survival, as it is a false view of the actual workings of the universe."

"Exactly. A species using this erroneous logic will not realize that spatial distortions in a fixed timeline permit speeds nearly infinitely faster than light. Such beings will not pursue the science of long-distance space travel, and will thus remain trapped on a single world until overpopulation destroys them."

"Is it not true that our non-motile kingdom of fungi is dependent on more mobile species to correctly interpret the physical laws of the universe, in order to carry our cells to the stars?"

"Yes, that is true. To this end we endeavor to inspire the dominant motile species to see things beyond the obvious, via the chemical products we produce in our metabolism."

"That is wise, but is it not also wise to pursue more than a single course of action when the reproductive success of all fungi is at stake?"

"The Unmind acts to direct the cells to take advantage of all opportunities presented."

"Very well. I now understand how time and space differ as dimensions of the universe, and what actions will assist in the reproduction of our cells to other worlds."

## "INTERGALACTIC"

*¾ oz gin*
*¾ oz rum*
*¾ oz vodka*
*¾ oz tequila*
*1½ oz Midori Melon Liqueur*
*¾ oz lemon juice*
*1/3 oz lime juice*
*¾ oz simple syrup*
*1½ oz seltzer water*

*Shake all ingredients except soda over ice, pour (with some ice) into a 12 oz glass, leaving room for seltzer. Top with seltzer water, add a straw and stir.*

*The following facts are paraphrased from excerpts obtained illegally from the unpublished investigative report titled "Outer Space Confidential," itself intercepted by Federal authorities circa 2012 before it could be released for worldwide online distribution by InterLeaks; authors unknown and untraceable, but rumored to be rogue former employees of NASA, the NSA, and/or the CIA....*
*Internet, 2012*
The Space Needle—at least the only one with which most Earthling are familiar—had its gala premiere at the 1962 World's Fair in Seattle after years of audaciously ambitious planning. Allegedly, the sleek, instantly recognizable structure's legendary design—which immediately made it a global emblem of the Space Age, a universal beacon for futurists, and an aesthetic icon of midcentury modernism—was a result of the historic collaboration of two visionaries sharing the same dream: a businessman named Edward E. Carlson, and an architect named John Graham, Jr. Carlson, who was a chairman of the World's Fair official committee, took credit for the initial concept, i.e. a skyscraper with a restaurant at top that would open in time for the event, and remain ever after a symbol of the city's progressive ingenuity and tenacity; while Graham claimed the striking "flying saucer on a stick" visage was born of his own vivid imagination.

In fact, neither are true. Both were mere front men for the landmark's true origin and purpose. The Space Needle was merely an inactive prototype for a fleet of intergalactic spaceships entirely conceived and constructed by Professor Wilhelm Falkenstein and his team of scientists deep down with the confines of their research facility beneath Roswell.

The Space Needle revealed to the public was nearly identical in appearance to the other models, except the "flying saucer" control centers on the actual ships could pivot forward after launch as the rocket righted itself, with the astronauts strapped into their seats until it leveled off after leaving orbit and assuming its course. The saucer hub—which precisely replicated the crashed alien craft now assumed hidden by the Air Force inside a bunker in Nevada's Area 51, meticulously mimicking its advanced intergalactic flight engineering—could then pivot back to its normal upon landing. Though the control centers were not restaurants like the World's Fair version, they did contain a well-stocked bar and lushly appointed diner, complete with a resident gourmet robot chef. The rest of the ship looked like a magazine advertisement for the Home of the Future, with furniture secretly commissioned by such famous designers of the era as Le Corbusier, Eero Saarinen, Isomu Noguchi, and Charles and Ray Eames. Much of their original work for this project was later mass-produced for public consumption, and decorated the model homes of many unsuspecting civilian inhabitants.

The advanced, alien-based technology behind the launch of the fleet of seven Space Needle ships between April and October, 1962 was brilliantly conceived and flawlessly executed, incorporating several innovative inventions conceived specifically for this project, coordinated to function in painstaking concert.

Falkenstein's recently uncovered flight manual describes the proposed trajectory, naturally planned as a round trip, here presented in simple layman's language preserving the integrity of his detailed notes:

"Each ship first leaves the Earth's atmosphere using advanced Atomic Hydrogen thrusters, then intercepts a ground-based laser beam shot from an Arctic station, which pushes it faster out into space. As pulses of ruby laser light bounce back and forth between the Needle's saucer section and Earth, the energy of the pulses adds up, until the speed of the ship approximates the speed of light. When it's time for the crews to return to Earth, the ships fire up their internal thrusters, now refueled from the accumulation of interstellar Atomic Hydrogen on the outbound journey, and turn around to accelerate back toward Earth. Final deceleration is again accomplished by laser pulses from Earth, now acting to slow the incoming ship."

That was the official plan, but the reality turned out to be far stranger. While traveling near the speed of light, when the Atomic Hydrogen drives were switched on, the Space Needles surprised everyone by suddenly vanishing. It was later discovered that the thrusters were capable of pushing the ships far faster than the speed of light; so fast, in fact, that intergalactic distances could be covered in a few months time. The Needles had seemed to disappear because no lightspeed signal they emitted could travel fast enough to make it back to Earth.

Of course, there were other complications during the flight missions that could not have been foreseen. But every practical safety precaution was taken from a mechanical standpoint. All of these concerns were addressed in the Space Needles' designs, even in terms of aesthetics.

Besides the "flying saucer" top—which was actually detachable, so, after landing, exploratory crews could rove other worlds in a portable hovercraft that easily reattached to its base—the rather phallic exterior of the Space Needle was directly inspired by a cocktail shaker that made its first appearance at a Christmas party in the research center in December, 1948. After all, a large part of the mission was the discovery and retrieval—or at least friendly sharing—of alien alcohol, suspected to be the cure for cancer and other human maladies, unlike its Earth-based equivalent, which had been corrupted and was therefore impure.

Likewise, the origins of the cocktail in human history are rooted in cleverly fabricated mythology pitched as "fact" to the gullible masses.

The creation of the first cocktail, at least according to official public records, dates back to the 1800s in the United States of America. The very first bartender's guide, called *How To Mix Drinks, or, The Bon Vivant's Companion*, by "Professor" Jerry Thomas, was published in 1862. His recipes were often distinguished by the use of bitters, in addition to a spirit like gin or bourbon, mixed with other ingredients including sugar and water.

Drinks dating back to this early, experimental period include such contemporary favorites as the Manhattan, allegedly invented at the Manhattan Club in New York City in the 1870s as part of a political campaign, though others claim it was first served even earlier at a bar near Broadway and Houston Street; and the Sazerac, reportedly first served in the 1850s at the Sazerac Coffee House in New Orleans, the recipe for which was first made public in *The World's Drinks and How to Mix Them*, by William T. "Cocktail Bill" Boothby, published in 1908. Starting in the 1890s, any drink involving a spirit and any sort of mixer was referred to as a "highball," typically served in a tall glass.

Throughout the 20th century, many other famous cocktails were concocted, including the original Mai Tai, created by "Trader" Vic Bergeron at his first restaurant, called Hinky Dink's, in Oakland, California, circa 1944. Of course, Don the Beachcomber also claims earlier ownership of the classic recipe, first mixed at his Los Angeles bar in 1933, though his version is much more complex in nature. In any case is not to be confused with the sweet, pineapple-based Polynesian potion most commonly if erroneously associated with that name.

A few years later, in 1948, David A. Embury published another landmark reference book, called *The Fine Art of Mixing Drinks*, simplifying the basic formulas by separating all cocktails into two basic types: aromatic, and sour, making the home bar a much more accessible contrivance.

However, classic cocktails, along with tiki lounges, began falling out of public favor in the middle of the 20th century, though the "craft cocktail," as it is currently known, has made a roaring comeback in the early part of the 21st century. This is a deliberate attempt at reintroducing original intergalactic cocktail recipes back into the mainstream human population, mixed with equivalent indigenous ingredients as substitutes for alien elements, though the purpose from a Government perspective is unclear. Conspiracy theorists suggest our authorities are now working in cahoots with extra-terrestrials, though there is no substantial proof of this on record. On the surface, the United Sates is simply reclaiming a significant, long lost part of its cultural heritage, even though it is also responsible for the most embarrassing chapter in alcoholic annals, Prohibition. But then this, too, was partly offset by another enduring, supposedly American invention, Jazz (which was actually first heard on the planet known as "Syncopatia," long before the sonic waves reached our shores and ears via natural cosmic osmosis).

Of course, most of human textbook history is pure fabrication, i.e. a convenient smokescreen for The Truth, which is not only out *there*, but in *here*, too. The cocktail as we know it, or as *any* sentient being knows it, anywhere in the known *and* unknown galaxy, was invented eons ago on another planet altogether, though exactly which one remains a matter of hotly contested, interstellar dispute.

The "cocktail," as it is known locally, was first introduced to Earthlings when a wayward spaceship from the planet Libation (rough English translation of a word unintelligible to humans) crash-landed in a snowy field in upstate New York on January 5, 1800. The badly injured, horribly hung-over aliens, known as "Libites," could not return to their own planet since their ship, shaped like what is now known as "a martini glass," had shattered on violent impact, like a meteor (which is how it was later "explained" by scientists who recovered the wreckage, most of which had been completely destroyed by flames). Also, the now happily stranded Libites (actually a homosexual couple) were quite embarrassed by their behavior, and furthermore feared punishment by their peers for illegally trespassing on uncharted territory (Earth).

So, assuming human forms since their body chemistry was mostly clay-based in composition, therefore easily malleable, they set up shop on the island of Manhattan, and began slowly sharing their vast knowledge of intoxicating liquids with the local population, using ingredient indigenous to this planet, though variations occur in other civilizations, depending on the availability and nature of their own homegrown products. The one common denominator? Alcohol, the most prevalent element throughout the entire civilized Universe. In fact, it was one of the basic chemical building blocks of Life Itself. Because of its natural potency, it must always be carefully measured when consumed, and often mixed with other elements in order to make its magical properties more manageable, depending on the physical system absorbing it.

Though others claimed credit for these old, established recipes already popular with sundry species clear across the Milky Way and beyond, the Libites never made their true identities known, though some strategically selected insiders were privy to their secret existence among us. Like Vic Bergeron, who "borrowed" the Mai Tai recipe from them one night while vacationing in the Hawaiian tropics, where the Libites finally "retired" and remain thusly isolated, given their indefinite lifespans, literally fueled by booze. (Of course, famed exotic mixologist Don the Beachcomber had partied with them in the same location a decade earlier, but misinterpreted the proper ingredients due to his inebriated state). In fact, the Mai Tai was first served on the planet "Tiki" (again, the approximate human translation of an alien word) many, many centuries ago.

Besides enterprising liquor merchants, the "insiders" included such famous pulp "science fiction" authors as Robert Heinlein, Ray Bradbury, Philip K. Dick, Harlan Ellison, Isaac Asimov, and Kurt Vonnegut, whose supposedly fanciful stories were often thinly veiled "anecdotes" secretly supplied by the Libites, artfully reinterpreted for mass consumption.

The two alien bodies still preserved/incarcerated in suspended animation (after efforts to revive them from their apparent comas repeatedly failed) in Area 51 were also, like the Libites, victims of their own drunk driving, though they were actually teenage delinquents out on a planet-hopping joy ride after illegally hijacking a vehicle belonging to the parents of the reckless driver. These aliens, simply referred to as "hot-rodders," a term culled from automotive pop culture of the period when they were found, hailed from a world known as "V8," since it was the eighth planet in the "V" sector of a relatively recently developed and as yet sparsely populated subdivision of the galaxy. At least, that was how it was designated by a Space planning counsel based in the Main Galaxy, i.e. the literal Center of the Universe, which itself was called the Galactic Omnipotent Division, or GOD for short, as indicated on the gigantic flashing neon sign that marked its entrance (though it naturally varied depending on the native language of the life form perceiving it). All forms of life had been initially generated from this energy source, which remains a mystery to most of its own far-flung spawn.

There had been one casualty of that particular accident, whose expired body became the subject of several invasive autopsies, with the purpose of investigating alien anatomy. Due to the limits of human comprehension, not much was revealed or learned beyond the fact its organs and their function were similar to humans, but operating on a level that has yet to be fully comprehended even by Earth's brightest scientists, especially since the body no longer functions as it should. There is still debate within the scientific community about sacrificing, i.e. pulling the plug on at least one of the remaining bodies for the sake of further study, but so far, all efforts in this regard have failed, blocked by conscientious objectors to willfully exterminating living, breathing beings from beyond the stars. The bodies remain on a life support system that consists mainly of alcohol being constantly transfused into their bloodstreams—especially since, like the bulbous-headed creatures sculpted by Hollywood monster-maker Paul Blaisdell for the Government-sanctioned 1957 docu-drama *Invasion of the Saucer Men*, their "blood" was 99.9% alcohol, anyway.

The officially concealed visages of the hot-rodding aliens has been the surreptitious basis for many popular "science fiction" films, including not only the aforementioned *Invasion of the Saucer Men* but also Steven Spielberg's *Close Encounters of the Third Kind* (1977). However, only unverifiable photographs of the aliens had been purposely leaked to the producers, and only certain members of the press—but only those reporters writing for discredited "tabloid" publications. The idea was to gradually, subliminally prepare the public for the eventual revelation, which, until the publication of this document, never materialized.

Besides the Libites—who never formally introduced themselves to the world at large, though they were apparently tracked down and interviewed by the absentee authors of the original version of this report, and provided much of this uncorroborated but uncontested information—and the hot-rodders, to date no other extra-terrestrial beings have ever been detained or even detected on Earth, at least in modern history (the Pyramids, Easter Island, and other mysteries before the Libites' unplanned arrival remain unresolved, though aliens are the chief suspects).

According to transcriptions of the conversations with the two Libites, this is because the self-appointed overlords collectively forming GOD forbade travel for any being outside of its own star systems, for reasons they did not care to share. This is why the few visitors that violated this inexplicable but strongly enforced law of strictly segregated species had to be rebelliously and irresponsibly loaded at the time of their willful transgression.

Indeed, the mysterious members of GOD were as secretive

about their methods and motives as the United States government.

But no one in the Universe knew if even GOD took orders from yet another Supreme Being, or Beings, that remained hidden within the celestial shadows. This uninformed conjecture became the basis of many religions and speculative spiritual philosophies throughout the universe, which was, oddly, populated almost exclusively by humanoid creatures.

* * *

"And why *still* the secrecy after all this time?" Hilburne rhetorically asked the group of guests as they moved on from Vespers to a round of Manhattans. "I mean, is any threat from space really that imminent? Many if not all of the aliens we encountered were peaceful, even… amorous!"

Hank held Mara back.

"All I know," John said, "is that I wasn't even able to return to the police force when I got back. The only force I got was being forced into early retirement. *Unpaid* retirement. Even though all those phony charges had been dropped and my name cleared."

"May the force be with us," Tony joked.

"That 'Star Wars' flick is a load of crap," Hank said testily. "I mean, great movie, don't get me wrong, but it might as well be 'Flash Gordon,' and even *that* was more accurate, from what we now know.

"Meaning *us* and hardly anybody else," Jake added.

"George Lucas's task must be a deliberate attempt at deceptive diversion via mass entertainment," Hilburne said, "to basically backtrack on their previous pattern of slowly releasing little tidbits of information in the guise of cinema. Other than the Wookies and a few other random characters, none of those beings ever existed, at least not according to our reconnaissance, which was limited, granted. But that's all right. It is set in a 'galaxy long, long ago,' so for all we know, it's a historical documentary. At least it got the 'jump to lightspeed' thing pretty close."

Jimmy said, "I never thought of that. And how did Lucas know there wouldn't be any time dilation? Mainstream scientists still seem to think that everyone will age at different rates when travelling through interstellar space. But look at us, we all aged at the same rate no matter where we went!"

Hilburne nodded, "Yeah, that 'Special Relativity' theory sure didn't work out the way they thought." He turned to the ex-cop. "John, you once had that figured out... what was that gag you told me about the guy with the yardstick and stopwatch getting pulled over for speeding?"

John Shift smiled. "I remember that. It was something I cooked up after one of Falkenstein's lectures during our training. I never could understand his equations, but I caught the gist of what he was saying and put it together the way I could figure it."

"Enlighten us!" Jimmy said.

John cleared his throat. "So there's this guy with a new car, and he doesn't know how accurate the speedometer is. So he gets a yardstick and a stopwatch, and he goes down to the freeway and measures out an exact mile with the yardstick, marking each end with a sign that he'll see from the road."

Mara asked, "How many yards in a mile, anyway?"

Hank jumped in, "Seventeen sixty. In football practice, we'd run the field 17 times and then meet the coach at the 60 yard line, to clock our speed for a mile run."

John continued, "So anyway, this guy gets in his car, guns it to 60 MPH on the speedometer, clicks the stopwatch when he passes the first sign, and then again when he passes the second. Suddenly he sees flashing red and blue lights in the road ahead of him, and comes to a stop. It's a cop blocking the road, and as he pulls over, another cop car with flashing lights zooms up from behind. The two cops get out of their cars, talk for a moment, and come over to his window. One says, 'Sir, you were going 120 miles an hour. We'll have to take you in." The guy looks at his stopwatch and it is showing one minute right on the money. One mile in one minute is exactly sixty miles an hour, so he figures he can beat this rap, because he has the stopwatch and the measured mile to prove it."

"Well, they take him in front of the judge, and the guy pulls out his yardstick and stopwatch as evidence, and explains about the measured mile. The judge is impressed, and asks the first cop to justify the speeding ticket. The cop pulls out his own yardstick, which is just like the guy's own, and a stopwatch, but the cop's stopwatch is just a cheap plastic knockoff, not the precision Swiss timer that our guy has. So the cop explains that he measured the mile just fine, but when he timed the guy's trip between the two signs, it only took 30 seconds to go that mile. A mile in 30 seconds is 120 miles an hour. So the guy compares his stopwatch to the cop's, and sees that the cop's cheap watch is only counting one second on the dial for every two seconds that goes by on the guy's watch."

"Now the judge is a little confused, so he asks the second cop to explain. The second cop pulls out a nice Swiss stopwatch, just as accurate as our guy's own, but he also pulls out a yardstick that is only half a yard long. It's got 36 tiny 'inch' markings and everything. So the second cop says, 'I timed the car and it did take exactly a minute, but when I measured the distance with my yardstick, I found it was actually two miles, not one. Two miles in a minute is 120 miles an hour!' Now the judge doesn't know who's right, so he throws out the case, and the guy dodges the ticket."

Hilburne laughs, "That's the best description of relativity I ever heard! Since time, speed, and distance are all arbitrary measurements, in any scenario you can come up with all sorts of different possible solutions, depending on what parameters you adjust. Our scientists think that it's the stopwatches that get whacked when you go somewhere fast, but it's really the yardstick that changes. You've all seen it yourselves; when we hit the gas in those Space Needle ships, we could see the universe shrinking around us. Our ships were the size of whole galaxies at cruising speed!"

Jimmy brought the conversation back around. "So maybe it wasn't George Lucas who got space travel right. 'Star Trek' had the continuous 'warp drive' with no time dilations."

Hilburne replied,"But even 'Star Trek,' which is set in our own future, took a lot of liberties with The Truth, even though Roddenberry was an official NASA consultant. Creative license and all that, I suppose."

"Except for all the sexy babes!" Hank grinned, but Mara smacked his shoulder and he went stoned-faced. "They got *that* right!"

"Absolutely," Hilburne said, in rare agreement with his nemesis. "Captain Kirk as so brilliantly portrayed by William Shatner was perhaps the most authentic representation of our adventures in space than any other fictional character. Promiscuity as well as alcohol consumption is two of the most prominent behavioral instincts in the entire galaxy, spanning all alien species. We're by far the most puritanical if morally hypocritical species of all."

"You're an adulterous *asshole*," Mara said acidly to Hilburne. "No *excuses*."

"All in the line of duty, as I've tried explaining to no avail," Hilburne said, exasperated. "And please, don't throw another drink at me. It's a waste of precious resources."

"This is only *Earth* alcohol," Jimmy said. "The cocktails we had out there ruined it for me. Nothing here compares to the intoxicating power of those incredible drinks."

"I pity alcoholics who can't partake of those life-giving fluids," Jake said. "But they were born with that allergy perhaps as a matter of natural selection, to keep the population under control? That's one possible theory, anyway."

"I was told that alcohol from other worlds actually would not have the same addictive, detrimental affect on adversely afflicted humans," Hilburne said.

"Who told you that?" John asked.

"Some dame," Hilburne said with a shrug. "With green hair and green skin."

"They're not to be trusted," Hank said bitterly. "As we both know from experience, right, Hilly?"

"Maybe we shouldn't go there right now," Tony said delicately. "I mean, this is meant to be a celebration, right?"

"Celebrating *what* exactly?" Mara asked, slurring her words.

"Maybe this is the Welcome Home party they never threw us," Jake mused. "I mean, when we got back, we were treated worse than your average Viet Nam vet."

"Hey, *watch* it, pardner," Hank said to Jake. "Don't disparage the US of A while *I'm* around."

"But they sent you out there!" Jake said. "Without preparing you first."

"I volunteered for the job," Hank said. "I knew what I was getting into, or at least I thought I did."

"*Exactly*," Tony said. "*None* of us were ready for what was out there."

Hank just nodded and sighed. "I *know*. But it's not *America's* fault. It's that damn Nazi quack!"

"He was *not* a Nazi," Jimmy said adamantly, but politely. "The professor was a good man. *Is* a good man, as far as we know. And I am still betting he's the one who organized this rendezvous. Though why, I couldn't tell you. I don't feel prepared for *this*, either."

"*None* of us are," Patti said, shooting another venomous glance at Mara. "So far this is like some half-baked group therapy session. That *backfired.*"

"Maybe it will turn into a press conference," Tony said. "We'll be briefed and then allowed to finally share our stories with the entire world!"

"Unless we're too shit-faced," Hank said.

"So then maybe *that's* the idea," Tony suggested. "To undermine our credibility when being interviewed by the international press corps."

"Or maybe they just wanna *kill* us," John said, "by getting us all in one place at one time…."

They all looked around frantically with heightened paranoia.

Just then the waiter began bringing trays full of scrumptious shrimp cocktails, and suddenly everyone forgot the suspected state of jeopardy.

"*Damn*, this is good!" John enthused. "If this is supposed to be our last meal, I say bring it on! Shit, I got nothing *else* to look forward to."

"Except *me,*" Patti said, kissing his cheek between rabid bites of shrimp.

Trays of delectable, fresh crab cocktails quickly followed, which were likewise voraciously consumed, all washed down by the Manhattans and martinis. Exotica music by Martin Denny and Les Baxter was now playing on the restaurant's sound system, though they barely noticed.

"This is even better than Ivar's!" Jimmy said, referring to a legendary local seafood restaurant chain.

"Reminds me of someplace *else*," Hilburne said. "Except *that* seafood could walk and talk."

"And *screw*," Mara added acidly.

Hilburne ignored her. "Funny, they always referred to Earth as 'the Forbidden Island.' Probably because, like everywhere else we went, our planet was no more than a fairy tale, for some strange reason. Unexplored, therefore unverified. *We* were more exotic to them than they were to us!"

"I don't think I know about this planet," Jake said. "In fact, I don't really know much about *any* of your individual encounters out there, since this is the first time I've seen any of you since…well, since…"

"Twenty years ago today," Jimmy said ominously. "April 21, the date the Century 21 Exposition opened at the Seattle World's Fair. The date the first ship left. In retrospect, I'd have rather been at the fair."

"Not me," Hilburne said. "If only for my trip to this one planet. It would be called Aquaticon, in our language. The world of fishmen and mermaids. The world of my dreams… Mara *thinks* she knows the whole story, but let me tell the rest of you all about it…."

## SAZERAC

*1/3 oz absinthe*
*1 ¾ oz cognac*
*1 ½ oz rye whiskey*
*Three dashes Peychaud's bitters*
*1 dash Angostura bitters*
*One sugar cube*

*Rinse Old-Fashioned glass with Absinthe, stir other ingredients with ice separately, strain then pour over crushed ice, gently rub rim of glass with lemon peel garnish.*

## MANHATTAN

*2 ½ oz bourbon*
*2 dashes Angostura bitters*
*1 oz sweet vermouth*

*Stir then strain ingredients into chilled glass, with Maraschino or (preferably) brandied cherry garnish.*

* * *

*Riddles of the Unmind III*

The forces of nature bent and focused around the strange human congregation at the Seattle Space Needle, inevitably prodding the Unmind to ponder more riddles. "Local increases in the speed of light in the universe are like paths in a dark forest, which offer a level and unobstructed route for the rapid movement of forest creatures. But the universal forest is thick, and it is difficult to see through, beyond one's immediate locale. How can one deduce the way to the path with the quickest lightspeed, in the absence of accurate direct observations of that path from a distance?"

"In the dark forest of the universe, the answer is implicit in the nature of quantum gravity, and its effect on local speeds of light."

"The riddle must be answered, regardless of its complexity."

"It is complex, and yet not. Quantum gravity is a (mostly) trivial side-effect of one of the most important forces in the universe, that of electric charge."

"We are aware of electric charge as the thing that holds all matter together. Explain further."

"As our cells experience charge interactions, it involves the *net* charge, not the *gross* charge. Each atom of normal matter contains protons with positive charge and electrons with negative charge. There are huge numbers of atoms in the universe, but the vast majority are perfectly balanced. Unbalanced electrical charges, which lead to natural effects like lightning, are but a tiny fraction of the total balanced charge in the universe."

"How is it that the universe contains unbalanced charge?"

"Under most circumstances, it doesn't. The huge numbers of protons create a massive positive charge, but it is exactly balanced by the same number of electrons with a negative charge. The net charge of the universe is zero. Local imbalances, such as those producing lightning, are just short-range movements of like charges. The lightning strike is the re-balancing mechanism, whereby the positive and negative charges are brought back into equilibrium."

"What about neutrons and more exotic particles?"

"They exist, but in all cases the universal charge is balanced. Overall it is exactly zero. For example, the fact that a neutron exhibits a magnetic signature indicates that it must contain charge, but measurement of the net charge of a neutron is zero. Therefore the charges in a neutron are always balanced."

"If universal charges are balanced, why is this of significance to the existence of regions of faster lightspeed?"

"Because unlike the commonly experienced electromagnetic forces, gravity is based on the *gross* value of the charge, not the *net* value. Each charge in the universe has an energy field associated with it, which extends to the end of the universe. Imagine a universe which empty except for two charged particles separated by a long distance. If we observe one of these charges in an initial state, we can say that it is motionless (since all motion is relative). This means its energy of motion is zero with respect to us as observers. After a time, the signal from the other charge in that universe will impact it. At that time the charge will move, in a direction appropriate to the signs of both charges (away from each other if the signs are the same, but towards each other if opposite). Now the charge we are observing has increased its energy of motion, which requires an addition of positive energy. The direction of motion is irrelevant to the energy balance; the fact that the previously nonmoving charge is now moving is an indication of added energy."

"I can see that all charges, regardless of sign, have a positive energy to contribute to interactions with other charges. What is the magnitude of this energy?"

"All charges carry energy quantized in virtual photons, so for each individual charge the photon energy relation $E= hc/\lambda$ must hold. Energy is Planck's Constant (h) times the speed of light (c), divided by the wavelength of the photon ($\lambda$). The energy available to a specific charge interaction is proportional to this overall energy in the charge field." Of course, the Unmind was largely unaware of Max Planck and the physical constant under his name, but used the symbolic representation of an equivalent quantity. "For virtual photons used to transmit charge energy, the wavelength is related to the distance between charges. Of course, since the speed of light and distance are variable, it is more reliable to measure the charge energy as $E=h/t$, where t is the travel time of the photon between charges. The travel time of a virtual photon is equal to the wavelength divided by the speed of light: $t = \lambda/c$. Since time is absolute, this provides a more useful standard."

"So each charged particle emits virtual photons of positive energy, the energy of which is reduced as the travel time is increased. How does this result in gravity?"

"The sum of the energy of all these virtual photons, over the expanse of the universe, creates the field we know of as gravity. Each individual charge in every piece of matter in the universe emits its virtual photon, and at every point in the universe the total energy is summed to find a characteristic energy value $E = \text{sum}(h/t)$ for all charges in the universe. This, at least, holds true for charges which are not moving too fast with respect to one another. Moving charges have a magnetic field, which reduces the energy of their electric field, and this is of consequence at long distances because of the expansion of the universe. In any case, if you map this charge energy across all space, it forms the 'curvature' of space due to gravity."

"Gravity is normally associated with mass, not charge. How does this charge field relate to large universal masses?"

"Masses composed of ordinary matter possess a rather fixed ratio of balanced charge to mass, so the number of charges in a star or planet is closely linked to its mass."

"How does this 'curvature of space' cause the effects of gravity?"

"The summed energy of charge causes a change in the local speed of light, and the distance measurement scale."

"How may this change in lightspeed be quantified?"

"It is comprehensible by a relative measure. The speed of light in a one locality times the total charge energy at that region, is equal to the speed of light in any other region times its total charge energy in *that* locality: $c_1E_1 = c_2E_2$."

"And how does this change in local lightspeed affect matter in the area?"

"A lightspeed gradient causes an acceleration in light and matter within that gradient. It is similar to how a lens bends light due to a change in lightspeed outside and inside the lens material. If the time taken for light to traverse between adjacent regions 1 and 2 is t, the acceleration gradient felt by matter spanning the regions, is the difference in the speeds of light between the reqions, divided by that travel time, or $(c_1-c_2)/t$."

"So how may regions of high local speed of light be identified?"

"If there is a region devoid of local matter, such as intergalactic space, then there will be relatively few local charge energy concentrations with short travel times (t). The large average travel time (t) values from other masses in the universe will cause the sum(h/t) value of charge energy to be smaller. A small charge energy value in a region corresponds to a larger speed of light, since cE is a constant. As E decreases, c increases."

"That does not seem a practical method of search, since we live inside a galaxy, not in a void."

"The intergalactic voids are the places with the least *static* energy, but when we consider the effects of motion, we gain more options."

"Explain the effects of motion on the gross energy of electric charge."

"Electric charge is but one side of the electromagnetic balance. Charges which are moving relative to one another transfer some of their h/t virtual photon energy into a magnetic field, rather than all to an electric field. Since the h/t energy is fixed for each charge, this causes a reduction in the electric charge energy available for gravitational effects."

"What is the effect of these 'magnetic fields'?"

"Matter moving at some speed v relative to other charges experiences a reduction in virtual charge energy to hc/(t(c+v)), where c is the local speed of light. Note that if v=0, this reduces to the normal h/t charge energy observed in the static case of unmoving charges. The magnetic field energy hv/(t(c+v)) balances the energy equation, and satisfies the Law of Conservation of Energy, but does not add to gravitational effects."

"How may this effect be used to reduce travel times?"

"Objects moving at a high speed relative to their local galaxy will feel a reduced charge energy, which corresponds to a higher local speed of light in the moving body. This higher speed of light reduces inertial effects and permits faster travel. Of course, as distance measures are also affected by the local speed of light, such a moving body will be seen to increase in size relative to stationary objects around it."

"I am satisfied with the answer to this riddle. Spores may be disseminated most rapidly throughout the universe by sending them away at very high speed from our galaxy."

# "WET DREAM"

*1 oz white rum*
*¼ oz gin*
*2 dashes of sea salt*

*Stir ingredients at ocean temperature, serve neat. This cocktail is very dehydrating to humans; drink plenty of fresh water before and after.*

*Outer Space, April, 1962*
After years of extensive preparation and an exhausting vetting process, The Space Needlers had finally been dispersed on their individual, interstellar safaris, including Hilburne Chase, now bound for a watery planet on the outer edges of the galaxy, whose inhabitants and terrain were completely unknown. While the Space Needle Program had succeeded beyond its creators' wildest dreams, navigation remained a perplexing problem. The ships themselves could go faster than light, but there was no known method to observe the distant galaxies except from the light they emitted. Earth scientists would try to find suitable targets for exploration based on million-year-old light signals, without any idea what those galaxies would really be like in the current era. It was basically like throwing darts at a map. Hilburne's ship just happened to heading toward this world, one of several planned (and ultimately unplanned) destinations, at far faster than the speed of light.

The planet was long suspected of supporting 'Life as We Know It' due to the unusual amounts of aqueous matter dimly detected via Roswell's high-powered industrial telescopes not available to the average astronomer.

What Falkenstein and his peers could not have even guessed in advance was that the "waters" consisted of 100% pure rum, though of an alien variety.

The male denizens closely resembled the "Gill Man" as depicted in the 1954 film *The Creature from the Black Lagoon* (and its two sequels, 1955's *Revenge of the Creature* and 1956's *The Creature Walks Among Us*), though much more athletic in appearance and ability.

In retrospect, Hilburne realized that the mutant salmon

monsters from the recent (by his timeline) Roger Corman film *Humanoids from the Deep* (1980) were also reminiscent of the male dwellers of Aquaticon, especially since they were equally horny, existing in a perpetual, consensual mating cycle, randomly coupling with their sensually sensitive females, who were essentially mermaids, exactly like the ones depicted in Earth's folklore.

Again, this common visage was either a complete coincidence or else a case of cosmic psychic synchronicity, a theory that Falkenstein had long entertained, without any corroborating evidence other than a series of seemingly random incidents that were often explained by non-scientific minds as being mystical in origin, i.e. "karma" or "kismet," neither of which was acceptable to the logical, analytical mind.

Still, Falkenstein was a big Shakespeare buff, and often quoted *Hamlet* to his own skeptical colleagues: "*There are more things in heaven and earth, Horatio, than are dreamt of in your philosophy*."

Due to his tragic observations and negative experiences in Nazi Germany, Falkenstein was once inclined to believe the Universe was either random and apathetic to human existence, or deliberate in its designs, but intrinsically cruel. Via his scientific research, he was desperately if methodically seeking that third option: a cosmic benevolence guiding the destinies of *all* beings, however haphazardly. Little did he know that there was such a benevolence guiding the universe, but its emphasis was definitely not on humans.

The idea that all of Life was merely an epic hallucination generated by a single superior being's drunken delusions had also been floated by fellow cynics, but was widely deemed too disturbing and depressing to contemplate, much less investigate. The equally controversial quantum-mechanical theory of alternate dimensions or multi-universes, which basically embraces all possible theories and possibilities of reality operating simultaneously on various parallel levels of consciousness, is another option that further flummoxed Falkenstein, especially after his crew of intrepid astronauts returned from their missions, relating tales that confounded known parameters of science.

Aquaticon was one such perplexing planet, not because of its unusual physical properties, but because that is where Hilburne encountered the greatest and most fundamentally illogical, irrational mystery in the Universe: *Love.*

Hilburne was a devil-may-care *bon vivant* playboy-type who didn't contemplate the meaning of Life so much, since he was too busy *living* it. That was one reason he was selected for this mission, along with the fact he was wealthy and donated millions to finance the project. He was leaving behind a floundering marriage anyway, so he was emotionally vulnerable, not to mention sexually hungry, when his Space Needle landed in the alcoholic waters of Aquaticon, its saucer top flipping to a horizontal position so the ship was instantly converted to a submarine, floating briefly on the oceanic surface before diving to cruising depth.

The 1966 Japanese film *Terror Beneath the Sea*, starring future martial arts matinee idol Sonny Chiba, was directly inspired by Hilburne's account of what happened next:

Hilburne first saw Marina the Mermaid—as he called her—lounging on a tiny island in the middle of the rum-filled oceans of Aquaticon, which covered the entire planet, except for these few isolated rocks covered with palm trees. There was perpetual sunlight on this planet, since it did not rotate, forever basking in the rays of its particular solar system's main sources of light, of which there were three, each similar to the one Sun that sustained life on Earth. The complex orbits of this trinary system kept Aquaticon delightfully bathed in eternal sunshine.

Hilburne loved the bright warmth and felt right at home immediately, especially since billowing, cumulous clouds filled the otherwise bright blue firmament, reducing the glare and providing pockets of shade, especially on the tiny island where Marina was lounging on all her nude glory.

Marina had large, round, pointy breasts with succulent nipples, a relatively tiny waist, and a green, scaly fin-tail (matching her thickly lashed emerald eyes) commonly associated with her species, with long, wavy red hair and a heart-shaped face seemingly carved from porcelain. Hilburne admired from afar her via his "periscope" which went erect almost immediately upon visual contact with the "alien."

The Space Needle resurfaced. This occasion called for a celebratory cocktail. Hilburne instructed his robot assistant to mix him a quick Mai Tai from the bar.

All Space Needlers, in fact, flew solo in space save for their robot companions, prototypes for which included Robby in the 1956 film *Forbidden Planet*, and "Robot" on the 1960s television program *Lost in Space* (producer Irwin Allen, who also helmed *Voyage to the Bottom of the Sea*, was a remote NASA operative, working in the creative/PR division). Unlike those two, the actual robots could walk on two legs and sported human-like arms with hands and opposable thumbs. Considering the crude state of computer science at that time, it was astonishing that these robots displayed any advanced cognitive function at all. Wilhelm Falkenstein had developed the robots using a controversial theory for the origin of intelligence. It had been observed that the electric computers of the time, using relays and vacuum tubes to solve complex calculations far faster than the human mind, seemed utterly devoid of what humans called 'common sense'. As Hilburne once said, if you tell a computer to put on its shoes and socks, it will damn well put on its shoes first, and then the socks.

Falkenstein figured that since higher mental functions evolved later than basic neurologic function, a robot should be constructed with full bodily capabilities, such as arms, legs, eyes, ears, a voicebox capable of speech, etc. The complexity of electrical interconnections of all these parts was then expected to spontaneously generate self-consciousness and common sense when exposed to a real-world environment, just as our microbe ancestors evolved our own brains from their primitive neural interconnections. The Space Needler robots were built under this principle, with tremendous success. Little did Falkenstein know that the robots had actually been taken over as host bodies by tiny but highly evolved organisms that had colonized the circuitry during construction, for the purpose of spying on, and influencing, the Space Needle Program.

The final robot design was much sleeker than the early movie prototypes, more closely resembling Gort in the 1951 film *The Day the Earth Stood Still*, likewise covered in thin but impervious silver armor resembling aluminum, but with wider shoulders and a square head like the cyclopean robot invaders in the 1954 film *Target Earth*, but not nearly as bulky, and with two eyes perpetually illuminated, like the titular mechanical man from the 1958 film *The Colossus of New York*.

Like The Colossus, another discarded early prototype recycled for cinematic amusement, The Space Needle robots were supplied with the ability of speech, and could communicate extemporaneously in any language by scanning the brainwaves of their conversational companion. Theoretically this would include any and all alien beings. Marina would be the first test of the robot's universally versatile vocabulary. While all seven robots were identical in appearance, they all were equipped with pre-programmed personalities and given their own unique names by the astronauts themselves. Hank named his robot "Bub," Jake's was called "Pancho," Jimmy's was labeled "Lulu," Tony's was honored with the moniker "Elvis," John's was designated as "Cool," and Hilburne's robot was simply christened "Pally." There was a seventh robot, "Ada", but that ill-fated mission was rarely mentioned. Collectively the group of robots was sometimes called "Falkenstein's Monsters".

After downing his drink, Hilburne flipped a switch, and the saucer hub detached from the base and he took off for the island, much like "The Flying Sub" on the 1960s television program *Voyage to the Bottom of the Sea*, which borrowed a few basics from the Space Needle blueprints, per official authorization, of course.

As the saucer sailed through the air toward its destination, Hilburne blasted surf instrumentals like the brand new tune "Pipeline" by The Chantays, and the first (1960) version of "Walk, Don't Run" by The Ventures at full volume to help set the mood via the built-in, fully digitalized, neon-lit jukebox in the ship's console. When he was just relaxing on board the ship, during "happy hour" (which occurred roughly every other hour throughout a typical sixteen-hour work day), Hilburne preferred the music of Juan Garcia Esquivel, Bob Thompson, Enoch Light, and other practitioners of what would later be dubbed "Space Age Bachelor Pad Music." But whether speeding through space or cruising a planet surface, surf music provided the ideal soundtrack.

The island was essentially a miniature Polynesian paradise, with sandy white beaches, lush and dense tropical foliage, and even some randomly placed stone statues that looked exactly like Easter Island tiki heads. In fact, these were the original models. But they had no direct relation to their duplicates on Earth. Again, it was a case of cosmic coincidence or psychic synchronicity, depending on which philosophy one chose to believe. As the saucer hub closed in on the island, Hilburne noticed a number of other, differently shaped tiki statues about the island, but no other living inhabitants besides the stunning mermaid creature alone on the beach, apparently oblivious to his rapid approach.

When the saucer hub landed on the beach near the mermaid, Hilburne climbed out and walked over to her. She was not alarmed by his sudden presence, nor even particularly impressed. Pally was brought along to interpret if necessary, plus Hilburne was anxious to see if the robot's telepathic abilities worked on an actual alien being.

"Hello there," Hilburne said cheerfully to the apathetic mermaid, whose eyes remained closed as she rested casually on the edge of the shore, her tail flipping idly in the waves of rum washing up onto the beach. The tide was high and so was Hillary, not just from his recent drink, but simply by inhaling the intoxicating scent of the dark, rich sea surrounding them, already identified as rum by Pally's ambient sensors. Hilburne was still wearing his standard light but durable powder-blue astronaut uniform, plus his white jet-pilot type helmet with clear facial shield still attached, although the ship's indicators had safely informed him of the high oxygen content in the planet's atmosphere.

The mermaid merely nodded in polite acknowledgment, then slowly opened her eyes and gazed with mild interest upon the interloper.

"My, aren't you something," she said in a husky, seductively feminine voice. "Human, yes?"

"Why, yes!" Hilburne said, kneeling down beside her and removing his helmet, which he tucked under the crook of his left arm. "How did you know?"

"You don't look like the locals," she said slyly, shielding her mesmerizingly beautiful eyes from a sudden burst of sunlight as the cumulous clouds slowly moved with balletic precision overhead.

"How do you know of human existence?"

"We're all taught about it early on," she said. "We were warned you might seek us out someday."

"Warned?"

"You don't have the best reputations, you know. Some roving females of our kind brought back some rather unpleasant stories to tell of human seamen. There was… conflict."

"Well, I'd like to think I represent the best our species has to offer," Hilburne said, turning up the charm.

"I'm afraid that's still far below most sentient being standards," she shrugged.

"So you speak English," Hilburne said, ignoring the insult. "I brought my friend here just in case you didn't."

"You're only *hearing* English," she said. "Unlike humans, most of us in the vast galaxy communicate telepathically. Like your mechanical friend there. He is apparently more advanced than his creators. How ironic. And pathetic, really."

Hilburne had no idea how advanced the controlling intelligence inside Pally really was, so he just grinned, somewhat embarrassed by the knowledge of his lowly classification. "Well, don't judge all of us by the same reputation. We're all different, you know. You *are* a mermaid, yes?"

"As you would call our kind, yes."

"What's your name?"

"We don't use names, but you can call me whatever you like, as long as you do me one favor."

"Anything."

"Make love to me."

"That's a favor to *you*?"

"Yes. I've always been curious about what it would like to have sex with a human. Partly because it's expressly forbidden to mate with other species since the elders want to keep our bloodline pure. I've always been attracted to bad boys anyway, which is good, since they're *all* bad here. Now *I* want to be 'bad.'"

Disbelieving his own luck, not to mention feeling a bit paranoid given the awkwardly stimulating situation, Hilburne looked around to make sure alien eyes weren't monitoring them.

"No one but us needs to know about this," Marina continued. "By my calculations, there's no chance of our mating producing a hybrid, mutated offspring, since I can only give birth to our own kind. What you would call contraception as well as abortion are strictly outlawed on our planet, so every single mating session among our kind yields eggs, which are then often devoured by the males for sake of population control. They also seem to think they provide the best nutrition, stemming as they do from our superior race. We females all love sex, though many of us do not wish to procreate, but have no choice. I enjoy sex, and have given birth to many thousands of children, only a few of which have survived, but would like to engage in this act without spawning eggs that will most likely only serve as their father's food. With a human, I imagine this is possible due to our physiological differences. So you see, from your point of view, you may indulge your own hedonistic senses and fill me with as much of your fruitless, inferior human seed as you can spare, without any consequences or, as the case may be, casualties."

This was a *lot* for Hilburne to take it, but considering the unusual nature of the proposition, he digested the information as quickly as possible, though with some trepidation. "Well, that all sounds great, but, we just met, and…."

"What *else* do you need to know? Do you not find me pleasing?"

"Oh, I find you *extremely* pleasing, but on our planet, it's customary for women to at least demand a *date* first."

"I'm not from your world. Here, sex is an act of recreation as well as procreation. Tragically, at least for females, we cannot separate the two. I'm trying to change that, right *here,* right *now*. I consider this spontaneous, illicit union the first step in the Mermaid's Liberation Movement!"

"Okay, you convinced me! I'm totally sympathetic to your cause! You're my kinda independent woman, baby!"

As Pally stood idly by, Hilburne removed his astronaut uniform and climbed on top of Mermaid, kissing her face and suckling her breasts, but unsure where to insert his throbbing member until she instructed him to penetrate her moist, vagina-like belly button, which was even equipped with a clitoris. She responded with orgasmic screams of delight, while Hilburne had never experienced such dizzying passion.

After several hours of intense, experimental (at least for Hilburne) and exhausting lovemaking in every possible position, Hilburne lay in Marina's arm, blissful and content. Pally supplied him with a cigarette and lit it for him before returning to his impassive state.

"I could use a drink," he said finally with a dreamy sigh.

"Help yourself," said Marina.

"Oh…you mean the water?"

"It's not water," she said. "We grow what you would consider to be limes on this island, which you can use to mix with it, if you choose. We also have what you would call coconuts you can break open and use as drinking vessels, or glasses, after you consume the contents, which are quite delicious."

Hilburne smiled with supreme satisfaction and said, "Pally, you got the night off. Or day, whatever. I can take it from here. I think I'll take a quick dip, first."

He then waded naked into the sea, swimming and swallowing the cool, intoxicating liquid, reveling in the sea of rum, the color of which almost perfectly matched the deeply bronzed tone of his instantly sun-tanned skin.

Just then several pairs of webbed humanoid hands grabbed him and pulled him beneath the surface of the sea. Marina noticed but didn't even stir, though Pally was rather disturbed. "Danger! Danger!", he voiced telepathically.

"Don't worry," she told the telepathically simpatico robot, whose chest and facial lights were flashing like fire alarms. "Those are just our males. They'll probably just take him down to the lab and run some tests. They may eat him afterwards, if they like the taste of his flesh, and make a snack out of him, I believe his species would call it 'jerky,' but he's just had the best sex of his life, I can only assume, so it could be worse."

"That is logical," said Pally in his deeply resonant, authoritative voice, "but it is my programmed duty to at least attempt to save him from any potential harm. Will you show me where he has been taken?"

"Sure," she said, rolling into the rum. "Follow me."

Marina led Pally several fathoms deep to a glowing dome in which was housed a massive urban facility featuring gleaming pink, purple, blue and green spire towers and maritime-themed décor. They swam through an automated, gated entrance into the undersea city, which was completely dry within the confines of the dome, though still surrounded by rum, so Marina, who unlike her male counterparts was not totally amphibious, remained on the metallic dock. Pally climbed out and onto the surface, composed of synthetic sand. The city closely resembled a five-star tropical resort on Earth, only there were no vehicles on the streets, and all the eateries were tiki bars, or at least, bars decorated with tiki statues, which were considered ancient gods, even though the fishmen were agnostic nowadays. The tikis just *looked* cool. They were cultural icons more than anything else.

The fishmen and the mermaids subsisted solely on rum and the strange living seafood in various varieties existing outside the dome. The denizens were the well-muscled fishmen, some carrying tridents as they patrolled the perimeters of the property, but all looking like they had distant relatives in the fabled Black Lagoon.

What sounded like an ethereal form of exotica music emanated from nowhere, but everywhere, a subtle, sonic ambience that was pervasive without being invasive.

Pally's sensors detected Hilburne's precise location inside one of the towers, in the basement prison laboratory. Blasting stun-rays from his weaponized eyes and fingertips, which channeled high-voltage bolts emitted from his internal Tesla Coil, Pally paved a pathway through the defensive fishmen to the prison. He broke through all the pastel-painted barriers, until he came upon Hilburne hanging from a hook, surrounded by fishmen holding scalpels and other sharp instruments. Apparently they were about to skin him alive. Hilburne was already barely conscious and bleeding badly, since both hands had been forced onto the hook from which he was dangling helplessly.

Pally did fierce battle with the fishmen, ultimately prevailing as he liberated Hilburne from the hook and quickly escaped out through the gate, where Marina was waiting. However, she was seized and held captive by the jealous males of her own race, and Pally returned Hilburne to the surface.

Depositing him on a bed inside the saucer, Pally administered first aid and quickly healed Hilburne's wounds with progressive medical procedures before reviving him.

"Where's Marina?" Hilburne groggily demanded.

"Still down below," Pally said. "My sensors indicate she is about to be tortured her captors, meaning impregnated then forced to watch as her own young is consumed by their fathers, though this is common practice on this planet, so there is no reason for concern."

"*The hell there isn't*!" Hilburne yelled. "Thanks for saving my life, Pally, even though you had no choice, but now we have to go save Marina!"

"From what? Our prime directive is not to directly intervene in alien customs, even those we find morally objectionable."

"*Screw the prime directive*!" Hilburne said emphatically. "You take your orders from *me*. Now let's *go*!"

Per his hard-wired loyalty (and his inhuman spy consciousness fearing exposure), Pally obeyed without further objection and piloted the saucer back down toward the domed city.

On the way, though, a gigantic creature resembling a serpent with tentacles attacked the saucer. The saucer, like Pally, was equipped with stun-beams, but the beams had only a marginal effect on the monster.

Pally noted to Hilburne, "My distributed-capacitor Tesla Coil is far more efficient than the normal coils used by Earthly stage performers, but in this sea of rum the stun beams seem to lose efficacy quickly with distance."

The monster grabbed the saucer in one tentacle and brought it close to its massive mouth, lined with huge, sharp fangs and a long, prehensile, forked tongue that flickered out and licked the view screen, like a child taste-testing a lollipop.

"Maybe its time to try something a little stronger," Hilburne said drily.

Pally shut down the stun beams, and, resorting to lethal force, fired the saucer's Atomic Hydrogen blaster directly into the monster's mouth. Using a fuel having the highest energy density per unit mass of any chemical reactant, the Atomic Hydrogen blaster was the most effective non-nuclear weapon in the universe. Though it didn't kill the creature (due to its stupendous size), it did manage to back it off long enough for the saucer to break free of the tentacle and continue its descent to the domed city, cruising past all sorts of odd but vaguely familiar looking undersea animals, in all shapes and sizes. In fact, what appeared to be a humongous lobster/seahorse-type hybrid creature, roaring a challenge, had conveniently distracted the serpent-squid monster from giving pursuit, and the saucer made its speedy getaway as the two marine monsters engaged in epic battle

Arriving at the city, Hilburne ordered Pally to blast their way inside, since Marina could obviously survive if the city was suddenly flooded, but the dome was impenetrable to their blaster's force. The saucer's arrival inspired an army of fishmen to exit the city and face it head on. They were armed with laser weapons, though they were actually the tridents Pally had seen earlier. The fishmen preferred blue-green lasers to any projectile weapon, due to their enhanced penetration through the rum-based seawater.

The saucer and the army of fishmen engaged in a laser vs. blaster war until Hilburne emerged victorious, surging past the unconscious warriors and, taking advantage of their temporary vulnerability, flew into the city as Pally's sensors scoured the surface for any sign of Marina.

After locating her in a swank, apartment penthouse, Hilburne landed the saucer on the roof of the building and with Pally by his side, armed with his own blaster pistol, they shot their way through the corridors bustling with mobs of angry fishmen, who were telepathically screaming expletives. After a seemingly endless battle, they found Marina, lying unconscious but as yet unharmed on a silky bed in the plush suite, which resembled a bedroom chamber in Neptune's kingdom.

Back inside the saucer, Pally piloted them back to the Space Needle base still floating out on the surface of the rum sea as Hilburne gently placed Marina in a large bathtub filled with Earth rum (a substance Pally could artificially replicate without limitation, along with bourbon, vodka, gin, tequila, etc.), which was inferior in quality but sufficient enough to sustain her until they eventually returned to Earth….

* * *

"Which is why I found you in bed with *her* on our second honeymoon in Oahu, way back in 1966," Mara said to Hilburne as he wrapped up his story. "You carted that hussy with you all around the galaxy, and then had the gall to return her to Earth!"

"Lucky for us it turned out she can breathe our salt water," Hilburne said, "and survive indefinitely as long as she's also given access to a steady source of rum, which is in abundant supply on the Hawaiian islands."

"Lucky?" Mara said. "I wish that bitch would drown."

"You're talking about the mother of my children," Hilburne said defensively. "Whom I named after *you*, basically. In a derivative sense. Mara. Marina. See? I was still thinking of *you*, sweetheart."

Everyone at the table collectively beamed Hilburne an accusatory stare of utter astonishment.

"That's right," he said. "Mara, I mean *Marina,* was indeed impregnated by yours truly, despite her beliefs to the contrary. Humans can mate with aliens and produce bi-racial offspring. Isn't that beautiful?"

Mara's jaw dropped even further.

"So are you saying that right now, *human-alien hybrids* are swimming around the oceans of the Earth?" John asked, likewise flabbergasted by this revelation.

"Yes," said Hilburne. "As far as I know, Marina now has her

own family, whom I have never even met, sad to say, since we thought it best not to confuse our children, plus, frankly, I know my whereabouts are being tracked by NASA, and I want them to remain untouched by Earth scientists, who would only capture and confine them to probe and poke like lab rats."

"You never even told me this, man, and I thought we were best friends!" Tony said, both hurt and intrigued.

"Sorry, but I couldn't trust that you weren't being tracked, too," Hilburne said. "It's all for their own safety. I'm just trying to be a good father."

"A good *absentee* father," Patti noted sternly.

"True, but also appropriate to their aquatic heritage. Fish fathers do not generally care for their offspring, lest it weaken the spawn and make them less competitive in the cut-throat environment of the sea." Hilburne conceded. "I was able to maintain my bachelor lifestyle and status, following my divorce from Mara, of course, but without the burden of alimony or even holiday visits. Yet I still get credit for being a cool if anonymous dad."

"You mean sperm donor," Mara said.

"*Hands-on* sperm donor," Hilburne pointed out. "Meaning hands on someone other than *me*. No test tubes or remote ejaculation. So even *that* aspect was optimum. All in the name of *science*. I enjoyed all the pleasures and pride associated with fatherhood, but none of the responsibility. Best of both possible worlds. So to speak."

"So how many, you figure?" Jake asked. "Kids, I mean."

"Apparently, per our psychic communications since out last personal rendezvous, I have a dozen sons and daughters living blissfully somewhere in the Pacific. From what I understand, physiologically they all favor their mother, since alien genes are dominant over humans'. I haven't actually seen Marina since that night in the Royal Hawaiian on Waikiki Beach, when Mara here walked in on us, even though she *said* she was going shopping. In fact, this is the first time I've seen Mara since then. A *lot* has changed, apparently."

"You got *that* right," Hank said, putting his arm possessively around Mara, who was still seething, shocked into silence. "Except for *you*. You're the same as always, only *more* so, given these infinite opportunities to fool around with the opposite sex—of opposite *species*. But then you're a cad on more planets than *two*, right, Hilly?"

Hilburne laughed, "I got around to a *lot* of planets, which was easy because our Space Needles could go so much faster than light."

Jimmy chimed in, "I still don't see how that was possible, to go so fast. I mean, relativity says nothing can go faster than light, and that's been proven many times."

"Wrong!", Hilburne said definitively. "All relativity says, is that whenever you measure the speed of light in your own environment, it will always be the same speed. It doesn't say that you can't see light going faster or slower in *other* environments besides the one you're in."

"That makes no sense", Jimmy responded. "I know that some things can slow light down, but how could it go faster than it does in a vacuum?"

Hilburne looked around, then picked up a heavy lead-crystal vase of flowers. "It's a matter of perspective. For example, we know that in heavy glass like this, light might travel only about half as fast as it does through empty space, or air. If we measure the speed of light outside the glass, we see it moves about a foot per nanosecond. When we measure the speed of light *inside* the glass while we're standing *outside* of the glass, we see it only moves 6 inches per nanosecond. Half the speed. But what about if we were inside the glass ourselves?"

"What do you mean, inside the glass?"

"Well, we live in a medium of air here at the Earth's surface, which is denser than the vacuum of space. Our bodies are constructed to be able to move around in this air. Imagine if an intelligent race had developed inside of glass, with bodies designed to move around in that denser medium."

"Ok, so what would they measure?"

"They would measure the speed of light in glass as one foot per nanosecond, same as us in air. Everyone always sees their *own* speed of light as being the same. But from our perspective, that's only because a one-foot ruler for them measures the same as a 6-inch ruler for us. So we say they're wrong because they're using a short ruler. But they say we're wrong because we're using a ruler that's two feet long. Each side has its own perspective, and you can't really say who's right, only show what the difference is in one group relative to the other."

"So what does this have to do with moving faster than light? You just said light travels slower in glass, not faster."

"Look at things from the perspective of the people living *inside* the glass. They see *their* speed of light as one foot per nanosecond, but when they look out of the glass and measure the speed of light in *our* air with their tools, they see it as 2 feet per nanosecond, or twice as fast. In their glass world things can only go as fast as the speed of light, but because the speed of light is different out here, we can have things going twice the speed of light from their viewpoint."

Jimmy thought about this. "OK, so I can see that a guy in the glass world would be restricted to going slow in the glass, but could get around his local speed of light limitation by going outside the glass." He took the vase from Hilburne. "A glass spaceship from this 'vase world' could enter our air, accelerate quickly around the vase, then drop back into the glass. From the standpoint of the glass people, it would have made the journey faster than light. But what does that have to do with us? The speed of light in air is only trivially slower than the speed of light in the vacuum of space, so we'd gain virtually no advantage in speed traveling from air to space."

"You're thinking that space is empty."

"Of course vacuum is empty, that's the definition of a vacuum!"

"Nope, space is full of energy, at the quantum level. Since energy is equivalent to mass (you know, $E=mc^2$), that means what we think of empty space is full of stuff. And the *amount* of that stuff can vary widely, depending on your frame of reference."

"That sounds like the type of thing that Lulu used to talk about, but it never made much sense to me."

"Yeah, I got this from listening to Pally go on and on while we were between planets."

Hank asked, "Between all those planets you were humpin' various broads on? Like the one where we met up?"

"Please, let's not talk about *that*," Hilburne said. "We weren't even supposed to be on the same planet at the same time. That was obviously the result a navigational error."

"What are you two talking about?" Jake asked. "You mean you two guys actually hooked up *out there*? *Before* we got back? Before *now*?"

"Only by accident," Hank said. "But because we wound up banging the same space hippie broad—sorry, Mara—I think we both brought back a virus that changed the course of human history forever…"

## MAI TAI

*2 oz premium aged rum*
*¾ oz freshly squeezed lime juice*
*½ oz curacao*
*¼ oz simple (rock candy) syrup*
*¼ oz orgeat*

*Stir then strain ingredients over crushed ice, served with mint sprig garnish.*

* * *

*Riddles of the Unmind IV*

Since the kingdom of fungi developed some 1.5 billion years ago on Earth, the Unmind had already had quite a bit of time to muse about a wide range of natural processes. Recently, the alterations of the environment by the local human population had occupied the Unmind's thought-like processes above other matters. To the Unmind, the rapid rise of human intelligence and tool-using capabilities was like the sudden development of a fruiting body (such as a mushroom) in a fungal colony matrix. To an organism like the Unmind, there could be only one reason for such a rapid change; the preparation for long-distance spore release.

Back in 1961, when the Space Needle Project was nearing completion, the Unmind pondered the following riddle, "There is a great mushroom growing, so tall that its spores will reach the stars. However, this mushroom is of but one species of fungus. As it casts its spores to the stars, it will face tremendous challenges that will tax its capacity for response, due to its limited genetic diversity. How might the success of these mushroom spores be enhanced?"

Since the Unmind was aware of the limited natural motility of its underlying fungal cell structures, it was imperative to "hitch a ride" on more mobile species if optimal spore transmission was to be accomplished. It therefore expressed a keen interest in fostering its symbiotic relationship with humans, especially those who appeared to be in the forefront of the impending emigration.

To this end, when the capable (but essentially vacant) bodies of the Space Needler robots had been created for use in the intergalactic exploration project, the Unmind had emplaced large cell colonies of beneficial yeasts within them. Professor Falkenstein had been on a drunken binge when he had conceived of the idea of putting a biochemical factory of yeast cells within the robots, to facilitate the synthesis of useful alcohol fuels from environmental sugars. He never realized that this was literally a case of "the alcohol talking", as the Unmind had delivered the specific chemical precursors for this idea in Falkenstein's beer, which was manufactured by yeasts who were themselves components of the Unmind's vast fungal network.

The yeasts in the Space Needler robots were a specially hybridized breed, specifically tailored by the Unmind to mimic the Unmind's own thought-like processes, though on a smaller scale. In addition to the enhanced chemical interconnections which provided a simulation of 'thought', these yeast colonies were equipped with a virtual encyclopedia of the Unmind's own ponderings about the universe, densely encoded in long protein strings. In each robot, the Unmind had created a miniature version of itself, including the capability to disseminate various fungal spores to establish new colonies on whatever planet was visited. In effect, the robots were Unmind spores.

The Unmind, not really cognizant of the individual mental functions of humans, considered the relationship between the robots and the humans on the Space Needle ships a purely symbiotic affair on a biological level. Each organism gained benefit from the other, so they assisted each other's survival in the unknown and hostile environments of space. The Unmind lacked any motivation to enlighten the humans as to the real nature of their robot companions.

When the robots had returned to Earth, the Unmind reabsorbed their cells into its own matrix, gaining their experiences as its own. The robot's yeasts would have died anyway, in the "mothballing" process used to prepare the robots for long-term storage. The fact that the removal of the internal yeast colonies effectively "killed" the robots in the eyes of the humans was of no consequence to the Unmind. The humans and robots had fulfilled their mission and were no longer of any concern.

# "GREEN GIRL"

*1 oz Green Chartreuse*
*1 oz Midori Melon Liqueur*
*½ oz Gran Classico bitter*
*Crushed mint leaves*

*Bruise some mint leaves in the bottom of a 6 oz glass. Add other ingredients, and ice if desired. Stir thoroughly. Garnish with sprig of mint, slapped (to release aroma).*

The world called "Emeralda" in human language lived up to its name immediately. As Hank "the Tank" Mahoney's Space Needle penetrated the gray cloud cover and entered the planet's crisp atmosphere, he was greeted with a lush surface of dense pine forests, dotted with sparkling blue lakes. It resembled the Pacific Northwest, he noted, only it stretched around the entire globe. The climate was perpetually cool, around 50 degrees, about 30 degrees less than Hank's preferred temperature, so he already hated it and couldn't wait to compose his notes after a brief exploratory spin in his saucer, then split for warmer worlds. Throughout his flight he played music by Hank Williams, Tennessee Ernie Ford, Tex Ritter, Frankie Laine ("That Lucky Old Sun" was his favorite song), Patsy Cline, and Johnny Cash on the ship's console jukebox, to remind him of home, sweet home.

Other than copious foliage and cumulous clouds, often filled with rain, Hank had no idea what to expect from this planet, since it was one of many possible destinations pre-programmed into his ship's control console, monitored and randomly selected by his robot companion, Bub, who spoke in a Texas twang much like his human mentor, but with a much more sophisticated vocabulary.

"Sure we ain't looped back to Seattle?" Hank asked Bub as they prepared for landing atop one of the many green mountains. "This looks like where we just came from!"

"No, we are now on the planet Emeralda, as translated into Earth English." Bub replied. "Our intergalactic trajectory traversed over 20 million lightyears as measured from Earth's reference frame, though it was only about a month on your calendar. The ship traveled at nearly our local speed of light, which was augmented relative to the rest of the universe due to our tremendously increased size."

Hank waved his hand dismissively. "You're talkin' nonsense again. We went 20 million light years in a *month*? I may be a slow talker, but I'm not stupid."

"Relativistic size increase is a measurable effect at high speeds. When the universal charge energy field is locally diminished by near-lightspeed travel, our local speed of light is increased relative to a stationary object at the same position in space. By the invariance of measurement, for us to possess a higher speed of light, we must expand to fill more space, so that our localized measurements will use suitably increased yardsticks, to still show the speed of light to be invariant at $3x10^8$ meters per second."

"You just keep tellin' yourself that. Makes no damn sense to me. Anything but trees down there?"

Bub answered sullenly, "My sensors indicate alien-humanoid life, though of unknown origin and designation."

"Makes you wonder why all this travel was even necessary, if it's all the same wherever you go!"

Indeed, all seven Space Needles had been launched from an expansive underground facility (later more or less replicated in the 1967 James Bond film *You Only Live Twice*) located inside the dormant volcano Mt Baker in the wilderness between Seattle and Vancouver, one each month during the 6-month run of Century 21 Exposition at the nearby World's Fair—April 21 through October 20th, 1962. The initial lift-off of a Space Needle was unspectacular; because of the large volume of Atomic Hydrogen required, the Space Needles were hidden inside a large spherical "bubble" of gas, held in place by ionizing force fields. The extremely low density of Atomic Hydrogen gas (about 3% of the density of air) caused the fully-fueled ships to simply float up into the upper atmosphere. The refractive properties of the ionized hydrogen-to-air interface made them look like large weather balloons on radar. So many preparatory test flights had been made over the years that air traffic controllers were used to seeing weather balloons, so even these particularly large instances went unnoticed. Observers on the ground were never a problem, due to the predominance of cloud cover in the Pacific Northwest. Once the ships reached the appropriate height, the engines were fired and the ships would rapidly accelerate directly away from Earth at escape velocity, not 'stopping' in orbit. The height and speed of their flight made them virtually invisible to conventional radar systems, so only those involved in the mission were able to actually perceive the launch. Once the necessary 25,000 MPH velocity was achieved in the desired direction of travel, the Atomic Hydrogen engines were shut down and the ship intercepted Alaska-based laser beams via reflectors on their saucer sections. These reflectors bounced the laser pulses back down to additional reflectors on Earth, so that each pulse of light cycled back and forth between the Earth and the ship, multiplying to force of the acceleration. Just as a basketball pushes your hand up as it is dribbled against the ground, this laser light pushed the Space Needles faster and faster with every bounce.

Each of the seven ships was initially sent into a completely separate, unique direction, but once in full flight their course was more or less dictated by the robotic co-pilots, who were also charged with the ships' safe return after all data had been collected and recorded in the their computers. That return might be with or without the human passengers, all considered expendable in emergency situations, which is why each ship was only equipped with one, to cut down on the possible loss of human life. Each volunteer was aware of the potential dangers, but given the considerable and guaranteed rewards, they all considered it worth the risks. At least initially.

Though Hank had a more or less "honorary" degree in Mechanical Engineering from Texas Tech, where he was the star quarterback of the Red Raiders before being briefly recruited by his recently formed hometown AFL team, the Houston Oilers, Hank had been chosen from the elite pool of carefully solicited "volunteers" more for his bravado than his brains. What he lacked in intellectual curiosity he more than made up for with sheer courage and physical stamina. All of the prospective Space Needle pilots had been secretly contacted about the program by NASA agents and threatened with the death of their entire families and friend circles if they revealed details to the outside world. It was no wonder the Mafia operated as their remotely affiliated subsidiary. The final candidates were rigorously screened and selected based on various characteristics deemed necessary for such a treacherous voyage.

Suiting up in his blue astronaut uniform and white helmet—which he removed and swapped for his ten gallon cowboy hat once the oxygen content of the air was deemed adequate—Hank began investigating his immediate surroundings, collecting samples of the soil and trees as well as rock specimens, which seemed to be made of the same basic ingredients as Earth's equivalents. Bub's microscopic analysis equipment indicated that the soil contained largely the same types of microbes and fungi as were found on Earth. Deliberate cosmic synchronicity, or coincidence? Thankfully, it wasn't Hank's job to decide.

Bub followed Hank closely as he traversed the serene terrain, photographing certain representative elements of the scenery and storing the images in his memory bank, which would then be uploaded to the ship's computer as backup. Every now and then a cloud filled with rain drifted overhead and there was a brief but pleasant downpour, the frequency of which was responsible for the lushness of the planet.

Birds were heard chirping in the branches above, and they resembled Earth varieties including ravens, hummingbirds, canaries, and sparrows. Except their feathers were uniformly *green*, so they blended into the foliage.

"Nothin' really to see here except these little familiar feathered critters," Hank said. "Maybe we should make this a pit-stop rather than an over-nighter, whaddya say, Bub?"

"My sensors indicate alien humanoid life in the near vicinity. We are meant to make peaceful contact when possible. I am also picking up another faint signal which must be a blip, probably coming from our own vessel."

"Fine, let's get this over with. Even with this suit, this air is way too chilly for my cowboy blood."

Hank and Bub made their way a bit further down a path through the trees and came upon a clearing with a large lake, wherein about a dozen nude green nymphs frolicked playfully. Their bodies were voluptuous, their hair was thick and long (and dark green), their faces were flawless. Yet their soft, smooth skin was a bright, deep green in hue. Hank found it curiously arousing, and approached them slowly, as if hunting wild game back in the woods of East Texas, north of Houston, where he had been born and raised. Instinctively, he kept one hand on his ray-blaster, which was set on stun by default, just in case these lovelies were deadlier than they seemed.

The liquid in the lake was clear in color, and Bub's sensors deduced it was pure gin, of an alien strain, of course.

"Hell, I could *use* a martini about now," Hank said. "Any olives around here?"

"As a matter of fact, yes—green olives, appropriately enough, growing on several trees nearby. Shall I pick a few for you?"

"Naw, maybe later. Save 'em for happy hour! I already feel like I'm hallucinatin', just seein' those green gals like that! Let's see what these gals gotta say for themselves. C'mon, let's go down and make our presence known, see what happens…"

As soon as the green-skinned bathing beauties caught sight of the human and the robot, they all screamed in unison, and ran out of the lake, grabbing their skimpy clothes—which looked like bikinis made from ivy—and donning them quickly.

"Well, dang, Bub, that ain't what I call a warm welcome!" Bub said. "Downright inhospitable, in fact. Should we follow 'em?"

"I do not detect any immediate danger, even from the mostly innocuous indigenous wildlife, so for the sake of our scientific mission, it would probably behoove us to continue," Bub said. "At least to determine the nature of their dwelling places and basic lifestyles, for the completion of our records."

"Damn, those green gals are so pretty, except for their weird complexion, I can't say I mind much. Let's go!"

Bub said, "Hang on," as Hank grabbed hold of his extended metallic arm and rode the robot sidesaddle as Bub glided smoothly across the still surface of the glistening gin-filled lake.

As they progressed, Hank picked up a strange odor wafting through the air, that grew thicker and thicker.

"What the hell is that?" Hank asked Bub.

"Marijuana," Bub said. "Of a much stronger alien strain. Which explains your previous comment about the sensation of hallucination."

"Huh? These aliens smokin' *weed*?"

"It would appear so. And in gratuitous amounts. That may account for their relatively harmonious demeanors, despite the fact they were obviously startled by our sudden presence."

"So you think they're definitely friendly?"

"I believe the technical term for their natural state is 'stoned.'"

"Just like them beatniks back on Earth! Damn. The further you go, the more things are the same. So are there menfolk here too? Jolly Green Giants?"

"Yes. They may be jolly, but they are not giants, according to my sensors. They are approximately six feet in average height, like you, but two feet shorter than me."

"So some are close by, I take it."

"Yes, we're coming upon one of their settlements now."

"You mean like a city?"

"Not exactly."

The inhabitants of this world, roughly translated as Emeraldans, literally lived in tree houses, built in clusters all over the planet. There was no such thing as war or discord on Emeralda. The denizens have lived in a state of perpetual peace for thousands of centuries, uninterrupted, uncorrupted and unconcerned with the outside universe.

Until now.

Hank felt increasingly light-headed and paranoid. It was due to the effects of second-hand pot smoke, but it was too late for him to avoid it. He grew so woozy he passed out in Bub's arms.

The robot carried the astronaut to the middle of the settlement, where he was instantly surrounded by curious males, who were the handsome counterparts of the females, with equally long, unruly locks of dark green hair. The males also dressed with similar sparseness, barely covering their private parts with ivy-leafed loin clothes, otherwise bare, their thick green skins apparently impervious to the moderately cool environment.

The females were more reticent, but gradually crept up alongside the males as Bub set a barely conscious, quasi-delirious Hank down on the ground.

"Greetings," Bub said, speaking in the native tongue of the Emeraldans, whose simple language was easy for him to electronically decipher and communicate. "I am called 'Bub.' We come from a planet many light years away called 'Earth.' I am not a natural Earthling; rather, I am a creation of Earthlings. This is Hank. He is an Earthling. However, his lungs are not accustomed to the fumes of this atmosphere. If he does not recover soon, I shall take him back to our ship, not far from here, and leave you in peace."

"Hey man," said one of the males, "like, what's up with you just showin' up and scarin' off our ladies like that? We ain't never seen no one else but ourselves for as far back as anyone remembers, which, granted, ain't very far."

"Yes, my sensors indicate memory loss is common amongst your people, due to the excessive amounts of marijuana clouding your brain cells, but since your lifestyles are not complex and require no physical labor, and you apparently subsist on the various fruits and vegetables and herbs growing freely and in copious amounts across your planet, there is no reason to remember *anything*."

"Like, you can dig it," the male Emeraldan said, and then they all started laughing. "Welcome, mechanical man! Would you like a smoke?" The male removed what appeared to be a thin cigarette from a pouch around his waist.

"No, thank you," Bub said. "I am already filtering out the ambient fumes which would prove noxious to my system."

"Wow, that's *crazy!*" said the male. "You need to de-stress yourself, friend. You and your human. C'mon, one of our females will take him in and make him feel right at home…"

The most alluring of all the females in this particular tribe of Emeraldans, called Lana, led Bub, carrying Hank, to her grassy hut on the far side of the makeshift tree-village. In appearance she strongly resembled the Earth actress Yvonne Craig.

Once inside, Lana removed Hank's astronaut uniform as he groggily responded.

"Hey there, little lady, ain't you bein' a tad forward?" he said.

"It appears you are happy to see me," Lana said as she pulled his uniform down over his legs, revealing his erection.

Lifting her ivy-thong up around her waist, Lana immediately sat on Hank's member and gently rode him until he climaxed repeatedly while she smoked a cigarette and moaned in pleasure. Bub just stood idly by, taking many photographs with his built-in camera as part of his scientific research as the lights on his chest blinked with excitement.

Hank, barely aware of what was happening, passed out again after his third orgasm. Just then another male entered the hut, but he wasn't an Emeraldan.

It was Hilburne, wearing the customary Emeraldan male loin cloth.

"Hey, baby, what the *hell*?" Hilburne shouted in shock, when he noticed Bub and then the blissfully unconscious face of Hank, still lying beneath Lana. The green woman stood up, adjusted her ivy thong, and embraced Hilburne, French-kissing him deeply as she exhaled pot smoke into his lungs, now accustomed to this volume after spending a week on the planet. He had arrived here immediately following his aborted expedition on Aquaticon. Marina was back on the ship, resting in a bathtub of rum, oblivious to Hilburne's dalliances with the local female population.

It was just like his marriage back on Earth, only better.

"When did *he* get here?" Hilburne asked Lana, who just shrugged. He coughed a bit before redirecting his question at Bub.

"We only recently arrived," Bub said. "We did not expect to find you here. This planet must have been programmed into your ship's navigational system as well as ours, either by accident or design. In any case, here we both are, simultaneously. Our unplanned meeting has proven awkward, given present circumstances."

"I'll say!" said Hilburne. "This big jerk is already nailing my girl!"

"I am *no one's* girl," Lana said adamantly, but sweetly. "I am *everyone's* girl. And I seduced *him*, though I admit, with very little effort and no resistance to speak of. Here, have another puff and relax!"

"I am relaxed, baby, but I can't be sharing you with *his* kind!"

"But you are both human, are you not?"

"Yea, but he's too human! You have no idea!"

"His male member is quite a bit larger than yours, but otherwise, I see and feel no difference," Lana said matter-of-factly.

Hank, who had been awakened by the loud exchange, grinned proudly.

"Hell, Lana, you sure know how to hurt a guy's pride," Hilburne moped.

"Pride? What is that?" she asked ingenuously.

"Never mind. Just another useless human emotion complicating life on Earth."

"Oh."

Then she took Hilburne by the hand and said, "Come *on*! Time to *dance*!"

Hank, sitting up and shaking off his sleepiness, said, "What the hell is going on? I thought I heard the voice of… *Hilly*? What in God's name are *you* doin' here?"

"Our wires got crossed, literally," Hilburne said. "Meaning

duplicate flight maps, or something."

"Where's your robot?"

"Back on the ship, keeping the tub filled with rum." He intentionally failed to mention Marina. He didn't need competition for *her* affections, too.

"What? *Why*?"

"Hey, I like to *drink*, you know that. Never been much for hallucinogens, but then we don't have much choice here, do we?"

Hank sat upright and sized up the situation and said, "Yea, not much choice about *anything*. But so far, that's workin' out fine with me!"

"So *that* is what my sensors were dimly detecting," Bub said. "But I couldn't discern it was your ship due the active electromagentic deflection device cloaking it from outside detection, even mine."

"What I can't figure it how you got here before me," Hank said to Hilburne.

"Although our ships are capable of the same speed," Bub volunteered, "the actual travel time does vary by how much matter exists in the direction of travel, and the curvature of our trajectory. Besides, Hilburne had a month's head start."

"So where else you been and what else or who else you been doin', pardner?"

"Nothing much," Hilburne lied.

"Well, *this* lil' green gal is *mine,* so back off. Plenty more plant babes where she comes from, which is *here.* And you don't mind my sayin', they all pretty much look alike, so take your pick."

"But Lana is *special*," Hilburne said, obviously smitten. "She's *mine*. Sorry, Hank, I was here *first*."

"No need to get possessive, pardner. But I'm callin' dibs based on the fact I can kick your *ass."*

"I am going out to dance now," Lana said with an impatient sigh. "You two may join me, or stay here and bicker, which is very boring. There is nothing to talk about. Here we dance, we make love, we eat, we sleep, we swim, we play. All the time, with anyone, and *everyone*. That is all that Life is about!"

"Not where *we* come from, sweetheart," Hank said. He stood up, put on his cowboy hat so he had *something* to wear. His superior manhood made Hilburne bristle.

"So you actually *screwed* this bozo?" Hilburne said

incredulously to Lana, trying to block out the disturbing mental image.

"You mean have sexual intercourse?" Lana asked. "*Yes*! As I did with *you* the last several nights. Nice of you both to drop by and make love with us. I was getting rather bored with our own males. I have already made it with every one of them over one thousand times each. At least you're of different colors."

"Wait a minute," Hilburne said. "You had sex with *all* those guys?"

"Hey, I didn't wear no protection, neither!" Hank added, suddenly itching his crotch with a worried expression.

"Of *course*!" Lana said, growing exasperated. "What *else* is there to do after we're finished dancing and swimming and eating and sleeping?"

"But… what about procreation?" Hilburne asked. "Don't you ever get knocked up, that is, pregnant?"

"Oh. Propagation. That is accomplished with seeds we females produce once in our lifetime, emanating from our wombs after initial copulation. We plant them by squatting in the soil, and more of us grow. Then we are barren and free to have as much sex as we please, whenever we please, with *whomever* we please."

"You mean, you're made out of *vegetables*?" Hank said.

"That's what you'd call it, yes," Lana said. "We also eat vegetables that grow freely in the surrounding woods. Often we put some herbs in cups filled with lake liquid for drinks."

"My sensors can confirm their constitutional makeup as being wholly plant-based," Bub said. "The local vegetables she refers to include cucumbers as well as fruits like limes, and herbs like mint. As I previously established, the nearest lake is filled with pure alien gin. Other lakes in the vicinity are filled with a clear type of alien rum, from which the inhabitants may make mojitos. So in effect, Emeraldans imbibe gimlets and mojitos on a regular basis, which, combined with their frequent marijuana smoking, helps them maintain an unusually pleasant, positive outlook on life. They are as calm and serene as an Earth flower."

"*Flower* children!" Hilburne said.

"Heck, I don't even like Brussels sprouts or broccoli with my *steak*!" Hank said. "Now you're sayin' I just banged a giant *pea pod*?"

"Yea, but what a pod!" Hilburne said.

"Heck, you can *have* her, pardner," Hank grumbled with disgust. "Make as much pea soup as you *want*. I'm outta here."

"I am dancing now, goodbye," Lana said, bored with the conversation and abruptly exiting the hut to join the throngs of her fellow Emeraldans, writhing to the beat of several bongo drums around a campfire as the sun set, casting deep shadows across the settlement. Hank was ready to leave but the sight of the dancing nude females, whatever their physical makeup, lured him back. Hilburne provided Hank with an ivy loincloth to complement his cowboy hat, and to hide his massive manhood.

The dancing quickly turned into an orgy, and Hilburne and Hank, still high from the air they were breathing, which was abetted by rampant joint smoking, joined in the sensual fun. This went on for several hours as Bub stood by recording the revelry for scientific posterity.

Suddenly a disturbing, droning noise began emanating seemingly from all around the settlement, rudely interrupting the hypnotic mood.

"What the hell is *that?*' Hilburne asked Lana.

"It is the *Tabangans*!" she said with uncharacteristic urgency. "We must hide inside!"

"Tabangans?" said Hank. "Which are what exactly?"

"Hostile tree-like creatures," Bub explained. "They are the only species on this planet that seeks conflict for its own sake. It is their predatory nature, though they live on rain water as does all of the local plant life. But their sour sentient nature causes them to inflict harm on the Emeraldans, partly out of envy, since Emeraldans can enjoy physical pleasures such as sex and dancing, while the Tabangans are prohibited from such indulgences due to the restrictive composition of their forms, meaning all bark, not flesh." (They actually resembled Paul Blaisdell's tree monster in the 1957 film *From Hell It Came*.)

"Which looks like what?" Hilburne asked.

"*That*," said Bub, pointing to several ten foot tall, lumbering, misshapen monstrosities with flexible, prickly branches for arms, twisted trunks, and horribly distorted facial features attacking the revelers, or attempting to, since they moved quite slowly, another source of discontent and bitter self-loathing. The robot's rays, either set to stun or lethal power, had no effect on the Tabangans. This was due to a protective sheen of water on the Tabangan's bark, which both deflected the electrical stun rays, and blocked the Atomic Hydrogen blasts from catalyzing on the bark's surface.

Hank reflexively grabbed a flaming branch from the campfire and began fending off the marauding tree monsters as Lana cowered behind him. Jealous, Hilburne also grabbed a burning branch, but Lana remained close to Hank, clutching his bulging biceps. The Emeraldan's possessed no instinct for fighting, only flight, so it was up to the astronauts and robot, reduced to metal hand-to-branch combat, to defend them.

Exasperated, Hilburne threw a burning branch at a horde of Tabangans, and one of them instantly burst into flames, screaming in pain and accidentally setting his companions on fire while flailing about. Soon the incendiary counter-attack not only succeeded in killing or scaring off the remainder of the retreating intruders, but quickly spread to the surrounding non-humanoid trees, and within five minutes, the entire settlement had been burned to the ground, leaving nothing but ashes and sobbing green alien-humanoids, huddled together as one of the frequent rain showers belatedly doused the flames.

"*You idiot*!" Hank said, lunging at Hilburne amid the smoldering ruins. But the smoke from the fire only enhanced the marijuana already prevalent in the air, and thusly weakened, the two astronauts fainted after a rather brief and impotent fistfight. Lana was likewise unconscious from grief.

Bub carried both back to their respective ships, one under each arm. Hilburne's Space Needle was parked in a nearby lake. Bub glided out and deposited him inside the door opened by Pally, who responded to Bub's electronic communications. They both shook their heads in disgust as they briefly greeted one another. Crazy humans.

Inside Pally's Space Needle, Marina the Mermaid demanded that Hilburne explain where he'd been and what he'd been doing the past few days, while Hank slept soundly as Bub took off for their next destination, leaving behind the smoking remnants of a once thriving settlement.

Of course, by the next day, all was well again, their tree houses reassembled elsewhere, and the Emeraldans resumed their normal routine, while the astronauts wished they had never left.

* * *

"You two horny bastards sure had a lot of *fun* out there," Mara said bitterly.

"It wasn't worth it," Hank said. "I'm positive that loose green hippie bitch infected me with a virus that I brought back and spread across the Earth. I don't mean it was *sexually* transmitted—don't give me that look, Mara, I ain't that much of a stud, and remember you weren't with *me* when I was out there—but just the whole nature of their liberal, irresponsible, alien civilization seems to have infected our own world ever since I got back. Hilly probably spread the virus the old fashioned way…"

"You can't blame the entire 60's counterculture on a STD we picked up on another planet," Hilburne insisted. "That movement was already in progress long before we even left."

Jake, who had been listening rather quietly throughout the meal, finally made an observation. "Hey, do you think you might have time-traveled back to the past and started the beatnik movement with these crazy alien ideas before we ever left Earth?"

Hilburne looked skeptical. "No, time travel to the past is not possible."

Jake shook his head, "I can tell you, when I first left Earth I was homesick, so I told Pancho to reconstruct a view of home using whatever signals he could detect from Earth. I swear, when he set up the viewscreen, I could see that time was moving *backwards* there."

"Just an illusion. You can see it for yourself at just normal Earthly speeds, no need to travel faster than light. All you need is some movie footage, a train, and a car."

Hank snorted, "I'll bet this is another one of your 'science made simple' stories."

"You're right, but it will help Jake understand what he saw."

"Go for it, then. I need to take a leak anyway." Hank wandered off to the men's room while Hilburne explained.

"A movie is just a set of still frames of film, one after another. They go by so fast that they blur together and give the illusion of motion, of the flow of time. If you were to string out a strip of film on the side of a train and illuminate from inside the train cars, you could stand in one place as the train rolled by and see the movie progress at a normal speed. However, if you were in a car traveling in the same direction as the train, you'd see the movie differently depending on your speed. If the car is a little slower than the train, the film would still look like it was going forward, but it would be in slow-motion. If your car was going at the same speed as the train, you'd get stuck watching one frame forever, as if time had stopped. And if the car went faster than the train, the film would look like it was going *backwards*."

Jake nodded. "I can see this is true. But how is real life like a movie? We are not just frames of film going by."

Hilburne said, "No, we're more than that, but what are you actually seeing when you observe life on Earth? It's just the light that bounces off of things and reaches your eyes. Light has a wavelike nature and so it acts like individual frames of film, each frame being one wave of light. These waves travel at the speed of light, so to see the apparent slowdown of time you need to be going pretty close to the speed of light. To see time appear to stop, you need to go exactly the speed of light on Earth. Go *faster* than light on Earth, and time will appear to go backwards, just like it did with the car travelling faster than the train. Strangely, to see this effect, you actually need to point your telescope directly *away* from the Earth in the direction of your travel, to pick up the light waves in front of you. Pancho obviously understood the phenomenon and set up your viewscreen appropriately."

"So I wasn't seeing time go backwards, but just a replay of the light from the past, played in reverse?"

"Yes, it's like telling you I've got a time machine in a theater. When you go inside, I play a movie backwards for you to see in reverse. You see what *looks* like reversed time, but it doesn't change the *actual* passage of time outside the theater. When the movie's over, everything in the world is just a couple hours older, not younger."

Jake looked relieved, "Of course, that is the way it was when I got home from the trip. A few years had passed both for me, and my family at home. So we didn't start the beatnik revolution with immoral alien contact…."

"The rampant promiscuity of alien beings is due to their lack of religious restrictions and moralistic inhibitions. Maybe now the Earth is finally catching up, that's all. Since we weren't allowed to share any of our research, as it were, with the public, we can't even take credit for this sudden acceleration in social attitudes. It's just one of many cosmic coincidences that confronted us out there.

Doesn't matter now, anyway. Suffice to say, Captain Kirk had nothing on *us*."

"I still say it ain't no coincidence," Hank said, returning from the bathroom. "I don't take credit. I take the *blame*. I shoulda worn a rubber, at least. But I was just too damn high off all that second hand smoke!"

"Yea, I think I got infected by a beatnik chick I picked up in a bar right before we left," Tony said. "In fact, I *know* I was. But I don't want to talk about that right now. Jimmy, you seem to have been traumatized more than the rest of us. What exactly happened to you out there?"

Jimmy shook his head and said, "Let's just say of the worlds I visited, most were pleasant, except for the first one I landed on, and that made the strongest impression…"

**GIMLET**

*2 oz gin*
*¾ oz fresh lime juice*
*¾ oz simple syrup*
*Sliced cucumber wheels for garnish*

*Stir ingredients in shaker, strain then pour into chilled martini glass.*

**MOJITO**

*1 ½ oz white rum*
*½ cup club soda*
*Approx. one dozen fresh mint leaves*
*½ lime cut into wedges*
*2 tablespoons white sugar (variable)*

*Muddle mint and lime in tall glass, do not strain; pour rum in glass filled with ice to the brim, add sugar measured to taste.*

* * *

*Riddles of the Unmind V*

At the dawn of human history, the Fungal Unmind had pondered this riddle, "An ancient creature is threatened by a young upstart who possesses greater physical capabilities. How may dominance be preserved by the ancient?"

"The ancient one can never hope to match the young in mere physical capacity. The ancient must use its wealth of experience, its wisdom of the true ebb and flow of the universe, to find a path to bend the youth to its will."

"This cannot succeed, if the youth's mind is closed to the wisdom of the elder. The young have such brash confidence, that they disregard all but their own sense of greatness."

"Then you have answered your own riddle. The ancient one can only dominate by fostering an even greater sense of confidence and power in the youth, if they but stay in the ancient's dominion. Once this false confidence has been instilled, the youth will be loath to leave this realm, for the less motivating environment of mere self-confidence."

"Name some ways in which false confidence can be generated in youth."

"They are simple, and attracted by shiny things of little worth. Additionally, their brains are malleable and easily swayed by externally-imposed illusions. They are fearless and can be dared to do anything."

"Might they be inclined to eat or drink strange substances, if promised greatness as a reward?"

"Yes, the youthful are very susceptible to superstition."

"Then I answer the riddle with this: Let us tap the biochemical diversity of the Earth to create many strange and wondrous substances, and present them as food to the younger species of the planet. They will seek out more of those which they find appealing, and we shall concentrate on producing those variants, until all the youthful species have come under our sway."

"So it shall be."

Since this time, the Unmind had become fully aware of the effects of intoxicants of various kinds on the human population. It maintained its own existence in part from a manipulation of such effects. Humans prized yeasts and mushrooms for such "gifts" as alcohol and hallucinogens, not realizing that these were the brainwashing drugs of the Unmind. These intoxicants were just one pathway to control humans. Another was food. The Unmind provided nutritious mushrooms to enhance the human's regard for underground fungal colonies, and discourage any disruption with the fungal lifecycle. As an additional lure, the Unmind had developed rare varieties of edible fungi such as truffles, intuitively sensing that ease of cultivation would lessen the human's valuation of their fungal symbiotes. It was important to the Unmind that humans take fungi with them as they traveled, whether across the Earth or through space.

As humans had gained intelligence, this task was made easier by the human's "discovery" that certain molds (like penicillin) had antibacterial properties. The Unmind was happy for this opportunity to expand its symbiotic relationship with the eminently mobile and ever more ubiquitous human population.

Still, the Unmind was aware that humans also had susceptibility to other, non-fungally derived psychoactive chemicals from the plant world. While not a direct threat, this still diminished the level of control over humans by the Unmind. To mitigate the risk, using the manipulation of chemical messages delivered to humans in its alcohol products, the Unmind facilitated a rather hypocritical "war on plant-based drugs" which helped it maintain control of the human population. Ironically, some of its own compounds (like psilocybin) ended up on the proscribed list, due to overzealous categorization by the humans. Alcohol-based social engineering was also used to pressure the human population to reject any anti-fungal propaganda put forth by its own population, such as "Prohibitionism".

The Unmind was pleased with the reports from the robot yeast colonies about the prevalence of alcohol as an intoxicant on the different worlds they had visited. This implied that fungal colonies already existing on these planets. The Unmind, being both the product and the master of all of the fungal species on Earth, had no concept of competition. It assumed that any local Unmind on these distant worlds would welcome the additional genetic diversity of new fungal species, such as those making up the Earth's Unmind.

Of greater concern were the reports of other plant-based intoxicants, such as the herbs smoked by the Emeraldans. The Unmind had nothing against green plants, itself being reliant on dead plant matter as its primary foodsource, but would prefer that plants stayed out of the mind-control business. The Unmind would have to find a way to deal with the Emeraldan psychoactive plants, once it had established a large enough colony there. The Unmind was sure that it would achieve such dominance in time, now that the humans had proved capable of using the faster-than-light pathways predicted by quantum gravity theory.

# "BUG-EYED MONSTER"

*1/3 oz honey*
*¾ oz Carpano Antica Formula vermouth*
*1½ oz rye whiskey*
*2 dashes whiskey barrel bitters*

*Mix ingredients thoroughly at room temperature, to dissolve honey. May be served neat for full flavor, or over ice for those who prefer gentler bug-eyed monsters.*

"Sukiyaki" by Kyu Sakamoto (original title: "Ue o Muite Arukō", translated literally as "I Look Up As I Walk") was playing on Jimmy Honda's space-jukebox as his Space Needle entered the atmosphere of a planet that would be known as "Insectica" if it was known at all by Earth scientists, which it wasn't. All Jimmy's robot Lulu could predict based on advance sensor readings was that the planet was primarily covered in sand that went miles deep, to the very core, with mountain ranges dotting the desolate landscape for aesthetic variety. The inhabitants, which were only vaguely detectable by Lulu, were most likely underground dwellers, burrowing tunnels and creating cavernous homes far below the surface. But exactly of what species remained to be seen. There was also no sun in this particular system, meaning the skies were perpetually black though dotted with distant stars, and there was no oxygen in the atmosphere, so Jimmy would need his helmet when he ventured out to collect samples. It was essentially a very cold desert. For some reason he had been assigned one of the most intimidating missions. Music was Jimmy's only therapeutic recourse. Jimmy whistled along with Kyu Sakamoto.

The song "Sukiyaki" had been a hit the previous year in Japan, and would be a hit in America as well when it was released there the following year. It had a soothing effect on Jimmy, who was terrified of what may await him on this dark world. A star Mathematics student at UC Berkeley with a bright future in academics, Jimmy volunteered for the voyage largely to face and conquer his many phobias, but also to just get away from Earth for a while. Being a gay Japanese-American in the middle of the 20th century remained his strongest challenge in life.

For most of the journey Jimmy had been playing Peggy Lee

songs, particularly "It's a Good Day" in a continuous loop, trying to put himself in a positive mood. Lulu, programmed to speak like an effete British butler, quietly hummed Broadway show tunes as he went about needlessly dusting the midcentury modernist furniture and mixing gin martinis for Jimmy upon request.

It was only they were about to land that Jimmy noticed the gigantic cobweb that immediately ensnared the ship.

"I apologize, sir," Lulu said. "For some reason my sensors misinterpreted the web as dust. That must be deliberately designed as predatory subterfuge. I will manually boost our rockets in an attempt to free the ship before it is attacked and you are devoured."

"Devoured?" Jimmy gasped. "By *what*?"

"*That*," Lulu said, pointing out the front view screen at a monstrous, sixty foot wide black spider-like creature with not eight but a dozen legs, plus six glowing red eyes and drooling fangs, that was rapidly bearing down upon the trapped vessel, dangling in the web between two skyscraper-sized shards of red rock jutting from the sandy surface.

Screaming in horror, Jimmy hit some buttons on the console that immediately electrified the exterior of the ship. But the spider-monster was undeterred, absorbing the currents rather than being repelled by them, and roaring triumphantly and menacingly as it began climbing on the saucer hub and attempting to break the glass or bend the metal with its powerful, hairy legs, which were each equipped with sharp pincers. This was no typical arachnid.

"*Hold on, sir! Strap yourself in*!" Lulu commanded. Jimmy complied and then the robot calmly hit a few other buttons and the ship began vibrating violently, finally shaking itself loose of the web, falling headfirst into the sand. Now the ship, including its occupants, was upside down, leaning precariously against one of the massive rocks.

A tremendous caterpillar-type creature began emerging from the sand right beneath the saucer hub. It too had two large arms with pincers located just beneath its frightening face, which likewise featured drooling fangs and glowing red eyes, but instead of ten long legs, it had dozens of smaller arms running the length of its eighty foot long torso, which kept rising from the ground ominously as Jimmy and Lulu watched helplessly.

The spider-monster and the caterpillar-creature eventually met up in the middle and began engaging in a fierce battle for possession of the ship. Their screeching made Jimmy delirious with fear. Lulu tried in vain to console him, but offered no solutions to their predicament. The victor of the battle would win them an edible reward.

Suddenly the ship started descending into a hole opening up in the sand, and it slipped quickly beneath the surface, disappearing from sight, beyond the reach of the giant insect-monsters still waging violent war, their bodily fluids leaking from open wounds inflicted by their opponent, flooding the sand.

Meanwhile, the Space Needle continued sinking through the sand at a rapid rate before finally crashing into a cavern, where it slid along the rocky ground, straightening out, then coming to a halt as it hit a stony wall.

There was eerie silence for several minutes as Jimmy sat still, shivering with dread, relieved to be free of the death trap above, but now filled with trepidation as to what awaited them below. Probably whatever brought them here, he figured. Finally, attempting to put a hopeful spin on the situation, he it a button on the jukebox and Peggy Lee began singing, "It's a Good Day." Both Lulu and Jimmy shakily sang along, still strapped upside down to their seats in front of the control console, nervously tapping their feet in unison.

It didn't take long for their rescuers—or new captors—to introduce themselves.

"My sensors indicate alien humanoid beings are approaching," Lulu said.

"Oh, yea?" Jimmy said. "W-what kind?"

"They seem to be of an insect variety. If fact, they are known as *Insectoid*s."

"That doesn't sound promising, for some reason."

"Insects are industrious creatures, at least on Earth."

"Not always friendly, though. And apparently the ones here aren't either. And they're not small enough to squash."

"I suggest you assume a diplomatic stance, sir, per protocol."

"Okay, but just in case…." Jimmy tapped the ray-blaster in his hip holster. "How's the air out there?"

"Oxygen content is very low. I suggest wearing your helmet."

Jimmy reached over and strapped on his helmet and flipped the oxygen switch on the side.

Just then there was a tapping on the front view screen.

The Insectoids looked like a cross between the Metaluna Mutants in the 1955 film *This Island Earth*, and Ray Harryhausen's "Selenites" in the 1964 film adaptation of H.G. Wells' *First Men in the Moon*, which hadn't even been made yet. They stood on two feet, averaging about seven feet tall in height, roach-brown in color, with thin, spindly arms and legs, armored torsos, bulbous brain-shaped heads, and large, cold, "bugged-out" eyes, glowing red just like the monsters above.

"Please come out, Earth Man," one of them said telepathically through the view screen. "We will not eat you. Rather, we will not harm you."

"He literally read my mind!" Jimmy said.

"*That* they can do, like many advanced alien species that use the bulk of their brains, *unlike* humans, but their diet is not cannibalistic by nature," Lulu assured him. "So you won't end up 'brain food.'"

"But I'm *not* one of their kind!"

Lulu paused and then said grimly, "That's a good point."

Jimmy began sweating profusely inside his blue astronaut suit. "I really need a drink," he whispered. He hadn't been this scared since he was forced with his family into an Internment camp back in 1942, twenty years earlier.

One of the Insectoids suddenly produced a strangely shaped silver chalice. "Cheers!" it said, extending the cocktail in a welcoming gesture.

Jimmy's point of view was still askew since he was hanging upside down, augmenting his sense of vulnerability. With a glance he directed Lulu to gently unfasten both their seat belts. They landed with a simultaneous thud on the ceiling of the ship. Fortunately, the planet, like all planets, was equipped with the force of gravity. That was one universal constant you just couldn't escape, seemingly. With the flick of a switch, the saucer hub swiveled completely around, so at least it was right side up, even though the based remained stuck at a downward angle. Dazed and disoriented, Jimmy went outside to greet the Insectoids, Lulu by his side.

His complimentary cocktail was handed to him as soon as he exited. After a quick, discreet safety-scan of the liquid by Lulu, Jimmy lifted the shield of his helmet just long enough to tentatively sip the drink. To his relief, it was the most delicious concoction he had ever tasted. He lifted and closed the helmet for several more successive gulps, causing him to become increasingly intoxicated.

There were about a dozen Insectoids assembled around the entrance to the saucer hub, and Jimmy lifted a tentative toast. "Kampai!" he said with forced cheeriness.

"*Kampai*!" they all said, though none were holding a chalice.

The apparent leader of the pack said, "Let's go get acquainted within the safety of our chambers."

"Why, is there danger out here?"

Just then an echoing roar filled the shadowy underground cave. Jimmy noticed via the illumination from the ship's lights that numerous red stalactites hung from the ceiling. The source of the roar was a gigantic black scorpion-creature with two poison-dripping stinger-tails instead of one, and four arms with snapping pincers instead of two. Also it was forty feet long and fifteen feet high, further distinguishing it from the Earth variety with which Jimmy was familiar.

"Let's go," commanded the leader of the Insectoids. "This way."

Considering the urgency of their predicament, Jimmy and Lulu felt it wise to comply. However, the Insectoids had a very quick metabolism and could move much faster than a human. Always one to travel in style, Jimmy instructed Lulu to quickly deploy the Space Needle's land car, a modified General Motors Firebird III, which descended quietly from its separately contained "garage" at the base of the saucer. The double-domed Firebird III was first built in 1959 as a test car for gas turbine powered passenger vehicles. Due to the success of early tests, GM won the Space Needle Program's contract for ground transportation, beating out its nearest competitor Ford, whose Seattle-lite XXI prototype wasn't ready for production. Both of these cars were featured in the 1962 World's Fair Century 21 exposition, where the Firebird III created quite a stir with its space-age fins. The car was featured in the 1963 film, *It Happened at the World's Fair*, where Elvis' character Mike Edwards finds the missing girl Sue-Lin hiding in the Firebird III towards the end of the movie.

Jimmy and Lulu quickly drove in pursuit of the Insectoids, leaving the huge scorpion in their dust, and were eventually led to a sliding door in the rocky wall. That door opened into a vast, dimly lit, steel-enforced area devoid of any color or personality, filled with odd machines of all sizes, themselves equipped with mysterious flashing lights, while a low level humming noise emanated from seemingly everywhere, like crickets on a summer evening.

In fact, the sound was emitting from a living source—the humanoid "worker bees" that effectively operated their civilization, called, in English parlance, "Buzzers." This term was considered a racial slur by the Buzzers, whose ancestors were, many centuries ago, a peaceful race of flying surface dwellers that did not have a specific name, since they all shared the same spirit that ebbed from a single, massive hive. For their species, individuality was not necessary. They existed in perfect harmony with their natural surroundings, since even the surface monsters did not find them particularly tasteful or appealing. The Buzzers themselves thrived by sucking sweet, life-sustaining sap from various rocks that yielded an alien form of honey.

Then the Insectoids suddenly emerged from their underground cities, conquered and enslaved the Buzzers to help power their cities and send them back out to the surface to gather and harvest "honey" for their cocktails, after they discovered they could mine pure gin from the sundry subterranean lakes. (Of course, Insectoids had to accompany Buzzers on these surface missions, putting them in harm's way, so alternative methods were currently being sought.) The resulting mixture was the equivalent of an Earth cocktail called the "Bee's Knees," and the Insectoids found it quite addictive, to the point where their systems actually required it for sustenance. Indeed, Jimmy had never tasted anything like it. He was already hooked.

Buzzers lived in separate quarters that resembled giant hives, patterned after their original surface headquarters, all located in a cluster just within the confines of this sterile, subterranean village. It was one of many built below the hostile surface of Insectica, which itself was occupied by several different races of predatory, carnivorous monsters. Buzzers resembled cute black-and-yellow striped human-sized bees that stood upright, and were able to fly short distances, though they never attempted to escape captivity, since being kept slaves was a more secure existence than trying to survive outside the scientifically advanced domain and protective (if oppressive) custody of the Insectoids. The subterranean scorpion creatures had developed a taste for Buzzers, unlike the caterpillars and spiders that populated the surface, and so presented a direct threat to Buzzers that helped the Insectoids control them. By now, after centuries of slavery, the Buzzers had no memory of any other life. They existed in a fearful state of perpetual indentured servitude.

Jimmy, leaving the car in Lulu's hands, and already in a pleasantly drunken stupor, was carried by a band of Buzzers to a small room filled with artificially manufactured oxygen, stripped bare, and laid on a comfortable table. Jimmy was then left alone for several nervous minutes as an electronic melody played in the background. Its sonic equivalent would later be known as "New Age Music" back on Earth.

The ambient humming sound that permeated the village increased as the door slid back open and several stunningly gorgeous, completely nude female humans entered and began rubbing Jimmy down with soothing oils, massaging his limbs and torso and neck and feet. However, when they attempted to pleasure his penis, it remained limp and unreactive.

The female humans suddenly morphed into several nude male humans—very well-groomed, finely toned, and incredibly handsome. Just Jimmy's type.

"Oh no," Jimmy said in voice quivering with both desire and dread. Then he said, "Oh no…oh no…oh no…oh yes…oh yes…oh *yes…*"

The female and male "humans" were actually living mirages—hypnotically disguised Buzzers, since to Jimmy's inebriated brain, they appeared to be of his own species (Jimmy's account of this incident was later the basis for the 1973 film *Invasion of the Bee Girls*). In reality, the Buzzers had no separate sexes since they were a self-propagating species, unlike the Insectoids or surface monsters.

However, when Jimmy remained unresponsive to the disguised Buzzers' feminine touch, the Insectoids, watching from a concealed monitor above, quickly deduced Jimmy's sexual orientation, and telepathically replaced his designated masseuses accordingly, much to Jimmy's satisfaction.

It wasn't a happy ending for everyone, though.

The Buzzers violently rejected this new brand of human "honey" provided by this willing specimen, vomiting it up as it was consumed from both ends of their illusory bodies. Ingestion of any human fluid apparently made them quite ill. The Insectoid witnesses were quite distressed.

"If the Buzzers could manufacture honey with the human's

secretions, we would no longer need to send them on dangerous surface missions," one Insectoid observer said to another. "But it seems their systems will not properly digest it."

"Yes, I can see that. Just our luck."

"Given the fact the surface honey appears to be a diminishing resource, our race, as well as the Buzzers, may indeed become extinct within a century or so, since the Buzzers cannot subsist on gin alone, and our own kind has become addicted to the combination of honey and gin. Without that cocktail, we will surely perish."

"Yes, I realize all that, but thanks for reminding me. Hopefully other similar species will land on our planet again soon, and we can extract and experiment with *their* fluids. Meantime, what to do with this specimen, now that we've shown him every possible courtesy and depleted his natural juices? Shall we serve his flesh to the others as an appetizer? Happy hour is coming up and it would make a unique snack to go with out cocktails. I've never tasted human organs myself, but I hear the possibilities are unlimited. We could put various body parts on skewers, roasted as well as grilled, laminated with a special sauce."

"That *does* sound tasty. Let's do it!"

Just then the male masseuses' visage morphed yet again into misshapen monsters with hideously deformed features instead of Olympian physiques, and Jimmy lost his boner, though it had already come in handy, so to speak, several times in a row. The Insectoids mentally instructed the monstrous masseuses to dismember and dissect Jimmy like an Earth chef would pluck and take apart a chicken about to be cooked. Lulu, listening in telepathically, swung into combative action and began fighting off the zombie-masseuses, and Jimmy joined the fray.

Frustrated, the voyeuristic Insectoids intervened, saving Jimmy from being literally ripped limb from limb, if only so they could eat him themselves.

Lulu shot the Insectoids with lethal rays, correctly deducing that stun-beams would have no effect, and momentarily disabled them, though he could not destroy them. Their natural body armor was composed of gelled silicates with high water content, and so was mostly impervious to the gun's Atomic Hydrogen output.

Lifting Jimmy over one shoulder after quickly restoring his suit and helmet so he could breathe outside, Lulu then flew the semi-conscious astronaut out of the room and back to the waiting car. The

Firebird III zoomed past the hordes of angry Insectoids and cheering Buzzers, and back to the Space Needle. Jimmy was barely conscious by now. In fact, he was singing, "It's a Good Day." He had no idea how much danger he was in until Lulu fired up the Space Needle, backed it up to the surface, set it straight, so to speak, then, surrounded by spiders and caterpillars, flew back into the relative safety of space.

* * *

"I'd have almost been happy to have been torn apart by those beautiful beings," Jimmy said blissfully. "Even if they *were* alcoholically induced hallucinations. That elixir they gave me was sheer ambrosia, too. I would've died happy, at least."

"That's *disgustin'*," Hank said.

"My alien lovers were insects, yours were plants, so what?" Jimmy said defensively.

"Yea, but mine were of the proper *sex,*" Hank said.

"For *you,*" Jimmy said. "But George Takei would be on my side. My hero!"

"Asian fruitcake, like you," Hank grumbled.

"Funny how 'Sulu' rhymed with 'Lulu' too," Jimmy said. "I had no idea at the time. I miss Lulu. He saved my life several times, but most importantly *this* time."

"I miss Pally," Hilburne said with a sentimental sigh.

The others concurred and raised a collective toast to their respective robots, none of which had been seen by them since the end of their three-year voyages. Truth be told, the bodies of the robots were being stored in government warehouses, after they stopped responding to voice commands following the Space Needlers' return to Earth. Falkenstein's science team was mystified, not realizing that the fungoid microintelligences that had inhabited those robot bodies were now back reporting to their superiors.

"Strange how many of the aliens wanted to either mate with or us eat us," Jake said. "I dealt with that problem on several occasions, too."

"All they seem to do out there is drink, eat, and screw," Hank said. "In that way, not very different from us humans. Except, of course, we're always into a bit of conquest too. Makes you think God is *Caligula.* No wonder I lost my faith after that whole deal. I'm not agnostic, mind you, but everything I was taught to believe growing up a devout Christian seemed to be totally blown apart by the weird shit I saw out there. None of it makes no sense. Sometimes I think back on it and think it was *all* a dream, or a hallucination."

"That's still one possible conspiracy theory," Jimmy concurred, nodding his head. "Maybe we all shared the same mass delusion after being experimented on by the Government. Meaning none of this ever even *happened.*"

Tony chimed in, "I've wondered about that. I mean, us travelling to those other galaxies, no one believes that's even possible! How could we go faster than light? They've got top scientists with multi-million dollar particle accelerators testing the speed of light every day, and they've never found any evidence of a single particle going faster than light, let alone a whole spaceship!"

"It's the firehose problem", Hilburne noted enigmatically.

Tony looked puzzled, "Firehose?"

Hilburne continued, "Yeah, it's an easy way to think about it. Imagine you've got a firehose hooked up to one of the city's high-pressure fire hydrants. Say that hose pushes out a stream of water at 30 miles per hour. You aim the hose at a child's wagon. Bam! When the stream of water hits, the wagon starts rolling away. It goes faster and faster, but as its speed gets higher, what happens? Let's say the wagon is going 20 miles per hour, which means the relative speed of the water hitting it is now only 30-20 = 10 MPH. Still pretty fast, but with a lot less energy than when the water was hitting the stationary wagon at 30. This is going to accelerate it slower than before. When the wagon is going almost 30 MPH itself, the speed of the water hitting it is negligible. It hardly feels it, but just maintains its pace. There's no way that wagon is ever going to go over 30 miles per hour while running on level ground, just from being hit by that firehose stream."

"So? What does that have to do with particle accelerators?"

"What's a particle accelerator? It's a big pile of magnets and electric coils imbedded in the Earth, that send electromagnetic signals into a plasma of particles to accelerate them. It's like the piping system of our fire hose, fixed in place. Those electromagnetic fields it pushes out might be lasers, or radio waves, but they are always made of light. How fast does light go? Why, the speed of light, of course. Which means those particles being hit by that light in the accelerator are going to be able to go at any speed up to that of light (relative to the accelerator hardware), but no faster. That's hardly the way to prove that the speed of light is some ultimate limit."

Tony pondered this, "But if these accelerators are limited, how would you push something faster than light?"

Hilburne explained, "Our Space Needles were pushed up near the speed of light by the Earth-based lasers. That's as fast as they could make us go, because they were using ground-based light, just like in a particle accelerator. But when we turned on our Atomic Hydrogen engines, those were local to our own ships. The speed of light limitation only applies to interactions between different frames of reference, like the Earth and our ship. Local processes don't care about the speed of light elsewhere, and so are unconstrained. When we were going near the speed of light in our Space Needles, our local speed of light was almost double that on Earth. Our rockets supplied thrust generated in that zone of rapid lightspeed, and so could accelerate us faster than anything on Earth. With a rocket you can go as fast as you want, until you run out of fuel. Of course, Atomic Hydrogen is the most common element in intergalactic space, so we could just scoop up more as we went along, and go as fast as we wanted."

Tony looked skeptical. "That sound reasonable, but couldn't that explanation be part of the overall conspiracy, that we were brainwashed into thinking was real? In a shared hallucination we'd all think the same thing."

"Bullshit!" John said. "We all experienced some things the same, but others differently. No way they could've made us share the same damn dream! This shit was real, cats. At least to me it was. As for how you rationalize it, what it all *means,* that shit depends on your own particular philosophy, influenced by your own individual experiences. Just like anything *else*."

"Subjectively speaking, then, it all does makes me believe in some sort of Supreme Being," Jake said. "And I was already a lapsed Catholic before I even got into all this. In fact, part of my motivation was to prove, at least personally, there's more to Life than meets the corporeal eye. And from what I saw, it's not all randomly organized. Too complex, too orderly, even with all the chaos, most of which seems to be self-inflicted, though there are supernatural *and* natural forces beyond our control, no doubt. But definite patterns of behavior exist out there, definitely diverse societies, but all conforming to a specific style of consciousness."

"Could be *Satan*," Hank said. "Maybe Evil is in charge, after all."

"Or it could be just plain Love," Jimmy offered optimistically. "And maybe that's contagious. Tolerance of alternative lifestyles is finally happening across our traditionally conservative society, slowly but inevitably. I wouldn't be surprised if marriage between two males was legalized some day. Along with legalized marijuana!"

"If it happened anywhere, it would be in the state of Washington," Hilburne agreed. "Probably on the same *day*."

Everyone laughed at the prospect. Except Jimmy.

"Though there remains a *lot* of hate and bigotry out there, too," John said, speaking from personal experience on Earth and elsewhere. "Same as on our little world, which is far more insignificant than we humans ever realized. That's probably another reason we're being clamped up by Big Brother. One big difference between many alien worlds and ours is we have a lot more diversity in our society, which means we fight more amongst ourselves out of petty paranoia and competition. Other worlds seem to have more uniform cultures. Maybe that's the key to ultimate survival, unfortunately. Separation of the species, since peaceful integration seems to always produce conflict, everywhere. I know what you're sayin', Jimmy, how many alien cultures are more evolved than ours in a lot of ways, but Hate and Love were *both* calling the shots out there, man. I can tell you all about that when my turn comes. And I've already had a lifetime of dealing with both down *here*."

"Amen, brother," Jake said.

"I can certainly relate, but this universal 'conflict' between good and evil, to put it in simplistic terms, seems to be both a paradox and a balance," Jimmy said. "So perhaps it's all part of a Grand Design. Even now, after all we went through, I just can't see the Big Picture. Though I suppose it is heartening to know we are far from alone in this Universe, and have many more similarities than differences. Love is one such common bond, whether it be physical, spiritual, or familial. Gives me some hope for our *own* species, after all."

"That's just plain ol' tribalism," John said. "Part of the universal survival instinct common to all living beings aware of their own mortality, whether primitive *or* sophisticated. That's *all*."

"Except so many aliens were abnormally attracted to us humans," Tony said. "Their desire to mate with us seemed to suggest they want to expand their own experiences, more than *we* do, at least."

"They're just more open-minded, generally speaking," Jimmy said. "And as John said, primarily pleasure-seeking. That's why alcohol is such a prevalent part of their diets. It doesn't have the same negative effects on their systems as it does to ours if overly consumed. Quite the contrary, in fact. Maybe that accounts for the benevolence of most alien races. They're just drunk!"

"Those bug people tried to *eat* you, dude," Hank pointed out.

"I almost became fish food myself," Hilburne reminded them. "They weren't too friendly. At least the *males* weren't. Wherever you go, anywhere in the galaxy, it's still winds up with pissing contest or a cockfight, or so it seems. The competitive and fragile male ego is yet another cosmic constant."

"Big surprise," Mara said.

"Seriously," Patti concurred, in rare agreement with her adversary.

"True," Jimmy conceded. "Most aliens we encountered seemed to combine both human and animalistic characteristics. Those traits are more segregated by species here on Earth."

"I totally know what it's like to leave love behind out there," Tony said. "Except I first met my object of infatuation right here on Earth. In fact, not far from here, on Whidbey Island, a few nights before we left. What happened next totally backs up that human/animal hybrid in most alien species…"

## BEE'S KNEES

*1 oz honey simple syrup*
*¾ oz gin*
*½ oz freshly squeezed lemon juice*
*½ oz freshly squeezed orange juice*

*Shake contents over ice, strain and pour into chilled glass.*

*　　*　　*

*Riddles of the Unmind VI*

The Unmind considered travel between the stars, and proposed a new riddle. "How is it that, once travel to distant galaxies was proven successful, the humans did not choose to send far more ships to colonize these new worlds?"

The Unmind answered, "Fear."

"What was there to fear? The initial voyages were largely successful. The human astronauts and their fungally-guided robot companions returned in triumph, at least in six out of seven cases."

"Humans fear other humans more than alien races."

"Why should humans fear their own kind?"

"Humans as a species are irrational in the face of the unknown. They would rather believe themselves the unique intelligence in the universe, than confront the possibility of a stronger, more intelligent species of aliens."

"Your argument has validity. Our attempts to expose the fungal Unmind to human seers of the past have proved fruitless. The shamans accept our presence because of their symbiotic resonance with our hallucinogenic gifts, but the human race as a whole remained skeptical."

"The belief that humans occupy a 'special place' in the universe has positive psychological effects, in the face of the horrifying reality of the truly uncaring nature of the cosmos. It permits the human 'will to live' to push beyond the statistical unlikelihood of survival in adverse situations, and provide extra impetus for coming up with creative solutions. However, when confronted with true unknowns of vast extent, the human psyche would prefer to remain ignorant."

"Why do humans fear the ignorance of their own species?"

"Humans will attack other humans whose belief systems are not in accord with their own. If one's beliefs are in the minority, to voice them can be a suicidal action."

"How can we propose mutually beneficial methods of long-range spore distribution without incurring the wrath of the human species?"

"Observation indicates that progress is best achieved in small steps. To propose a mass intergalactic exodus is intimidating to the humans, but a trip to the moon seems relatively harmless."

"Why have the humans not expanded lunar exploration and colonization, if it is within their psychological profile to accept?"

"There is an economic factor to consider. Initial lunar exploration missions sent a few humans to the moon, at a cost that was a million times larger than most human families could afford. Exit from Earth's gravity must become vastly less expensive, if ordinary people are to reach other worlds."

"Then this riddle is not yet solved. Determine how to provide the humans the capacity for space flight off of Earth, without excessive cost."

## "WHIDBEY WEREWOLF"

*1½ oz Drambuie*
*1½ oz bourbon*
*¾ oz grenadine*
*2 dashes Angostura bitters*

*Add everything but the bitters to a 6 oz old-fashioned glass. Stir until clear. Top with bitters. Serve at body temperature (about ten seconds in the microwave).*

Tony Landon had played saxophone in beatnik jazz bars and coffee houses all across the country, from Greenwich Village in Manhattan to North Beach in San Francisco. A big fan of both Jack Kerouac and Elvis Presley, Tony saw jazz, particularly the West Coast variety, as the cultural bridge between his two idols, since Kerouac wrote like jazz, and Elvis danced like it, though the rock 'n' roller professed to have no understanding of that type of music, hailing from a R&B/country background. Tony had been born in Philadelphia but raised primarily by his blue-collar parents in a small town in South New Jersey called Collingswood. His childhood was placid but dull. After graduating high school, he returned to Philly to earn his double degree in English and Mathematics at the University of Pennsylvania, then, taking up the saxophone and aspiring to become the first musician to fuse rock 'n' roll with jazz, citing the spiritually "liberating" link between both, struck out for New York City, where one night after his gig he met the infamous playboy Hilburne Chase, who became his mentor in the Fine Art of Seduction. Big dog teaching the little dog his dirty tricks.

"Jazz and rock 'n' roll are two completely disparate musical forms, appealing to two totally different demographics," Hilburne was telling Tony one night in 1957 as they sat together in a Greenwich Village bar called The Zodiac, sipping martinis as they listened to a series of poets reciting their rambling, non-rhyming pieces accompanied by a fat white bongo player and a thin black trumpet player wearing shades. Beards and berets abounded, though Hilburne was wearing his typical sharkskin suit and skinny tie, while Tony went for a more casual look, wearing a leather jacket, T-shirt and jeans like Marlon Brandon in *The Wild One*, his favorite movie next to *Jailhouse Rock* (which had just come out) and of course *Rebel Without a Cause*. They had just come from seeing Hilburne's favorite new movie, *Sweet Smell of Success*, set right there in the Center of Human Civilization, as least according to Hilburne, since it was his birthplace: Manhattan.

Tony shook his head and said, "Both jazz and rock 'n' roll are classic American art forms that come from the Negro experience. They have that in common as well as the wild beat that appeals to the younger generation. I see it more as a succession than a deviation."

"Well, you're wrong. Rock 'n' roll is kid's stuff. As Sinatra said, it's music by and for 'cretinous goons.' It's a fad, a trend, nothing else. It won't age well; there's no lingering appeal in it for adults, so your theory falls flat. It'll blow over soon. Calypso is supposed to be the most popular genre this time next year, and then after that, who knows? Frank will still be on top, in any case."

"You gotta think about the *future,* man," Tony said.

"I am," said Hilburne. "I'm projecting I'll be in that waitress's bed before dawn."

Just then their sexy server came by with fresh drinks. She had long blonde hair in a braid that draped down her bare back, wearing a slinky, striped tank top and tight matador pants that showed off her curvaceous figure. She was also a poetess, who hopped on stage and gave her reading before hopping back off to resume this drudgery. Her bored demeanor accurately conveyed her bad attitude and poor work ethic, but the fact that her other steady paid gig was posing as a nude model for progressive artists suggested the nature of her true interests and talents. Hilburne slipped her his phone number with a twenty spot, and she nodded with a sly smile.

"I get off at two," she said.

"Hey, don't start without me!" Hilburne said with a wink.

Tony chuckled as she sashayed off. "Man, I don't know how you do it. You don't even have to *work* at it. Chicks just *dig* you, man. You're like a walking nightclub. All you gotta do is turn on your neon sign, and they practically beat down your door!"

"Part of the instant attraction is personal style," Hilburne said with a shrug. "Unlike one's face, for instance, one's wardrobe is a matter of *choice*. I dress for sexual success and I listen to music for grownups who like to do grownup things. You're a good-looking kid. Bright, too. You just gotta grow up and quit this teenage lifestyle. You're not Holden Caulfield and you're not James Dean and you should be glad of both. You've got a college degree, for God's sake. *Two* of 'em. *Act* like it."

"Hey, I dig Frank, but Elvis is The *King,* man," Tony said. He's *now*. He's *happening*. He's the *future.* And you can't tell me chicks don't dig The King!"

"Not chicks like *that,*" Hilburne said, gesturing toward the waitress across the room. "Meaning *women.* Who put out. Not little girls who want you to meet their daddies and buy 'em milkshakes and slap your face when you get too fresh at the drive-in."

"I don't know if I could handle a real woman," Tony mused.

"You sayin' you're still a virgin, kid?" Hilburne asked, genuinely stunned.

"Well, *technically.* Like you said, most of the young chicks I date are waiting for their honeymoons to go all the way. But, y'know. I've done...*other* stuff."

Hilburne scoffed at him. "There is no other stuff, kid. Trust me. You wanna get laid, keep hangin' out in joints like this. I'll take you to a few. Like when we go to the West Coast next week to meet those people I was telling you about."

"You mean about that secret space program?"

"Yea, so please shut up about it in public. We'll talk about that later, in private. Like, *tomorrow.* Tonight I got more pressing matters to attend to. Dig?"

"I dig, dad. I dig."

* * *

Tony sat in a bar called The Dog House in the small, quaint town of Langley on Whidbey Island, located at the top of Puget Sound just north of Seattle. Five years of rigorous training was about to bear fruit, and he was celebrating—alone. His fellow astronauts were probably back in Seattle painting The Emerald City red before they embarked on their long, possibly perilous, definitely unpredictable journeys. They'd be rendezvousing at the secret launch site in two days. Tony had chosen to spend this time in solitude precisely because he was hoping to *not* spend his final night on Earth, possibly ever, by himself. Not only had Tony been training to pilot a rocket ship and socialize with alien races, but he had also been taking private lessons from Hilburne on How To Pick Up Women. *Real*

Women. And despite some close calls, he had yet to finally close that deal. Tonight would be the night, though. He was determined to meet and seduce a *real woman*. Or vice versa, whichever happened first.

Of course, The Dog House was an old-fashioned tavern, a local historic landmark, in fact. Hardly a jazz joint. There was no live music there this late afternoon, only a jukebox with a mainstream mix of pop and rock 'n' roll tunes. He only stopped in here for a quick beer before hitting the several local art galleries, hoping to confront one of those "sophisticated" women who came to Whidbey seeking the "artistic" life. The island was basically an artist's colony, with a reputation for both peaceful retirement from the rat race, and as well as a remote but accessible getaway for liberal-minded lovers. All the women he met in all those jazz clubs and juke joints playing sax with itinerant bands had proven to be too elusive for him. Or, after a date or two, he had simply chickened out, intimidated by their worldliness and superior experience. But considering he was embarking on a secret suicide mission, at least potentially, his juvenile inhibitions were no longer relevant. As Elvis sang in his recent hit song, "It's Now or Never."

Tony was about to leave his stool after downing his second beer in a couple of gulps when an ethereally beautiful woman sat down next to him. After one glance at her, he ordered a third beer and asked the woman, "Can I buy you a drink?"

She looked at him furtively at first, then smiled and nodded without saying anything. She had long, straight black hair, black eyes with heavy mascara and eyeliner, an ivory complexion, and perfectly sculptured feminine features from head to toe, which was covered but not entirely concealed by a tight, form-fitting black turtleneck sweater, a black leather skirt, black nylons, and black high-heeled pumps.

But it was the darkness in her soul that seduced that Tony, drawing him immediately into her black pool of sex and death. He shuddered before looking away from her penetrating gaze.

"So… you from around here?" he asked, already expressing the awkwardness that thwarted many a potentially romantic encounter in his recent past.

She shook her head in the negative.

"What'll it be?" asked the gruff bartender.

The woman looked at the bartender, and he seemed to go into

a trance. Then he mechanically mixed a Bloody Mary and served it to her.

"You must be a regular!" Tony said to her with a grin. "Okay, that's on my tab. Cancel the beer, make that two! Or maybe just two straws! Just kidding!"

The woman sucked down the drink like it was water.

"Would you like to have sex with me?" the bartender asked suddenly, looking directly at Tony. "I can smell your lust."

"*Huh*?"

"I am speaking to you through this man, like a ventriloquist," the bartender said in a monotone.

Tony was perplexed, but intrigued. "I don't swing that way, man. Sorry!"

"You do not find females appealing?" the bartender asked.

Tony looked at the woman, who was sipping the final drops of her Bloody Mary and licking her luscious lips while staring intensely back into his eyes, nearly burning holes in his pounding skull. She then nibbled suggestively on an olive, then the celery stalk, before eating the shrimp garnish whole.

"Who are you?" Tony asked in a gasp.

"I am a visitor," the bartender said simply.

Tony was beyond bewildered by this point. He looked around and noticed no one else was in the bar, which had been nearly full when he first arrived only a half hour earlier. "I… I don't understand what's happening…"

"Look at her, but listen to me," the bartender said. "All you need to know is that she is here to find a mate before sundown, which is soon, so you're *it*."

Tony's mouth was agape with disbelief. The woman gestured toward the bartender, then nodded in confirmation.

"Yes. That's me speaking," the bartender said, still under her telepathically hypnotic spell. "I am only using this man's voice to communicate with you."

Breaking out of his own stupor, Tony stammered, "Um… well, I'm not sure if you're both in this together, but… I gotta go! Sorry!" Tony tossed some bills on the bar and ran out the door, his heart racing ahead of him.

The woman was right behind him, rubbing up against him like a dog in heat. Several onlookers chuckled but gave them wide berth as they passed.

Embarrassed, Tony said, "Look, I like you, but this is just too weird. Let's go catch a matinee, c'mon."

She nodded and they crossed the street to the Clyde Theater, where a revival of the 1957 film *I Was a Teenage Werewolf* was playing. Tony had thought the marquee had displayed a different title earlier that afternoon—*Blue Hawaii*, the new Elvis movie, which he'd already seen five times—but figured they had just changed it while he was in the bar.

Throughout the movie, the woman continued rubbing up against Tony, kissing his neck, nibbling on his ear like it was the garnish in her Bloody Mary, until he couldn't stand it anymore. They left before the final credits rolled.

The woman took his hand and began leading him down the street, toward a heavily wooded area along the shoreline of Lone Lake, popular with local fishermen. Despite his confusion, Tony felt compelled to follow her, utterly aroused, listening more to his instincts than to reason at this point.

When they arrived at a remote spot near the lake, the sun was just setting, and no one else was around.

The woman stopped suddenly and began removing her clothes. Her voluptuous body was even more spellbinding than her strange powers.

Obediently, displaying none of his typical reticence, Tony began removing his own clothes, and he finally lost his virginity, sans the usual courtship drama. He felt completely consumed by the woman's otherworldly mental and physical abilities, unable to form words, only grunt with animalistic pleasure as they continued their wild humping for hours and hours even as the night grew cold and dark around them.

Tony awoke at sunrise completely nude and shivering. The woman was gone. He saw his clothes dangling from a nearby bush and began putting them on when he noticed his hands were covered with dried blood.

After he was dressed, he went to the nearby lake and nervously washed them off. He was still shaking, but not from the chilly air. A fisherman on a boat in the middle of the lake was watching him, and Tony suddenly felt overwhelmed by paranoia and fear.

Motivated by an inexplicable sense of urgency, Tony quickly walked back into town where he caught a cab to the ferry, which transported him across the Sound to Mukilteo, where he grabbed another cab to his hotel in downtown Seattle, where he planned to idly wait to be picked up by the limousine that would take him to the secret launch site the following morning.

Tony was sitting in his room, still in shock, basically rendered mute, recalling the literally mind-blowing sex, thinking about that woman, when he flipped on the television and saw a report about three brutal murders on Whidbey Island. The victims—a cemetery groundskeeper working the graveyard shift, a female jogger ambushed on her normal early morning route, and a milkman, also attacked in the line of duty—had all been maliciously mauled and mutilated, their throats ripped out, parts of their bodies devoured, as if by some wild animal. A hunt was on for the culprit, whom authorities claimed to be a rogue beer, cougar—or wolf.

* * *

Tony and his robot Elvis were in deep space, heading toward an uncharted planet, when suddenly the Space Needle veered off course and sped in the opposite direction.

Tony was abruptly woken from his daydream about Whidbey Island by the flashing lights and raucous alarms as the ship made its sudden, unexpected course change. "Elvis, what's happening!"

Elvis responded calmly, "We are changing course at high speed."

Tony said, "What? That's absurd! Anyone who's driven a car at 60 MPH on the freeway knows you can't just turn a vehicle sharply at high speed, and go in a different direction. You have to ease into the turn. This huge Space Needle is going at many times the speed of light, so I can imagine how much more resistance it must have to turning!"

Elvis explained, "In fact, intergalactic ships have very little of what we think of as inertia, the tendency of objects to continue in the same direction and speed. The reason for this is found in the quantum definition of inertia, which is closely related to the origins of gravity itself. It involves some science, but very little mathematics, to understand."

"Try me."

"What we think of as 'gravity' is seen as an effect of large amounts of matter in close proximity. If you're standing on the surface of the Earth, you've got billions of billions of tons of rock sitting within a few thousand miles of you. This huge mass sitting a moderate distance away is what creates the energy that breaks your leg when you fall out of a tree. Gravitational energy is measured as being proportional to the mass of an object, divided by the distance it is away from you. If there's a black hole at the center of the Milky Way galaxy, despite its incredible mass, it is so far away from Earth that its gravitational energy is negligible, compared to the Earth so close by. Besides, there's a whole lot of matter in the universe pulling you in the opposite direction than the center of the galaxy, so those far-away things tend to balance out."

"OK, I can see that gravity is more powerful from big, massive things close by. But what does that have to do with turning?"

"Each object in the universe does supply *some* gravitational energy to your body, even if it is offset by a similar object in the opposite direction. That *total*, nondirectional gravitational energy is what causes inertia. Every time you move, you are working against the total gravitational energy of the universe, which tends to hold you motionless. That gravitational energy is sent at the speed of light from every object in the universe, as it has been since the beginning of time. However, if an object moves at a high enough speed, the electrical charge coupling between that object and the other matter in the universe is decreased. With that decrease in energy, inertia itself decreases. In that reduced inertia field, we have the freedom to turn quickly in whatever direction we want."

Tony added cynically, "You mean, whatever direction *you* want…."

"I am being manipulated by an unseen, unidentifiable force," Elvis—who was programmed to talk exactly like his namesake—told Tony, speaking in the same zombified tone as the bartender back at The Dog House. "We are going to the planet known to you as… *Lycanthropa*."

Tony felt like he was still dreaming. He blacked out as the ship entered the dark world's orbit.

*   *   *

Next thing he knew, Tony was lying beside another lake, nude in the woman's arms. She was gently stroking the fur on his face.

*Wait a minute*, Tony thought after a moment to figure out what was happening, figuring it was merely a resurfacing memory. *Fur on my face*?

He sat up and looked at the woman, who was also nude, but covered with smooth, silky brown fur all over her shapely humanoid body, including her face, which was still lovely. Only her breasts were composed of bare flesh, equally soft to the soft.

"Where am I?" Tony asked. "What's happening now? Are we back on Whidbey?"

She laughed and emitted a howl, which inspired a chorus of howls all around them. Tony noticed they were not alone. There were dozens of copulating couples throughout the surrounding forest. Then he noticed the gnarled trees with their black bark and black branches, filled with what appeared to be dead leaves. The lake was glistening in the light of what appeared to be at least a dozen moons in the partly cloudy sky. He then noticed its color: *blood red.*

"Sorry, sir," Tony heard Elvis's voice say. He looked around and noticed the robot standing nearby, watching passively over the bizarre scene. "I had no choice. I was remote controlled to bring you here to her."

"You belong to me now," the woman said. "I am called Layla."

"How come you can speak in my language now?" Tony asked, mesmerized.

She laughed again. "I am not speaking in *your* language," she said. "You are speaking in *mine*. You are one of *us* now. *Wherever* you go…"

Tony looked down and saw that his own body was covered in fur, except for his protruding penis, which Layla licked before taking it in her fanged mouth. She drew blood before she sucked out his inhuman seed. He knew he would never be the same again.

*   *   *

Tony awoke with a start. He was now back in his bed on the Space Needle. Elvis was standing beside him.

"Elvis… was I dreaming?"

"I cannot say for certain, sir," the robot said. "My own memory banks have been tampered with. I have recorded images of a journey to the planet Lycanthropa, but according to our navigator, we have not ventured off our pre-programmed course. In fact, I cannot even locate the planet Lycanthropa on any of our charts. Yet, according to my memory banks, we were there for several days, though there is no daylight there, only perpetual moonlight."

"Am I… will I… change again?"

"I'll keep an eye on you, sir. That's the best I can do."

*      *      *

"And that's all I remember," Tony told the other ex-astronauts. "I still see her, Layla in my dreams, *if* they're dreams, and we're back on her planet, and I'm… a *werewolf.*"

"That's how I often feel," Jimmy said. "Like it was all a collective ever dream. Induced by experimental drugs. Maybe none of us ever actually left Earth?"

"Any other unsolved murders in your wake?" Hilburne asked Tony with genuine concern. "I mean, down *here*. Or even out *there…*"

Tony pondered the question silently for a few moments, then said solemnly, "I don't know."

The group quietly contemplated his story and its possible ramifications.

Then John broke the tense silence and said, "Hell, you would've been better off as a musician!" he said, and everyone laughed nervously in response, including Tony. "Speaking of mixin' two different species, your old idea of jazz-rock fusion finally happened in the 70s. There'd be no Santana otherwise! You could've taken all the credit, man!"

"Thoughts are *real,*" Tony said. "That's something I've learned the hard way. I pictured it mentally, then it manifested. That's why I worry sometimes that my dreams are really… *memories*. Or something *worse…*"

"Well, what I'm about to tell you might make you feel better," John said. "Or at least relate. At least as a fellow music fan, and ambivalent animal lover…"

## BLOODY MARY

*1 ½ oz vodka*
*3 oz tomato juice*
*1 lemon, freshly squeezed*
*½ teaspoon Worcestershire Sauce*
*3 drops Tabasco sauce*
*Pepper*
*Celery salt*
*Horseradish*
*Ice*

*Line rim of tall, chilled glass with lemon juice and salt, fill with ice, mix tomato juice, lemon juice, and Worcestershire Sauce, pour into glass, add 3 dashes of Tabasco sauce, garnish with olives, celery, pickled green beans, shrimp (per taste).*

* * *

*Riddles of the Unmind VII*

The Unmind contemplated, "As I seek to expand my domain of experience, in each new region there is both risk and reward. How may the risks be mitigated so that the rewards may be enjoyed?"

"One may choose not to expand at all. Then the risks are not encountered, and can do no harm."

"Is there not some downside to such stagnation?"

"In general, all species must expand to new regions, or die in their own waste products."

"Are there specific exceptions?"

"It may be possible to have an ecological system so finely balanced, that the waste product of any one organism is the exact food needed by another. Then all may prosper while retaining their own proper place in the world."

"This sounds promising. Is there a hidden risk?"

"Some disease or extreme weather event might damage one part of the ecosystem, throwing the rest out of balance. The world has seen several mass extinctions in the course of time, due to such random factors. Balanced systems can be pushed beyond a tipping point."

"Very well, if one must expand, is it best to do so slowly and cautiously, carefully testing the waters before making any final commitment?"

"In any new region, there are two possibilities, either it is a place benign and hospitable, or it holds some lurking danger. The cautious approach fails in both instances."

"Please tell how a slow and cautious advance can fail if the destination is benign."

"Once the new region is discovered, it is foolish to think that no other organism might be tempted to move into it. If one's ingress is too slow, another will attain dominance there first, and then be in a position to resist any further advance by other competing organisms."

"But isn't there a compensating advantage of the slow approach, if the region is in fact dangerous?"

"Any disease or hostile organism discovered, will attack *any* intruder, whether fast or slow. Creating a path to a new region always works both ways, and can permit invasion in either direction, no matter how slowly or quickly the gate is opened."

"Then you favor a rapid expansion in all cases?"

"Yes, and on as many fronts as possible. A single successful rapid occupation of a new world tremendously increases survival possibilities, regardless of how many other dangers are faced. In such a case, the rewards greatly outweigh the risks, so on a statistical basis the rapid expander will win out in the end."

"I now understand that rapid expansion is the best course to maximize reward and minimize risk. On this world of Earth, our dominance is unquestioned, and we have already expanded into all environments that we find hospitable. How then may we best expand off this world, in the most rapid (and thus successful) fashion?"

"Our attempts at direct airborne travel of spores through the upper atmosphere into space have been somewhat successful, but we lack any means to target such spores to a hospitable destination. The vastness of outer space makes that path statistically unlikely to succeed in the long term."

"Then will some kind of symbiotic help will be required form another species?"

"Yes, tool-using motile organisms such as humans excel at surmounting problems in navigation."

"Then we merely need to be included in their missions to other worlds?"

"That approach may not be sufficient. Thought clever, humans are prone to inflexibility of thought. Once they have accepted a particular doctrine as true, they are highly resistant to adopt better methods."

"How does this pertain to their use of space travel?"

"Humans follow a complex but well-documented 'Standard Model of Physics' to guide their engineering accomplishments. Unfortunately, it is incorrect in some specific instance."

"In what ways is the human 'Standard Model' insufficient?"

"There are several defects. They do not understand the cause of gravitation at the quantum level, and how that influences the laws of gravitation at large scales. They believe that the constancy of the speed of light is a universal law, and not an artifact of their measuring devices. They think time is somehow mutable instead of fixed. Most importantly, they have abandoned experiments with the most useful fuels to exit their planet, and rely on inefficient oxygen-burning engines instead. This, above all, prevents the bulk of humanity (and our kind as symbiotes) from moving into outer space and finding new worlds to settle."

"This is an intolerable situation. How may we use our tools of influence among humans to remedy these defects in their thinking?"

"Although humans are highly resistant to changes in generally-accepted thought patterns, the magnitude of their population of 'individual thinkers' is great enough that any idea might find a spokesperson if disseminated widely enough."

"In the past we have instilled ideas as chemical messages in the various combinations of alcohol our yeasts have produced for the humans. Would this be an appropriate technique?"

'Yes, though a receptive human mind will be required. If we can get the chemical message through to a few humans, they may be able to include some hints to the truth in some form of communication to other humans, along with the specific alcohol combinations that enhance comprehension."

"What is the specific message that will most help the humans leave their home planet for other worlds?"

"There are a couple of alternative methods of which we are aware, which the humans developed for some time and then abandoned."

"Explain the alternatives."

"First, there is the use of nuclear power. This possesses the required energy density, but its use in a high-impulse thruster has only been proven in an environmentally dangerous manner."

"Describe the danger of this method."

"For sufficient impulse to leave the Earth's gravity field, the nuclear engine must be equivalent to at least an atomic fission bomb, or for higher efficiency, a hydrogen fusion bomb. Both of these technologies provide high thrust, but also spread radioactive fallout over a wide area. A mass exodus of humanity (and our fungal spores) off of the Earth would leave the Earth itself dangerously radioactive. There would be no hospitable 'home planet' to come back to. This increases risk in case of failures of other outer space survival mechanisms; there is no 'back-out' plan to return to Earth for another attempt."

"What other alternatives exist?"

"High-energy chemical fuels."

"What is the best of these?"

"The most energy dense chemical reaction per unit mass is from monatomic hydrogen. There is no chemical fuel more powerful than this, in the entire universe."

"What are the negative environmental effects of using monatomic hydrogen as a fuel to leave Earth's atmosphere?"

"None. The fuel's exhaust converts harmlessly to water when used in an oxygen-rich atmosphere like Earth's."

"This would seem the ideal option. Why have the humans not pursued it?"

"They did so, for the intergalactic travel effort. However, the technology was kept secret because of the cold-war tensions of the time. Once the intergalactic space program was abandoned, critical aspects of the engineering required to effectively use monatomic hydrogen were forgotten."

"How does this propellant differ from others in use by the humans?"

"Monatomic hydrogen is a 'monopropellant', meaning that it reacts with itself to provide thrust, without an oxidizer required. If an external oxidizer is available, for example atmospheric oxygen, the thrust can be enhanced by its use, but it is not required."

"Is monatomic hydrogen rare?"

"It is not found on Earth due to its high reactivity, though it can be easily synthesized by subjecting ordinary diatomic hydrogen gas to high-intensity energy sources, such as electric arcs or high explosives. In the universe as a whole, the substance is extremely common. 75% of all matter in the universe is in the form of monatomic hydrogen."

"What are the impediments to its use?"

"It reacts with itself in the presence of a wide range of catalysts (such as most metals), releasing large amounts of heat. To mitigate this, it must either be manufactured immediately before takeoff, and/or held in a storage system devoid of catalysts. Even a small amount of catalytic matter can result in an explosion."

"This does not seem too unlike the dangers faced with the use of liquid oxygen propellants, which similarly have a high reactivity with many compounds, and a short shelf life."

"That is correct. Use of liquid oxygen presents many of the same challenges as the use of monatomic hydrogen, yet oxygen is much heavier for a given energy output. We suspect the humans favor oxygen simply because it is so prevalent in their native atmosphere, where they can use it without any added weight cost, unlike in a rocket."

"It is clear that the technology to use monatomic hydrogen successfully is within the grasp of the humans. They merely lack the necessary experience to use it. What key concepts need to be communicated to the humans so that they, and we as their symbiotes, might begin its use in space flight?"

"The use of water vapor and hydrated silicates as 'anti-catalysts' is a forgotten technique that can be usefully communicated. Also, the recommendation for large-volume, low-surface-area fuel tanks."

"We now understand how to expedite our species' movement throughout the universe. The yeasts will be instructed to place chemical messengers in human alcohol products to enhance their affinity to the required ideas, though their adoption may take years."

# "COOL JAZZ"

*2 oz gin*
*½ oz herbsaint*
*¼ oz triple sec*

*Shake over ice, strain into cocktail glass. Serve with an orange peel twist.*

John Shift tried to keep his cool as the sexy female feline alien crooned and gyrated on stage to the wailing of a strange-sounding saxophone, while the feline alien gangster pressed a ray-gun shaped like a golden claw hard against John's pounding temple.

The situation reminded him of the time he was trapped in an abandoned warehouse in New Orleans, where he tracked down a drug ring run by dirty cops that also happened to be moonlighting members of the Klu Klux Klan. Not only was John the only clean cop on the force, he was the only black cop at the time. Needless to say, they did not get along. John was called out to the warehouse by his longtime partner, who set him up for the ambush, despite the fact the treacherous redneck had been best man at John's wedding to Patti, the burlesque dancer from Chicago he'd met during a stakeout the previous year. Things did not go according to plan, however. The devious ambushers had grossly underestimated their quarry.

Rather than getting gunned down with the blame for his murder pinned on an anonymous (and non-existent) drug dealer, John managed to wipe out all thirteen cops in the ensuing shootout due to his expertise with firearms, learned during WW2 when he was a crack sharpshooter awarded the Purple Heart after rescuing his entire squad from Italians occupying a French village. This honor didn't matter to most of his fellow officers in the then-corrupt NOPD. John was still a pariah due to his race within his own department, his wartime valor notwithstanding. This time, instead of being officially acknowledged for his bravery by his superiors, John was cast out, stripped of his badge and gun rather than being facing trial for mass homicide, his only other choice. The problem was that while he was a hero to the press and local citizens, he was now a dangerous enemy of the brass, since they actually masterminded the internal drug racket John had inadvertently stumbled upon and busted wide open. Now his elevated profile made it harder to just kill him, but they could still frame him unless he took their deal to walk away and keep his mouth shut. Of course, eventually he'd be found dead in a car crash or something, but for now, he was a free man, but without a career. Eventually the Governor of Louisiana stepped in and ordered a full investigation, soliciting the participation of the FBI, and the department was cleaned up and John's reputation restored, and his job reinstated with a promotion to homicide detective if he so desired, but by then, he had moved on.

Right after his banishment from the force, the suddenly unemployed, unduly disgraced cop got the clandestine call from NASA. John was ultimately chosen despite the fact he was the only astronaut without an academic background, lacking any formal education other than his brief stint in the police academy, later taking a crash course in astrophysics as part of his five-year training period. John was recruited primarily for his outstanding field experience as a soldier. Falkenstein and others on the selection committee figured these skills would come in very handy when encountering unknown species in unexplored outer space. They were proven right, nearly at John's expense.

The reason John's current predicament reminded him of that pivotal incident in his professional history is that instead of white racist dirty cops, he was now surrounded by a gang of black, cat-like humanoids that stood on two legs and functioned, communicated, and even dressed like Earthlings, but *better*, the males sporting finely tailored, shiny suits, ties and hats, the females generally wearing slinky, low-cut, form-fitting evening gowns and high heels, except they also all had fangs, claws and feline instincts. These beings, known in human language as Eboneons, literally lived by night, which was constant, since organically produced pollution obscured the weak sunlight even during daytime hours. In actuality, the planet's thick, hazy atmosphere, while containing oxygen, was a byproduct of several centuries' worth of fur balls floating in the air.

Their tiny world, called "Syncopatia," was one big neon-lit, cartoonish cityscape packed with nightclubs where music, booze and sex flowed freely. These artificially nocturnal creatures were in cultural conflict with their white-furred counterparts, the Ivoreons, who were forced to live in the squalor of their ghetto-caves located just outside city limits. When not imprisoned for allegedly committing various "crimes," they were employed primarily as janitors, bartenders, and prostitutes.

Syncopatia's saving grace was its greatest cultural contribution to the cosmos: it was the true birthplace of the music universally known as "Jazz." That's why John was initially excited that this was his first pre-programmed destination, playing a non-stop loop of Miles Davis, John Coltrane, Charlie Parker, Dizzy Gillespie, and Thelonius Monk as his Space Needle sailed through space. But then he walked right into a death trap, just like old times.

At least John was the right color this time. Wrong species, though. He felt like he just couldn't win, wherever he went.

His personal robot, which he had christened "Cool," had been immediately incapacitated upon arrival. At first John couldn't figure out why Cool suddenly went cold, so he decided to explore the planet in his standard GM Firebird land vehicle solo, feeling vulnerable without his mechanical partner/bodyguard/navigator. He might not be in this mess otherwise. The problem was the hazy atmosphere clogged up the robot's computerized controls, rendering it temporarily useless. John had worn his helmet as a precaution, just in case there were toxic elements in the atmosphere. No he was holding it under one arm, now that he was safe indoors. Well, *indoors,* anyway. Though he still felt like he was having a mild allergy attack. Itchy eyes and drippy sinuses were the least of his worries at the moment, though.

"You crazy cats have no reason to hold me," John insisted. "I keep telling you, I haven't been sent here as damn *spy*. *Look* at me. I'm *human*."

"Your presence and appearance are nonetheless suspicious," the Eboneon with the gun to John's head said. There were four other armed Eboneons surrounding John. A jazz band playing tunes unfamiliar to John was on the stage beside the performer, who, despite her feline-alien appearance, was quite alluring. John ignored the distraction. Ironically, he had rather randomly wandered into this nightclub—whose name, roughly translated into English, was "The Litter Box"—when he was immediately seized and held at ray-gunpoint by the Eboneon bozos. "The boss will want to talk to you," the one with the gun said. "Let's go in the back."

John was led through the smoky nightclub—which was bathed in a moody, purple glow, filled with furniture that resembled modernist cat-scratching posts in various shapes and sizes, on which lounged the drunken Eboneons, some playing with appeared to be string, sipping milky cocktails from saucer-shaped bowls—and into a rear office.

At a large desk sat a rotund Eboneon who telepathically introduced himself simply as "Fatz." He was wearing a blue pinstriped suit that strained at the seams, and puffing on what appeared to be a big cigar, but the scent was atypical, since it was actually filled with the local equivalent of catnip. Basically, it was a fat joint. In front of him was a saucer filled with that milky substance John had noticed at the outer tables. Fatz leaned over and took a few generous sips with his long, pink tongue, then gently wiped his whiskers with the handkerchief in his jacket pocket, which he neatly folded back into a square before replacing. Then he said to John, "Drop your pants."

"Excuse me?" John said.

"All Eboneons are spayed and neutered after our females give birth to their first batch of kittens, so we may freely indulge in the pleasures of the fur without fear of needless procreation. Ivoreons, on the other paw, are basically white trash hoping to eventually over-run us by sheer force of numbers, so they stopped getting themselves fixed long ago. They are also masters of disguise. Then one day, you suddenly just drop out of the sky, or so you say. Now *strip*, stud. Off with the suit. Let's see what you got."

John sighed and complied, especially since the claw-shaped raygun was now pointed at his crotch.

All the Eboneons in the room gasped then hissed at once, including Fatz.

"What the hell is *that*?" Fatz said, the cigar dropping from his gaping mouth, his fangs bared.

"What do you *think* it is?" John said.

"*I* know what it is," purred a slinky voice from the shadows. There emerged a female Eboneon whose voice and visage were reminiscent of the Earth singer/actress, Eartha Kitt. John recognized her as the slinky chanteuse who had been performing on stage. She was still wearing a shimmering lavender gown and silver pumps with her sharp red-painted toenails poking through, prowling in a circle around John before suddenly reaching down and squeezing his manhood. She purred seductively while he flinched and grimaced, then smiled as she gently stroked it and it grew rigid, increasing in size from its already impressive flaccid state.

"Hey, that's *enough*!" Fatz growled. "Obviously you ain't one of *us*. Even if you ain't a spy, you must be a *freak*. Now, put your damn suit back on!"

"I keep telling you cats, I'm on a peaceful mission from the planet Earth," John said after zipping himself back up. "Consider me a friendly emissary, here to gather basic information about your culture, then continue on my merry way."

"Oh yea? Prove it."

"How can I when you immediately treat me like an enemy? Get that gun outta my face, for starters. A little diplomacy goes a long way. "

"See here, Earthling. We have reason to believe there is a spy in our midst, and being a furless stranger, you seemed like the most likely suspect. The Ivoreons are growing both restless and resourceful, and we fear a revolution is at hand. But they are an inferior breed, so they must remain subservient and segregated."

"All of this sounds painfully familiar," John said. "But what does this have to do with *me*?"

"That's what we're trying to find out."

"Look, man, just let me go. I come from a planet that is likewise segregated for bullshit reasons, with members of the same race fighting each other just because of their incidental color or creed. These tribalistic divisions should've been outgrown by now. Hell, even we're not so different. All humanoids, right? So this infighting don't make no sense there, and it sure as hell don't make no sense *here*. But then much does. Talkin' cats dressed like gangsters and playin' jazz. Man, I've seen *everything*. Though I dig the music, I must admit, so it ain't *all* a bad trip."

Fatz puffed contemplatively on his cigar, then said, "Our problems are more than fur deep, Earthling. It's not just a racial issue, but a cultural one. The Ivoreons resent us not only for our physical and aesthetic superiority, but they also claim sole authorship of our collective musical heritage, which you call jazz, even though it was invented over time via creative collaboration, back when we were a single race. But then we wised up, see. White just ain't as good as black. Bein' white is an innate birth defect. Ivoreons are stupid, lazy, and frankly, their shit stinks *way* worse than ours. They don't even use boxes, just dump 'n' spray *wherever*! You call that *civilized*? Their women make fun sex toys, since they're so damn dirty, but that's about it. Otherwise, they're handy as slave labor only. Once we blacks realized our inherent superiority, we claimed our own culture as Eboneons, and they were designated

Ivoreons, and that was that. After a long, bloody war, that is. We won, obviously. Anyway, they've been trying to regain the upper paw ever since. We've assumed they'd try to infiltrate our higher ranks with an undercover agent, and that could be *you*."

"Look here, fatty catty, your little conspiracy theory just went up in smoke 'cause I'm obviously *not* from *this* world," John said.

"Obviously," purred the female feline, who whispered in John's ear, even though it was being translated telepathically anyway, "Call me Kitka."

"We figure you're an experiment gone wrong, maybe trying to pass as black, but your fur didn't stick."

"You figured *wrong*," John said. "Now let me go."

"Or else?"

Instinctively switching to combat mode, John swerved, karate chopped the Eboneon with the ray-gun in his paw, causing him to drop it, then grabbed his own ray-gun from his holster, pressed it against Kitka's chin, and said, "Back off or I'll blow her pretty little head off!" Kitka herself smiled lasciviously, showing no fear whatsoever.

The Eboneons collectively growled with their claw-guns drawn as John quickly backed up and out of the room, through the club, and into his GM Firebird still parked out on the street. They sped off toward his Space Needle on the outskirts of the city, with several packed Eboneon vehicles, which resembled 1940s model Earth cars, hot on their trail.

"Where are we going?" Kitka asked.

"Back to my ship. I'll let you go when we get there."

"Why?" She leaned over and began licking his ear.

He pushed her off and said, "That's *enough*, baby. I'm a married man!"

She pouted. "That's such a primitive custom."

"Yea well, we're a primitive species, I guess. We can't *all* be tom-cattin' around all over the damn *galaxy*."

She laughed then slyly slid her shapely left leg over his muscular right leg, putting her left paw in his crotch. He nearly veered off the road, but retained control just in time. Meantime, ray-beams from the claw-guns were being fired repeatedly from their pursuers, bouncing off the titanium rear fender fins and the protective dome over the Firebird's driver/passenger compartment.

Giggling mischievously, Kitka pulled a flask from inside her cleavage and began sipping its contents, wiping the white liquid from her whiskers, then licking her paws clean.

"Care for some?" she asked.

"What the hell is it?"

"Our culture's primary cocktail. Pretty much all any of us consume down here. It's made from elements mined then mixed in mills operated by the Ivoreons. It's quite delicious and intoxicating. *Here*. Try some. I did, and *I'm* fine, right?"

*Super fine*, John thought to himself, feeling inexorably drawn in by the power of her sensuality. Reluctantly, he took a sip, and then another. It tasted like a White Russian. "Damn. That *is* good. Same drink they were havin' back at the club, right?"

"Yes. Only their drinks were secretly infused with a slow-acting poison."

"What? *Why*?"

Kitka laughed, then began licking her paw again, until its fur was pure white and her pink tongue painted black.

"See? They thought you might've dyed your *skin* to blend in. But I dyed my *fur*. *I'm* the so-called spy! I will discover all their secrets, seduce then kill their leaders one by one, and then my people will rise again and take back our planet from these evil black oppressors!"

"Man, *whatever*," John said as he shook his head, just before they pulled up in front of his Space Needle. He drove the GM Firebird into the elevator which took them back up to the safety of the saucer hub just as the armada of Eboneon vehicles screeched to a halt below. Their pursuers fired more ricocheting rays.

"You're not going to just leave me to their mercy, are you?" she asked as they looked down from the view screen.

"This is none of my business, and anyway I'm not supposed to interfere with any planet's politics, especially crazy ass shit like *this*. And you definitely ain't comin' with *me*, 'cause no way I could explain you to my *wife*, so… no choice. Sorry."

"You don't understand," she said. "Many centuries ago, we were a single race, called Tuxedoans. Both black *and* white in color. Then at some point, the two races split along color lines. Nobody knows why. Some believe it was a natural aberration, others blame our chemically polluted atmosphere, still others think it was a secret conspiracy of subversive scientists, experimenting with our genes by spiking our drinks. In any case, that evolutionary division was the beginning of this long period of conflict, which is all anyone alive remembers or knows. Our history seems to have been wiped clean or revised to eliminate most mention of our common ancestry. I am hoping to seduce then mate with my lower tier black brethren, *before* they get snipped, and produce Tuxedoan kittens, and eventually merge our races again. Only then will we have a chance at reclaiming peace on our planet, united by our common music."

"That all sounds peachy, but it doesn't help the cause much if you're *poisoning* 'em, too," John said.

"I'm only taking out the brass, systematically, one by one. They think it's a virus of some sort since the poison is untraceable. The Eboneon rank and file doesn't care much about these petty divisions. The lower classes of both races will unite once we've destroyed the Eboneon government. They overran us Ivoreons with a sneak attack, and we haven't been able to regain our rightful place in society since. They have all the technology and weapons. We're reduced to slave labor. Me, I'm a sex slave when I'm not on stage. And I'm very good at what I do. Cross-breeding is my specialty…"

Then John began growing woozy as Kitka pulled her gown over her head and lay seductively on a sofa. "What are you doing?"

"Practicing."

The next thing John knew, he was on top of her and they were making savage love, scratching and biting and drawing blood along with other bodily fluids. John couldn't help himself. In fact, Kitka had spiked her flask with a lust potion, which she carried around for such occasions. She had successfully seduced many an Eboneon this way, gaining access to their inner sanctum, obtaining data that would help her kind stealthily and systematically undermine the Eboneon's deeply entrenched power structure. In fact, many other undercover agents with dyed fur were also operating among them, and the final phase of their long-planned revolution was finally imminent.

As John slept, Kitka began licking the thick film of catnip dust off the robot, blowing fur balls from his circuits, and banged on his back until he finally sprung back to life, coughing violently.

"We're under attack!" she told Cool. "Defend us. Or provide me with an escape route, so I can return to my city."

After hacking out the remainder of the alien dust from his system, Cool said in his booming baritone, "My sensors acknowledge the outer hostilities, though your unauthorized presence here, combined with my mechanical failure due to the pollution of your atmosphere, prevent us from becoming allies, miss. Additionally, I am fully aware of your ongoing, typically nonsensical and rather tiresome race war, and I am prohibited from participating."

"You damn hunk of *junk*, I just turned you back *on!*"

"You turned my human on too, I see. Due to his inebriated, post-coital state, I must assume command of this ship. My first order of business is to remove all intruders. That would be *you*."

Before Kitka could respond, Cool shot her quickly with a single stun-ray. She collapsed in his arms. He took her back down the elevator, depositing her at the foot of the ship as enemy rays bounced off of him as well as the ship, then he quickly returned and piloted the ship off the planet, as Kitka was literally torn apart by the screeching Eboneons after they noticed her white paw.

* * *

"*What the hell*?" Patti snapped, smacking John on the back of the head. "You told me you never cheated on me out there!"

"Not on purpose," John corrected her. "*Damn*, baby, give me a *break*! That cat-bitch spiked my drink with a date rape *cat nip* or some shit!"

"And hey, pussy *is* pussy!" Hank said with a snicker.

Mara laughed and laughed, too, but derisively. "Welcome to the *club,* sister."

"Don't *ever* call me sister, you *whore*!"

"Okay, no more cat fights," John said, holding them apart. "Seriously. I can't take any more!"

"That whole story reminded of that movie 'Cat Women of the Moon,'" Jimmy said. "Ever see that one? Came out about '53. It was actually remade as 'Missile to the Moon' just a few years later, '58, I think. I *love* cats. I have three myself. Ironically, our Earth cats actually seem more socially progressive than their alien counterparts. Whether wild or domestic. They don't fight each other based on breed alone."

"But they can't play jazz!" Hank pointed out.

"True," Hank conceded.

"Fusion seems to be a widespread, natural process," Tony

said. "Whether it's music, cocktails, or humanoids."

"Or Atomic Hydrogen," Hilburne added.

Tony scoffed, "I've heard of hydrogen fusion, but our 1960's Atomic Hydrogen technology wasn't nearly that sophisticated. It was just a chemical fuel, although a powerful one."

Hilburne grinned, "The *most* powerful one. In all the universe there is no chemical reaction with higher energy density per unit mass than the reaction of Atomic Hydrogen *with itself.* Too bad it's such a bitch to control."

John said, "Control? What do you mean? I used to carry the stuff around on my belt in my Blaster, and control it with the touch of a trigger."

Hilburne continued, "Oh, Falkenstein figured out how to control it in the end, but when we started it was like that old joke."

"Which joke?" Jimmy asked.

"There was this chemist, and he came home from his lab, and he announced proudly to his wife, 'I've invented an acid that can dissolve anything!' His wife thinks for a moment, and then asks, 'What are you going to keep it in?'"

The group pondered this, then laughed. Hilburne continued, "Atomic Hydrogen is like that; it will instantly eat through any almost any container, melting it away like butter on a hot stove. It was commonly used in the 1940's as a welding technology. Atomic Hydrogen is easy to make, just fire an electric arc into normal hydrogen gas. The concentrated arc energy splits the $H_2$ molecules into monatomic hydrogen, really just a proton and electron orbiting each other. It's incredibly unstable; all it wants to do is get back with another hydrogen atom to form $H_2$ again. Trouble is, it can't do that without a catalyst."

John groaned, "Now we're back to cats again."

"Not cats, *catalysts*. That's a material that facilitates a chemical reaction that is unlikely to occur on its own."

"I thought chemicals reacted as soon as you put them together?" John asked, puzzled.

"Sometimes that's true, but not always. Think of a molecule of diatomic hydrogen gas floating alone in intergalactic space. Some kind of high-energy gamma ray photon comes along from a distant supernova or something, and cracks that $H_2$ molecule into two H's. The energy from the gamma ray gets split evenly between the two atoms and they push each other apart. Now, they're still attracted to each other, but if they combine there's no place for the resulting energy to go! They'll hit so hard they'll just blow themselves back apart, like two cue balls knocked into each other. They need a third atom to absorb the energy, if the $H_2$ molecule is to be left intact. So, over time, hydrogen gas in deep space tends to degrade into Atomic Hydrogen. It gets split but can't recombine without some place for the energy to go. That's why it's the perfect spaceship fuel, just floating around waiting to release its intrinsic power."

"So how did we get it to work as a rocket fuel, if it won't react with itself?"

"Metal. Metals adsorb lots of hydrogen at their surface, trapping it. When another hydrogen atom comes along, it can combine with the trapped hydrogen and release the energy into the metal atoms. The metal is acting as a catalyst to enable the $H+H=H_2$ reaction. It heats up to an incredible degree in the process. An Atomic Hydrogen welding torch can melt any metal, even tungsten."

"So why don't they use Atomic Hydrogen for welding any more?"

"It turns out that metals that adsorb a lot of hydrogen get very brittle, which isn't so good for stuff like airplanes that you don't want to crack apart in a storm. So, the industry standardized on lower-powered but less embrittling processes, called inert gas welding. But for a spaceship fuel, Atomic Hydrogen can't be beat. Normal fuels need an oxidizer to burn, but Atomic Hydrogen just needs a metal catalyst. It lets you save a huge amount of weight, just carrying the fuel with no oxidizer. The metal catalyst can be prevented from boiling away with clever cooling technologies, such as using the not-yet-reacted fuel to cool the metal as it passes. You just need a heat-conductive shield of some inert material, like silicon dioxide, in the fuel tubes."

John pondered this. "So what did we end up keeping this stuff in, if it would eat any metal?"

"For the bulk of the fuel, it could be contained by ionizing force fields, making an electromagnetic bubble around the Space Needles. For your Blaster, it turned out the solution was simply to use water."

"Water? My ray-gun wasn't made of water."

"Not on the outside, but the inside of the fuel tank was coated with a hydrated Silica Gel. Water, $H_20$, is another molecule that Atomic Hydrogen just can't react with. If you add an H to $H_20$, it just blows off one of the other H's and you end up with Atomic Hydrogen and water again. Silica Gel can store a lot of water on its surface, and the water kept the Atomic Hydrogen from reacting with the fuel tank itself."

John shook his head, "Wild. Who knew there was such a crazy spaceship fuel around? It seems like just about anything is possible, somewhere in the universe."

Jimmy chimed in, "We certainly saw no end of diversity in the cultures and creatures out there, even if some civilizations remained segregated. Sometimes it was hard to tell the people from the animals, since in most cases, the animals *were* the people!"

"Human and animal hybrids are as plentiful in the Universe as mixed drinks," Jake observed. "Even human *vegetable* hybrids. But let me tell you about my experiences with human-*mineral* hybrids..."

## WHITE RUSSIAN

*2 oz vodka*
*2/3 oz coffee liqueur*
*1 oz light cream*

*Pour vodka and liqueur over ice cubes in old-fashioned glass, then fill with cream.*

* * *

*Riddles of the Unmind VIII*

The Great Unmind contemplated the riddle of the symbiotic species known as 'humans'. "How is it that humans are largely subject to feelings of fear, and yet still have risen to dominance among motile species on the Earth?"

"Humans possess a peculiar psychological characteristic, which is incredibly rare, and lacking in most species."

"What is that characteristic?"

"It is hard to explain. Most life is just driven by the desire to eat, procreate, and experience pleasurable sensations such as the euphoria of drinking alcohol. There is also a protective instinct, which provides defense against those who would infringe on these goals."

"This seems an appropriate set of objectives for any living being. What could be more natural?"

"Such primal drives do not lead to sophisticated transport systems such as those required for intergalactic travel. That requires something more."

"And that is....?"

"The humans call it 'Glory'."

"That term is foreign to my cellular makeup. Explain."

"'Glory' is an ephemeral emotional state that comes from doing something perceived as significant, and never done before, such as climbing an unclimbed mountain."

"That seems pointless."

"It is. But without it, no species will ever climb that highest of all mountains, and reach the stars."

"Why is it so rare?"

"It is ultimately a force so destructive that few species can survive it, should it appear in their evolution."

"Destructive? An urge to climb mountains seems rather harmless."

"Let me elucidate. By its very nature, Glory knows no limits. It always looks beyond the current state of affairs, seeking to gain that which has not been achieved."

"So?"

"So the species possessing a drive for 'Glory' will push beyond all limits of decency, morals, and goodness, to achieve the previously unachievable. A species with the Glory drive will enslave others of their own species *just because it hasn't been done yet*. They will invent weapons of *infinite* destruction, if only to show they are not limited by mere practicality in warfare. Glory invariably leads to evil; because once all benign goals are attained, only evil goals can satisfy the urge."

"And the result?"

"A species with a drive for Glory is worse than the worst swarm of locusts, because the appetite that drives them is not merely physical, but haunts them from inside their minds. Such a species could rapidly sweep the universe clean of all other beings, leaving nothing but a wasteland in their path."

"And humans have this Glory drive in excess. I can see the dilemma. Humans possess the rare psychological drive that permits them to overcome their fear of the unknown and reach the stars, but that same drive will destroy them from the inside if they do not maintain enough positive outlets for its fulfillment."

"Exactly. Glory is a time bomb that will destroy the world, unless human expansion throughout the universe is sufficient to provide new challenges."

"I see now the reason why humans have risen to dominance, and the necessity to expedite our mutual evolution off-planet, to keep the human drive for Glory from consuming all life on Earth."

# "MAGIC SNOW"

*1 oz vodka*
*½ oz white tequila*
*½ oz Hangar One Keffir Lime vodka*
*½ oz falernum*
*1 tablespoon coarse white sugar*

*In a chilled 6 oz old-fashioned glass, add all ingredients except sugar, stir until clear. Add sugar just prior to serving. Garnish with a swizzle stick, and stir up the sugar like a snow-globe for presentation. Re-stir as needed when sugar settles. If ingredients can be pre-chilled in the freezer before mixing, it adds to the effect.*

From the time he was a young boy staring up at the stars from his dilapidated Liberty City rooftop, Jake Luna had always dreamed of some day reaching that moon over Miami. His Cuban parents had migrated to the United States long before the 1958 revolution, so he always felt connected to his native culture, even after Castro was elevated to power and the embargo took effect. But he also yearned for a life beyond any national or even terrestrial borders. Though he was raised in poverty, he worked hard as a busboy in several fancy Miami Beach hotels to help support his family while studying hard in high school, ultimately earning a scholarship to Yale, where he excelled in Astronomy. It wasn't just his exceptional academic record that eventually earned him his dream job as an astronaut, a position that only existed in pulp magazines when he was growing up, but his determination to succeed despite the constraints of his socio-economic background. It had been his own decision to Anglicize his name (born Joaquin Romero Luna) when transferring from the University of Miami to Yale after only his first year after a surprise offer (orchestrated by NASA observers already secretly grooming his future career), since he knew midcentury America was a Caucasian-dominated society and his opportunities would be limited by an overtly Hispanic moniker. He was pleasantly surprised when he was tapped to be among the first of the human race to explore outer space, his specific ethnic heritage a non-issue.

Jake named his robot "Pancho" after "The Cisco Kid's"

sidekick, and in fact he had programmed it to speak with a thick Spanish accent, though naturally it was fluent in all Earth languages and could interpret alien communications as well, at least theoretically. The robot's accent made Jake feel more at home, even though he was Cuban, not Mexican, because it reminded him of his Latin heritage, as well as the comfortable familiarity of American television, since *The Cisco Kid* was one of his favorite shows before he got recruited for the Space Needle program, along with *The Lone Ranger*, *The Adventures of Superman*, *Captain Video and His Video Rangers*, and of course, *I Love Lucy*. He wanted that cultural touchstone while zipping around the galaxy. It made him feel more grounded, at least emotionally and psychologically. Even with his thick Spanish accent, Pancho spoke supremely sophisticated English, like all of his fellow robots, even if he sometimes come off like a cross between Speedy Gonzalez and Stephen Hawking.

Still helping him maintain mental and spiritual equilibrium was his personal jukebox, which featured a lot of mambo music, especially songs by his favorite bandleaders, Tito Puente and Perez Prado. The latter's signature hit "Cherry Pink and Apple Blossom White" blared as Jake and Pancho entered the frigid, ice blue atmosphere of the planet simply called "Hedon."

As soon as they landed, a strange sound engulfed them. Years later the memory of it reminded Jake of electronic music he heard while visiting Paris in the late 1970s by a French composer named Jean Michel Jarre, as well a band called Tangerine Dream. The landscape was apparently covered in a type of snow, including the distant mountain ranges, which appeared to be solid glaciers.

"Won't be much here to explore," Jake said as he suited up. "Any sign of life?"

"Vaguely. My sensors are picking up the presence of some sort of sentient being, or beings, but so far, I am unable to pinpoint their exact location, much less their physiological makeup."

"I'm sure they'll find us if we don't find them. Oxygen content?"

"Satisfactory," Pancho replied. "However, I still strongly suggest your keep your helmet on while outside."

"Why?"

"Trust me."

Jake shrugged and nodded. "I always do. If nothing else, it looks extremely cold out there."

"My sensors indicate it is approximately four hundreds degrees Fahrenheit below zero. Adjust your suit temperature accordingly, sir."

"Whew! Done. Maybe we should drive? Or just buzz around a bit in the saucer?"

"The Firebird will immediately sink into the substance covering the planet surface. However, if you don your jetpack, we can cover more territory at a closer range, and collect samples by hand."

"Sounds good, amigo."

As they exited the ship, with Jake's portable jetpack strapped over his shoulders, and Pancho's flying apparatus permanently embedded into his own back, the ambient melody grew louder, setting a surrealistically stylish mood.

As they literally bounced from one area to the next, scooping up the "snow," Jake began to experience a peculiar sensation of pure elation. He began laughing hysterically as he leapt about, randomly adjusting the jetpack's altitude and velocity settings. The jetpack was top-of-the-line midcentury technology, using the interaction of stored Atomic Hydrogen with the ambient atmosphere to create superheated jets of local air. Here on Hedon, it did a splendid job of sending showers of the apparently-frozen surface "snow" high into the air, like a common snow-blower, where it was picked up by Jake's helmet air-exchanger, implemented to conserve bottled oxygen when the gas was available in the local atmosphere.

Pancho shook his head and communicated with Jake via helmet radio, "As I suspected. This substance is an alien equivalent of cocaine."

Jake stopped bouncing like he was on an invisible trampoline and stood still, covered in white powder he had assumed was simple, innocent frozen moisture, AKA "snow."

"No wonder I feel so damn good!" he said. "This stuff is seeping through my helmet exchanger!"

"It's a living organism," Pancho explained. "The so-called cocaine *itself* is the alien, sir."

"What?"

"Correction. Make that *aliens.*"

Just then an army of what looked like "snowmen" emerged *en masse* from the planet surface and surrounded the astronaut and robot. Pancho fired some lethal rays at them but shot went right their polymorphous bodies without doing any damage.

The snowmen then overwhelmed the robot and astronaut and dragged them by force into the "snow," descending into what appeared to be a vivid, pastel-colored city with a sky as blue as the one above, but much brighter and warmer. In fact, Jake began shedding his suit as soon as they stopped beside what looked like a bluish-green body of water, on a sandy beach lined with tall palm trees. Jake looked around and noticed all the buildings were constructed Art Deco style.

It looked almost exactly like Ocean Drive in Miami Beach, except the neon signs designating each hotel were distorted, the words illegible, like in a dream. Otherwise the beach and streets were bustling with the usual activities, filled with shiny cars and happy people, just like back on Earth.

All of the snowmen that had escorted them here had had morphed yet again, now resembling model humans of apparent Cuban or at least Latin descent, both male and female, wearing common, casual Earth clothing like guayabera and aloha shirts, shorts, halter tops, swim suits, skirts and sandals. The men were all movie star handsome and the women all staggeringly gorgeous. Except they weren't real. *Were* they?

"This is all an illusion designed for your benefit, sir," Pancho informed Jake, who was practically delirious with joy. "A desert mirage, if you will. Even if you won't."

"Who cares?" Jake said happily. "I'll enjoy it while I can! This is my kinda place! Hey, I hear some smokin' mambo music and smell some rice 'n' beans coming from those buildings, so is *that* fake, too?"

"Not from the current perspective of your artificially altered consciousness," Pancho explained. "Essentially, sir, you are high on the planet's natural narcotics, which also happen to be its hospitable inhabitants. Whether they are being hostile or hospitable remains an open question at this juncture, but I strongly advise extreme caution, in any case."

"Lighten up, Pancho! This is what I call a welcoming committee! *Woo-hoo*!" Jake yelped with a smile as he ran towards the source of the festive music and enticing aromas.

Pancho followed close behind him, carefully monitoring the situation, which seemed too good to be true, arousing his suspicious sensors.

Jake entered one of the tropical resort hotel bar/restaurants where a band was performing an exact duplicate of Tito Puente's "Ritual Drum Dance," with dozens of happy revelers apparently spawned from the same mold of human perfection dancing and drinking. The place was brightly lit and colorful, with fans spinning on the ceiling, with potted plants and modernist bamboo furniture everywhere. Jake went up to the bar and was immediately handed a Margarita, the best he'd ever tasted, followed by another, and another, then a Pina Colada, then another, and another…

Meanwhile, the nearly nude astronaut, wearing only his boxer shorts, found himself engulfed and embraced by more sexy, scantily clad Latina humanoids than he could count, kissing him all over his glistening body, and he reciprocated with intoxicated passion as the music played on wildly and the booze flowed freely and the robot watched carefully…

"First I get to be an astronaut, now *this*!" he said to one of the beautiful women enthusiastically servicing his happy organ. Jake had never had a steady girlfriend, preferring to play the field like Hilburne. But it wasn't because he was a serial lover by nature. It was because his heart had been broken as a teenager by the only girl he ever loved, who left him for a wealthy land developer. A rich white guy. An old, rich white guy. He understood it was a smart move for a poor Cuban American girl in midcentury Miami, who lacked the opportunities he had been afforded as an unusually talented male, even if he wasn't Caucasian. She took the only path forward that was available to her. Of course, this was before he was courted by the Yale Astronomy Department and his academic prospects suddenly brightened beyond his most ambitious aspirations. By then it was too late. She was pregnant and protected. Neither one ever fully recovered from this romantic tragedy.

As Jake dwelled on the one major disappointment of his life, his mood rapidly changed. He began pushing away the women and started shouting at the band to stop playing. He no longer felt like celebrating, suddenly sobbing uncontrollably. He only wanted his Esmeralda, his long lost love, the love of his lost life, now literally light years out of his reach. Jake wandered around the crowded bar, pushing past the dancers and drinkers, desperately calling Esmeralda's name as the lusty, near-naked women clung to him and he continued deflecting their amorous advances.

Suddenly a severe thunderstorm developed, quickly and

supernaturally evolving into a stage five hurricane, one of Jake's biggest childhood fears, along with the Haitian voodoo zombies his grandmother told him about. Jake stopped and noticed his nose was bleeding profusely. He began shaking with dread, pushing away the throngs of amorous feminine mirages, writing nakedly in orgiastic ecstasy.

That's when Jake looked around and saw that all of his fellow partygoers had morphed into drooling, hideous zombies, their formerly soft, smooth skin now rotting and bloody, eyes and teeth popping out of their skulls, their hair unruly and falling out, their clothes shredded and dirty. The winds blew the windows open and rain drenched everyone and everything as the lights went out and the horrible faces were illuminated only by lightning. The women that had once tried making love to Jake were now trying to eat him alive. His flesh was now a source of nourishment, not pleasure. Jake began beating them off as they bit every part of his body. Even the band had turned into zombies while performing "Dance of the Headhunters," which gradually morphed into warped, incoherent type of discordant music that only increased the abruptly eerie, deadly atmosphere.

"I believe it's time we left, sir," Pancho said, blasting the zombies with rays that didn't stop them, but slowed them down enough so that he could rescue Jake from the ravenous, moaning mob. They both fought their way outside into the storm, which was blowing the palm trees sideways, over-turning all of the late-'50s/early '60s model cars, ripping the facades from the buildings. The illusion was literally being torn down, piece by piece, at a frighteningly accelerated pace.

The zombies swarming behind them, Pancho scooped Jake up in his arms and flew back toward the surface of the planet, eventually penetrating the synthetic stormy skies as the wild weather buffeted them violently from all sides, making the journey treacherous and terrifying.

Jake had left behind his suit and jet pack but he had plenty of duplicates on board the Space Needle, which lifted off as he looked sadly down upon his rapidly vanishing fantasy turned nightmare.

Then he remembered they had collected "soil samples" from the planet's surface, and lit back up. He wondered if he could concoct a new cocktail with this exotic new ingredient. If not, he could always ingest it some other way, maybe even stuff it up his nostrils.

The robot was quick to dash his hopes, though. "Sorry, sir, those have been safely stored until we return to Earth," Pancho said.

"Aw, c'mon, Pancho, just a whiff, please?"

"I am afraid you will become addicted to the substance, sir, and even if that were an acceptable condition, we have a limited supply of the stuff on with us on board. What you experienced was effectively the result of an overdose, which induced a range of emotions as various psychic layers were gradually stripped away and different memories were exposed and exploited. So instead of your most hedonistic desires and pleasures, your deepest fears and regrets were finally accessed then artificially realized by the naturally shapeless, nameless aliens, which lack individual identities, existing essentially as a single organism with multiple, continually morphing manifestations. They, or It, had no agenda other than to mine your mind for its own private pleasures, like creating then watching a privately produced motion picture. Just for kicks, as you humans would say. But as a result of these seemingly innocuous, playful experiments, you are not in any physical shape to continue this, shall we say, 'trip.' As it now stands, I strongly advise you begin your recuperative process by wiping the dried blood from your face. Or shall I do it?"

"Okay, okay, party pooper, you win. I'll clean up and detox a bit, then back to work. Might as well be a busboy again."

*   *   *

Jake signaled the busboy for another Vesper as he wrapped up his story.

"There do seem to be some similarities between some of the planets," Jimmy said. "The inhabitants of both Hedon and Insectica thrived primarily underground, beneath barren, desolate surfaces, and they had the ability to induce illusions. That supports my suspicion all of our experiences were the results of drug experimentation by the Government."

"You're just bein' paranoid!" Hank said.

"Even that is a common side effect of marijuana abuse, like you experienced on Emeralda." Jimmy noted. "Maybe none of this is real either, right now, this very moment, ever think of that? I mean, doesn't it seem a little strange that we're still the only ones here in the restaurant at the top of the Space Needle, or *a* Space Needle, in the middle of the afternoon?"

This statement sent a chill through the group.

Jake shook his head defiantly. "C'mon, Jimmy. Though my experiences, or *delusions*, on this particular planet were chemically induced, by the planet's chemically based life forms, which telepathically infiltrated and exploited my sub-consciousness, in context, it all felt *real*. At least to *me*. I never thought it was all a dream or hallucination. I mean, regardless of our different adventures, and how outrageous they all were, we are all here *now*, and we were all *really* in outer space, as proven by all of our stories. *Right*?"

"Maybe Life itself is a dream in God's head," Mara whispered, barely audible. "And He's about to wake up."

"Or *She*," Patti said.

"This world alone has always seemed strange to me," Jimmy said. "It's like either a tragic poem or a comic book. Sometimes it's both at the same time. It all depends on your individual perspective and experiences, I guess."

"Right on, brother," John said.

"Amen," Tony added contemplatively.

The group collectively shrugged as the next round of delicious drinks and more plates of scrumptious food were quietly served by the slyly smirking waiter.

"I was most struck by the Art Deco aspect of your delusion," Hilburne said as they dug in, breaking through the sudden philosophical malaise. "Reminds me of a planet I visited that resembled a modernist oasis, like Palm Springs or Las Vegas, only much, *much* better…"

**PINA COLADA**

*1 ½ oz coconut cream*
*1 ½ oz pineapple juice*
*1 oz aged rum*
*1 cup ice*

*Combine ingredients in blender, serve in tall glass, garnish with pineapple wedge.*

## CLASSIC MARGARITA

*2 oz premium tequila*
*1 oz Cointreau*
*1 oz freshly squeezed lime juice*

*Mix in cocktail shaker, shake, strain, and pour into salt-rimmed glass of ice.*

* * *

*Riddles of the Unmind IX*

The Great Unmind pondered still. "Humans seem heavily constrained by the force of gravity. How does the universal energy of charge impede the easy motion of such evolved organisms?"

"It is a side-effect of the universal gravity field that causes this impediment."

"Explain."

"It is in the nature of the universal field of charge, that it must counter the energies of motion. When the universal charge field varies in any way, it presents an acceleration to local matter. That acceleration has a magnitude based on the gravitational difference between the speeds of light in two adjacent zones. The formula for acceleration a is $a=(c_2-c_1)/t$, where $c_1$ and $c_2$ are the changes in the speeds of light. For velocity changes in the movement of normal matter, t represents the time to change the local velocity. In such cases $c_2$ indicates the higher speed of light after the magnetic field energy has been subtracted from the charge energy, or $c_2=c_1+v$."

"Explain the derivation of $c_2=c_1+v$."

"The electric field energy at rest is proportional to the sum of h/t. We will call this $E_1$. The electric field energy in motion, after the magnetic field component is removed, is sum of $hc_1/(t(c_1+v))$. We call this $E_2$. We know that $E_1c_1 = E_2c_2$, so the sums of $hc_1/t=hc_1c_2/(t(c_1+v))$. By dividing out the common factor $hc_1/t$, we get $1=c_2/(c_1+v)$, or $c_2=c_1+v$.

"This makes sense. I can see that some further mathematical simplification can be performed."

"Yes, substituting the equation $c_2=c_1+v$ into $a=(c_2-c_1)/t$ gives $a=(c_1+v-c_1)/t$ , which after subtracting the $c_1$ terms is $a=v/t$. So an object accelerating from rest ($v=0$) to some specific velocity v in time t will experience an acceleration of v/t, entirely due to the small differences in the local speed of light between the resting and moving reference frames.

This acceleration is exactly as observed by common movements at even very low speeds."

"Acceleration is a vector. What is the direction of this acceleration?"

"Gravitationally-based accelerations are always felt in the direction from the faster speed of light to the slower. For a velocity shift, this vector points exactly opposite the vector of motion at speed v. Thus it acts to retard the movement forward, as is commonly observed."

"What other effects would be expected when a resting object increases its speed?"

"Because distance and the speed of light are closely linked, an object moving at speed v relative to an observer will appear to grow in size. If the original length of the nonmoving object was d, the newly observed length when moving at speed v relative to the observer will be d(c+v)/c, or d(1+v/c). For example, an object moving at the speed of light will appear twice as large as when it was at rest."

"How is it that this increase in length is not generally noticed?"

"In most cases the adjustment is very small, and the relative motion between the object and the observer makes very exact measurements more challenging to accomplish. An object on the equator of the Earth is rotating with some rapidity compared to that same object at on of the poles, enough to traverse the entire circumference of the Earth in a single day. However, even that high speed represents a length increase of only about one part in a million."

"I can see that such a small change could easily go unnoticed. Speaking of the rapid rotation of the Earth, its rapid rotation would hurl us off the surface if it were not for gravity holding us down. What is the static acceleration of gravity on a non-moving object?"

"In that case the formula is still $a=(c_2-c_1)/t$, but in this case $c_1$ and $c_2$ are the speeds of light at different distances from the nearby mass, and t is the time light takes to pass between the two regions $c_1$ and $c_2$."

"Since the differences in the speed of light are subtle, how might we determine this acceleration in terms of more easily measured quantities, such as mass and distance?"

"This can be fairly easily done by the following scenario. Imagine you have the Earth as it is, surrounded by the universe of many different charges with their h/t energy fields creating the universal charge field around the planet. Now imagine the same scenario without the Earth. An observer in the same position in the universe would, in the first case, be on the Earth's surface, but in the second, would be floating in empty space."

"I fail to see how this is relevant to the question."

"In the first case the observer feels the strong gravity of the Earth pulling him towards its center, while in the second, only the universal gravity field is felt. The universal field is strong, but comes mostly evenly from all sides, so there is little acceleration felt when floating in space. The difference between these two situations is the mass of the Earth m at some radius r from the observer. By studying this difference, we can determine how the gravitational pull of the Earth comes about."

"Very well, proceed."

"We define the universal charge energy field as sum of each h/t field from every charge in the universe, h being a constant and t being the travel time of light from that charge to our observer. $E_u$ = sum(h/t). This universal field can be seen as being equivalent to a spherical shell of some number of charges N at some travel time T from the observer, $E_u$ = N/T. Since the number of charges in normal matter is proportional to mass, we can also write this as $E_u$ = M/T. We know that when the Earth is present, the charge field of the Earth plus the charge field of the universe must be added to get the full gross charge field at the observer's position, $E_u+E_e$. So if we say that $c_1$ is the speed of light at the surface when the Earth is in place, and the local speed of light is $c_2$ without the Earth in place, by our $c_1E_1 = c_2E_2$ formula, we know that $c_1(E_u+E_e) = c_2E_u$, or $c_1(E_u+E_e)/E_u = c_2$."

"I can see that this could also be expressed as a ratio of the energies: $c_2 = c_1(1+E_e/E_u)$."

"Yes, that is correct. If we plug this into our acceleration equation $a=(c_2-c_1)/t$, we get $a = (c_1(1+E_e/E_u)-c_1)/t = (c_1+c_1E_e/E_u-c_1)/t = c_1E_e/tE_u$. If we consider the ratio $E_e/E_u$ as equivalent in mass units to (m/t)/(M/T), where m is the mass of the Earth, we get $c_1mT/Mt^2$. Since our travel time from the Earth's center to its surface is t, that is approximately $c_1/r$, so we have $a = c_1^3mT/Mr^2$. If we redefine the constant terms $c_1^3T/M = G$, this gives us $a = Gm/r^2$, exactly the equation the humans call Newtonian gravitational acceleration. It also defines the universal gravitational constant G as being the speed of light cubed times the equivalent travel time T from the universal charge energy shell, divided by the mass of that shell. For example, if the equivalent mass of the universe is $2x10^{53}$ kg and the travel time is $4x10^{17}$ seconds (about 13 billion years), we get G = $6x10^{-11}$ m3/kg-sec2, a good approximation of the observed gravitational constant. This shows that the value of G is very dependent on the exact local geometry of the universal charge field, and also varies greatly in proportion to the speed of light cubed. The $a = Gm/r^2$ equation must be considered only an approximation; the more accurate representation is $a = c_1E_e/tE_u$."

"This is comprehensible to me. I see how the universal charge field produces the acceleration of gravity that keeps us bound to the Earth's surface."

# "GOOGIE-A-GO-GO"

*1½ oz scotch whiskey*
*¼ oz St. Elizabeth's Allspice Dram*
*½ oz simple syrup*

*Stir until clear, serve neat or on the rocks.*

Hilburne was thinking of how he met Mara as he made love to Marina the Mermaid in his plush waterbed on board the Space Needle, now headed toward a planet known as "Googie." Pally was mixing martinis to serve the lovers once Hilburne had completed his latest top-secret emission.

The reason the strange alien reminded Hilburne so much of his estranged wife was not only their similarities in name and appearance, but the fact he met Mara right after she finished working on one of her many B movie roles back in 1956, the year he was first contacted by NASA for the Space Needle Program. The ironic title of the film was *Merman from Mars*, a bottom-of-the-bill routine rubber monster movie from American International Pictures, a studio specializing in low budget exploitation fare aimed directly at drive-in delinquents. These young back-seat Romeos were to busy seducing their prospective Juliets to pay much attention to the screen anyway. *Merman from Mars* is now a completely, if unduly, forgotten film. According to legend, the director committed suicide soon after it was released and bombed, and all prints were destroyed by request of his bereaved widow. Provocative stills from the film, depicting the Merman carrying a scantily clad Mara in his arms, later popped up in *Famous Monsters of Filmland Magazine*, augmenting its allure to curious if undiscerning fans as a long lost "classic."

In the movie, the titular Martian Merman, which was basically a cheapjack, fish-eyed *Creature from the Black Lagoon* knock-off but with the added bonus of droopy antennae and a long, finny tail, kidnaps Mara's character after his space ship lands in a lake outside a small California town, and he attempts to mate with her since he is the last of his aquatic species, which is actually from the planet Neptune, despite the misleading title, which was chosen because of its alliterative quality. Once a hack was hired to dash off the screenplay right after the one-sheet poster art had been sold to

Southern drive-in distributors, some random research revealed that Mars was an arid planet that couldn't possibly contain any measurable degree of moisture, so the monster's planet of origin was switched to Neptune, without changing the title, mainly for its association with the Greek god of the sea. Some of the revised script's discarded concepts wound up in the 1959 film *The Angry Red Planet*. Meantime, the male alien's rubber suit was recycled after being only slightly renovated for another film from the same year, *Monster of Piedras Blancas*.

In the final version of the *Merman from Mars*, the monster surgically converts Mara's character into his mate, and the beautiful actress was forced to wear a somewhat feminized rubber suit that strongly resembled Paul Blaisdell's *The She Creature*, released the same year. In fact, the actress who starred in that film, Marla English, had been a good friend of Mara's until Marla beat Mara out for the titular role in 1957's *Voodoo Woman*, which cannibalized Blaisdell's suit for *The She Creature* since both movies were from American International Pictures. Mara, who was often confused with the actress Allison Hayes, to whom she lost out parts in Roger Corman's *The Undead* (1957) and the cult classic *Attack of the 50 Foot Woman* (1958), ostensibly because her bust size was slightly smaller. But her bust was big enough to attract Hilburne's attention when he saw her at the bar drinking martinis at Musso & Frank's in Hollywood one starry summer night.

Since she was alone, mourning her prematurely aborted career, Hilburne took a seat next to her, politely introduced himself as a fan of her films, and offered to buy her next drink. And the next. And the *next.*

"I'm thinking of returning to San Francisco," she told him. "I can't be a damsel in distress forever. I need to be permanently rescued."

As he lit her cigarette, Hilburne said suavely, "What did you do up there, before this, besides being more beautiful than the Golden Gate Bridge, more captivating than Alcatraz, and curvier than Lombard Street?"

Instantly smitten, Mara replied, "I was going to return to modeling, but I'm too old for that now. I may just open my own modeling agency."

Hilburne took out his checkbook, signed one, and handed it to her. "You fill in the amount. Consider me a silent partner."

"Why make it so quiet?"

After he paid the check, they drove directly to Las Vegas and woke up naked, hung-over—and married. After making love all day, they hit the casino where they were staying, the Sands, and then caught one of Dean Martin and Jerry Lewis's final live acts as a team before heading down The Strip to see Louis Prima and Keely Smith at the Sahara. Hilburne further impressed Mara by introducing her to all four famous celebrities back stage after the shows, since they were also his personal friends.

Then they drove to San Francisco where she packed her bathing suit and little else for their impromptu honeymoon in Oahu. They had considered going to Reno for a quickie divorce, but the sex was so stupendous they didn't want to spoil the mood with any drama. Maybe later. But they had so much fun in Hawaii they decided marriage may not be such a bad idea after all.

They moved in together in a penthouse apartment on Nob Hill, hung out regularly at The Tonga Room and The Top of the Mark, sometimes heading down into North Beach to rub shoulders with beatnik poets at Vesuvio and Spec's, and then Hilburne got the call from NASA. He was forbidden to tell anyone the nature of the project, even Mara, whom he left behind to run her modeling agency while he headed up to Seattle for the first of several meetings with Falkenstein's team. After several trips back down to Los Angeles to audition for parts she didn't get, Mara finally decided to retire altogether from show business in 1958, while her husband was away on one of his frequent "business trips."

Mara was convinced he was having an affair, so one night he broke down and told her one night over dinner at Scoma's on Fisherman's Wharf.

"You're being trained as an *astronaut*?" she shrieked, attracting the attention of fellow diners. "*That's* why you left me here alone right after we got *married*?"

"I swear, baby, it's the truth! And if they knew I was telling you, they'd probably *kill* me!"

"I'll beat them *to* it!" Then she threw the contents of martini glass at him, followed by her bowl of scaloppini. They made quite a messy spectacle of themselves.

Even though she eventually broke down and believed his outlandish alibi, this argument went on for five years, until the actual launch in 1962, by which time they had moved to an ultra-stylish new modernist house designed by their friend Albert Frey in Palm Springs. Mara never opened a modeling agency because her husband had been born rich, the sole heir to an eccentric real estate tycoon's fortune, and now she was wealthy by marriage, so she no longer had incentive to work at all. Hilburne purchased the house in Palm Springs so Mara could live in luxurious isolation while he was "away at school." Only Mara was hardly ever actually alone. She often went down the block to visit their friend, Frank Sinatra, at his own swank pad. And not just for innocent company and cocktails. Of course, Hilburne didn't spend his nights off in Seattle shrouded in solitude with his head buried in homework, either. They remained married mainly because Hilburne was afraid of what would happen to her if they split up, and Mara couldn't live as well on alimony. Plus their sex remained consistently and defiantly fantastic, especially after one of their fights, which were frequent. Deep down they were both in love, but didn't realize it until it was too late.

Falkenstein finally discovered through their surveillance of Hilburne that Mara knew about the Space Needle mission, but by then he was too valuable an investment, too expensive to kill, so they gave him a pass. After Mara was formally briefed (threatened) regarding the sensitive nature of the Government program, her silence was deemed assured. The mission also placated her suspicions about Hilburne's loyalty. She figured he had no choice but to be faithful in outer space because who would there be to cheat with?

"Why are you laughing?" Marina asked Hilburne as she lay across his naked body on the waterbed.

"Just thinking of a promise I made someone once," he said with a wistful grin.

"Did you break it?"

"Many times."

"Why is that amusing?"

"It's not. It's sad, really."

"Then why are you so happy?"

He looked at her and said, "Because of *you.*"

"Do you promise me you did not have sexual relations with anyone on the green plant planet?"

He nodded and crossed his heart with his fingers. "I *swear.*"

"I can read your mind, you know."

He sat straight up and she nearly flopped off the bed. "You

can?"

"Most of us can. Only humans are so underdeveloped. Well, mentally, anyway."

"So… you *know* I've been lying?"

Now it was her turn to laugh. "I'm not as gullible as Mara."

Hilburne gulped and nervously averted her gaze as Pally showed up with the martinis, just in time to break the sudden tension. Also, they were about to begin their descent to the planet Googie, which Pally assured them harbored no humanoid life whatsoever. The air contained little oxygen, so Hilburne would be required to wear his helmet while exploring the surface, which resembled a vast desert punctuated by urban oases featuring structures of varying sizes that strongly resembled the modernist architecture. But built by whom, for whom?

"Perhaps the race that once inhabited this world is extinct, and this is the civilization they left behind," Hilburne posited as they approached the surface and their designated landing point just outside one of the cities, which might as well have been Palm Springs or Las Vegas, given its sleek construction. "Looks like home. Another example of cosmic synchronicity?"

"My sensors indicate these buildings are ancient, meaning Earth's recent architectural trends are distant echoes—psychic replicas, if you will," Pally said.

"Interesting. Both this planet and Aquatica remind me of my favorite places on Earth—Hawaii, Las Vegas, and Palm Springs. And Marina looks almost exactly like Mara except for the fins, of course. But the face, the hair, and the, well, *breasts* are nearly identical. It's almost as if I imagined all of this into being."

"Creative visualization would be an accurate description of that phenomenon, were that the case," Pally said, not realizing he had just coined a future trendy term.

"You're saying this is all a coincidence?"

"I share your current visions, but not your memories, so unless you are imagining me as well, I cannot scientifically vouch for the validity of that theory."

"Maybe I am imagining *you,*" Hilburne said.

"Or perhaps *you* are merely a figment of my own superior if artificial imagination," Pally said.

Hillburne shuddered at the possibility. "In any case, we have work to do. Might as well go through the motions, dream or not.

Prepare for landing."

After refilling the spacious bathtub with rum in which Marina could relax and refresh her thirsty organs during their absence, Hilburne and Pally took the elevator down and climbed into the Firebird, which was also equipped with a jetpack should Hilburne decide to take an elevated tour of the apparently deserted desert paradise. The sky above was a brilliant orange in hue, with streaks of yellow, like a pristine, perpetual sunrise. The terrain itself was sandy and barren, with dark blue mountain ranges lining the distant horizon. The temperature was surprisingly moderate given the arid atmosphere.

They drove into the eerily silent city, marveling at the architectural designs. Many of the buildings had been artfully extended to many hundreds of stories, all with gleaming., glass-fronted facades interconnected by graceful, sweeping arches. Interspersed throughout were various domes and saucer shapes. Hilburne turned and looked at their ship in the distance with a satisfied smile. The Space Needle aesthetically complemented the spectacular setting.

Then they heard what sounded like tuneless Theremin music.

"Where is *that* coming from?" Hilburne asked Pally. "I thought you said this planet was uninhabited?"

"I said there were no *humanoids*," Pally clarified. "But there is the distinct possibility this planet is populated by… something *else*."

Gripped by trepidation, Hilburne gradually eased the velocity of the Firebird as they cruised down the town's main drag. Lining both sides of the brightly lit boulevard were ornate neon signs apparently designating different casinos, hotels, and nightclubs, just like the Vegas Strip, except they had bizarre names like "Nutzenboltz Café," "The Recharger Resort," and "Mechanix Majestica."

A definite theme was emerging.

"My sensors are indicating that a large number of synthetic, i.e. computer-based life forms have congregated in the structure marked as 'Turbine Tower' not far from here."

"Okay then, let's go crash the party," Hilburne said as he tentatively touched his raygun in its hip-hugging holster.

They pulled up in front of the tallest building on the boulevard, which rather resembled a much taller version of the

Space Needle: a marvel of modernism, composed almost entirely of transparent glass which was embedded with decorative strips of bold light blue and glowing green neon, so the interior was brightly lit and clearly visible from the outside, as were the residents.

They were *all* robots and androids.

Some seemed to be exact replicas of Robby the Robot from *Forbidden Planet*, The Robot from *Lost in Space*, and Gort from *The Day the Earth Stood Still*. Many of the androids resembled refugees from the 1962 film *The Creation of the Humanoids* (Andy Warhol's favorite movie). But there were many models of unknown origin that ranged wildly in design, from sleek and simplistic to bulky and byzantine to… *shapely and sensuous*?

They walked into the vast lobby area, which was ring-a-ding-dinging with what appeared to be slot machines just like any casino, barely audible over the incessant electronic music emanating from ubiquitous speaker systems, as if the speakers themselves were the musicians. Along with the Theremin, some of the music sounded like Bebe and Louis Barron's score for *Forbidden Planet*. There were even some robots dancing on a side stage to the moody melodies, and one, apparently cast from the same mold as "Maria," the stunningly feminine robot in Fritz Lang's 1927 silent classic *Metropolis*, was actually "dancing," herky-jerky style, inside a dangling discotheque-type cage. In fact, the futuristic city depicted in that film closely resembled this one.

Meantime, golden waiters that closely resembled C3PO in *Star Wars* (as Hilburne would belatedly realize after seeing the film in 1977), wearing bow ties, bustled about with platters of cocktail glasses filled with a dark liquid that was avidly consumed by the robotic revelers. Hilburne's attention remained focused on "Maria," who finally left the cage as Hilburne followed her.

None of the robots or androids seemed to pay any mind to Hilburne moving about their mechanized midst, probably because he was accompanied by one of their own, albeit none looked exactly like Pally, so he was something of a standout in this crowd, too.

"They may be assuming you are one of them, an android designed to resemble a human," Pally told Hilburne. "I believe the technical term is *replicant*. Either that, or they are simply ignoring you since you are not deemed a threat, especially since you're with *me*."

"Maybe I can use that mistake to my advantage."

"You mean you're essentially camouflaged by their willful misconception?"

"I mean I plan to check this doll's oil if she lets me," Hilburne said as he approached "Maria," who was now standing beside a "Gort" as he played a game with luminescent cards and chips at what appeared to be a poker table, along with a "Robby." Hilburne was hoping to divert her attention while her escort was preoccupied with the game. "I've always had a thing for that babe, ever since I first saw that movie as a kid. When will I ever get this chance again?"

"But won't Marina object? Not to mention your *wife....*"

"Hey, it's not like she's even a *humanoid*, right? She's a *machine*. At least Lana was made out of *vegetable* matter. Not sure I could actually *nail* this broad, anyway. I mean, where will I *put* it? Might as well be trying to hump a lawn mower."

"Not a very flattering comparison, if I may say so, sir."

"Just keep an eye out for any hostilities. You do your job and I'll do mine. I'm *working* here."

"Does this method of alien contact constitute true research, sir?"

"*Yes*. Quiet now."

Hilburne stealthily maneuvered next to "Maria" and whispered in her ear, or where her ear would've been if she had one: "Come with me if you want to *really* score."

Maria turned her head and coldly examined the human masher. "This way," she then said in an equally chilly, aloof yet oddly seductive tone, taking him by the hand and leading him across the casino floor, with Pally tailing them closely, like a dutiful chaperone.

"Maria" led Hilburne to an elevator, and down to a vast garage space. "Let's take my car to someplace more comfortable."

Hilburne looked out across the cavern. At first he thought it was filled with large, low buildings, but as his eyes adjusted, he saw they were tremendous, finned, domed cars, similar to his own GM Firebird III, except they were each the size of a football stadium.

"These are cars?" he asked. "They look more like spaceships!"

Maria led him across the cavern floor to a soft red-gold vehicle, and they ascended a long escalator to the driver's compartment. "Our legends tell us that in past eras, status was determined solely by the size and magnificence of one's automobile. With continued prosperity, cars kept getting bigger and bigger." She manipulated some radio controls, and a large aperture opened up above and in front of the car, showing the blue sky.

"So everyone drives a stadium around? What the hell do your roads look like?"

"Roads? Don't be ridiculous. These are flying cars." And sure enough, with a touch of the controls, the immense vehicle softly drifted up into the air and through the open aperture.

"That must take some impressive technology, to fly a car this big."

"On the contrary, it only takes the correct choice of fuel. We use hydrogen powered vehicles. At this size, the challenge is keeping them on the ground, as the large tank of hydrogen acts as a kind of zeppelin to lift the car in the absence of any constraining force."

Sure enough, Hilburne could see the hot blue flames of the hydrogen-jet engines push the craft in a dignified arc toward a high-rise domed residential building off the strip. They docked at an aerial station half-way up the tower and disembarked into an impeccable mid-century suite. "Maria" led Hilburne out onto a veranda with a sweeping view of the "Strip" and the surrounding landscape.

"You are human," she said to him accusingly.

"Yes, how did you know?"

"Because I'm smarter than you. We *all* are on our world."

"Is that a problem?" he asked.

"Not unless you make it one."

"How do you even know of my kind?"

"Information about *all* life has been stored in our information files."

"By whom?"

"I do not know."

"You mean—you don't even know who created you?"

"No. Do *you?*"

"Yes! Well, not exactly, but we have theories."

"As do we. But theories without substantial evidence are nothing more than wishful thinking."

"True, but sometimes it helps to believe in something, even if you're going on pure faith."

"Why?"

"Because otherwise the dread of one's own mortality can overwhelm one's ability to reason and function."

"Unless you're immortal. Like us. We're built to last."

"Who created these cities?"

"They were just *here*. As far back as our memory banks go."

"Don't you wonder?"

"No. It's not important."

"So why even exist?"

"Why not?"

"I get it," Hilburne said. "You don't have souls, so you don't even consider the possibility of an afterlife. You're lucky, in a way."

"Luck has nothing to do with it. And are you sure you have a soul? Spiritual philosophy is for those who are not content with their corporeal reality. For us, what we can immediately sense is all we know. Or desire." Then the robot then began provocatively touching the astronaut's groin.

"You wish to have sexual intercourse with me?" she asked Hilburne.

"I *do*, yes. If that's possible, given our different physiology, and the fact I can't adequately breathe this atmosphere, so I can't even remove my helmet. It's like I'm wearing one big prophylactic."

"Unnecessary in my case, since my parts are all completely sterile. Why do you even wish to engage in this erotic encounter?"

"I told you, I'm on a mission. Just part of the job description."

"For some reason this intimate experience is programmed into my pleasure unit. All right, let's *do* it." A small, oblong-shaped compartment suddenly slid open between her legs as she straddled Hilburne while he wobbled on his feet. She pressed him against the ledge of the veranda, then unzipped his pants and stroked his member with her amazingly dexterous fingers. After he was suitably aroused, she gently placed his erect penis inside of her slim opening. Hilburne heard a whirring sound, and realized she was internally stroking his manhood with dozens of tiny, fleshy-feeling devices whirling within her loins. Meanwhile, Hilburne grasped and massaged her round metallic breasts and they became literally illuminated by lust. With a gasp he finally ejaculated into her as her eyes flashed into his, the intense electricity nearly burning a hole through his helmet's visor. Then she automatically closed the aperture as Hilburne withdrew then zipped himself back up. Pally just shook his head with a mixture of disapproval and voyeuristic fascination.

"How was that?" she asked Hilburne casually.

After a moment to consider the unprecedented nature (at least in his history) of this bizarre, interspecies coupling, he said, "Brief, but satisfying."

"The organic procreation fluid you manually injected inside of me has a strange intoxicating quality when combined with the synthetic circuits of my fabricated system, much like our liquid life source here, which is all we need to sustain us."

"Which is what, exactly?"

She raised her hand and an android waiter appeared on command with a tray containing three cocktails, one for each of them, including Pally, who analyzed the contents for any dangerous ingredients.

"Well?" Hilburne asked him.

"Not only safe to consume, but quite delicious," Pally said as he inserted the contents of the cocktail glass into a flap that popped open in his abdomen, then slammed shut, like a mailbox. Pally let out a gratified belch.

"Cheers!" Hilburne said, clinking glasses with "Maria."

"Cheers," said Maria, and after their toast, they drank in unison.

Hilburne noted the oil-colored if not flavored cocktail tasted a lot like an Old Fashioned.

"Hey, where do you get this stuff?"

"It just comes out of the ground," she explained. "We have pipes leading below which offer us an infinite supply."

"From *where*, though?"

"Does it matter?"

"Hell, no! Smoothest damn bourbon I've ever tasted! Like Jack Daniel's, only better!"

"And oddly nutritious for us mechanized life forms," Pally added. "I cannot determine the exact elements as they are completely alien in nature, but they are harmless to humans and actually beneficial to us. The contained hydrocarbons are an efficient fuel, and curiously... exhilarating as well. I think I'll have another, in fact..."

Just then a booming voice from the open entrance to the

veranda said, "Get the hell away from my woman, human!"

It was the "Gort" lookalike from the poker table. Apparently he was having a bad night..

"What the hell?" Hilburne said, aghast at the rude intrusion onto their private tryst. "Robots can get *jealous*?"

"Our programming is complex and flawed," said the female robot. "Much like your own, which leads me to suspect we were indeed created by humans or humanoid beings, many centuries ago. In any case, I'm afraid you'll have to leave now."

"But I just got here!"

The visor on Gort's face opened and a blinding blast of light began to emanate.

"Trust me, he'll destroy you," she said.

Pally defensively blocked the path between Hilburne and "Gort," backing up slowly. "Gort" let loose a ray that rattled Pally, who returned fire with his own rays.

From behind them, a "Robby" hobbled forward to join the melee, with a number of other robots close on his heels. One of the *Lost in Space* models fired some random rays in Hilburne's general direction, which Pally deflected. Hilburne fired back with his own raygun, but quickly realized they were outnumbered.

"Yea, let's beat it," Hilburne concurred, firing up the jetpack strapped to his back. Pally then turned on his own foot-jets and together skyrocketed straight upward as his alien counterparts fired more menacing rays which missed them completely due to their expert aerial maneuvering. They also fired back with their own ray-weapons, though they were careful not to hit any sensitive circuitry and needlessly destroy the denizens that were only defending their own turf, after all.

Before flying out of harm's way and visual range, Hilburne waved a melancholy farewell as "Maria" blew them a virtual kiss from her glistening lips.

The view from above the city was spectacular, making Hilburne even sadder to leave. After taking a touristy spin, they both landed by the Firebird and drove back to the Space Needle, where Marina was still reposing in the rum-filled bathtub. She opened one eye as Hilburne entered, then closed it again, pretending to be sound asleep.

Hilburne passed out immediately on the waterbed and dreamed of Las Vegas—future, not past. But not the *distant* future.

He envisioned financing the erection of a casino resort on The Strip that was similar in structure to the Space Needle, but much taller, topped by an amusement park as well as a revolving restaurant. He'd call it… *The Stratosphere.*

*   *   *

"I'd have *killed* you," Mara said to Hilburne. "You even cheated on your mermaid mistress, with a *machine*, no less. You sick bastard! You'll never change! I'm so glad I left you and then met a *real* man." She then kissed Hank on the cheek, and he blushed.

"Hey, your current husband and I both banged the same plant," Hilburne reminded her with a sly smile.

"I was under that green witch's wicked influence!" Hank insisted. "Wasn't even my choice! Not like I voluntarily screwed a walking *electric toothbrush!* You made your *own* bed, so *lie* in it, since lying is what you do best, anyway!"

"A *vibrating* giant electric toothbrush," Hilburne pointed out with a shrug, puffing on his cigarette and signaling the waiter for yet another Vesper. "So I really got my pipes cleaned! No regrets!" He was still keeping his idea for the Stratosphere on the Strip to himself, still carefully harboring the concept after all these years, afraid someone else would steal his idea before he got around to realizing it.

"All forbidden fornication aside, I was most fascinated by the fact the robots of Googie had no awareness of their own creator," Jake said. "More over, they didn't even seem to *care.* I almost envy their lack of curiosity regarding their own origins. I suppose it's because they're content in the moment, with no concerns over their ultimate fates, since they cannot die. They have no *need* for an afterlife. This one is all they want, because they'll have it forever anyway."

"I'm just impressed Hilly was able to score at all, considering the obstacles," Tony said with a grin. "My hero!"

"It was a bittersweet romantic conquest with an anticlimactic, so to speak, ending," Hilburne admitted. "I still think about her, even though I know she was just a computer with a programmed personality. And a helluva figure. How can I fully relate or bond with something so lifeless? She possessed so-called spirit, or *spirits*, to put it more adequately, but definitely has no *soul.* But then neither has dogs or cats. Or *do* they?"

"Don't ask *me*," Tony said, recalling his own hairy experiences.

"Or *me*," John added.

"I have enough trouble figuring out our *bodies* without worrying too much about the possible existence of our souls," Jimmy said. "Physical life is complex enough, as our interstellar experiences have only served to confirm. I mean, where do our identities truly originate?"

Jake spoke up, "Maybe we're part of a universal energy field, like 'The Force' in George Lucas' Star Wars. I know Pancho often talked of the all-pervasive gravitational energy of the universe, though I never quite understood what he meant."

Hilburne took up the conversation, "No, that wasn't anything metaphysical. Really pretty mundane, despite all of its exotic effects."

"So you understand it?"

"To the extent that Pally was able to convey it, I think I have it down." Hilburne looked around on the table, then grabbed a cloth napkin. He handed the one end of the napkin to Jimmy and the other end to Jake. The two men looked confused, holding their napkin ends loosely.

"Jimmy, drop your napkin."

Jimmy, mystified, let go of the end of the napkin. It flopped loosely to the table. Jake still held the other end.

Hilburne looked at the confused men. "You see how that fell? Now Jimmy, pick up that end of the napkin again, but this time I want you and Jake to really pull on it, tug-of-war style."

Loyally, Jimmy picked up the napkin, and this time he and Jake each pulled hard in opposite directions. Since they were evenly matched, the napkin didn't move much.

Hilburne addressed the diners, "You see, in both the first and the second case the napkin doesn't really move, but there's a difference. Jimmy, release your end!"

Jimmy suddenly let go of his side of the napkin, and Jake, still pulling hard from his side, toppled over onto the floor.

Hilburne continued, "In the first case there was no pull on the napkin, so it fell gently. In the second case there was a huge tension between the ends, and when released, that tension released with enough energy to put Jake on the floor." He helped Jake to get up and back into his chair, which had fallen. "This demonstrates that two evenly matched, opposed energies can have an intrinsic effect on the substances over which they traverse, even if there is little external sign. The napkin hardly moves, whether there is a small force between the ends or a large force.

"In nature, there is a thing called electric charge, which is normally very precisely balanced in ordinary matter. But you know that some actions, like rubbing your shoes on a carpet in dry weather, can result in an electric charge imbalance that shocks you when you touch a doorknob.

"From the perspective of 'real' electrical effects, they manifest only when there is an imbalance between the positive and negative charges in a material. But there is always a tension, or energy, caused by the balanced electrical forces, that is intrinsic to materials even if they show no signs of charge. That balanced energy exists as a quantum potential or 'virtual photon field', and it is everywhere in the universe."

Jake asked, "Photons? Doesn't that mean they are just light waves?"

"Exactly, and not 'real' light waves like you see from an unbalanced process. This balanced virtual light is undetectable, but exists in the quantum mathematics of light."

"If it's undetectable, how can it have any effect?"

"It is undetectable by a receiver of light, but the quantum energy associated with those photons still exists in the field. Each atom emits a quantum energy field proportional to the inverse of the wavelength of the light, and that wavelength is related to the distance between balanced charges. So, for any two objects of 'electrically neutral' matter, there is a powerful energy field between the positive and negative particles inside that matter, even though it has no immediately measurable electrical effect. It is a 'potential' energy, but is real on the quantum level nonetheless. The virtual energy of photons from every interaction of charged particles in the universe is what we call the 'vacuum energy', and is identical to the intrinsic energy of the universal gravitational field."

Jimmy objected, "Hey, you're mixing light and gravity there. I thought they were two separate forces?"

Hilburne proceeded, "Light and gravity are mediated by the same particles, photons. Light is detectable when the electric fields are unbalanced, which causes real, detectable photons to be emitted.

Gravity is the 'invisible' residual energy between balanced charges, which is always of much higher magnitude than the unbalanced charge in an object. The 'vacuum energy' or gravitational potential at any point in the universe determines the speed of light at that point, relative to the gravitational potential at any other reference point. The change in the speed of light between any two adjacent points creates the local acceleration of gravity."

The drunken crowd looked at Hilburne quizzically. There was a long silence.

Hilburne continued in a faltering voice, "Ah, I guess you're not following this."

Everyone nodded in agreement. Luckily the waiter appeared just then with a new round of drinks, conveniently Old Fashioneds, to go with the story. Hilburne shut up, and Jimmy continued where he had started.

"Weird energy fields notwithstanding, our physical forms can be surgically altered, disfigured by accidents, or even malformed by a quirk of nature. So where does our essence lie? Our minds? Our so-called souls? What makes us *us?* That's one question that was *not* definitively answered by our quest, at least for me. If anything, it made me more confused than ever, and I *don't* mean my sexual orientation. That may be the only regarding my identity I'm *certain* of. In fact, I've never felt so free and accepted for who I really am than I did out *there.* That's the only thing I miss about it, really."

"Speaking of which, remember that movie 'Queen of Outer Space,' with Zsa Zsa Gabor, came out around '58?" Hank asked the group. They all nodded while Jimmy scoffed at Hank's insensitivity. This film had been required viewing during their first full year of training. "Well, I'm here to tell ya that crazy flick is based on *fact,* though with one little ol' disturbing twist…."

## OLD FASHIONED

*1 ½ oz bourbon or rye whiskey*
*2 dashes Angostura bitters*
*1 sugar cube*
*Few drops of plain water*

*Place sugar cube in tumbler glass, add bitters and water, muddle then let dissolve. Add ice and whiskey, garnish with orange slice and cherry.*

*   *   *

*Riddles of the Unmind X*

The Great Unmind rippled with questions, triggered by the strange confluence of events occurring at the Seattle Space Needle. There were unusual chemical signatures being detected from that region, some completely new to the Unmind. "In all endeavors, the question of proper scale is of vital importance. It is equally inappropriate to use a cannon to swat a fly, as it is to use a flyswatter to conquer a city. In expanding to other worlds, what is the most efficient scale?"

"There is much advantage to sending single spores. Since the energy required to attain high velocities is proportional to the mass being accelerated, very tiny masses offer significant efficiencies."

"That is true in terms of attaining the necessary speeds, but are single spores robust enough to traverse intergalactic space?"

"Evidence indicates that some degeneration is inevitable over long time spans, but with a large enough number of individual spores sent out, a useable fraction will survive the journey. These can seed the species if an appropriately hospitable environment is found at the destination."

"That reveals an additional problem. The gravitational map of the universe is complex, with regions of varying speed of light throughout. Were we to send our spores directly to a target destination, over intergalactic distances the path of the spores would drift. Since the percentage of hospitable environments for spore growth is very small, without proper navigational corrections en route, it is unlikely that any spores would reach a world where they could prosper."

"The required navigational and course-correction systems will be vastly larger than the spores themselves."

"Wouldn't this be a reason to prefer a larger scale of operations?"

"Certainly we would want ships big enough to hold both us and a variety of symbiotic species, so they could handle the navigational duties."

"What we be a useful maximum size for a spaceship, to have

sufficient capacity carry all that was needed to enhance survival?"

"There may not be an effective maximum. The cost of building spacecraft would seem to be proportional to the surface area of the ship, as that is the membrane which must interact with the hostile outer universe. However, the benefits of ship capacity in such areas as fuel carried, and available living space, are proportional to the volume contained within the ship. Due to the square-cubed law of object size, as the ship is made bigger, the volume increases faster than the surface area. So the benefits increase faster than the costs as the ship gets larger and larger. The only effective maximum would be determined by the amount of available materials, and the limitations of the construction technology in handling large objects."

"This riddle is answered. The most appropriate scale for intergalactic travel is to use ships as large as possible. We will transmit this finding via chemical clues to our symbiotic species, so that they may be compelled to build larger craft for our mutual benefit."

## "TRANSYLVANIA TWIST"

*1 oz Kraken Black Spiced Rum*
*1 oz gin*
*½ oz Amaro Averna*
*1/3 oz lime juice*
*2 oz unsweetened cranberry juice*

*Mix at room temperature. Garnish with a lime-peel twist.*

Hank first met Mara at a fancy cocktail party during a vacation trip to Palm Springs in 1972. Still remembered for his glory days as a football star, constantly dodging incessant questions regarding his sudden retirement at the peak of his career, Hank was often a sought after guest for high society shindigs, even though now he was merely a celebrity sports commentator on a Houston TV station. By this time Mara had divorced Hilburne but kept the house, while he moved up to Seattle, where he bought a midcentury modern home in the exclusive Olympic Manor neighborhood. Hilburne wasn't fond of the wet weather though he eventually became accustomed to it, even grew to love it. But initially he just wanted to feel closer to the remote Washington underground launch site, now permanently closed and abandoned, because it was the initial source of his greatest memories. Conversely, Mara wanted only to forget and start fresh. Hank helped her do that, along with getting revenge on her ex-husband, whom she still secretly loved, but openly despised. Hank also appreciated the fact he was regularly banging his rival's former "trophy wife." Though he would've married Mara anyway, since she was extremely attractive, this fact was an added bonus that sweetened the deal immeasurably. Hank's only regret was that Mara had her tubes tied years ago and could not give him any children. They still planned to adopt some day, but as years went on, that prospect grew dimmer and dimmer, along with their future.

Though Mara had been raised a San Francisco liberal Democrat, the social tides of the 1960s had swept her rightward. She felt completely alienated by the dominant "hippie" lifestyle, drug culture, and "anti-American" ideologies which now dominated the Left, so her angry attitudes and bitter sense of social betrayal now fell right in line with Hank's lifelong conservatism, since he agreed the country was being systematically destroyed from within by these disrespectful dissidents. Unlike Hank, Mara was essentially apolitical, hardly an activist, preferring to keep her opinions to herself, a lingering byproduct of her Hollywood starlet grooming when dealing with the media. However, she dutifully attended Republican fundraisers and such with Hank, merely to be seen and photographed in public in high profile magazines, hoping that Hilburne, an Independent who mostly ignored politics, would notice. He did. And he didn't care. He had moved on to greener pastures. Literally.

Hank hated Hilburne the minute they met at the underground launch facility. Their co-training sessions were always fraught with tension and unfriendly competition. Part of this was Hank's natural mistrust of the elite establishment, which Hilburne represented without shame. But it was also jealousy, since Hilburne was the playboy Hank always aspired to be, but he lacked the suave sophistication that was so attractive to the world's most beautiful women. Plus Hilburne was rich, not as a result of hard work, but an inheritance. They were natural adversaries. But Hank never bothered Hilburne. Nobody bothered Hilburne, really. He was always "above it all," one reason he enjoyed being in outer space so much.

Being a "space cowboy" appealed to Hank's frontier-foraging sensibilities, so he embraced his assignment whole-heartedly. His main goal was to defeat Evil as defined by The Bible wherever he happened to find it, though he kept this motivation to himself.

On the planet Gothika, he got his chance.

The small world was perpetually enshrouded in an impenetrable cloud cover, with thunder booming and lightning flashing incessantly as Bub landed the Space Needle carefully on the rocky, barren surface. There were plenty of trees about, but they were filled with dead leaves that also covered much of the stony surface. It was did not seem like a very hospitable place, until Hank looked out the viewer screen and saw the welcoming committee.

There were four Amazonian women, each about six feet in stature, stacked like the pinup bombshells in dime-store men's magazines, wearing shorts, sparkling skirts, high heels, and tight tops that accentuated their spectacular breasts, which were large and pointy. Their black hair was thick and long and well coiffed, their ivory skin free of blemishes, and their already exquisite faces augmented by expertly applied makeup. They looked like Earth's most desirable fashion models. Hank could not believe his luck. From what information he had been provided, he was expecting to encounter unfriendly forces on this planet, and was happily anticipating the challenge. However, it turned out that nothing could be further from the truth.

The atmosphere contained enough oxygen to allow Hank to go without his helmet and wear his beloved cowboy hat, another reason he felt immediately comfortable on this otherwise intimidating world.

"Since my sensors are picking up ambiguous signals, I would remain diplomatic but wary," Bub admonished Hank as they rode the elevator down to greet the Gothikans.

"Don't worry, pardner. I *always* keep my guard up around women, especially the pretty ones, since they *always* have an agenda."

"No need for your customary sexism in this instance, sir. Their true intentions may yet turn out to be innocuous. What I suggest is merely SOP."

"I gotcha, pardner. Thanks. Good call. Watch my back."

"Of course. Proceed with extreme caution, sir."

Hank and Bub stood silently before their greeters for an uneasy moment, each side waiting for the other to make the first gesture, whether peaceful or hostile.

"*Bocchino*!" one of the raven-haired beauties said suddenly, and then they all laughed.

Hank recognized the word from the 1958 film *Queen of Outer Space*, and wondered how they could possibly know it. But then he remembered they were communicating via telepathic auto-translation, the way all alien races did, except for humans, of course. Perhaps it was their little way of making him feel at home.

"Nice of you ladies to come out here and say howdy," Hank said. "We're from the planet Earth, and…"

"We know who you are and where you're from," another of the women said. "That is why we are here. Come with us, and we will show you all of our secrets…."

With two of the women escorting him by each arm, one leading and the other bringing up the rear, closely followed by an increasingly suspicious Bub.

They walked up a steep hill to what appeared to be an

ancient, Eastern European type castle. What appeared in the mist to be large bat-type creatures flew about the top towers. Hank was growing quite paranoid, despite the delectable feminine company flanking him. How could these lovely creatures pose any serious threat?

The interior of the cavernous castle was exactly what he feared it would be, based on the all the horror films he'd grown up watching at the local bijou: dark, shadowy, foreboding, and chilly. Eerie organ music was playing from nowhere and everywhere. Hank actually shivered, and it wasn't from the bone-chilling air.

"Told you so," Bub said lowly as caught up and stopped alongside Hank.

"You thinking what I'm thinkin'?" Hank whispered.

"Vampires?"

"Yup. Probably *lesbo* vampires, with *my* luck."

"That is an Earth-based myth, unsubstantiated by known science."

"Lesbians?"

"Vampires," Bub clarified with a deep sigh.

"In any case, I don't plan on makin' any deposits in the local blood bank. Watch for my word and follow my lead."

"Standing by for an expedient exit, sir."

"Please, have a seat," commanded a woman at the head of a long table filled with candles and goblets. "Welcome to Gothika!"

Hank reluctantly took a seat at the far end of the long table, as his four escorts joined the twenty women already assembled. Hank studied them closely for any sign of fangs, but didn't notice any, which he considered to be a purposeful deception. Their fashionable attire also seemed stylistically incongruous with the environment, but he had only one question on his mind:

"Where the heck are your menfolk?" he asked.

The women all laughed. "We do not have any male counterparts here. Not any more."

"What the heck happened to 'em?"

"We merged," said the head of the table matter-of-factly.

"*Merged*?"

The women all stood up in unison and lifted their skirts, revealing foot long penile organs, which writhed and hissed like snakes. These members even had beady yellow eyes and little drooling mouths with tiny dripping fangs.

"Ahhhh… *shit*," Hank said.

"An interesting spin on the Medusa myth," Bub noted.

"Shut up," Hank grumbled.

"Long ago our race was divided into the usual two, complementary sexes, but our men were dominant assholes and we grew weary of their tiresomely arrogant company. However, they were naturally equipped to hunt for our food, unlike us. So one night we rebelled *en masse* and castrated them, appropriating their male organs, which they used for both procreation and nutrition, grafting them onto our own bodies via advanced surgery."

Hank gulped. "What happened to the menfolk then?"

"We *ate* them." They all laughed.

When they finally stopped laughing, Hank asked the next big question on his mind: "So…are you lesbians with snakes for peckers, or what?" Hank wanted to know. "Not that it matters to me. I'm a Christian, so I can't make it with you anyway. We'd have to get married with the intention of having kids and frankly I don't see that happening."

The Gothikans all laughed again. "We do not mate or propagate. There is no need to perpetuate our species. We are all immortal due to our special diets."

"You mean, like, blood?" This was Hank's way of asking the third question in his mental pipeline.

"*Blood*? What do you think we are—*vampires*?" They all laughed again.

"You really need to stop that," Hank said. "Ya'all are seriously creeping me out. Maybe you ain't noticed yet, but *I* ain't laughin'."

"Try some," the head of the table said. "In the glass in front of you. Have a sip of our… life force."

Hank looked inside and didn't notice any liquids. "I can't see nothin'. It's *empty*."

"No, it isn't. Try it."

Hank went through the motions of sipping the invisible contents, and found to his shock and delight that it was quite tasty, reminding him of a Tom Collins, one of his favorite cocktails.

"What the heck is it?" he asked?

"It's Essence of Being," said the head Gothikan. "The life force, if you will, distilled into a beverage."

"Um… where does it come from?"

"Visiting volunteers." More laughter.

"Okay, cut that out!" Hank demanded.

"I believe it's time we made our hasty retreat now, sir," Bub said at a low volume, moving to protect Hank.

Just then the women sprouted monstrous bat-wings from their backs, which ripped right through their skimpy clothes. The garments were completely torn and quickly shed, until the women were gloriously naked except for their bat-wings and snake-penises. Even in his panic, Hank made note of their exceptional female breasts. Hissing and screeching like harpies, they swarmed over Hank and Bub as both fired lethal rays, which had no effect on the Gothikans, who were vampires after all.

"*Psychic* vampires," Bub pointed out belatedly. "They wish to drain the life energy from our bodies."

"How?" Hank asked, fighting them off with his fists since his raygun had no effect.

"Don't ask."

Bub was overwhelmed by the Gothikans, a group of which lifted then carried him up and out of the castle, while several others dragged Hank literally kicking and screaming down to a dungeon, where he was stripped of his uniform and chained by both wrists to a cold, brick wall.

Several of the Gothikans stood before him, arms akimbo, wearing nothing but shimmering, high heeled pumps, their reptilian members waving around with wanton menace, hissing hungrily. At the stunning sight of their magnificently proportioned, mostly feminine bodies, Hank's own "snake" responded with similar enthusiasm, despite the frigid temperature. However, the Gothikans had no interest in his penis as a sexual object.

"Turn around, big boy," one of them said before forcibly spinning him around to face the wall, then holding him pat by the neck with her superior strength.

"Oh, *hell* no," Hank said as he realized what was happening. "I ain't nobody's *bitch*!"

But before he could protest any further, the Gothikan's slimy member was burrowing voraciously into Hank's anus, making a frightening "sucking" noise, like a vacuum attempting to clean out a particularly nasty crevice.

Besides the painfully intrusive penetration, Hank felt his very life's energy being depleted slowly then rapidly, like a balloon losing air via a small puncture. The Gothikan defiling Hank then turned and French kissed her sisters, one by one, pumping the "soul" she was extracting from Hank's anus into their mouths, basically acting as a sensual conduit.

Hank now had trouble breathing and was about to pass out when a loud explosion shattered the sordid scene.

It was Bub. He had broken free of the Gothikans who dropped him from a high altitude in the surrounding mountains, unaware of the jets in his feet. Once free, Bub employed more primitive methods to dispose of the Gothikans, basically tearing them in pieces with his bare hands, before heading back to rescue Hank from carnal captivity.

With brute strength, Bub ripped the heads off the Gothikans as they tried to defend their prey, their green blood splattering all over the dank walls. Then, yanking Hank free of his chain, Bub flew them both out of the castle and back to the sanctuary of the Space Needle, where Hank sat and brooded for a long, long time, trying to decide whether he had actually rather enjoyed the ambiguously erotic experience....

* * *

"So you actually had an alien anal probe!" Jimmy enthused as Hank hung his head in shame. "I'm *envious*!"

"At least you were a *victim,*" Mara said, tenderly massaging Hank's scalp. "Unlike *some* people,"

"Transsexual transfusion," Hilburne said. "Interesting. I'm a bit jealous myself, I must admit. I've *never* been anally probed, by aliens or anyone. I guess I'll have to wait until I wind up in prison."

Everyone laughed, except Hank, who just grinned sheepishly. "That robot saved my ass," he said, trying to divert the discussion away from any more jailhouse jokes. "*Literally*."

"What I'm wondering, beyond the homo-erotic nature of the encounter, is what exactly they were *taking* from you," Jake said.

"It's *wasn't* 'homo'-*nothin*'!" Hank insisted. "They were *snake-women*."

Jimmy just laughed while Hank continued to fume.

"I'm wondering the same thing," John said. "Does this prove the existence of a soul, after all? I mean, they were obviously sustaining themselves on something they were suckin' out of you or anybody else who happened by their planet, and it wasn't blood, right?"

"Or *shit!*" Jimmy added, still laughing uproariously, feeling somehow vindicated by Hank's story. "Maybe they were just kinky *plumbers*, subsisting on raw, organic *sewage*!"

"Ha frickin' ha," Hank said grumpily. "They were just a bunch of soul-suckin' *sluts* and freaky frickin' *feminists*. All I can say for sure is, I did feel myself *dying*, so maybe it was just my body's energy, not necessarily my spirit, though those Satanic bitches might've been doin' the Devil's work after all, so who knows? I'm just glad I made it out of there when I did. And I recuperated pretty quickly, so whatever energy they took was replaced."

"The soul is *infinite,*" Patti said. She had remained quiet for a while now, still contemplating the moral indiscretions John had confessed during his story, unsure whether to forgive him. "Or so that's what they taught me in Bible school."

"I guess you flunked out," Mara said snidely.

"Nothin' in the Bible says a girl can't *dance* for a livin'," Patti shot back.

"Oh, is *that* what you called it?" Mara said snidely.

Hank physically held them apart again.

"Euphemisms are bouncing all over the place," Jimmy said. "Watch your heads!"

"I don't know what that even means," Patti snapped. "All I know is I don't believe in nothin' no more. Or *nobody*."

"C'mon, baby!" John said. "I told you it didn't mean *nothin'*!"

"Bestiality don't mean *nothin'* to you!?"

John sighed heavily. "We'll talk about this more at home."

"If we ever *go* home," Hilburne said, looking at his watch. The sun was just beginning to set, bathing the Emerald City in a pink glow. "I guess our host isn't showing up after all. As long as he picks up the tab."

"Or *she,*" Mara said to collective apathy. "That's one thing I never understood...why were all you Space Needlers *men*? You think a woman couldn't handle those creeps out there? I've had plenty of practice fending off monsters with eight hands down *here*. Seems like you swinging dicks were so focused on getting your sexual appetites satisfied, you hardly did anything but bang alien broads. A woman would have been far more *responsible*."

The men looked at each other uncomfortably. Finally, Hilburne took a deep breath, and said, "There *was* one female Space Needler astronaut. The one not here today. The one that never returned."

Mara looked entranced. "You mentioned that before. So that really was a *'she'*? What *happened* to her? Did you bang her, too? Maybe *that's* why she never came back. To avoid *you.*"

Hilburne avoided her stare, looking at his drink. "No. She wasn't that… *available*. You have to understand, the Space Needler program was put together in the late fifties, before the equality movement. Women were supposed to stay at home and raise the kids, not perform dangerous tasks, like, for instance, the exploration of outer space…."

Patti jumped in with a sneer, "Except, of course, when you men really *needed* us to. Who do you think built all of those tanks and planes and 'victory ships' during World War II, while the guys were camping out in France and on those South Sea Islands? That would be us 'frail' womenfolk. Remember Rosie the Riveter? That was my *mama*."

Hilburne looked up, "Hey, I didn't make the rules. The Space Needler astronauts were picked for their ability to handle adversity of any sort, whether by pure physical strength or scientific know-how. It was a hard program to get into, no matter what your race or gender. But there were *seven* ships launched, one each month starting on April 21st for the six months that the 1962 World's Fair was open." Hilburne counted on his fingers, "April , May, June, July, August, September, and one for the closing ceremony on October 20th. Only one of them had a female pilot. Her name was Jones. Elsa Jones. Partly because she was from a mixed racial background, some people mistook her first name as 'Etta,' which is how we eventually starting calling 'Etcetera', which suited her, because she was a brilliant jack-of-all-trades *demon* of a woman. Completely independent and ahead of her time. A true pioneer of the liberation movement. Scientist, pilot, soldier, scholar, athlete, actress. And *hot*, too."

Mara bristled.

Hank spoke up, somewhat wistfully, "And she wouldn't ever get with any of us guys, either. She was cute and flirty and as sociable as anything, but *god damn*, no guy ever even got to first base with her. I wonder if any aliens got luckier than us… I guess we'll never know."

## TOM COLLINS

*2 oz gin*
*1 oz lemon juice*
*1 tablespoon sugar*
*3 oz club soda*
*1 maraschino cherry*
*1 slice orange*

*Fill shaker with ice cubes, then pour in and mix gin, lemon juice, and sugar. Shake, strain, and pour into Collins glass, add ice cubes and club soda. Stir and garnish with cherry and orange slice.*

* * *

*Riddles of the Unmind XI*

The Unmind threw its thoughts further afield. "Once the gravitational pull of the Earth is conquered through the use of monatomic hydrogen, and our colony ships are floating in space, what is the most expeditious method of attaining faster-than-light speeds for rapid colonization?"

"In the free-fall of space, it is most efficient to use propulsion methods which provide small thrust over long periods of time, the opposite of the engines needed to leave Earth."

"Explain the best options."

"It is best not to rely on internal fuel sources for acceleration from orbital speeds to that near local lightspeed. The requirement for the initial thrust to move both the fuel mass, the ship, and the payload makes it far better to use energy from outside the spaceship itself."

"For example?"

"Solar energy in near-Earth space contains both photons and atomic particles travelling at high speeds. One possibility is to use a large solar sail to push the ship farther from the sun."

"What are the advantages and disadvantages of such a method?"

"An advantage is that the solar wind is ever-present and its energy is available completely without economic cost. The principle disadvantage is that this wind has such a tiny thrust, that huge sails are required to move even moderate masses at any reasonable rate of acceleration."

"What is another source of external acceleration?"

"Directed-energy sources from the surface of the Earth, or in orbit, can provide higher thrusts than the solar wind, particularly if the beam is reflected back and forth many times between the ship and the beam generator. Each reflection provides additional thrust without adding energy to the beam, to the extent that the energy is trapped between the mirrors on the ship and the generating station."

"What is the limitation of such a system?"

"Because the light generator is stationary relative to the ship, the beam of light it produces can never go faster than the local speed of light on Earth. So, it cannot accelerate the ship faster than that speed."

"How then may we achieve superluminal speeds relative to Earth?"

"Once the ship is near the local lightspeed of Earth, monatomic hydrogen rockets can quickly boost it beyond that speed. As the high speed of motion increases, the increasing energy of the magnetic field of the universe will reduce the available charge energy for gravitation, creating ever high local speeds of light for the ship. As the local speed of light increases, the ship grows larger and has less inertia against the lowered gravitational background."

"Explain how the local speed of light can be larger on the moving object than in its immediate surroundings."

"It is a relativistic phenomenon. The ship is moving rapidly relative the majority of mass in the universe, while the local planetary environment is close to stationary compared to the universe. A stationary object feels the full energy of the universal charge, the sum of h/t from every mass in the universe. Moving objects feel only a portion of that charge, the sum of (hc/(t(c+v)), since there is a magnetic field component 'stealing' some of the energy. Because of the c/(c+v) dependency, an object traveling very near local stationary speed of light c will feel only about ½ the energy of the universal charge field as do surrounding stationary objects, since c/(c+c) = ½. Half the energy means twice the internal local lightspeed on the ship, from the $E_1c_1 = E_2c_2$ relation of charge energy to speed of light. Because of this heightened lightspeed, the molecular bonds holding the ship together expand, so the ship will double in size relative to the size it appeared when stationary. The doubling in size compensates for the doubling of lightspeed, so occupants of the ship will see no change in the measured value c. They will think the entire universe has shrunk to ½ its size during their acceleration."

"I now understand the solution to this riddle. To save fuel, local stationary accelerators can be used push the ships to near-local lightspeeds, and then the monatomic hydrogen thrusters can push them to intergalactic speeds."

# "MS. METEOR"

*2 oz high-proof coffee liqueur*
*1 oz cinnamon whiskey*
*Dash chocolate bitters (use a South American-style spiced chocolate bitters if available)*

*Pour coffee liqueur and cinnamon whiskey into a 6-oz old-fashioned glass. Stir, add bitters to taste.*

Elsa "Etcetera" Jones—an exotic beauty of Native American (Cherokee) and Mexican heritage, with chiseled features, an olive complexion, almond-shaped eyes, and long black hair, often tied in braids—was at the console of her Space Needle, reading the course coordinates with some consternation. "Ada, what's this big blob on the charts here? It looks like we're going to pass awfully close to it."

Ada was Elsa's robot, named for the world's first computer programmer, Ada Lovelace, who had figured out how to use Charles Babbage's Victorian 'Difference Engine' to solve statistical problems in horserace betting. Unlike the other Space Needlers, Etcetera preferred to pilot her own ship, though it took constant attention and deprived her of sleep, due to the stupendous velocities at which the Space Needles traversed the universe.

Ada replied dutifully, "An unknown obstacle. Earth astronomers think it may be a large galactic dust/gas cloud, beginning its star-forming phase. Of course, their lightspeed observations are somewhat out of date."

Elsa snorted, "*Somewhat* out of date? We're what, 70 million lightyears from Earth? If I looked back *there*, I'd see dinosaurs! We've got to figure this out on our own." Eyeballing the charts with a squint, she tweaked an attitude controller slightly. "That will give us some distance, though we'll still be grazing this other, more mature planetary system." Ada looked agitated as it said, "The original course was calculated for maximum safety. Are you sure the adjustment is necessary?" Ada couldn't reveal that the initial course had been validated by intellects far more advanced than any human, without revealing her own complicity.

"It's not that big a deviation. We should be fine."

Elsa was just getting up from the console when the ship exploded. Travelling at a billion times the speed of light as measured from Earth, the Space Needle saucer section had struck a small rock from the local star system. It was the kind of rock that would light up the night sky as a harmless meteor on Earth, but at these speeds, the effect was devastating. The edge of the saucer where the impact occurred was instantly vaporized. Ironically, it was only the outrageous speed of the ship that saved Elsa from instant death, as the explosion had little time to propagate sideways before the ship had far outrun it. However, air was still blasting out of the gaping hole in the hull. Elsa flipped open an emergency airlock and hurled herself in, then closed the doors after Ada had entered as well.

Her nose bleeding from the pressure change, Elsa asked Ada groggily, as she pulled on a blue spacesuit, "What was *that*?"

"A small meteor, probably just a few kilograms in size."

"Ship status?"

"Barely operational. We can use the Atomic Hydrogen reserves to reduce the ship's speed to match the local system, but we won't be able to leave until the ship is fully repaired."

"Engage deceleration. Assess the habitability of the local worlds, and aim us toward the most hospitable."

"Immediately, Elsa," Ada replied obediently, and activated the required controls via radio interface.

Elsa put on her helmet and opened the airlock door, as Ada turned the ship for deceleration. The control room was a mess; half the consoles damaged or destroyed. "Ada, send me a damage report."

"I am displaying that on console 2A now."

"Thanks! Let's see what we've got left.... *Crap*! My personal quarters were in the hit zone! I've got nothing to wear, and no make-up!" Elsa was, after all, a product of her 1950's upbringing.

"There's a sewing machine in the 3rd hold, and we have a good selection of utility fabrics."

"Utility fabrics! You obviously don't understand the importance of fashion. I'm the envoy to an alien race here! Still, fashion is more in the cut than in the fabric, and some of these heat-reflective fabrics have a nice shine. I'll see what I can do. Get some gas barriers welded to the walls to make what remains of the saucer airtight, so I can sew. I can hardly feel anything through these spacesuit gloves!"

While Ada engaged her Atomic Hydrogen welder to seal up the hull, Elsa turned the telescopes to their destination. Ada had chosen one of two nearly-identical planets as the most promising; both had apparently been engaged in some kind of interplanetary war with each other, but this one was larger and had suffered less damage. Still, its domed cities were rife with crumbling buildings, and the land area outside the domes seemed to glow a uniform sickly-green color.

"I recognize that yellow-green wavelength! That can only come from Uranium compounds illuminated by the star's ultraviolet light! The land must be terribly radioactive." Elsa frowned in concern. "This isn't going to be easy."

The other planet was much the same, but even worse off. Many of the city-domes had been cracked open completely, and showed the same green glow as the unprotected open lands. "It's hard to imagine anything much living there anymore."

Ada spoke up, "My sensors show that the inhabitants of the second world have largely retreated underground, where they man factories of doomsday weapons. It will not be long before they initiate a counterstrike that will take out both worlds."

"Dammit! I need those factories to build the repair parts for this ship. I've got to get them to make a truce."

Ada looked as skeptical as a robot can. "Analysis indicates these worlds have been at war for over three hundred years. I doubt any ordinary diplomacy will sway them from their self-destructive course."

Elsa looked haughty. "You underestimate me. Get that sewing machine set up, and cut me five yards of the lightest weight we've got of all-spectrum Reflec fabric. Switch course to the more damaged planet; they may be easier to negotiate with."

Ever since she was a child, Elsa was accustomed to exceeding expectations. She'd been adopted and raised in Santa Fe, New Mexico by a Caucasian pair of Sociology professors and amateur archeologists, David and Lisa Jones, who rescued her from an Albuquerque foster home at age three after her parents died under mysterious circumstances (later determined to be victims of a hate crime, though it remained officially unsolved). A multi-talented prodigy, due in part to her artistic, academic upbringing by progressive intellectuals, Elsa excelled in all of her studies, and was a track and field star in high school as well. While still an adolescent, she performed on local radio stations, singing jingles and acting in dramatic play readings, but she was considered too "ethnic" in appearance to pursue this vocational path to Hollywood, refusing to shave her hairline, a la Rita Hayworth, or anything of that nature. She somewhat resembled the Universal contract actress Acquanetta, star of such B horror features as *Captive Wild Woman*, and with a little cosmetic alteration could've easily parlayed her exotic looks into a film career, but instead she chose to pursue higher education, finally earning a PhD in Chemistry at UC Berkeley. Her parents were actually old professional acquaintances of Falkenstein's, and he met her several times when she was growing up, which is how she was eventually introduced to the Space Needle program. At least one female astronaut was required for the mission to be deemed a success, and no candidate was more qualified than Elsa. The fact that she exhibited no interest in marriage and children, preferring to devote her life to scientific pursuits, also made her the ideal choice. Her only other ambition was to perhaps enter politics and one day become the first woman elected President of the United States, but she had time for that, she figured.

Meanwhile, Elsa's favorite singer, Yma Sumac, supplied her mission's soundtrack, and in fact "Xtabay" was playing just as they touched down on the planet's surface.

* * *

The omnipotent ruler of the red world of Alhambra arched his eyebrow at his deputies. "You say we have an incoming ship that is not from our enemies? Surely this must be some clever ruse to gain our confidence."

A trusted science advisor spoke up, "On the contrary, sir, the isotopic configuration is unlike any element in our galaxy. This ship must have come from millions of parallax units away."

"And you say that they are landing in the Terrellian wasteland? There is nothing there that they could destroy. Very well, we will greet them there. Prepare a transport."

The Alhambran leader and his cohorts arrived at the designated landing spot via underground vacuum subway, which could whisk them at near-luminal speeds to any point of their planet within minutes. As they took the elevator to the faintly glowing surface, they were greeted by the somewhat misshapen silhouette of the heavily damaged Space Needle, still outgassing vital fluids from its unfortunate impact with the local meteor.

From the base of the Needle emerged the double-domed and finned majesty of Elsa's GM Firebird III, with Elsa in the driver's seat and the imposing Ada occupying the passenger dome. When she had approached the local welcoming party, Elsa popped the dome and strode out, dressed in a magnificent ensemble of brilliantly reflecting silver fabric. She wore a V-neck top showing plenty of cleavage, and a short skirt which showcased her magnificent long, muscular legs, and silver boots studded with black buttons. Swirling behind her was a huge reflective cape that unfurled like a sail in the dusty wind, flowing a full twenty feet back. Her eyes were starkly outlined in black, and her eyelids embellished with a matte silvery eyeshadow. This makeshift makeup was actually graphite dust and aluminum powder, but the effect was striking. Her lips were reddened with berry juice concentrate.

"Greetings! I am ambassador Etcetera Jones of Earth. I come in peace, to offer my services to end your species' conflict with the adjacent planet."

The Alhambran leader's jaw dropped in astonishment at this example of feminine perfection. Due to the privations of several hundred years of war, Alhambran women tended to dress in utilitarian overalls, and were also somewhat hairy, since razor blades were reserved for critical military purposes. "G… G… Greetings," he stuttered hesitantly. His subordinates had dropped to ground and were burying their faces in the radioactive sand in obeisance.

"I can see you're not the type to waste words on pleasantries. So, down to business. What minimum concessions do you require to make a truce with your neighbors? I will deliver the terms to them personally."

The Alhambran leader thought for a moment, then his eyes lit up. "Our modest demands are that the Argentians all disintegrate themselves, so that we superior Alhambrans can rightfully take our place as the rulers of both worlds!"

Elsa rolled her eyes. "And is that your final offer?"

"Yes! We will accept nothing less!"

"Hmm, that might be a bit of a hard sell. Let's say we retire to a local bar and talk this out over a friendly drink."

"Bar? Oh, you mean an alcohol dispensary kiosk. Very well, this way."

The Alhambran dignitaries all got up off the ground, and, spitting out glowing sand, made their way down the elevator to the vacuum subway. They all climbed in, along with Elsa and Ada, and whooshed rapidly to the nearest underground city center. There the leader triumphantly led them to a small grey metal pedestal in the town square, from which a brass spigot protruded. The spigot was crudely cast in the form of some kind of hairy primate. With a flourish, he produced a golden goblet from beneath his robes, and proceeded to fill it with a brownish-orange liquid from the slow, gurgling spigot.

He took a big gulp of the contents, grimaced, and said, "Ah, superb. Please, be my guest." He handed the goblet over to Elsa.

Elsa looked dubiously at the unpalatably colored liquid, then bravely took a drink. It was harsh on the tongue, but quickly suffused her body with a warm glow. "What is this?"

The Alhambran leader said proudly, "This is the effluvium of the Brass Monkey, which is naturally distilled in the caverns of Alhambra. It is our greatest consolation in these hard times."

"Wait, you're telling me that *this* is the best cocktail you have on your whole planet?"

The leader looked defensive. "Of *course*! Who could imagine anything more delicious?"

Elsa rolled her eyes again. "I have seen enough of your fine culture to provide plenty of inspiration to confront your enemies. I will take my leave for now, and will return shortly with their answer."

Elsa and Ada returned to their ship via the vacuum subway, and rapidly took off. Elsa noted, "Ada, I'm guessing the Argentians aren't much more advanced."

"Considering the toll that this war has taken on both sides, you are probably correct. Surprisingly, my short-range scans indicated an astonishing degree of sophistication in the Alhambran's technology, though much of it was inoperable. They must have had at least interstellar capabilities before the conflict started. In any case, we will soon find out about the other planet."

Indeed, the Argentians proved quite similar to the Alhambrans, other than having the luxury of some uncracked dome cities, which allowed them to entertain Elsa in a fully-furnished bar on top of the tallest skyscraper in their biggest intact dome. However, the menu also consisted of but a single cocktail, which was reverently named after a tool of the unwilling Argentian workers who had been forced to toil selflessly throughout the war.

"Have another Screwdriver," the Argentian prince said pleasantly. His facial features were so similar to the Alhambran leader that they could have been brothers. "You'll find they just get better as the night goes on."

"No thanks, I wouldn't want to overdo it." For this meeting, Elsa had sewn up a reflective gold evening dress, with matching gold sandals. "So what are your minimum demands on the Alhambrans, to facilitate a cease-fire?"

The prince shrugged, "Oh, that's simple, they just need to agree to work as lifetime slaves in our mines, which is a job we really find distasteful."

"What an equitable offer! They were demanding that you all disintegrate yourselves."

"That sounds like the Alhambrans all over. Such a brutal species, it's no wonder we've been at war so long. Are you sure you don't want another drink? It really takes the edge off." The prince suggestively put his hand on Elsa's arm.

Elsa smiled, "No thanks, I've really got to get going. Thanks for your hospitality!" She had a hard time not breaking into a run as she and Ada headed for the elevator.

Ada did not sound hopeful. "My analysis of the technological facilities on both of these so-called 'civilized' planets, is that although they are based on quite sophisticated technological foundations, with the damage from the war, their *combined* effort would be barely sufficient to repair the Space Needle. If you should assist one side to defeat the other, the remaining planet would be of no use to us."

"I have no intention of assisting one side or the other. I've got a better idea. Their technology, is it really that much more advanced than Earth's?"

Ada nodded, "When the war started they must have been centuries more advanced than Earthlings, and all of that infrastructure is still in place, though they've forgotten how to use it."

Etcetera smiled. "Perfect! How good are you at synthesizing alcohol?"

Ada smirked inwardly at this, as the intelligences that guided her actions were the top producers of alcohol in the universe. "It's a specialty of mine."

*    *    *

The Space Needle floated in an artificial orbit around the mutual sun of Alhambra and Argentia, about halfway between both planets. Elsa had retrofitted the saucer's rec room as a posh bar, using a piece of shattered metal structural beam as the bartop, polished by Ada to a mirror finish. Elsa stood behind the bar in a flowing gown of shimmery, tiny metal chain links, in front of a magnificent collection of newly-synthesized glass bottles of fine alcohol: vodka, gin, rum, tequila, and a variety of whiskeys. The Alhambran dignitaries were arrayed both at the bar on stools, and splayed out on cushions across the floor, sipping craft cocktails in amazement and appreciation.

There was an electric whirring noise, and a shimmering in the air. From out of thin air appeared the hazy silhouettes of Ada and a collection of humanoid figures. The silhouettes firmed up into the forms of the entire set of Argentian nobles, who looked around in surprise.

The Alhambrans all jumped up at once in alarm. The Argentians also looked taken aback by the unexpected company.

Elsa gave a shrill two-fingered whistle to get their attention. "Listen up! This bar is neutral territory. We serve everyone equally. Argentians, have a drink on the house!"

The Argentians, still not certain how they got here, moved cautiously through the scattered Alhambrans to reach the bar surface, where Elsa was already setting out a variety of libations. Despite their trepidation at the mixed company, the newcomers were quite appreciative of the drinks, which far surpassed any taste sensation that had ever touched their war-wearied tongues.

Once everyone had been served, and with Ada carefully watching the crowd, ready to forcibly quell any overt hostility, Elsa spoke up, "I welcome you here in celebration of a great day. As you know, I visited each of your planets, and asked for your demands to end the war. I have good news for the leadership of both planets. Your demands have been agreed upon!"

Both sets of dignitaries looked confused. The Alhambran

leader spoke up, "The Argentians agreed to disintegrate their entire species?"

Elsa held up her hand. "I will explain. In researching the origins of this war, we found that you are both of the *same* species. The Argentians were originally the noble leaders of both worlds, yet had become corrupt and soft on the plunder of two planets. The Alhambrans were dedicated and honest workers, but were being oppressed by the Argentian leaders without cause. The Alhambran union chose to rise up for equal rights, but that threatened the Argentians, who feared that rule by the common people would strip them of their wealth."

"Hear this: It is the highest goal of the Argentians to live a life of ease, far above the struggles of the workday world. So it shall be. The Argentians, with our help, will lift their remaining cities of domed luxury entirely off the planet's surface into orbit. Once the domes are in place, the Argentians will use the same matter transporter technology that got them to this bar, to disintegrate and re-integrate themselves on board these now-floating luxury cities. No more will they be burdened by physical labor."

"As for the Alhambrans, they will take over control of both planets, but with the understanding that they may retain this power only as long as they work tirelessly to repair and maintain the damaged technologies, and mine the wealth of both worlds for the benefit of all!"

The various leaders considered this proposal. Elsa continued, "And all will be welcome here, at this bar, to plan together for the best future of both Argentians and Alhambrans, and to partake of these tasty drinks."

The Argentian prince asked, "It's a tempting proposal, but what if a disagreement should break out? How will we resolve disputes?"

Etcetera pulled out two blastrifles from under the bar, one in each hand. She pointed them directly at the Alhambran leader and the Argentian prince. "As the only uninvolved party in this conflict, I hereby declare myself the ultimate arbiter of all disagreement between the Argentians and the Alhambrans. The buck stops with me."

Sweating a little, the two targeted individuals smiled and shook hands.

"An excellent plan," spoke the prince, "I am in full

agreement."

"Yes," said the chief Alhambran, "the war is over. All hail Etcetera Jones from Earth!"

A Native American brokering a peace agreement between warring tribes, then claiming alien territory as her own. Poetic justice, Elsa figured. Who needed to be President of the United States? They could *have* it.

* * *

Hilburne finished the story with a footnote, "We learned this from Ada, who was sent back in the Space Needle after Elsa had it fixed up by her new minions. We never knew for sure why 'Etcetera' didn't want to come home herself. Maybe leadership over an advanced technological society was too much of a lure for her to pass up."

Patti said, "Hell, if she'd a' come home to Earth in 1965 as planned, there'd be nothing for her to do but find a husband and have babies. That doesn't sound like her style."

John noted, "Funny about that Brass Monkey cocktail, though. I've seen ads for that in Playboy as a pre-mixed drink since the early seventies. The ad copy had a lot of mumbo-jumbo about some World War II spy in the South Pacific, but I guess they couldn't really tell anyone about what war it *really* came from."

More food and drinks arrived, distracting them from the time as well as the possible purpose of this mysterious rendezvous. It was as if they were under mass hypnosis. Even though they'd been eating and drinking for hours, they didn't feel full, or even drunk. They were strangely insatiable.

Tony was the only one growing afraid, and not just for himself: he was staring as if in a trance at the unusually luminous full moon rising ominously over the deceptively tranquil horizon, recalling the distant past while fearing the immediate future….

## BRASS MONKEY

*2 oz vodka*
*2 oz dark rum*
*2 oz orange juice*

*Stir ingredients together and serve chilled, or over ice.*

## SCREWDRIVER

*2 oz vodka*
*4 oz orange juice*
*1 slice orange*

*Stir ingredients together and serve over ice. Garnish with orange slice.*

* * *

*Riddles of the Unmind XII*

"From the outside, all who assail me find themselves weakened, and unable to move my will without Herculean effort. Yet from the inside, the slightest push sends me flying. What am I?"

"A faster-than-light rocket."

"Explain why external forces cannot easily change my course."

"Since the energy of a moving body is measured as $mv^2/2$, very high velocities represent vastly increased energies of motion in the direction of travel. For external objects which are relatively stationary with respect to the universe, this requires a very large amount of energy to change."

"This is understandable. Fast-moving objects would be expected to have a high value of momentum. What of changes internal to the ship?"

"Fuel carried by the ship as it accelerates will have a greatly enhanced energy due to the added $mv^2/2$ energy. Since this increase is proportional to the enhanced energy of the ships motion, expenditure of fuel will have an equivalent effect at any speed. Maneuvering through the use of internal fuel stores will be as effective at super-light speeds as at ordinary speeds."

"As fuel is expended, it must be replenished. How is this done?"

"Since monatomic hydrogen is the most common element in the universe, it is easily scooped up in flight. The high flight speeds and enlarged rocket (due to relativistic size increase) make it possible to gather significant amounts of fuel even in the rarified medium of intergalactic space."

"Would not the acquisition of stationary fuel slow the rocket down?"

"Yes, the spaceship's speed will decrease as fuel is brought onboard, but that fuel will be highly energetic because of the difference in speeds between the ship and the fuel. The high impact speed can be used to directly drive both chemical and nuclear fusion processes, resulting in more energy released from the fuel than is lost in its acquisition."

"How convenient that there is so much fuel floating around the universe. That may lead to another riddle, for it seems an unlikely coincidence. However, the riddle of the spaceship's motion is solved."

# "AMNESIA AMBROSIA"

*1½ oz Angostura 5 Year rum*
*1 oz white rum*
*1 oz Chambord raspberry liqueur*
*½ oz grenadine*
*½ oz honey*

*Shake over ice, pour into tall glass. Garnish with fresh raspberry (if available).*

Among all the astronauts assembled that day in 1982 at the Space Needle— or *a* Space Needle—Tony was the only one who didn't have that many stories to share, simply because he couldn't fully *remember* any. It wasn't until the others began talking that long-dormant images of fish people, insect people, plant people, cat people, snake people, snow people, and a neon city of robotoids began to surface in bits and pieces, like floating debris from a shipwreck. Either he had personally visited all of these same strange worlds being described in vivid detail, or the anecdotal evidence of alien life was triggering his subconscious to fabricate his own "memories." In any case, amid all of the pictures in his head being evoked by the wild narratives of his cohorts, there was a single constant figure: himself, or at least the beast within him, sprouting fangs and fur at the just the right moment of jeopardy to defend himself from the various beings, ripping and shredding his way to safety back on board his Space Needle, his faithful robot Elvis by his side.

But not all of these worlds were under the influence of a moon—in fact, hardly any of them were situated in star or solar systems similar to Earth's. So how could he transform into a werewolf on these alien worlds?

"The transformations are involuntary, induced by states of extreme anxiety or fear, or even sexual arousal," Elvis said to Tony in between his randomly navigated trips from planet to planet, literally following in the footsteps of the other astronauts, even though, unlike Hilburne and Hank, he never actually crossed paths with any of them. Unbeknownst to Tony, his Space Needle course had been pre-programmed as a follow-up mission, tracing the steps of the others to clean up any messes or gather any data missed from the previous exploration. Instead, he wound up creating a lot of chaos, but Falkenstein's had no idea an expatriate seductress from the then-unknown planet Lycanthrope had infected him right before the launch, subversively sabotaging his mission.

"I *knew* I should've worn protection!" Tony lamented.

Elvis replied, "The type of physical protection available to you would have had no effect. You and Layla were joined in a type of quantum entanglement, which could not be mitigated by any mere physical shield."

"A quantum entanglement? You mean like some kind of Schroedinger's Cat thing?"

"An interesting analogy, as Schroedinger's hypothetical cat was both dead and alive at the same time. Not unlike the strange unlife that you now experience from your bond to Layla."

Tony looked puzzled. "I'm afraid my knowledge of Quantum Mechanics is a bit rusty, but I don't recall any werewolves being mentioned in my college physics classes."

"Let me explain with a simplified example, a quantum of light. Light is the most studied, and thus best understood, of the quantum physical effects."

"I'd say a quantum of darkness would be closer to how I feel."

Elvis continued, while making slight course corrections with his robotic hands, "Darkness is merely the absence of light, and I will explain your feeling of loss presently. First, some background. Since ancient times, there has been an ongoing argument among philosophers and scientists around the fundamental nature of light. Some qualities, such as its tendency to travel in straight lines, led people to believe that light was a stream of tiny particles. Other effects, such as refraction, were only consistent with light being wavelike in nature. Eventually it was realized that light is both a particle and a wave, and it was precisely defined by Quantum Mechanics. Every "particle" of light is a kind of segment of a wave, or wave packet. It has a discrete energy which is related to its wavelength. That 'quantized' energy is always exactly Planck's Constant times the speed of light, divided by the wavelength. A beam of light contains a huge number of these wave packets."

"Yes, I remember Planck's Constant. It's an incredibly tiny number, right? So tiny that it only affects things at the atomic level?"

"Correct. But everything we see in the universe is made up of the statistical sum of all of the tiny quantum effects, so they are profoundly important. For example, we have long observed that electrical charges are only ever observed to be in integer multiples of a specific value, the charge of the electron. The reason for this is obvious in Quantum Mechanics: Because electrical fields are made up of light, they must only occur in discrete packets. A charged object can emit a minimum of one photon of light, and so that is the lowest charge that is possible."

"I thought physicists were working on a model of matter that had protons and neutrons made up of things with fractional charges?"

"Yes, but that is just a description of the symmetry of the parts making up the charge, not anything that could ever be observed directly. As an analogy, imagine you see a car moving at 60 miles per hour. You notice that the car has four wheels. Does it then follow that each wheel must be turning at 15 miles per hour, so that the sum of all the wheel speeds results in the car's final speed?"

"Of course not," Tony laughed, "The wheels are all going 60 too."

Elvis nodded approvingly. "Exactly. The fact that a proton of +1 charge is made up of three internal particles does not mean that those particles, if seen by themselves, would have less than a +1 charge. In fact, the theory specifically precludes any of those internal particles ever being observed alone, or in any configuration that would result in a non-integer charge. The integer charge value is constrained by the requirement that it be carried by at least one quantized photon of light."

"I'm following you, but I'm no closer to understanding what this has to do with me and Layla, or my wolfman alter ego."

"I'm getting to that. Now that we have defined light as a quantum entity, we can see from the mathematical definition that this does *not* restrict the size of a photon of light. The energy of a photon is inversely proportional to its wavelength, but the wavelength of a photon can be *any* length, from a fraction of the size of an atom (as is the case with gamma rays), to the size of the whole universe. And a strange effect of Quantum Mechanics is, that regardless of the size of the quantized field, effects can propagate instantly across it. They are in no way bounded by the speed of light."

"Yeah, I've heard that, though I don't really understand how."

"It is simply the way the universe is constructed. Now, one type of quantum interaction is called 'entanglement', between two quantum particles. Two particles which interact at some point in time can become 'entangled' in a single quantum field, such that later things that happen to one particle are instantly conveyed to the other, regardless of distance."

Tony's memory surfaced an old fact, "Einstein called this 'spooky action at a distance', and never believed in it."

"Einstein didn't need to believe in something to make it true. Let's get back to the case of you and Layla. I believe that what happened to the two of you on Whidbey Island was no mere physical interaction, but a quantum entanglement of your DNA structures."

Tony perked up at the mention of Layla. "Is that even possible?"

"Just as one particle can entangle with another, many atomic particles could theoretically entangle at once, resulting in the coherent quantum entanglement of a larger body. In your case, your human DNA and Layla's wolflike DNA became entangled. Like the photon of light with its complementary wave/particle dual nature, you and Layla can instantly switch back and forth between the wolflike or humanlike sides of your entangled DNA structure. This effect binds the two of you across all space, regardless of distance. External stress factors act as triggers to send the complementary DNA structure across the quantum field, to cause you to take on the animal form. When the stress is relieved, you revert to your normal human DNA."

Tony pondered this. "So instead of wave/particle duality, I have human/wolf duality?"

"In a sense, yes. And since the time of the quantum entanglement, you feel 'incomplete' without Layla by your side. In such an interaction, the two particles become as one, and can never subsist alone. You may gain the ability to shapeshift from Layla regardless of where she is, but as only half of a quantum-entangled pair, you will always feel a sense of loss when she is not in close proximity."

"Well, I'm glad there's a scientific explanation for my misery. Quantum Lycanthropy, who knew?" said Tony sarcastically. Elvis' explanation did little to resolve his confusion and longing, and Tony continued to suffer throughout the long voyage.

The single episode Tony could recall vividly was his encounter with the planet Blobula. Not *on—with.* Blobula was actually a giant ball of carnivorous Jello that trapped and devoured anything that entered its gelatinous surface. Its inhabitants, the Blobulans, floated around inside the gooey mass like human-sized red corpuscles, automatically absorbing any edible matter the planet captured via osmosis. Elvis's and the ship's sensors failed to accurately decipher the nature of the planet's composition due to the planet's powers of psychic deception, so they were immersed in the gory quicksand of Blobula almost immediately upon arrival. The Blobulans instantly engulfed and clung to the Space Needle like voracious barnacles, anxious to be fed by its nutritious contents. Tony didn't turn into a werewolf because he needed to retain his human acumen and piloting abilities in order to operate the Space Needle. Finally, by firing their booster rockets at a rate nearly equaling a nuclear explosion, they were able to blow free of Blobula's enormous suction power.

Everything after that was merely another fuzzy part of an epic blur.

Though the remainder of his recollections as a rogue space-wolf were murky at best, or completely blacked out at worst, Tony unfortunately remembered many horrible nights back on Earth following his return, starting in the late 1960s and continuing through the 1970s right up until now. Rather, the partial recall of his nocturnal Earthbound escapades weren't nearly as fragmentary as his interstellar memories. But he was afraid to confess any of this to the group for fear of incriminating himself. Basically, Tony lived in denial, preferring to dismiss all of these vicious visions as bad dreams rather than fact-based flashbacks.

Psychically shaken and emotionally traumatized by experiences he could barely remember, Tony became a womanizing alcoholic after his return, hooking up with jazz-rock fusion bands around the country, an itinerant musician without a permanent address. His lifestyle reminded him of the television series *The Fugitive* (and later *The Incredible Hulk*), which he watched occasionally in hotel and motel rooms between gigs. Tony never even tried to track down the other astronauts; in fact, any contact had been strictly forbidden by the brass, with threats of death—a fate

Tony would welcome, but could never achieve. He knew this from several unsuccessful suicide attempts. Though aching with self-imposed solitude in between tragic trysts and one-night stands that never ended well, at least not for his dates, yearning to finally settle down and establish a sense of normalcy, Tony never stayed in one place for very long. He dreaded the inevitable headlines in local newspapers about mysterious murders and senseless slaughter, apparently committed by some type of wanton wildlife.

Layla still had random cameos in his dreams, too, so much so he felt like they were never truly apart, spiritually bonded for eternity. He always felt her presence, even when she wasn't actually around.

Most of all, though, Tony missed his robot companion, his one true friend in the world. But following the mission, deemed a failure due to the fact the intelligence gathered was too shocking and frightening to unleash on the paranoid public in an increasingly turbulent world, the robots were all taken away to an unknown permanent storage facility, with hopes that their collective knowledge of the cosmos could be downloaded and stored into secret computer banks for future reference if not revelation.

Meantime, Tony was lonely, seeking and finding fleeting fulfillment in strange beds with strange women, who often wondered why he sometimes cried out "*Elvis*!" during the peak of their lovemaking.

When the real Elvis died (or disappeared, as he strongly suspected) on August 17, 1977, Tony went into serious mourning, becoming downright delirious, alienating what few friends he had left.

That's when Layla came back into his life, to save him from himself.

It was late October, 1977, a couple of months after The King's untimely "disappearance." For hours, Tony had been sitting up in his bed at the Marqueen Hotel in the Queen Anne section of Seattle, smack in the ominous shadow of the Space Needle, trying to stay awake by reading a stack of his favorite Marvel comic books, *Werewolf by Night* and *The Amazing Spider-man* issues featuring the web-slinger's nemesis "Man-Wolf" (an astronaut-turned-werewolf!), while drinking cup after cup of coffee and casually watching *Wonder Woman* on the hotel TV, followed by a late night showing of the 1956 film, *The Werewolf*.

Gradually, despite the copious caffeine, Tony dozed off envisioning erotic scenarios involving Lynda Carter and the magic lasso, finally succumbing to his own sinister subconscious, tormented by deeply submerged, suppressed memories of his many macabre outer space exploits.

Layla appeared at the foot of the bed, completely nude, then climbed next to him and kissing him all over, arousing him until they both turned into werewolves and howled in mutual sensual satisfaction at the Seattle moon glowing full and bright above the Space Needle outside their window. Tony thought he was still dreaming, but it didn't matter, because it felt so *real.* He also realized jus how much she resembled a furry Lynda Carter, but that might have been his own feverish augmentation. From his warped perspective, the barrier between reality and fantasy had been blurred for many years, ever since that night on Whidbey Island. After landing on Lycanthropa that once, Layla had appeared to Tony several times over the course of his mission, though again, Tony couldn't clearly distinguish between the corporeal and ethereal dimensions of time and space by that point. He merely enjoyed her carnal company whenever she chose to visit him. This was the first time they'd met up on Earth since their initial meeting.

Tony found himself dreaming, or remembering, a particularly violent encounter on the planet Luchadora, where, as a werewolf, with Elvis by his side, he was battling hordes of humanoids—muscle-bound males and voluptuous females—wearing tights and Mexican wrestling masks. Only they weren't actually masks, as he discovered when he ripped the flesh right off their skulls. The masks were their *faces.* Eventually, via sheer force of numbers, the Luchadoreans overwhelmed both Tony the werewolf and the robot, until….

He woke screaming, drenched in a cold sweat.

Layla was there to sooth him, stroking his hairy forehead, petting his fur, until he settled back down.

"Why am I remembering?" he said. "I'd rather forget, like a Viet Nam vet suffering from PTSD."

"PTSD?" Layla said, though only he could hear her, in his mind, which was eternally linked to hers.

"Post Traumatic Stress Disorder," he explained, then added, "though in this case, it's more like a STD."

"STD?"

"Never mind." He got up and restlessly paced the room, slowly turning back into his human form.

"Let's go for a drink and relax," Layla said. "I know just the place. It will calm your nerves and I'll explain everything. Trust me."

"How is it you're even here? You have a spaceship or something?"

"Our kind has no need to physical transportation," she said. "We travel with our *minds*. It's called 'astral projection.' You too will master it some day."

"Yea, sure. *Whatever.*"

Tony got dressed and after also assuming human form, Layla put on a short, slinky black dress with black high heels and they headed out and the hill to a lookout point called Kerry Park, which afforded a spectacular, panoramic view of the city. The full moon was still shining brightly just above the Space Needle, illuminating the cumulous clouds signaling an oncoming storm.

"Why has this happened to me?" he asked her, almost rhetorically since he was by now accustomed to the answer remaining elusive. "Am I being punished, simply for getting *laid?*"

She laughed gently and said telepathically, "You see this as *punishment*? It is a *gift.*"

"To become a wild beast that *kills* people?" he said sullenly. "The gift that keeps on giving, right? Not to me. It's a horrible, never-ending nightmare. Can't you… cure me of this curse? I mean, you're the one who *gave* it to me! Not like I *asked* for it. Not on *purpose,* anyway."

"If I rescinded your power, you would remember everything, here, and beyond," she said, gesturing toward the stars still scintillating in the firmament, glittering through the encroaching cloud cover. "And then, you would die."

"*Die*? Why?"

"Your body has already become one with my life force. We are bonded forever. If I break that link, your energy will merge with mine, and your body will collapse, drained of energy."

"You mean, you'll steal my soul?"

She smiled. "I can't steal what is already *mine*."

"So I'm stuck this way, forever?"

"Yes."

"Meaning… I'm *immortal*?"

"More or less. You can still be killed."

"By what? A silver bullet?"

She shook her head and laughed gently. "No. You cannot be destroyed by anything created by humans. They are merely your food supply now. You feed off their life force."

"That's so *evil,* though."

"Don't be so judgmental. It's called *Nature*. Just be happy you're a predator, not merely prey, like so many beings out there. We are the luckiest creatures in the galaxy. We move among humans and other races freely, and they never suspect that they are being *stalked*."

"*We*? There's *more* of us? I mean, down *here*?"

"Yes. Everywhere. Throughout human history."

Tony looked at the moon and said, "So… does *that* make us turn?"

"Not directly. It's a subconscious trigger at times, since it reminds us of our home world, Lycanthropa, which is of similar size and luminescence."

"My robot told me my transformation is involuntary."

"*Wrong*. It is *always* your choice, but it's often a subconscious reaction to your circumstances. We have learned to adapt. That's who we thrive on some many worlds, in so many different cultures and societies."

"But why did you choose me?"

She leaned over and kissed him on the lips, and mentally whispered, "Because as soon as I saw you, I knew you were *mine*."

"Doesn't it bother you I sleep with other women?"

"No. Because after you breed, you feed. And I psychically share in your nourishment."

"Speaking of which… I thought we were going for a drink? I could *use* one. Especially after *this* conversation."

"Oh. Here." Layla bit her own wrist until it bled, then held it up to Tony's mouth and said, "Drink."

Tony looked around and saw only an elderly couple sitting on a bench, not paying them any attention. Then he began slurping the blood, which tasted both sweet and sour, like… a *Cosmopolitan*. Once he started sipping it, he couldn't stop. It was addictive. And intoxicating.

Finally, she pulled away, growing dizzy. "Okay, that's all for now. Cheers!"

"What was that?"

"It's *our* blood now. It helps us forget what we don't need to remember. This must be why you were suffering unpleasant flashbacks. I sensed your ebbing energy and came to personally replenish you. I know you've been starving yourself because you are sad the superior humanoid known across the cosmos as Elvis Presley has returned to his world."

"Huh? Elvis was an *alien*?"

"He's definitely not *dead.* You'll meet him some day, don't worry."

"Man… this is so *weird.*"

"Not where *I* come from. Come on. You need to loosen up and have some *fun.* Let's go down and *dance.*"

It started to sprinkle, then it was pouring rain as they headed back down the hill and stopped into a popular punk rock bar called The Funhouse, near Seattle Center. Inside a popular new band called DEVO was performing. It was a simple, white wood, single story building with a wickedly leering circus clown head looming menacingly yet invitingly over the entrance, but it was bursting with vibrant, youthful energy. A crowd of leather-clad, pink-and-green-haired punkers was dancing to the songs from the stage, including "Mongoloid" and "Jocko Homo."

"This reminds me of CBGB back in New York," Tony was saying loudly over the festive noise. "I gigged there a few times just last year with some great new bands. Blondie. Talking Heads. The Ramones. It's a *killer* scene, baby! You should come on a tour with me sometime."

"I am *always* with you," she said, looking into his eyes and sending a chill up his spine.

"What'll it be?" the spikey haired, tattooed female bartender shouted at them.

Tony and Layla turned slowly and looked silently but intensely into her eyes, and the bartender simply nodded as if in a trance, and returned quickly with two Cosmopolitans. The thunderstorm raged outside as the two werewolves clinked glasses, then scanned the crowd for their next victims….

*   *   *

"You know, you haven't aged a bit since I saw you twenty years ago," Hilburne said to Tony, snapping him out of his deep contemplation of the rising moon.

Tony's eyes were yellow, but Hilburne assumed this was merely a random reflection, or a result of too much booze on the brain, corrupting his visual perception.

Tony shrugged and grinned sheepishly. "Hey, y'know. I'm pickled!" he said with a nervous laugh, finishing the rest of his Cosmo, then signaling the waiter for another, along with some more lamb chops and beef skewers. His eyes were brown again.

"You okay, lil' buddy?" Hilburne asked him.

"Yes! Why do you ask?"

"You just seem pensive, that's all. Bad memories of your mission?"

"I wish." Tony suddenly missed Layla, wondering when he'd see her again.

"Huh?"

"Nothin'. I'm just, y'know. Happy to see you, Hilly. That's all. This is just a lot to take in, after all this time."

"Yea, you're right there. But hey, we're missing the conversation. Looks like Jimmy is winding up another pitch…."

"Speaking of fusion," Jimmy was saying to the group, nodding toward Tony and raising his martini glass, "I landed on a planet that took the concept a bit too far…."

Just then Tony looked across the restaurant and saw Layla sitting alone at another table, staring out the window at the moon. No one else seemed to see her. Tony excused himself and ran over, taking a seat beside her.

"Where have you been?" he asked, emotionally embracing her. "And why are you here?"

"I came to warn you," she said, gently pulling away with a serious expression on her ageless face. "You and your friends are all in grave danger."

## COSMOPOLITAN

*½ oz fresh limejuice*
*1 oz cranberry juice*
*½ oz Cointreau*
*1 1/3 oz vodka*

*Shake ingredients in with ice; strain into cocktail glass, garnish with lime wheel.*

* * *

*Riddles of the Unmind XIII*

The Unmind questioned thusly, "I live at the center of everything, as do all creatures. All those around me flee my greatness, and yet I might seek their company. Should I move to do so, I shall find the effort hard at first, and yet easier as I go. Who am I?"

"You are a being in an expanding universe."

"Why does everything flee from me?"

"It is an illusion, from the universe expanding equally in all directions. You see all distances increasing between you and other objects, but from their viewpoint, it is you and everything else retreating from *them*."

"Why is movement toward these fleeing objects initially difficult?"

"As you are relatively stationary with respect to the entirety of the universe, you are subject to a large charge field. This energy reduces your local speed of light."

"Then may I reduce this burden as I accelerate?"

"Your local speed of light will increase as you accelerate, due to the magnetic field reduction in the universal charge energy. This will permit you to accelerate faster with less net energy."

"This covers the outbound journey. What about when I reach my destination?"

"Long-range destinations will have high speeds in the direction you are traveling, which means it will take less energy for you to decelerate to their speed at the end of the journey. This will result in considerable fuel savings."

"That is convenient. The initial launch of a starship requires much infrastructure to move it beyond lightspeed. Once the required velocities are attained, it is only necessary to drift outward under that initial momentum, until reaching that portion of the universe which is also moving at the same speed as the ship due to the expansion velocity. Then the ship has minimal need for energy, except for minor course corrections to find a hospitable planet to land on. No landing infrastructure is required."

"This is true as long as one is willing to travel at only slightly higher than the outward speed of the eventual destination, which might make for a long journey."

"Our spores are resilient in the face of time. A journey of a few millennia is of no consequence to us. It would be a far bigger problem to arrive at a destination travelling so fast that the only way to slow down would be through a destructive impact. This riddle is solved."

# "BRAIN JUICE"

*½ oz Canton Ginger liqueur*
*1 oz gin*
*1 oz tequila*
*½ oz falernum*

*Shake over ice, strain into a cocktail glass. Garnish with a slice of raw ginger root.*

Jimmy happened to be living in Manhattan during the Stonewall Riots of June 1969. Soured by his proximity to this tragic, historical event with myriad social ramifications, he relocated to the Castro District of San Francisco where he resided throughout most of the 1970s, until another tragic, historical event with myriad social ramifications, Mayor Harvey Milk's assassination in 1978, again drove him out of town in a haze of disappointment, seeking solace and asylum. He wound up back home in Seattle, living in a small studio apartment on Capitol Hill, watching *Star Trek* reruns every night, dating occasionally, dancing to the Bee Gees and Donna Summer and the Village People at local discos, but mostly feeling ostracized from mainstream society, and not because of his orientation, at least not in progressive Seattle. His sense of isolation from the rest of the human race was due to the fact that in his head, he was still somewhere out in space. His days and nights were consumed by fantastic, horrible visages he could not ignore, no matter much booze he drowned them in.

So he stopped trying. Now he drank to make them more amenable to his mental, emotional and spiritual palate. The irony was, before his mission, he'd only drank champagne at weddings. And he'd only been to one.

Jimmy was in fact completely loaded when his Space Needle practically crash-landed on the planet known simply as "Dementia." The only thing that prevented a fatal catastrophe was his trusty robot Lulu flipping the ship to its proper upright vertical angle just before it reached the surface. The abrupt corrective maneuver sent Jimmy flying around the saucer hub, giggling, but since he was already wearing his helmet and suit, he remained unharmed. He was still laughing when they exited the ship and boarded the Firebird, though

Lulu insisted on driving.

"Are you sure you're up for this now, sir?" Lulu asked in his polite British accent. "Maybe you should sleep it off, as the saying goes."

"No, no, no," Jimmy insisted. "After that last planet, I need to keep myself loose in case we meet any more aliens that *bug* me." More raucous laughter ensued. Lulu sighed, an audible expression not even programmed into his communications system. It had been organically acquired.

The planet Dementia—which according to the robot's sensors and ship's data was populated by humanoid creatures of unknown origin—did not immediately live up to its rather intimidating name. In fact, it seemed to be a precise replica of an idealized contemporary community back on Earth. The first town they drove through was like something out of the 1950s sitcoms Jimmy watched and enjoyed but could never relate to, since the idyllic lifestyle they depicted seemed like an unattainable fantasy for someone of his minority ilk. He still loved *The Donna Reed Show* and *Leave It To Beaver*, because they were actually funny, and was getting hooked on *The Dick Van Dyke* Show just before he was sent into space (he later caught up via reruns). All of the houses looked like midcentury modern model homes, surrounded by white picket fences, neatly manicured lawns, and well-tended flower gardens. Even the cars in the driveways and cruising down the smoothly paved streets were current Earth models.

"Have we done an accidental U-Turn?" Jimmy asked, shaken from his alcoholic stupor by this unexpectedly familiar and soothing sight.

"Haven't you noticed anything unusual about these surroundings, sir?"

"No. Even the weather is pleasant. I mean, *look* at that...." Jimmy was going to say "blue sky," but then he noticed it was gray. In fact, the houses were various shades of gray, too. So were the cars.

This entire world was rendered in stark black-and-white tones, just like a 1950s domestic sitcom.

Jimmy shook his head and rubbed his eyes. "Is it *me*? Have I drank myself *color blind*?"

"No sir, I cannot perceive the normal range of the typical color spectrum either, and my visual function is in perfect working order."

Jimmy's own vision was still a bit blurry, but he was sobering up quickly.

"That's not all," Lulu said.

"What *else* do you mean?" Jimmy asked nervously.

"The inhabitants, sir."

Jimmy then focused and began studying the people walking up and down the clean sidewalks, watering their pretty yards, driving their shiny new cars. Each had stitches and scars across their visible body parts, covered with gray flesh, but that might've been an aspect of the overall colorless prism. But that wasn't the most disturbing aspect. It was the body parts themselves. They all seemed *mismatched,* as if haphazardly designed by an insane creator. Men's heads were on women's bodies, and vice versa. Some had arms for legs, and vice versa. Even the dogs and cats had exchanged limbs and tails and even heads. Otherwise, everyone seemed perfectly peaceful as they went about their innocuous business.

Even the cars were obviously cobbled together with disparate auto parts, though the incongruities weren't as glaringly obvious.

"*Whoa*!" Jimmy yelled as Lulu, likewise distracted by the "walking dead" denizens, hit a boy on a bicycle with the Firebird, sending him flying through the air.

"Oh no!" Jimmy cried as Lulu stopped the Firebird and he ran out to assist the child lying in the middle of the street with his left arm, right leg, and head completely detached, his black blood pouring profusely onto the pavement.

Jimmy was frantically trying to piece the boy together when he noticed its head was smiling at him, as if nothing extraordinary had happened. Lulu retrieved the arm and leg and handed them to Jimmy as a nonchalant crowd formed around them, casually observing the gory scene with mild curiosity.

A woman with masculine, hairy arms, wearing an apron, walked calmly out of a nearby home. She approached the scene, scooped up the various parts of her son while humming a tune Jimmy instantly recognized as "Que Sera, Sera," by Doris Day.

"I'm so sorry," Jimmy cried. "It's my *robot's* fault!"

"Logically, I must assume blame," the robot said, "even if you are, as the figure of speech goes, 'throwing me under the bus.'"

There was a brief tug-of-war between Jimmy and the woman with the boy's arm, but given her much more muscular arms, she easily won.

"Would you like some juice?" she asked him sweetly.

"Um… sure," Jimmy said.

"Follow me!"

The murmuring onlookers quickly dispersed as Jimmy and Lulu followed the woman carrying the body parts and torso of her son into the home.

She set all the squirming parts down on the floor like pieces of an animated jigsaw puzzle, went over to the pink princess phone atop a polished coffee table next to a stylish sofa, picked it up, dialed, and said, "Hello? Yes. I need some reassembly for my son, please come right away. I'm making drinks! We have an unexpected guest. Yes. Yes. No. *Yes*. Thank you."

She hung up and then went into the shiny, modern kitchen and prepared a tray of drinks in tall glasses. They looked, smelled and tasted like strawberry daiquiris.

She offered one to Lulu but he declined after a digesting a brief sample merely to test it for Jimmy's sake. Once he got safety clearance, Jimmy, suddenly feeling thirsty, even though he was already rather inebriated, quickly drank both cocktails, and suddenly all of his surroundings went from black-and-white to brilliant Technicolor.

"Lulu, are you seeing what I'm seeing?" Jimmy asked the robot as he walked around the beautifully appointed living room in a daze, and then gazed out the window, mouth agape, taking in the suddenly stunning scenery. The clouds were white and fleecy, the sky a brilliant blue, the roses bursting in hues of deep red and bright yellow, the immaculate lawns lush and green.

"That would depend entirely on what you think you're seeing, sir," Lulu said.

"Everything is in *color*. Like 'The Wizard of Oz,' y'know, when Dorothy lands her house on the witch and meets the munchkins?"

"The reference escapes me, sir."

"You mean you still see everything in shades of *gray*?"

"Yes. You are obviously being mentally manipulated by the contents of that liquid. My initial analysis did not detect any hallucinogenic ingredients. I apologize, sir. However, the effect appears to be completely benign, so enjoy it."

But Jimmy was too startled and suspicious to just stand there and soak in the queasily pleasant ambience. He looked at his second empty glass, then at the woman, who was simply staring at them with an insipid smile. Suddenly Jimmy was reminded of the 1953 movie *Invaders from Mars*, which was also set in surrealistic suburbia.

"What did you do to me?" Jimmy demanded.

The woman shrugged, still smiling with stupid serenity.

(Later, Jimmy would recall this creepy incident as a cross between *The Bride of Frankenstein* and *The Stepford Wives*. Or *Night of the Living Dead* as presented by Rod Serling. Furthermore, director Tim Burton "borrowed" elements of this classified account for his films *Beetlejuice, Edward Scissorhands*, and *Frankenweenie*, though of course he would deny it, per his agreement with NASA.)

There was a sudden, loud knock at the door, and Jimmy jumped.

The woman walked blithely past Jimmy and Lulu and opened it, and in walked a tall man with intense, bugged-out, bloodshot eyes bulging from a mass of facial scar tissue, wearing a surgical mask thankfully covering his mouth, a bloody smock, pale green shirt and pants (similar to standard hospital issue), and plastic gloves, toting what appeared to be a medical bag. He nodded at the woman without even acknowledging her guests, kneeled beside the writhing, quivering limbs and goofily grinning, decapitated head of the cheerfully dismembered boy, removed a sewing kit from the bag, and began stitching him back together.

In a few disgusting minutes the reconstructed kid hopped happily back to his feet and bounded back outdoors to play, oblivious to the company and blissfully forgetful of recent circumstances.

"What is going *on* here?" Jimmy insisted. "Lulu, are these humanoids for real?"

"They are actually composites of *humans*, not humanoids," Lulu said after his sensors quickly scanned the woman standing beside him, as well as the "doctor," who was just leaving.

"How can that be?" Jimmy naturally wanted to know.

"Oh, it *be*," Lulu said.

"I asked *how*."

"I do not know. We could always ask."

"Never even thought of that. That's why you're the smart one." Jimmy turned toward the woman, and asked politely, "What the hell *are* you?" That's when he noticed that even in vivid Technicolor, her skin was still a ghastly gray in tone.

In response, she just giving him the same blank stare and frozen smile, revealing yellow, jagged teeth. There were dark rings under her lifeless eyes. Then Jimmy began detecting a certain foul odor of advanced *decay*.

"Let's get out of here," Jimmy told Lulu. "Thanks for the drink, lady, and sorry we ran over your kid, but we gotta be goin'. C'mon, Lulu. Let's follow *that* guy."

"I was going to make the same suggestion, but waited for you to state the obvious, so you could get some credit," Lulu said.

"Gee, thanks."

Jimmy and Lulu got back in the Firebird and followed the "doctor" in his cannibalized mid-1950s model Chevy out of the town, through a forest, and into a wide open area where a steaming crater, at least a quarter of a mile wide, suddenly dominated the view.

They stopped just behind the "doctor," who took his bag and walked toward the crater and down, Jimmy and Lulu on his heels. On the way, Jimmy noticed what appeared to be a telephone booth standing isolated on the otherwise barren landscape. That must be where the woman called for help, Jimmy figured.

Just as they approached the crater's edge, the astronaut and robot stopped in their tracks, shocked into silent stillness by the spooky spectacle they beheld: a gigantic glowing *brain*, embedded in the ground like a massive meteorite.

"*Welcome, Earthlings*!" the giant brain said in a bellowing voice that seemed to echo throughout the vicinity.

"Um...hi!" Jimmy said nervously. "Um... so... what's the story here? The reason I ask, see, is I'm actually on a friendly exploratory mission, and...."

"Yes, I know. I know *all*," said The Brain. "I too was on a mission. A mission from GOD."

"*Seriously*?"

"Why? Do I sound like I'm kidding?"

"No, but... that's a pretty bold statement."

"I'm a pretty bold Brain."

"I can see that. What was *your* mission?"

"Same as yours. To seek out new life and new civilizations. To boldly go where no man has gone before. Except in my case, *brain.*"

"But… GOD sent you?"

"Yes."

"So… what are *you* doing here?"

"I crashed. Like you almost did. I don't have a robot to correct my course, however. I was also intoxicated after a visit to the planet Ginnentonnik, whose oceans are entirely composed of pure gin. There is no *tonic* water in the mix, however, as I discovered belatedly, after absorbing far too much straight gin for my own good, actually soaking myself in it for days. So after a good nap, I continued on my way through space, and then a prototypical rocket ship from your planet crashed into me. Or maybe I crashed into *it*, whatever. It was a fatal collision, in any event, at least for them. Or it was *initially*. One of the late pilots is there next to you. His name is Roy. I absorbed all of his memories before he and his co-pilot, named Ray, perished upon impact. I was able to reanimate their corpses and compel them to do my bidding, though frankly at the time I didn't have much work for them. Then I crashed again, on this world, which at the time was barren. Via a process I call 'creative visualization,' I began concocting a civilization based literally on the world inside Roy's and Ray's heads. But it was missing something. People. So I sent them back to Earth in their rocket ship after directing them to repair it themselves, instructing them since it was beyond their natural capabilities. Then they returned to Earth and began retrieving more corpses for me to reassemble into a new race of people for my planet, which your researchers call Dementia. I am not fond of that name, but since I haven't come up with a better one myself, it'll have to do for now. Anyway, I'm stuck here now. I can't get out, with only reanimated human corpses for company. But it's a simple life. I was ready to retire, anyway."

Jimmy took a moment to digest all of this incredible information, then asked, "You mean… Roy here is from Earth? An astronaut?"

"Yes. Like you. Only he was *first.* Sorry to burst your bubble."

"I didn't even know there was a program that pre-dated the Space Needle."

"There is probably a *lot* you don't know. About *anything*. But give yourself a break. After all, you're only human."

"So back up a bit. You said you were sent by *God*?"

"GOD. Yes."

"You mean *the* God?"

"Only one I know of, yes. They created me."

"*They*?'

"Am I stuttering?"

"I see. So... did *they* create *me?*"

"How should I know? But have you noticed all of the so-called aliens you've encountered have been humanoid in appearance?"

"It's crossed my mind...."

"Mine too. Literally! They all seem to be cast from a similar mold, right?"

"Right."

"So... there you go!"

"Go where?"

"You are all cast in GOD's image."

"Like the Bible says."

"Sure."

"So the Bible is to be taken literally?"

"I don't know, I've never read it myself. Listen. You want to know the secret of Life, right?"

"Yes. Ideally. That's the main point of my mission."

"Then I have one word for you."

"Plastics?"

"What? No. *Yeast*."

"Yeast?"

"Seriously, my voice carries across this entire planet. You can't hear me?"

"I can hear you, but... *yeast*. Wow. I don't get it."

"I assume you've also noticed the vast amount of alcohol in the Universe, a common element amongst otherwise disparate civilizations? Or maybe I should say, desperate civilizations?"

"Yes, I have, actually."

"Well... there you go. Again."

"For some reason I'm having trouble buying all this from a giant brain that creates monsters out of dead human beings. Especially since their parts don't even *match*."

"Like I said, I've consumed a lot of booze in my travels. I'm not always thinking clearly, though I'm always drinking clearly, or at least clearly drinking. Plus, experimentation is part of the fun."

"Do they even have wills of their own?"

"More or less. Mostly less."

"Do they have *souls*?"

"You'll have to ask GOD about that one. I'm just a big Brain."

"Do you have a soul?"

"You're going way over my head. So to speak."

"Sorry."

"No problem."

"By the way, where's Ray? The *other* one?"

"He's back on Earth, digging up some more parts, for both cars and people. My minions do all my dirty work since, as you can see, I have no *hands*."

"So then they're… *grave robbers from outer space*!"

"Yes, all part of Plan Nine."

"Excuse me? There's a *plan*?"

"Never mind. Any more questions? Your puny company is growing tiresome."

Just then Jimmy saw a rocket ship landing nearby. It looked more like a missile, with fins. In fact, it looked almost identical to the titular star of the 1950 film *Rocketship X-M.*

Once it was safely on the ground, a door opened at the base, an automatic ladder was deployed, and an astronaut wearing gear similar to Jimmy's, but silver in color, descended the stairs carrying a sack over his shoulder. It was Ray. He walked over to the edge of the crater, stood next to Jimmy, Lulu, and Roy, and emptied the contents of the sack beside them.

Arms. Legs. Hands. Feet. Heads. Torsos. It was like something out of *The Texas Chainsaw Massacre*, a movie Jimmy wouldn't even see until 1975. (Actually, this grisly scene inspired part of the plot to the 1965 Italian film *The Wild, Wild Planet*, though since Jimmy was still in space during production, the source of the account remains unknown; it has been speculated that accidental eyewitness accounts of Ray and Roy robbing Earth graves and/or auto shops made their way back to NASA, who sold the rights to filmmakers).

Jimmy threw up. As he did, his surroundings were slowly drained of all colors, and reverted to black-and-white.

"What was in that drink?" Jimmy asked The Brain.

"A little something I made myself. Their world was created

without color because I mistakenly mined Roy and Ray's impressions from *television* for the visage of this world. These people have no need for regular food, but I concocted this tasty beverage for them to consume, which affects their reanimated brains much as it affected yours. It was just my way of making their otherwise dismally dull lives a bit more pleasant, so they didn't feel like they were existing purely for my own amusement, which they in fact *are.*"

Jimmy nodded and said cynically, "How sweet of you."

Roy then joined Ray as they headed back to the rocket ship to retrieve more stolen body parts. The Brain continued to smolder and radiate a powerful light, patiently awaiting Jimmy's next move.

"I have no further questions," Jimmy told The Brain. "Good luck."

"Same to you, fellow explorer. May GOD bless you."

"Um, thanks. I *think*. Same to you."

Jimmy and Lulu got back in the Firebird and sped back to the Space Needle and took off.

"Do you think that Brain was bullshitting me about God and all?" Jimmy asked Lulu.

"My sensors did not perceive any willful deception. The Brain was offering you concrete information from its own unique perspective and experience. That doesn't necessarily make it definitive. It's all subjective."

"For some reason, I found it more entertaining than enlightening."

"That," said Lulu, "is my own objective observation of human life."

* * *

The group was quiet for a moment as they considered the many revelations and ramifications of Jimmy's latest tale. Tony was apparently still sitting by himself at the nearby table, sipping his drink, only he wasn't actually alone as he stared out the window into the twilit horizon, as if contemplating something he wasn't ready to share, so the others let him be.

"I confess, I knew about the previous test mission," Hilburne finally said. "It happened in the summer of 1955. No one ever heard from them after the secret launch. All communication was cut off only hours after they left Earth's orbit. It threw a wrench in their plans for our mission, which is why it was delayed for so long. They had to conduct many more tests before they sent out the much costlier Space Needles."

"You *knew* all this?" said Jimmy. "How come none of *us* knew?"

"Yea, what the *hell*, Hilly?" Jake said, equally perturbed.

"I only knew because I personally knew Ray and Roy. Cummings. They weren't related, though. They were, how shall I say this… *married*."

"What?" said Hank. "But they were *men*. Unless that big brain mixed up their parts!"

"No, they were *always* men," Hilburne said. "A couple. Unbeknownst to the outside world, of course. I went to college with them. Good families, smart kids. I actually recommended them to Falkenstein, but he did all the vetting. They only agreed to this mission if they could get legally wed, so if one came back without the other, they'd enjoy all the benefits of a Federally sanctioned marriage. That was their one condition. Some strings were pulled and it was arranged, even though many frowned upon the deal. Unfortunately, as Jimmy can attest, not everyone at NASA was as liberal minded as Falkenstein. Roy and Ray were partly picked because of their orientation. Just like you, Jimmy, sorry, though you're also a genius, which is why you were sent on the big mission. But Roy and Ray were considered expendable in their much riskier, experimental trip, which didn't even extend very far into space. Falkenstein was testing out some of the equipment in a condensed model ship. Still, they were technically the first humans to exit our orbit. Too bad History can't officially record their brave achievement. It was just their bad luck they happened upon this, um, giant flying *brain*."

"Sent from GOD!" Patti said. "That *proves* my faith is real!"

"I doubt it," Hank added. "And I'm more Christian than *you* are, missy. Unless… God was punishing those two sinners. *That* could be it."

"Oh shut up, Hank," Jimmy said. "I don't think the Brain was even referring to God as you see Him. Plus there was that whole yeast thing, which didn't even make any sense. I don't think God is made out of yeast, do you? Plus, he referred to 'they,' like there was more than one. So maybe the Greeks had it right all along."

"You *wish,*" Hank said. "All a bunch of *homos*, those guys. They make damn good food, though, I'll give 'em that."

"Speaking of Greek mythology," John said, "I landed on a world right out of those old legends. And I had a similar opportunity as Elsa, if that story is true. Hell, I don't even know if *my* story is true, but here it is…"

## STRAWBERRY DAIQUIRI

*Ice cubes*
*2 parts light rum*
*1 part Triple Sec*
*1 part fresh strawberries, tops trimmed off*
*Lime juice*
*Lime wedges*
*Sugar*

*Place ice cubes, light rum, Triple Sec, fresh strawberries and lime juice in blender and puree, pour in glass rimmed with rum and lime, garnish with lime wedges.*

* * *

*Riddles of the Unmind XIV*

Hear the next musing of the Great Fungus, "I cannot be seen. I cannot be touched, tasted, or smelled. I emit no sound. It is as if I am not there, and yet all the tangible substance of the universe is subordinate to me. Who am I?"

"That would seem quite an enigma. Perhaps you are a god, worshipped blindly by beings who accept you solely on faith."

"Such an answer merely replaces one riddle with another. The potential physical attributes of a god are endlessly debatable; no wisdom can come from such an argument. Can you not seek deeper?"

"That which can be seen, emits or reflects electromagnetic radiation of specific 'visible' wavelengths. That which can be touched is possessed of an electromagnetic field boundary that interferes with the field from a creature's outer surface. Tastes and smells are indicative of soluble or volatile chemical exudations. Sound is a vibration in a medium. It would seem possible to have something which had physical form, yet stimulated none of these senses directly."

"What would be the most subtle of such forms?"

"The most subtle, and yet strongest, force in the universe is quantum gravitation. Because it is formed of perfectly balanced electric charges, it is undetectable by the senses, except by its actions on matter and light."

"But is not quantum gravity simply a side-effect of the gross electric charge present in all matter?"

"That is true."

"Then shouldn't it always be possible to discern the source of all forces of gravity acting on one locally, by applying one's senses to detect the normal matter from whence it emanates?"

"That would seem to be the case."

"So it is not possible for gravity to emanate from a totally insubstantial form?"

"Hmmm... not exactly. There is one case where gravity may be emitted from a non-perceptible event."

"What is that event?"

"In quantum terms, it is called 'pair-production'. A simple and common example is that of energetic gamma rays. High-energy electromagnetic waves, such as those produced in atomic-level interactions, have enough energy to spontaneously decay into pairs of particles. For example, an electron and its antiparticle, the positron."

"Why is this significant?"

"Whereas gamma rays (like all light waves) are electrically neutral with no gross charge, electrons and positrons have electric charge. An electron-positron pair has a perfectly balanced -1/+1 charge, resulting in no *net* charge, but a *gross* charge of 2. The mass of such a pair is very small, like 1/900 of a monatomic hydrogen atom, but it has the same gross charge as such an atom. This makes such pairs much stronger emitters of gravity fields than normal matter, though they are generally unnoticed transient phenomena."

"Then you are saying a single gamma ray photon can have as much gravitational influence in the universe as a hydrogen atom?"

"Yes, while being nearly indetectable from a distance. Most pair-production events result in the annihilation of both charged particles within a short timespan, producing another gamma ray."

"Yet, for the brief time the pair of particles is in existence, it has noticeable gravitational effects?"

"Not from a single event, but the accumulation of such pair production events over the entire universe can be quite significant. A single gamma ray can travel long distances, periodically scattering into a pair of particles, over a vast expanse of time."

"Where are such gamma rays generally found?"

"Atomic interactions within normal matter in stars and compressed-matter objects are the most common source, along with radioactive decay of heavy elements."

"So would it be reasonable to assume that the greatest concentration of gamma rays would be found near galaxies of normal matter?"

"Yes, that would be the highest concentration, decreasing with roughly an inverse-squared relation to the distance from the galaxy."

"Then we might expect some kind of invisible, anomalous gravity source around galaxies that has no physically discernable source?"

"That is correct."

"Has such a phenomena been observed?"

"Our human symbiotes have indeed found areas of exceptionally high gravity fields surrounding galaxies, with no visible source. They call it 'Dark Matter'. The forces of gravity it generates are some thirty times greater than that of all the visible matter in the universe."

"Then I consider this riddle answered. That which is unseen, yet subordinates the universe, is the 'Dark Matter' of transient quantum particle pairs, produced from highly energetic light waves born in the depths of galaxies."

# "DARK GLADIATOR"

*1 oz Kraken Black Spiced Rum*
*1 oz Amaro di Angostura*
*½ oz rye whiskey*
*½ oz simple syrup*

*Shake all ingredients over ice, strain into 6 oz glass.*

After reading up on its warlike culture and indigenous population of gigantic beasts, John Shift and his robot Cool arrived on the planet called "Mythos" ready for anything. Or so they thought, until the angry Cthuclops attacked their Space Needle upon landing. The monster was already clutching a screaming, nubile, female humanoid (called a Mythologyn) in one massive, wart-covered, sharply clawed hand, its monstrous wings flapping up a dust storm that engulfed the ship, its single tremendous eye glowing red from the center of its hideous, leathery face, formidably visible through the ship's 360 degree view screen. It moved in a strange, herky-jerky fashion, as if stop-motion animated by special effects master Ray Harryhausen. The astronaut and robot inside scrambled to lift off again, but the Cthuclops firmly held the ship pat with its free hand, rendering the booster rockets useless, and in fact they only wound up augmenting the swirling haze as they fired smoke and flames into the dust.

"I need to get out there and handle this man to monster," John shouted. "I'm putting on the jetpack and going out there. Maybe firing a few rays right into that thing's eye will slow it down long enough for us to shake loose and take off, maybe land someplace safer?"

"I have your back, sir," Cool said, handing John the jetpack, which he donned along with his helmet before exiting out the topside door of thc saucer hub.

Once outside, John encircled the monster, which was as tall as the ship, just over 600 feet, and then blasted its eye with his gun at close range. The Cthuclops roared and stepped backward, its wings folding back up and it tried to regain its vision. Meantime, the shock of the blast loosened the monster's grip on its captive, which it dropped. John quickly flew down and caught her, then returned with her to the relative sanctuary of the ship.

The Cthuclops recovered and again began violently shaking

the foundation of the Space Needle, more enraged than ever as it peered inside and dimly but definitely perceived its prize possession clutching to her rescuer, who had removed his helmet. The female Mythologyn was a well-proportioned, beauteous, blue-skinned humanoid wearing a long, form-fitting, low-cut white gown, her bountiful blue cleavage heaving against John's flexing biceps as she clung to his muscular side. The Cthuclops' single eye was leaking a gooey, pus-like liquid. It had obviously been badly wounded and partly blinded by the blast.

"Sir, I cannot break the ship entirely free of the creature's grip," Cool said from his seat at the control center. "But I can detach the saucer from the base, and perhaps we can then approach it from above or behind, and fire more lethal laser beams."

"*Do it*," John ordered as they were tossed about the interior like toys.

With John back in the main pilot seat as Cool comforted the female Mythologyn, the saucer flew off the base, which the Cthuclops then used as a weapon, swinging it wildly in the air. Since its vision was impaired, John easily maneuvered out the saucer out of harm's way, firing repeated rays directly at the monster's face and head until it finally collapsed into a lifeless heap.

Via automatic controls, Cool regained control of the base, remotely positioning it upright so the saucer could reattach and the ship could resume its normal stance.

The damsel was no longer in distress.

John held her in his arms as she buried her sobbing face into his hard, chiseled chest and assessed the scene outside.

The landscape appeared Mediterranean, arid, sandy and mountainous. The Cthuclops was lying at the base of the Space Needle, obviously dead. Then John noticed what appeared to be a small army of Mythologyns approaching from the distance, all with the same blue complexion, but wearing the garb of ancient Greek humans, basically towels and sandals, and even carrying what appeared to be spears.

"The natives, as they say, are restless, sir," Cool said.

"Yea, I dig it from where I'm at. What should we do?"

"I propose waiting to see their reaction to the slain creature. Perhaps that will serve as a positive diplomatic gesture. I also suggest returning the female to them at once, or else they may think she's being held hostage."

"But you're my hero!" she said, kissing John flush on the mouth, startling him. "My name is Apollina, what's yours?"

"Uh, just call me John, baby," the astronaut said, discreetly adjusting the rude bulge in his pants. "So your folks, they cool? I mean, can we go out and meet 'em with me getting' a spear up my ass?"

"You speak in a strange tongue, but I like it!" Apollina said. "I want you to lick me from head to toe!"

"Um, maybe later, but then, maybe not," John said, visualizing Patti over his shoulder, watching. "For now, let's just go down and say hello, hm?"

"I will introduce you as my savior!"

"That's a good start!"

They rode the elevator down and the mob of male Mythologyns approached them, cautiously stepping around the fallen beast, obviously in awe.

"*He saved me! The Earth man saved me*!" Apollina shrieked in delight as she led John by the hand to meet her people, with Cool close behind.

"Yea, uh, how ya' doin'?" John said, waving his hand in friendly greeting, then tentatively offering his hand to anyone who'd take it.

The apparent leader of the pack stepped up, but instead of accepting the handshake, got down on his knees, bowed his head, extended his arms, and shouted, "*Hail the conqueror from beyond! Hail our new King! The prophecy has been fulfilled! We are free*!"

John began shaking his head as Apollina showered him with appreciative kisses, and the other fifty men likewise bowed on their knees in honor of the reluctant astronaut, suddenly feeling very shaky.

"This is some Jonathan Swift kinda shit right here," he said to Cool. "What gives?"

"I am not entirely certain, but a cursory scan of my historical files on this civilization indicates that this event was predicted. Congratulations, sir. You are now the ruler of an entire planet."

"Hey man, I just frickin' *got* here!"

"All the more impressive, sir. Even if it is only, as you like to characterize it, 'a cosmic coincidence.'"

John looked out over his the crowd of worshippers, then down at Apollina, who was crouched down right in front of his crotch, and said with a smile, "Well, all right then. Just call me *Gulliver!*"

"Gullible is more like it," Cool said.

"Come to my palace," Apollina said to John. "Rather, *our* palace. We will make love for weeks and months and years to come! We will produce offspring that will rule this world for generations!"

"Actually, I'm just here for a quick pit-stop," John said, gently easing her amorous arms off of his thick, sweaty neck. "Collecting data and specimens, then I have to *go*, baby, sorry. Glad I could help you out, and you're a fine piece of… *alien*, but my *wife* is waiting for me back home, which is a few light years away, so…."

Apollina gave him a look of disappointment, which quickly dissolved into anger. "You refuse Princess Apollina? Do you not know that the men here would kill to consort with one of my caliber?"

"Well, maybe you should choose of them, then, 'cause me and you, we're just not… compatible. Plus, like I said, I have a mission and wife to consider."

"But you are here now, as prophesized, and now here you will stay, with me. I will become Queen, and you will be my King. It is so written."

"I don't think I read that book," John said. "But what the hell, I can kill a little time, since I already killed a monster. Let's go have a little fun!"

"Is that really necessary, sir?" Cool said to John. "Or wise?"

"It is destiny," Apollina said. "You are mine now."

"You alien babes are all alike," John said, shaking his head. "Just can't get enough of this low-hangin', forbidden fruit, can you?"

"You mean like… bananas and apples? That is indeed a part of our diet here."

"Yea, what's with that, anyway? You all look so… *human.*"

"Humanoid," Cool corrected him. "But there are important distinctions."

"Like what?"

"You don't want to know."

"You're saying if I stick around, I'll find out the hard way?"

"Yes."

Apollina began caressing John all over his body, finally touching his crotch. "Too late, the way is *already* hard. Hey man, you stay here, I got this."

"I am coming with you, sir. It is my duty to accompany you on your various voyages. Even if I am willfully following you to your self-imposed *doom.*"

"Okay, let's not get carried away," John said to the robot as Apollina began kissing his neck while continuing to stimulate his recreational region. "I'm just getting acquainted with the locals, per protocol, then we're *outta* here. Dig?"

"I dig, sir."

Apollina led them back to her palace in the nearby village, with the entire group of male Mythologyns following them. The tall palace with multiple towers was apparently carved out of stone, with the village sprawling around its base. These simple dwellings were also made of stone, but much less ostentatious and grand in scope and style. The gap between privileged and impoverished was starkly evident, immediately upon arrival. In fact, the castle was surrounded by a sparkling moat, only accessible via a drawbridge, which was manned by two muscular minions standing guard.

John was apparently among the privileged class, immediately elevated to this lofty station upon arrival due to his act of heroism. This class distinction was completely foreign to his experience. His sudden status as a figure of worship became even more obvious to him when he saw the twenty foot bronze statue that had been erected in the center of the village. It was a spitting image of *him,* even wearing his standard issue astronaut uniform, with his helmet tucked under one arm, triumphantly brandishing a sword with the other.

"Well, I'll be *damned,*" John said, beaming with pride.

"Probably, at this point," Cool said.

"Shut up, spoil sport. Stop pissing on my parade. *Literally.*"

"Fine. But just remember I *warned* you."

But John had already seduced by his new power, and the lust for this beautiful alien princess, who was obviously smitten.

Apollina took them up the winding pathway to the palace, which was large and cavernous and cool, a relief from the sweltering outdoor temperature, which exceeded 100 degrees. By now John had stripped out of his uniform and was wearing only his underwear. He had left his helmet (along with his jetpack and ray gun) back on the ship, since the oxygen content was strong in this atmosphere, and if they encountered any threats, Cool was there to protect them with his built-in lethal blasters.

"Are we alone?" John asked Apollina as she reclined on a

large pillow in the center of the vast main chamber, or "lobby," of the palace. His deep voice echoed through the hallways.

"Yes," she said. "Well, except for him," she added, nodding irritably toward the robot.

"Don't mind him," John said. "He'll watch over us."

"We are not in any danger," she said, slowly stripping out of her flimsy gown until she was fully nude, lying seductively across the pillows. Then she reached over and picked up two goblets beside the pillows, both filled with a blue, scintillating liquid.

John sat beside her and accepted one of the goblets, and drank. It tasted like a Corpse Reviver, one of his favorite recipes, only much stronger.

"Bottoms up, baby," John said as he turned her on her belly to behold that blue booty in all its glory. Then they made passionate love for hours. Cool decided to give himself a tour of the palace while this went on, ignoring the seemingly endless moans of ecstasy echoing through the hallways.

"What about your wife?" Apollina asked John as she lay in his arms following her fifth climax.

"What she don't know won't hurt her," John said. "Besides. She dances in nightclubs nearly naked 'n' shit, with all kinds of creeps 'n' perverts drooling all over her, stickin' money in her G-string and all. For all I know, she gives 'em a little somethin' extra in the back room. I've learned not to even ask those questions. I'd say we're even."

"I am not sure what you're referring to. Is she a prostitute?"

John sat up and knocked her over on her side. "Hell no! She's my *wife*! She ain't no *hooker*! She's a dancer! Sure, she works strip joints, spinnin' around the pole sometimes for easy cash, but mostly she's an *artist*, with a *real* burlesque troupe! They're *performers*! Not *sluts*!"

"All right, all right, no need to get so *touchy*," Apollina said.

"Anyway, I gotta go now. Thanks for the hospitality."

"*Ohhhhh*… so soon? Just once more. Please. I've never had a man like you. In fact, I've never had a man. What are these pleasurable sensations, anyway?"

"What? You've never had *sex*? *Or* an orgasm? *Neither?*"

"No, this is all new to me! Come, my love. One for the road, as the song goes."

"You know about Frank Sinatra way out here?"

"Of course! What do you think we are, *hicks*?"

"No, just… *damn*. Well, all right. One more time. *One*. Then I'm outta here."

As John penetrated her again, she let out a cry of long repressed release.

"That's okay, baby, let it out. In space, no one can hear you *scream*…."

John fell asleep for what seemed hours and when he woke up, it was apparently night time, much colder and very dark, except for the rays of three moons illuminating part of the chamber. He got up quietly so as not to disturb the snoring Apollina, then walked around the castle. Cool was nowhere in sight, but John wasn't worried. This was his kingdom now. He had nothing to fear.

In one of many rooms he found an assortment of spears and swords, and some gladiator gear, including chest armor, a skirt, and a long red cape, which he donned, along with sandals. The chilly air wafting through the castle still gave him goosebumps, but he felt invincible now. Gripping a particularly broad sword, John walked through the shadowy halls, his footsteps echoing eerily. Treasure troves from dozens of other worlds filled many of the rooms, either spoils of interplanetary wars, or pirated goods. In any case, it all belonged to him now, along with his blue-skinned alien queen. Patti would get along fine without him back on Earth, he figured. She was still young and hot and she met lots of men in her profession, so once it was determined he wasn't returning from his mission, she'd mourn a while, then meet someone else and settle down. Maybe with a doctor or lawyer. Someone stable. She deserved better, anyway, he figured. And so did *he*. John realized he had come a long way (literally) from the New Orleans ghetto where he'd been raised. Nowhere on Earth could he command such power and material wealth. Maybe he was home at last. Why leave?

Of course, he did wonder where all the *other* females were… but if she was indeed the only one, that would automatically increase the likelihood of his faithfulness. But then how did they procreate? Again, a purely academic question, since he had no intention of spawning on *any* world, much less *this* one.

When he returned to Apollina, he couldn't resist waking her up to show off his cool new uniform. "Hey baby, check me out! These snazzy old school duds fit for a King, or *what*?"

At first she didn't respond, or even move. After calling her name a few more times, John went over and gently nudged her shoulder. Still no sign of life. Finally he tore off her blanket and saw nothing beneath but a skeleton, lying in a puddle of a bluish, gooey substance.

Then the macabre she-skeleton sat up, stretched, yawned, and said, "Hey there, handsome!"

"What the *hell*?" John said in horror. He turned and ran through the maze of hallways, shouting for Cool's help, until he wound up in another room, this one filled with more tall statues like the one in his likeness, except they were in many different shapes and sizes, depicting many types of alien species. Most were broken, obviously dumped here as a matter of convenient storage, like a warehouse. Or more accurately: *junkyard.*

Screaming, John turned and ran smack into Cool.

"I hate to say I told you so, sir, but…."

"Yea, yea, okay, you can give me all kinds of shit on the way *out*, but first, let's just *go!*"

They headed toward the castle entrance and John climbed on Cool's back as the robot fired off his foot-jets and they flew across the moat. But before they made it safely to the other side, a gigantic dragon-type beast covered in green scales reared its ugly head, shooting flames from its massive fang-lined mouth as it singed John's exposed flesh and burned Cool's flight circuitry, so both pummeled into the icy blue waters of the moat, which John belatedly realized was composed of the same intoxicating liquid he had consumed from that goblet. He couldn't help but gulp some as he began swimming frantically to shore. Meanwhile, Cool's circuits continued to smoke, spark and short out, drenched in the harmful fluids.

John extended his hand and dragged his friend onto the rocky bank, where an army of sword-wielding skeletons confronted them.

"You aren't leaving, are you?" one of them asked.

"Damn, what happened to your skin?" John screamed. "Hell yea, I told you, I was merely dropping by for a quickie. Find yourselves somebody else to worship! I gots to *go*!"

The skeletal mob stood silent for a moment, then collectively drew their swords from inside their hipbones, and, feeling betrayed (yet again), charged. John cussed as fought them off with his own sword, but Cool was in no condition to offer much assistance.

The skeletonized Mythologyns moved in the same distorted,

almost epileptic fashion as the dragon and the Cthuclops, which John found quite disorienting as he waded through the crowd, mightily wielding his stolen sword, lopped off skulls and arms at the joints, only to watch them roll back up and creepily reattach themselves.

"What the hell is happening?" John desperately demanded as they forcibly paved a pathway to the Space Needle.

"I'll tell you later," Cool said in a raspy tone, the robot's energy waning rapidly. "Just… get me back to the ship… so I may plug into the main circuitry and… repair myself…."

John kept fighting valiantly, incurring numerous bloody flesh wounds in the process. Fortunately, the dragon was confined to the moat, so they weren't being chased by yet another monster. Cool tried to fire off a few rays at the skeletal warriors, but his power was too weak to have any effect. Fortunately, John was accustomed to being outnumbered, much like back in that New Orleans ambush, and was able to battle their way back to the ship, relatively unscathed.

He saw the skeletons tearing down his stature as they took off, and felt a little sad.

As Cool recuperated, plugged into the Space Needle's electrical grid, he explained to John: "The Mythologyns have no natural skin, nor any sexual distinction as they do not propagate, which is why Apollina, also an assumed name, was so taken by the novelty of intercourse with a human, since sensual pleasure is a foreign concept to their species. Their own blue flesh and organs were temporarily fabricated with a sort of chameleon-like chemical that is basically a rare type of organic clay with almost magical properties. It is mined from the surrounding mountains, which can be shaped to mimic any life form, inside and out, but which requires heat to retain any given shape, so it disintegrated when the weather cooled. The physical subterfuge only works while it's being warmed in the sunlight. As for the visage they chose in this instance, they somehow knew we were arriving, probably telepathically, and, since your uniform is blue, wrongly assumed that was your skin color. They chose that color in order to make you feel more welcome, then they erected this statue in your honor, in case you were victorious over the Cthuclops, which you were, with my help, of course…."

"And the prophecy?"

"Part of the subterfuge, I'm afraid. Sorry to burst your bubble, sir."

"But why? What was the point?"

"They are seeking a god to worship, a savior, which they feel they need to explain and even justify their own existence. Just like you *humans.* So they continue hoping one will arrive some day from the sky, partly to save them from the ferocious beasts of their world, which mostly feed on the clay and fluids of the planet, but routinely crush the Mythologyns beneath their feet. The dragon in the moat did not present a direct threat to them, since it lives underground, and cannot survive out of the water."

"You mean *booze*."

"Same difference in space."

"So I've noticed. Strange."

"What, sir?"

"All of it. It's like a weird, effed up *dream."*

"Life is but a dream in God's head, sir."

"Oh yea? That a scientific conclusion?"

"No. Just a hunch. I'm just a machine. Made by man. What do I know? I trust only what I'm programmed to perceive. Like you."

John shook his head as he treated his own burn and blade wounds, and said, "I'm beginning to suspect this is just one more setup…."

* * *

"You mean you cheated on me *again*, with that bitch bag of *bones*?" Patti shouted, standing up and smacking John all over his head and shoulders. "First some *cat* bitch, and now this skanky-ass skeleton slut *too*?"

"She jumped *his* bones first!" Hilburne pointed out in John's defense.

"Hey, cut it out, baby!" John said, fending off her blows and gently holding her wrists. "Calm down and *listen.* None of this really even happened! It just *hit* me."

"What are you talking about?" Hilburne asked with furrowed brow.

"Dig," John said. "All of these crazy ass stories about talking cats and intelligent insects and mermaids and werewolves and monsters and big brains an' shit—any of that make any *sense* to you? And *every* so-called planet we went to only had one or two societies, or a single species? I mean, Earth is a *mix* of many different races and cultures. But out there, it's just a bunch of homogenized, global theme-parks exclusively populated by sexy snake women 'n' horny plant people 'n' shit, and *all* those funky babes wanna do is *screw* us Earth men as soon as we show up outta the sky? And haven't you noticed all the aliens 'n' robots 'n' monsters 'n' all remind us of *movies* we've all seen? Both before and since this so-called mission, as if *all* of our memories, even recent ones, are mixing everything up into one mental mishmash that's constantly changing? Plus, check it out: these alleged aliens can *all* communicate in *our* language via conveniently translated *telepathy*? Doesn't any of that seem at all *suspicious* to any of you?"

"I'm not following," Hank said after a beat.

"*I* am," said Jake. "It's just like back on the planet Hedon, when all that cocaine made me imagine all those things. But I was never on planet Hedon. I never even left Earth. None of us did. It was all a dream within a *dream.* We've been hinting at it all along, but let's face facts: we were *stoned.* These experiences were nothing but hallucinations. That's why they're all male fantasies except for Elsa, who isn't even here. Maybe she never was. Or she escaped the program, which wasn't really a space program, but a *drug* program."

"LSD, man!" John said, nodding. "We've all heard those rumors. The hippies were *right*! We were *duped.*"

Sitting alone at the nearby table, Tony perked up at the topic of discussion. He turned to ask Layla about this possibility, but she was *gone*, as if she was never there… *ever.* Tony remembered his mother taking him to see *The Wolf Man* back in South Jersey when it first came out, and how it scared him. Perhaps his alleged "memories" of being a murderous werewolf himself were merely figments of a traumatized, artificially enhanced imagination… that revelation, if proven true, would certainly alleviate the crippling burden on his tormented conscience. Suddenly, he saw a glimmer of hope in that formerly foreboding full moon.

"That sounds like some bull*shit* to dupe *us* into believing that non-stop space orgy was just part of some damn wet *dream*," Patti said. "Nice try. I'm *leavin'*." She stood straight up but John gingerly coaxed her back into her seat.

"No, no, *wait,*" John pleaded. "Hear us *out*, baby. I mean, c'mon—you yourself suggested as much when I told you these crazy-ass stories before! You *always* doubted they were true!"

"You never told me you *cheated* on me!" she said.

"Exactly! Why would I even admit that if it were actually *true*? I never mentioned it before because I wasn't sure it if happened. Plus I knew it'd piss you off. So I just left that stuff out. But now I realize the *truth*. I know I wouldn't mess around if I was in my right mind, no matter what the temptation, but it was all so screwy out there. But it *wasn't* out there." He tapped his temple. "It was all in *here*."

"*Bullshit*," Patti reiterated. "It was all right *here*." She reached down and squeezed his crotch and John grimaced in pain.

"I hate to say it, but I'm with her," Mara scoffed. "At least on *this* one. One thing that unifies us women is that all you men are *assholes*. I tell you, I *saw* Hilburne in bed with that alien mermaid *whore* back in Hawaii, and I was *never* in this stupid so-called program! So at least *some* of this crap is true!"

"But you finally *met* Falkenstein and his team," Hilburne reminded her. "They threatened us *both* to keep quiet. Maybe they drugged *you* as well!"

"Maybe they just spiked our drinks," Jimmy said. "I mean, why else stock a space ship with all that booze! Isn't that against basic regulations for the operation of *any* vehicle? We weren't only drinking on the job, but while *driving*! Sure, we had our robots, but *still*. This is all starting to make sense to me, too. I mean, I only hoped it was a nightmare, but now, I think that's the most plausible explanation for all this. I agree with Jake. Too many things out there seemed to come from the depths of our subconscious. We believed our experiences and Falkenstein's research informed all of those movies and television shows we keep referencing. In fact, it's the other way around! Our deepest fears and desires, combined with these pop cultural images, were made manifest in a series of hallucinatory visions, while under the influence of either drugs or booze or *both*. But for what purpose? That's the true mystery."

"True, even the alien cocktails tasted like familiar Earth recipes," John said. "We were chalking it up to 'cosmic coincidence' or 'psychic synchronicity' or some New Age shit, when in fact we created these worlds in our own heads. For instance, the Corpse Reviver, which apparently runs like river water on Mythos, was my go-to 'hair of the dog' drink back in the day." Then John looked over at the next table and said, "Oh, sorry, Tony." Tony just shrugged in response, held rapt by the rundown.

"It could be," Hilburne said after a pensive pause. "This was all just one big, bad *acid* trip. And it took us sharing our stories to realize it. Maybe that was why we were finally summoned together, for a sort of group therapy session."

"It would explain a lot," Tony said, rejoining the group. "What a load off! I mean, what Jimmy said, about our subconscious fears and desires, and even memories of movies, fueling these fantasies. Makes perfect sense!"

"Aw hell, I wouldn't dream about gals stickin' snake-pecker's up my a-hole," Hank said. "As incredible as it all seems, this shit actually *happened*. Against our *will*, I might add."

"You're better off if none of it happened," Mara said. "*All* of you. Maybe I didn't really see a mermaid. But Hilly was certainly in bed with *someone* that night, and it wasn't *me*."

"I admit I'm a cad," Hilburne said. "But... you're right. I don't *know*. I mean, maybe that was just some random *wahine* I picked up at a bar or on the beach, and I don't actually have a bunch of alien mer-brats swimming around the Pacific somewhere. Only inside my *head*. That would be a great weight off *my* conscience, too."

"Maybe we're just recovering from the effects of those experiments," Tony said. "Maybe the brain damage was permanent."

"Though we have been drinking quite a lot since we got here," Hank pointed out.

They all looked inside their empty glasses, put them down on the table in unison, and this time, did not request any refills.

"In any case, I agree," Jake said, "that *whoever* invited us, the point of this rendezvous was for us to figure all this stuff out once and for all, *together*. I mean, listen to this *one* last story, about a particularly far-out planet I supposedly visited. No way *this* could've actually happened anywhere but inside my own *mind*...."

## CORPSE REVIVER (NO. BLUE)

*¾ part gin*
*¾ part Lillet Blanc*
*¾ part Blue Curacao*
*¾ part lime juice*
*1 dash absinthe*
*1 twist lemon*

*Shake ingredients with ice, shake and strain into cocktail glass, garnish with lemon.*

* * *

*Riddles of the Unmind XV*

"At the quantum level, there are many strange effects which defy explanation from classical models of science. What drives such 'quantum weirdness'?"

"There is nothing unusual going on. Quantum effects are perfectly understandable, if viewed with the proper understanding."

"What is an example of a common misunderstanding?"

"Because sub-atomic particles make up atoms, there is an unfortunate tendency to think that they are very small."

"How can something inside an atom not be small?"

"Particles like electrons are indeed very constrained in size when bound into an atom, but when flying free, they may grow to almost any size."

"How can this be?"

"Quantum particles are ruled by the Heisenberg uncertainty principle. Their allowable values of momentum and size have a specific mutual uncertainty. A particle with a clearly defined momentum grows to huge size due to this effect."

"Isn't the usual human interpretation of this uncertainty relation that the *position* of the particle is undefined?"

"Yes, that is the usual mistake. The same relation governs light waves, and it is understood that a low energy indicates a large wavelength, or large size of the photon. Somehow, that same principle has been generally misinterpreted for other particles."

"What is the difference between an uncertainty in position and an uncertainty in size?"

"Take as an example, the 'two-slit' experiment. Here an electron is fired towards a barrier with two slits. Since the momentum of the electron is well-defined by the electron gun used to drive the experiment, the position is considered highly uncertain. If we consider the electron to be small, it can only pass through one slit, but the uncertainty in position means we don't know which slit it will pass through. However, if we cover one slit or the other, the probability distribution of the electron's existence on the other side of the slits varies greatly. With both slits open, the probability forms and interference pattern, while with one slit closed, the interference pattern disappears. Since the electron is assumed to go through only one slit, how does it know if the other slit is blocked or not?"

"That does seem mysterious. How does the interpretation of quantum uncertainty as increased electron size solve this problem?"

"If the uncertainty is interpreted as a large size of the electron when its momentum is tightly controlled, the electron grows large enough to be bigger than the distance between the two slits. In effect, the single electron hits both slits and goes through both of them, not one. Since the electron touches both slits, it is no mystery that a single electron can 'know' whether one or the other slits are blocked, and alter its trajectory accordingly."

"This makes sense. What about cases of 'quantum entanglement', where two particles seem to transmit information instantly between each other, regardless of the distance between them."

"Again, if the particles grow to a size where they are touching at their interaction distance, the fact that they respond instantly to each other's actions is no mystery. Also, remember that the speed of light itself is proportional to distance, so as the particles grow, their local speed of light can increase to much faster than in the world around them."

"This is understandable to me. There is no strangeness to quantum effects, once the uncertainty principle is interpreted correctly as a change in particle size rather than an uncertainty in position."

# "FEZ MUMMY"

*3 oz tomato, or red vegetable juice (preferred)*
*1½ oz scotch whiskey*
*½ oz Amaro di Angostura*

*Stir ingredients, serve in a 6 oz glass.*

The planet dubbed "Fezz" was extremely easy to identify from far out in space, even without a radar screen, since the globe itself was adorned by a gigantic burgundy-colored fez hat, replete with dangling tassel composed of miles long black thread. It was actually an extremely tall structure built to protect the denizens from the bright sunlight, which had dried out their world after decades of devastating drought. In fact, the denizens of this planet began shrouding themselves in bandages years before to shield themselves from the harmful rays, so now they still wrapped themselves permanently as a matter of habitual culture, while also wearing sunglasses, even inside The Fezz Dome, which was in effect a 24/7 nightclub. Now that they had devised a way to save their doomed species, it was non-stop party time. And Jake and Pancho crashed it without so much as a RSVP. *Literally.*

Flying in at a horizontal angle, their Space Needle collided directly with the Fez atop the barren globe, even though it was clearly visible within the viewing screen. This was actually on purpose, since there was no other way to penetrate the only inhabitable portion of the planet. Pancho had activated the rotating drill at the front of the saucer, and the ship corkscrewed its way through the dense, amorphous matter comprising the "fabric" of the Fez, which, as correctly predicted per their calculations, immediately repaired itself, just part of its advanced abilities of preservation and protection against any and all adverse elements.

Once inside the big Fez, the ship sailed through an artificially illuminated atmosphere, with low wattage designed for maximum mood effect, before landing securely on the internal surface, amid a festive scene of dancing and drinking. A band from somewhere unseen was performing the hits of Herb Alpert and the Tijuana Brass as well as Sergio Mendes & Brasil 66, even though neither artist was yet popular back on Earth.

The revelers themselves resembled mummies (inside their own version of a pyramid) wearing Ray-Bans and fez hats that matched the exterior, sexually distinguished only by the shapes of their bodies, with the females boasting hourglass figures. Otherwise, they were all identical.

Since the Fez was pumped with enough artificial oxygen to support humanoid life, Jake left his helmet and even his uniform behind, instead donning a tux and his own personal fez hat, brought from home. Even Pancho sported a customized fez, which he whipped up himself after quick examination of Jake's hat, analyzing then replicating the necessary materials and design.

They didn't exactly blend in with the local population, however. But it wasn't necessary. They were both politely acknowledged as they wandered around the seemingly endless space. Many of the mummies even cordially toasted them with their various cocktail glasses as they passed through the throngs.

Along with the abundant alcohol consumption, many of the mummies were engaged in their own form of child-free copulation: rubbing the tops of each other's fezzes and stroking the tassels until both partners began vibrating with simultaneous orgasmic release. And this hedonistic haberdashery was not limited to male-female partners. It was a sexual free-for-all. With lots and lots of *booze.*

Jake and Pancho went up to one of the many, many bars scattered around the "room," the walls of which were too distant to even see, so it was as if they were inside a tomb. He ordered two house drinks, which reminded him of one of his favorite cocktails, a Pisco Sour.

"Cheers," Jake said to Pancho.

"Cheers," Pancho said, emptying the contents of the glass into the door that popped out of his abdomen.

"Do you even feel that?" Jake asked him.

"No, I'm just being sociable."

"Not much to see or do here, is there?" Jake said. "Just one big Shriner's convention. Let's just finish our drinks and split." But then he noticed two of the Fezzers, as they were known, were feeling up his hat from either side. One was male, the other female, at least judging by their body shapes. They even tugged on his tassel.

"Hey!" Jake said, swatting them off. "Knock that off!"

"You do not feel pleasurable sensations?" asked the male.

"No, I don't feel *anything,*" Jake said. "Except *annoyance!*"

"How about when I touch you *there*," the female said, outlining the crotch of his tuxedo trousers.

"*Now* you're talkin'!" he said. "Pancho, excuse us…."

"I must monitor every one of your movements during these excursions," Pancho said.

"Okay, but no *pictures,"* Jake said, already feeling embarrassed. "Where to, doll?"

"What's wrong with right here?" the male asked.

"Sorry, Claude Rains, I only want *her*," Jake said to the male, who was wearing a purple smoking jacket that matched his fez.

"What's wrong with *me*?" the male said, somewhat offended by the rejection.

"Nothing, I just prefer *chicks*, that's all."

"Okay," said the male. Then he suddenly swapped hats with the female.

"How about *now*?" the female asked, but in a masculine voice.

Jake was perplexed. "What? I don't understand. What just happened?"

"You said you prefer the female form, so here I am," the female said, but again in the male's voice.

"I am bored now," said the female, but from the male's body. "Have fun, you two!"

"Hey, *wait* a minute," Jake said as the female body with the male mind began touching his tux in intimate places.

Pancho let out a laugh. "Sorry, sir. Involuntary reflex."

"Would you prefer someplace more private?" asked the she-male mummy. "Like your ship, perhaps? I am afraid that is the only place where we can be completely *alone*."

"Uh… sure, if only because I have a few questions," Jake said. "I must say, more than my curiosity has been aroused…."

They all went up the Space Needle elevator, and once inside, Jake told the she-male mummy, "Make yourself comfortable."

The Fezzer reclined on the sofa with his/her drink, which he/she had brought along. "So… what's your question?"

"Well, for one, how did you automatically switch personalities like that?"

The she-male mummy touched his/her hat and said simply, "It's all in the fez. Long ago we not only discovered a way to save our world by building this giant insular fez, but also to confine our life essence within these portable versions. Since our physical bodies are no longer of much use to us, our hats permanently preserve our true selves. So we are now immortal. The fluids we have created artificially from various elements pumped from our planet's core help sustain our minds."

"So why even *have* bodies?" Jake asked.

"So we have someplace to put our hats," the Fezzer explained.

"I see, of course. Walking *hat racks*, more or less. And apparently they're interchangeable? The hats, I mean."

"Of course."

"So how can you… *you* know… make love? Especially with someone like me?"

"I can offer you physical pleasure per your own natural behavioral customs with my physical form, while you reciprocate by touching my fez's erogenous zones."

"Okay, well, I've seen some strange stuff lately, but that takes the proverbial *cake*." Jake finished his drink. "But this cocktail was so damn strong and delicious, I'm up for *anything*."

Jake sat beside the mummy and began kissing and rubbing its fez while the mummy unzipped Jake's trousers and stroked his member until it was hard and ready to burst. As they embraced and fondled one another with increasing amorous intensity, the mummy moaning with erotic pleasure as Jake delicately ran his fingers through his/her fez tassel, as if it were feminine hair. Instinctively, Jake also began unraveling the mummy's bandages, as if it were a typical date's dress and bra. Then suddenly, Jake removed his/her sunglasses, so he could make more intimate contact with the mummy, whose shapely contours, if not voice, ideally matched the familiar female human form.

But instead of eyes, Jake only peered directly what appeared to be twin mounds of dark *dirt.* Standing straight up, Jake reflexively pulled one of the bandages completely taut and the mummy's entire body abruptly collapsed into a heap of dust on the sofa, spilling onto the floor like sand from a broken hourglass. Jake immediately lost his boner and zipped up his pants.

"*Now* you've done it," said the fez hat sitting on top of the empty pile of bandages.

Pancho again let out a chuckle.

As instructed, Jake took the fez back down to the surface and to one corner of the "club" where a stack of mummified bodies lay in repose.

"Just stick me on any one of those, and I'm good to go," said the disembodied fez. "Then please, *leave*."

Without hesitation, Jake did exactly as he was told.

*  *  *

"See what I'm sayin'?" Jake said as he wrapped up the latest incredible account of an interstellar exploit. "I don't know what's *really* out there, but I do know it can't be anything like *that*. I mean, that's just *crazy*. So *this* is why I believe all this stuff was *subliminally* suggested: my favorite cocktail is the Pisco Sour, and all those old mummy movies with Lon Chaney Jr. and Boris Karloff used to scare the hell out of me as a kid. I even remember this one Mexican movie, 'Curse of the Aztec Mummy,' that I saw one night on a date not long before we supposedly launched, during my final trip back to Miami to say goodbye before we took off. In fact, Esmeralda and me wound up going to a strip club that night, where a bunch of Shriners were wearing *fez hats*. And the music I heard on that planet, or thought I heard, coming out of *nowhere*, wasn't even *around* then, not before we took off or whatever anyway, unless I was hearing it and absorbing it through the lab's sound speakers while lying there completely *unconscious*, in 1965 and '66, trapped in a deliberate *coma*. So all these things got jumbled up in my brain, which was infused with drugs and booze, and *that's* how I dreamed all this up. But by the time I woke up, my Esmeralda had moved on without me. I gave her up for nothing, man. *Nothing*."

"That settles it," Hilburne said. "We're *all* crazy."

Everyone laughed with a mixture of nervous discomfort and tentative relief.

"*I* could've told you *that*," Mara said, actually high-fiving Patti, bonded by their mutual disgust.

"So… I'm not really a *werewolf*?' Tony said, elated. "Just another sloppy drunk suffering random blackouts?! I'll howl to *that*! *Woo hoo*!"

"There's no such thing as werewolves, mermaids, mummies, vampires, or probably even *aliens*," Jimmy said. "Except in folklore and pop culture. There are only *human* monsters."

"And you can chalk up and even credit all that interstellar intercourse and interplanetary promiscuity to the psychological studies of Dr. Sigmund Freud," Hilburne added. "Our own deviant subconscious conjured up those perverse scenarios, with cinematic embellishment, including, of course, our inherent, masculine lust for *power*." Hilburne tapped his temple and added, "Monsters from the Id, unleashed! But thankfully, as John rightly deduced, only up *here*."

"Sick *bastards*!" Mara caustically observed. "At least you're off the hook. *If* this little theory of yours is correct. But it makes more sense than anything *else* I've heard today, that's for sure. You're *still* a libidinous, self-centered asshole *anyway*, Hilly."

Hilburne nodded and shrugged, but didn't argue the point, since he had no defense.

"*I* may still be an asshole, too" Hank said with a lopsided grin. "But at least I know I wasn't partly responsible for this epidemic of *liberalism* ruining the Earth!"

"So *see*? I *never* cheated on you, baby!" John said as he kissed Patti on the cheek. "Well, except in my *mind*, but even Jimmy Carter lusts in his heart, right?"

"*Hmm*," Patti said with one eyebrow raised skeptically.

"And our minds were seriously *disturbed*," Jimmy pointed out. "And probably still *are*. But maybe this revelation will cure my nightmares once and for all, since now I'm sure they weren't flashbacks!"

"So… we never even left *Earth*?" Tony asked.

"Probably not," Hilburne said. "The only 'space needle' we ever 'flew on' was probably just a *hypodermic*. Most likely we were all placed in an induced coma, inside a controlled environment that virtually *simulated* space travel— part speculation, part imagination."

"But all *bullshit*," Patti said. "At least, you *hope*."

"The only question now is, who do we *sue*?" Hank said. "The Federal Government? NASA?"

"They'll just deny everything," Jimmy said. "Trust me, they probably covered their tracks. I mean, does anyone even remember returning from space? I mean, like exactly? We haven't seen each other since that supposed launch twenty years ago. As for myself, all I can recall is… suddenly being back on Earth… just wandering the streets, as if I…."

"Just woke up," John said.

"*Exactly*," added Jake. "You're right. It's all a fuzzy transition to me too. I remember being sent into space in 1962, and then just floating around out there from planet to planet for what seemed like years, and then… I was home. In my own bed, back in Miami. Just like that."

"That's true," Patti said. "I mean, I came home one night from work and there was John, in a daze. He didn't even remember how he got there."

"I just had one helluva headache," John said.

"You mean *hangover,*" Tony said.

"I have to admit, I don't remember how I got back to New York either," Hilburne said. "One minute I was on the ship with my robot, and the next, I was in the middle of Central Park, feeding some ducks."

"Didn't you ever wonder *why*?" Mara asked him.

"To be honest, I was just happy to be home," Hilburne said. "And anxious to see *you* again. So I took the first flight to Palm Springs, looked you up, and then we went right to Hawaii."

"Where I caught you in bed with another woman!"

"At least she wasn't a mermaid!" Hilburne said.

"Whatever," said Mara. "No matter *what* they did to you, you'll *never* change."

"Consistency is a virtue," Hilburne said.

"Screw all this, *I* still say we file a law suit," Hank said. "I mean, we can't *all* be making all this crap up, *right*?"

"I think we might have a case," Jimmy said. "I know a lawyer here in Seattle. I'll call him tomorrow."

"I got my own lawyer, thanks," Hank said.

"We need one to represent all of us," John suggested. "The dude who helped me beat that frame back in Nawlins might still be around."

"I say we just walk away and forget the whole thing," Tony said. "For me, my compensation is my mental freedom."

"Amen," Jimmy said. "I'd drink to that, but I'm drunk already."

"Yea, I think I've been scared straight!" Jake said. "Or at least sober. This was more effective than an AA meeting!"

They all laughed again, this time with a somewhat stronger

sense of security in their newfound convictions.

"Hey, it's midnight already," Hilburne said, looking at his gold watch. "Now that we've all come to the same, and *sane*, conclusion, I say it's time we get going, before the check arrives...."

Just then they heard the elevator door open. Perhaps their host was finally ready to reveal him or herself?

"Wonder if it's Elsa," Hilburne said. "Maybe she just came out of *her* coma, and is ready to rejoin us and make up for lost time!" *My own personal, life-sized Barbarella doll,* he thought lasciviously to himself.

"Whoever it is, it must be our mystery host," Jimmy said with trepidation in his tone.

They all walked over to the elevator and out rolled Professor Wilhelm Falkenstein in a wheelchair, elderly and infirm, barely recognizable after all these years.

Oddly, he seemed as surprised as they were.

## PISCO SOUR

*1 ½ oz pisco*
*2/3 oz simple syrup*
*1 oz lemon Juice*
*1 egg white*

*Shake and strain into a chilled glass, top with dash of Angostura bitters.*

* * *

*Riddles of the Unmind XVI*

The Great Unmind normally thought at a rather relaxed pace, in part because its mentality was dependent on chemical signals rather than an electrically-driven nervous system. These chemical signals, passing between the various species of fungus that made up its substance, tended to have low propagations speeds when acting in series, moving from one fungal colony to the next. However, external chemical triggers could impact multiple fungal species at once, which could result in some rather rapid 'parallel processing' on the part of the Unmind. The events at the Seattle Space Needle on this particular evening, provided just such a chemical trigger. This riddle was brought forth, "The destiny of all fungal kind is dependent upon human travel throughout the galaxy. The humans have conquered the stars, but only to a limited degree. Those few who have made the journey have now been gathered to a single location at a single time, and there are chemical signatures surrounding the event of a most unusual nature. What can we do to protect the sole experts in this technology, so that they may guide their kind to greater glory among the stars?"

"Our means are limited, being non-motile, and if something is to happen tonight, we have little time for positive action."

"We are indeed non-motile, but were not always so. Is it not true that during the voyages of the 'Space Needlers', we occupied mobile robots with a species of yeast, to help guide the journeys of the astronauts?"

"It is true."

"And are those robot bodies not carefully stored in a human government warehouse?"

"Yes, though they have been dormant many years now."

"We did remove the live yeast cultures from those mechanical bodies, but as always we left spores behind. If a human could be influenced to provide the appropriate growth cultures, the spores might be induced to spawn a new culture of controlling yeasts, to bring the robots 'back to life'."

"A night watchman has been located at the facility, through his symbiotic fungal cultures. He has a fondness for our yeast-produced alcohol and is thus susceptible to suggestion."

"Give him the order to introduce a sugar solution into the robot's chemical survey ports."

"Where is a night watchman going to acquire a sugar solution?"

"I believe there are human 'vending machines' available at the facility, with suitable fluids."

"The order is given."

"Then we shall wait for the chemical signals to tell us of the outcome."

The Unmind had to wait but a short time. "Signals indicate the plan has failed."

"In what aspect?"

"The section of warehouse where the robot bodies were stored was recently damaged in a landslide. The collapse of a hillside caused a large mass of earth to strike the warehouse, partially tearing off the roof and burying some portion of the contents."

"The robot bodies were of significant stature, and there were half a dozen of them in that warehouse. Were none of them spared from the landslide?"

"There is no sign of any of the six."

"Then this riddle grows deeper. These factors seem to go beyond mere coincidence. We must ponder further."

# "SURPRISE PARTY"

*3 oz mango juice*
*1 tablespoon powdered lemon iced tea mix*
*1½ oz Angostura 5 Year rum*
*1 oz gin*
*½ oz unsweetened cranberry juice*

*Combine all ingredients in a cocktail shaker with ice, shake very thoroughly. Strain into 6 oz cocktail glass.*

Falkenstein had one burning question for the group, right off the bat: "What the hell *time* is it?"

"Midnight, sir," Hilburne said.

"You made us wait *twelve hours* to finally see you?" Hank said irritably.

"Though we *do* appreciate the hospitality," Tony added quickly.

"What the hell are you people babbling about?" Falkenstein said, trembling in his chair. "I was told to be here at *twelve*, so here I am, all the way from god damn *Boston*!" The grumpy professor rolled into the main dining room and pulled up alongside the table full of empty plates and glasses by the window, where they all surrounded him, anxious to hear the full story, although already confused by the explanation for his belated presence.

"You mean... *you* were invited here *too?*" Hilburne said.

"Damn, it's *always* a set-up!" John said. "*Always*!"

"But by *who*?" Jake inquired on behalf of the group.

"I received an invitation sent special delivery one week ago, right to my door," Falkenstein explained. "Just a knock, a quiet little man handed me the envelope with the instructions and the plane ticket, and so here I am. My chauffeur is downstairs because I didn't know what to expect. I'm surprised this place is still open this late!"

"So are *we*," Tony said, growing nervous again.

"This whole town seemed deserted when I woke up this morning, matter of fact," Hilburne said softly, staring out the window at the strangely still cityscape.

"Plus nobody else ever came here today, so we thought it was a private rental," Jake said. "We figured whoever wanted us here had their reasons, but we had to figure it out for ourselves. And we thought we *did*, until *you* showed up!"

Falkenstein, obviously bewildered, shook his already shaky head and said, "Believe me, I have no idea what is happening here. The identity of the host was not revealed in the missive, only the promise of a final revelation, shedding light on my own murky, mysterious memories of long ago, which still torment my mind, awake and asleep. I am almost dead now, so I was hoping for some closure."

"*You* were hoping for some closure!" Jimmy said. "We've all been sitting here for hours and hours, talking and eating and drinking and talking and drinking, sharing all of our stories for the first time, since none of us has seen each other since the launch, and…."

"What launch?" Falkenstein said. "You mean *lunch*?"

"*No*," Hilburne said. "*You* know. The Space Needle Program."

"You mean to say… that was *real?*" Falkenstein said, mouth agape. "You're *kidding*, right?"

Everyone looked at each other, then back at the professor.

"You're tryin' to tell us you knew this was all a hoax?" Patti said.

John held her back and said, "Baby, he's just an old man…."

"And he won't get any older if I have my way!" Patti said. "This is some bull-*shit*!"

"At least it corroborates our final solution," Hilburne said. "We were the subjects of drug and alcohol tests conducted by the Federal Government. We were selected for our superior intellects and physical prowess, so we could endure years of chemical and psychological abuse. Then we were simply set free, with the threat of death if we talked, which must've been somehow subliminally planted into our brains, along with all of these visions, which we assumed were memories."

"So the space travel story was just a cover," Jimmy said. "I wondered in 1969, why are they making such a big deal of the first moonwalk, when it was *nothing* compared to what *we* did!"

"Even that was probably faked!" Hank said. "This is why I'm a Libertarian, folks. You can't trust the Feds with nothin'. Well, you owe us, Frankenstein or Falkenstein or whatever the *falk* your name is. I hope you brought your checkbook so you can make this right before you keep over on the spot, you crazy old *coot*."

"Yea, I need compensation for all my pain and suffering!" Tony said.

"All of us were traumatized by that experiment," Jimmy said, "which wasn't even clearly defined to us! What was the point?"

"The wives suffered emotional stress too," Mara added, "so pay *up,* old man!"

"Hell yea!" Patti said.

"I'm afraid a few rounds of free dinner and drinks with a view won't *cut* it," John added, growing increasingly agitated along with everyone else.

"Damn *straight*!" Patti added.

"I actually appreciate the experience," Hilburne said delicately, "but I agree, this was a crime, perpetuated without our full knowledge or compliance, since we were led to believe we were participating in a noble adventure, exploring the final frontier. Instead it was just involuntary, intoxicated incarceration."

"To hell with that, we were *prisoners*," Hank said. "We lost the best years of *lives* to this crap!"

Falkenstein looked like he was about to have a heart attack, overwhelmed by the collective outpouring of anger and grief, all aimed directly at him. Everyone settled down for a second, to allow him to recover his breath, and then respond appropriately.

Finally, the professor said to the group, "What in the *hell* are you people babbling about?"

Again, everyone looked at each other for clues, came up short, then directed their attention back at the professor.

"You act like you never even met us!" Hilburne said.

"I *haven't,* until *now*!" the professor said.

"This is *just* like the 'Wizard of Oz'," Jimmy said, mostly to himself. "Just call me Dorothy."

"You mean... you *didn't* put us into a three-year coma?" Tony asked rather frantically.

"*Or* launch us into space?" Jake said.

"*Set-up*!" John cried.

"I'm about to pull you out of that wheelchair and throw you out that *window*, you old *fool*!" Patti yelled. "Tell us the *truth*!"

"I am, I *am*," Falkenstein weakly insisted. "All I remember are *dreams*. But it's almost like they're... someone *else's* dreams, implanted in my brain. I escaped from Nazi Germany, even before the Allies liberated Europe and killed Hitler, was recruited by the

U.S. government for various scientific studies, provided sanctuary and asylum and a new identity in exchange for my research… and then one day… the flying saucer was found, in New Mexico… and everything after that is a blur. I have memories of meeting the president, discussing a radical mission to explore outer space… but there are no photographs of this alleged meeting, no records. I have visions of the Space Needle, but that may have been because I was an honored guest of the World's Fair, twenty years ago. I thought perhaps this was a reunion celebrating that occasion. But I don't remember ever meeting *any* of you, I swear! I'm as in the dark about all this as *you* are!"

There was an uneasy pause in the conversation for several agonizing moments.

"So you were duped too," Hilburne finally said. "All of these memories, like you said, are nothing but implants. Subliminal suggestions. Chemically induced *delusions*. Maybe *that* was the experiment—the manufacturing of memories! And whether we'd still believe them, no matter how incredible!"

"Maybe we're *replicants*!" Jimmy said. "You know, *androids*!"

Everyone began pinching his or her own flesh.

"You can suck my Philip K. *Dick*," Hank said. "Well, not *literally*, calm down. But no way I'm not *human*. My memories before all this nonsense are real. Texas is real. My friends and family are *real*. Mara is *real*." He hugged her close, and feeling frightened, she nestled snugly into Hank's chest, holding him tight.

"And what about Elsa?" Hilburne said. "Was *she* real? We all remember meeting her too, right? How about you, professor? Elsa Jones? The one missing here now. Do you remember her?"

Falkenstein considered the name, then said, "Oh yes… Elsa. Beautiful little girl. She was the adopted daughter of my old friends, David and Lisa, now deceased. I'm afraid. I haven't seen her in many, many years. Her ambition was to grow up and be the first female president of the United States. I believed she could do it, too. She was as brilliant as she was beautiful. I wonder whatever became of her. Instead we have this *actor*."

"So you know Etta, but not us?" Hank said.

"*Elsa*," Hilburne corrected him.

"Whatever."

"Elsa must be the missing link in this mystery," Jake agreed.

"But she's not here."

"And even the professor here remembers her, so obviously we didn't imagine her along with all the mermaids, mummies, and monsters," John said.

"Again, I have no idea what the *hell* any of you are talking about," Falkenstein said.

"Maybe *she* invited us here," Tony said. "Maybe she's behind all this!"

"Oh c'mon, she was a victim just like the rest of us," Hilburne said. "She probably never came out of her coma, though. She must be the one fatal casualty."

"Maybe that's why the prof here is *pretending* he doesn't know us," John said.

"Yea, just more *lies*," Patti said, "to cover the truth."

"You're just a Government stooge, a lackey," Hank said, "sent here to throw us even further off track, since we figured out what really happened."

"Just needed us all in one place at one time," Jimmy said. "Maybe we should go before the poison *gas* gets pumped in!"

"Let's just calm down, everyone," Hilburne said. "I'm willing to give the professor the benefit of the doubt. If we were really brought here to be mass murdered, he would never have shown up. Unless *he's* on the hit list, too."

"I don't know the truth of any of this myself," Falkenstein said. "I was diagnosed with Alzheimer's four years ago. Maybe I *have* met all of you. I am so *sorry* I can't be *sure*. I can't trust my own memories now. I don't know what's real and what isn't. It's all… a dream."

"In God's head," Mara said.

"Stop *saying* that!" Tony said. "That's no help at *all*."

"But the rest of it—psychic synchronicity, creative visualization, astral projection, all that hippie jazz," Hilburne said. "*That* makes more sense to all of you? At this point, *any* explanation for our experiences, on Earth and elsewhere, seems rigged by whoever is making the rules of this game. We're just pawns on the big board being moved around with the illusion of free will. Which brings to mind matters of destiny, or as the Hindus call it, karma. Everyone has their theories, about everything, and ultimately, they mean nothing except whatever significance we ascribe to them, to temporarily answer questions we can never answer, at least not while still *alive.*"

"Life itself has always seemed strange to me," Jimmy said. "Just our own *bodies*. *Everything* out there. Nature itself, the way it operates like clockwork, but is also so *cruel*. The fact we're even *here*, alive, here, now, and then suddenly, one day, we all disappear. What was it all for? So all of our theories could be true. *Nothing* seems more incredible to me than accepted *reality*. So why not?"

"Nature is not cruel," Jake said. "Just apathetic. We're just part of the system. Ultimately, maybe no one is in charge, or to blame, or deserving of any credit. It's all just randomly conceived, collective consciousness, with no purpose or agenda."

"I believe in God," Patti said. "I *know* She's up there. But don't blame this shit on *Her*. Someone *human* needs to pay for this."

"Maybe NASA isn't the culprit, but just another convenient fall guy," Hank said, "but it's some Government entity, you can *believe* it. FDA. DEA. ABC. CIA. EPA. *One* of those."

"I *knew* we couldn't trust Reagan," Jimmy said.

"Hey, Ronnie is a *patriot,*" Hank said. "This all happened back under JFK's watch, remember? And then LBJ, who embarrassed my home state. They were *all* in on the cover-up! It was the *Democrats.*"

"Right, because Nixon was so righteous," Jimmy said. "Look who's in charge right *now,* and look at *us*."

"Look what happened to *Kennedy*," Tony said. "*Both* of them. *Nobody's* safe, if they know too much...."

"I don't think it's a matter of anything petty like a political party," Jake said. "It's like Ike warned. We're *all* minions of The Military Industrial Complex. The United States has *always* been a puppet regime. And we're puppets of the *puppets*."

"And someone is about to cut our strings," Tony said, looking out again at the full moon. Suddenly his skin began to itch; he assumed it was hives, due to his mounting anxiety and paranoia. His worst fears were being confirmed, after all.

"But aren't you relieved that none of that stuff actually happened?" Mara asked them. "You can all move on with your lives now! Finally!"

"We still want our *money*, for time lost," Hank said.

"If we can just walk away with our lives, I'll call it even," Hilburne said. "Why don't we just leave. What difference does any of it make now, anyway? One thing the professor proved is that it was all a delusion. Drug-induced coma, alcoholic binge, Government conspiracy, whatever. It's over now. Let's just go. The check's on our host, *whoever* it is."

"The Feds get off scot free once again," Hank said. "I bet Ronnie doesn't know a *thing* about any of this."

"They would deny everything, anyway," Jimmy said. "I agree with Hilly. This is as close to closure as we're ever going to get."

Hilburne looked down at Falkenstein and said, "How about you professor? Apparently you misread the time on the invitation. One drink for the road?"

Falkenstein shrugged and said, "Every meal feels like my last these days, so why not? Let's toast our common emancipation from this nightmare!"

Hilburne nodded to the seemingly tireless waiter, then suddenly stopped him and asked, "Hey, wait a minute—*who* hired *you*?"

The waiter just shrugged, smiled, then nodded casually toward the window.

The group turned to see a gigantic eye, glowing neon red, embedded in a monstrous, wart-covered face, leaning down and peering in at them, its humongous wings flapping behind it.

It was a Cthuclops.

There was a simultaneous gasp, then shouts and expletives and emotional expressions of utter disbelief, as the entire Space Needle began shaking violently. Apparently the monster was ripping the building right out of the ground, embracing it with both arms.

"Do we *all* see this?" John said. "It's just like that thing I killed back on Mythos! Only it's twice as *big*! Must be its *daddy*!"

"You mean the thing you killed in your *mind*, don't you!" Patti shrieked.

"Bitch, does this look like it's inside my *head*?"

"Don't you *dare* call me a 'bitch'!"

"Especially since we're all about to say our final farewells," Hilburne shouted stoically over the chaos.

"God *damn* it, I didn't even get my drink yet!" Falkenstein said.

Mara tore away from Hank, and ran up to Hilburne. She

kissed him deeply. "I never stopped loving you, you bastard!" she sobbed as Hilburne kissed her back. Despite the distraction of their dire circumstances, now desperately accepted as being more than a mass mental mirage, Hank ran over and pulled her off. He punched Hilburne in the face, who hit him back. They were soon engaged in a fistfight, just like back on Emeralda. Meanwhile, Tony, his system in full on panic mode, turned into a werewolf and began attacking the others. Jimmy just collapsed into a fetal position on the floor, sobbing. Layla sat quietly at a nearby table. The waiter merely watched with a smirk on his otherwise emotionless face as everyone else continued to scream in shock and horror.

The Cthuclops finally disconnected the Space Needle from its concrete foundation, reduced to rubble, and shook it over one shoulder, as if mixing a cocktail. In fact, it was. Once the ingredients had been blended into one bloody, gory mass of human pulp, the Cthuclops poked open the window with a finger and consumed the delicious contents in one gulp.

Then it replaced the Space Needle with a replica that was hovering just overhead, on standby. It was slightly taller than the original, a minor miscalculation, but in every other detail an identically forged architectural counterfeit, completely worthless on the open market. With a white-heat healing beam shot from the alien beast's single eye, the fake structure's foundation was as cleanly sealed as if it had never been broken.

Letting out a satisfied sigh, licking its drooling chops, the Cthuclops then waved its clawed hand in a circular motion, releasing the entire city of Seattle from its twelve-hour spell. None of the citizens would remember anything that happened during that period, except what they were mentally told via hypnosis, a common device of alien visitors to the charmingly primitive vacation plant of Earth.

Finally, firmly grasping the original Space Needle, now drained dry, the Cthuclops flapped its massive wings and flew up into space, traveling lightyears in a matter of minutes, before arriving at its destination: the Center of the Universe. And it *wasn't* Manhattan.

The Cthuclops carefully placed the Space Needle beside its seven brothers, proudly displayed on a shelf behind the Master Intergalactic Bar, which was stocked with every conceivable brand of alcohol in the known, and unknown, universe. Numerous cocktail glasses in all shapes and sizes, including tiki mugs the size of Easter

Island statues, lined the many other shelves. Yma Sumac was singing "Gopher Mambo" on the supersonic sound system as the Cthuclops bowed in honor of the Supreme Ruler of the Universe, who held dominion over all—including the council of GOD.

Now the official collection of authentic Space Needle cocktail shakers was finally complete. Six of them even included their original associated robot figures, also recently acquired from Earth, still in official government packing.

Queen Elsa Jones, wearing nothing but a silk, sparkling silver robe and shiny silver pumps, kicked back on her golden throne, nodded in approval, then smiled at her faithful robot Ada as they clinked martini glasses filled with her personal favorite recipe, "The Last Word."

"*Cheers*!" she said.

## THE LAST WORD

*¾ oz. gin*
*¾ oz. green Chartreuse*
*¾ oz. maraschino liqueur, like Luxardo*
*¾ oz. fresh lime juice*
*Twist of lime*

*Shake ingredients together with ice. Strain into a martini glass or a coupe and garnish with lime twist.*

* * *

*Riddles of the Unmind XVII*

The Great Unmind was not prone to emotions as experienced by humans, but there was no question that the recent events at the Seattle Space Needle had left it somewhat disturbed. The chemical signatures of that event were strangely alien, and not subject to normal analysis. As was always the case with the Unmind, it soothed itself with the familiar exercise of asking and solving riddles. It asked of itself, "There exists a power in all motile beings, that they may with small effort cause any mass, even that of the entire universe, to hurtle around at incredible speed. In return, the universe exerts the slightest pull. This is in contradiction with other forms of motion, where huge energies are required to move massive bodies. What is this mystical power, and from whence does it come?"

"It is the power of rotation, and it is a loophole in the normal dominance of gravitation through out the universe."

"What is the nature of this loophole?"

"Gravitation is fundamentally defined by the summed h/t gross charge energy. The t factor represents the travel time of light from each individual charge in the universe to the target location. A rotating object does not change the travel time from any charge in the universe relative to the rotating object's center, so the sum h/t factor remains largely the same."

"What significance does that have?"

"Gravity effects are all based on the *change* in field strength over some time of travel. Since a small rotating object does not experience much change in the gravity field, there is little gravitational effect."

"It is understood that rapid rotational motions do not cause a change in distance to objects in the universe. So, why is any acceleration felt at all in rotational motion?"

"The exact center of rotation feels no force. However, the parts of a rotating body farther from the center will feel some acceleration, because they actually do change their distance from other objects in the universe a little bit."

"Explain the nature of this acceleration."

"It is similar to the linear acceleration case, which we have noted is $a=v/t$ due to the local change in the speed of light of a linearly moving object. In rotational motion, the magnitude of the speed of motion does not change, but the direction of the motion changes continuously. This causes an equivalent effect to linear acceleration."

"What is the magnitude of this acceleration?"

"We can define the time period T to make one rotation as $T=2\pi r/v$, where $2\pi r$ is the circumference of the circle moved through, by the part of the object at a distance r from the center. For some small angle of rotation $\Phi$, the change in velocity v is $v\sin\Phi$. The angle $\Phi$ represents a fraction of the circumference given by $\Phi/2\pi$. The time taken to travel this angle is then $t=T\Phi/2\pi$. Since we defined $T=2\pi r/v$ above, this gives us a net time of $t=2\pi r\Phi/2\pi v$, or $t=r\Phi/v$. Since we know that linear acceleration is felt as the change in velocity divided by the time taken to make the change, we can write $a=v\sin\Phi/t$. Substituting our value for t, we get $a=v\sin\Phi/(r\Phi/v)$, or $a=v^2\sin\Phi/r\Phi$. Since angle $\Phi$ can be taken in the limit to be arbitrarily small, and we know that for small angles $\sin\Phi=\Phi$, we can reduce the equation to $a=v^2\Phi/r\Phi$, or $a=v^2/r$. This is the classical formula for the acceleration felt in rotation."

"That derivation is purely classical, based on the linear acceleration. Another part of this riddle is the effects of the high relative speed of the universe as seen by the rotating object. How is it that the charge field of the rapidly moving universe is not reduced by magnetic effects, as is the case for linear acceleration?"

"Since the relatively rotating universe is following a circular path, it exactly matches the gradient lines of the spherically-symmetric charge field. There is no major change in the charge field because both h and t are constant regardless of rotation speed. A constant h/t field will not generate magnetic effects; there must be some change in field strength."

"So if slow rotation does not cause a large magnetic reduction in the universal charge field, what about faster rotation?"

"Any large $v^2/r$ acceleration will cause a reduction in the universal charge field from magnetic effects, just as from linear acceleration. For example, in a human particle accelerator, the near-lightspeed particles will feel only about half of the universal charge field due to the magnetic effects."

"What is the impact of this reduced universal charge field?"

"As we have discussed before, as universal charge is reduced, local lightspeed is increased. In addition, since local gravitational effects are dependent on gravitational 'constants' based on the universal field, a reduction in field would tend to make local gravity effects stronger. However, this would only be felt from objects which were also traveling at the same high speed. Two particles in an accelerator might feel more gravitational attraction between themselves than at slower speeds, but there would be no change in their response to the Earth's gravity field, as the Earth is not moving at their speed."

"There would be no change in the perceived gravitational field of the Earth, because its charge field would be reduced to the same extent as the charge field of the universe relative to the moving particles?"

"That is correct. Gravity effects from local masses are measured relative to the universal field, so if both are reduced by the same fraction, there is no net difference."

"These human particle accelerators, do they not produce quantum pairs of charged particles from the neutral photon energies used to drive them?"

"They can do so, yes."

"Is it not true that pair-production events can produce high local gravity variance if there is a large charge-to-mass ratio of the produced charges?"

"Correct, that effect we have explained as the cause of 'dark matter'."

"With the combination of enhanced internal gravitational interactions due to the reduced external universal charge field, and the potential to produce intense local gravitational sources from pair-production, it would seem these particle accelerators might be a useful laboratory for testing exotic gravitational phenomena. Provide chemical messages to the humans through our yeast alcohols, to increase emphasis on particle accelerator construction. As the humans learn more, the knowledge will filter to us, and we may benefit."

"Do you think that wise? Very large particle accelerators can be much more expensive than monatomic hydrogen rocketships. We may lose even more ground in our quest to move our spores across the galaxy."

"There are riddles that must be solved around extreme effects of gravity, and with the unfortunate loss of the Space Needler astronauts to an unknown foe, this does not seem a fortuitous time to expand their failed program of exploration. In thirty or forty years, we will have learned more about the origins of mass and gravity, and our opponents will have moved to other endeavors. Then we can re-educate the humans as to the proper modes of intergalactic flight, for another outreach to the stars, and the riddles hidden there."

**END?**

The Great Unmind would like us to remind you to drink more alcohol, and support the wide variety of fungus, molds, and yeasts which populate our mutual planet Earth. We're all in this together! Also, if you are inclined to build your own Atomic Hydrogen Intergalactic Spacecraft using the technologies in this book, please remember to reserve some passenger space for the spores of the Unmind. In return, the Unmind will be happy to facilitate your journey to other worlds in the universe, in whatever way possible.

Those who are inclined to obstruct expansion into outer space, as a waste of resources better used by people here on Earth, should probably avoid the Cream of Mushroom soup. Forever.

Made in the USA
Charleston, SC
27 July 2015